Tomorrow
Will Be
Sunday

HAROLD HORWOOD

Tomorrow Will Be Sunday

DOUBLEDAY & COMPANY, INC. GARDEN CITY, NEW YORK

1966

*All of the characters in this book are ficti-
tious, and any resemblance to actual per-
sons, living or dead, is purely coincidental.*

For Marguerite
with love and gratitude

Note of Thanks

To MR. HARRY BOYLE, who commissioned the material on which this book is based.

To MR. FARLEY MOWAT, who read early drafts and offered vital criticism.

To my father, ANDREW HORWOOD, who supplied much of the background material and acted as my business proxy while I worked on it.

CHAPTER ONE

❦ ❧

In a little valley on the shore of a great bay, set between a beautiful sound and a chain of offshore islands, lies the village of Caplin Bight, where the boy Eli was born. He and his companions never called it a village. In Newfoundland it was an outport—one of a thousand, all devoted to fishing. There were few towns in Newfoundland when Eli was a child, little industry or manufacturing—just the outports strung along the coastline, some with three or four families, some with three or four hundred, and the great, distant market city of St. John's, which sold the fish and brought the rum and molasses from the ends of the earth.

Caplin Bight was somewhere in the middle range of outports, with forty-six families, all but three or four of them fishing families. But in Eli's boyhood the population was already starting to drift away, a few to St. John's, or to the mines or paper mills, but most to the States, where the Boston suburb of Chelsea was populated largely by expatriate Newfoundlanders grown filthy rich by dint of hard work in a burgeoning industrial society.

Eli, the son of Elias and Martha Pallisher, was a dark, slender boy with the appealing eyes, soft features, and gentle expression of the Eskimo people, who had contributed perhaps a quarter of the genes that dictated his growth. By the time he was ten the people of Caplin Bight had already marked him as an odd child. He refused to join in the frog-torturing expeditions so dear to the hearts of the village boys. He flew kites, when kite-flying time arrived in the windy days of fall, but he made them of a strange pattern that he got out of a book, weird, boxlike things that nobody believed would fly, until they soared higher and freer than any of the diamond-shaped kites of the village tradition. He played with a group of children, like any other child, but he was just as often seen alone, not moping about, looking for something to do, but intently pursuing some private project of his own.

Eli had peculiar tastes in pets—a dragonfly that everyone said would sting him to death, and that he fed on house flies and mosquitoes, watching its trap-door mouth consume his offerings with hour-long fascination; a spotted rock sculpin that he kept in a tub of salt water and taught to come to the surface to take scraps of food from his hand, until his mother pronounced the whole thing to be unnatural and ordered him to put it back into the sea. He began a shell collection, and a collection of lichens, spending half a day searching the forest for a bit of the emerald-green lungwood that grew, rarely, on sticks of dead birch. But he lost interest in such pursuits as regularly as he started them, and his parents were afraid he had rolling-stone tendencies.

The boy had a habit of asking questions that his elders found annoying. On Sunday afternoons he would hang around the government wharf, listening to the conversation of idle men until they forgot he was there and spoke of matters supposed to be hidden from the ears of a child. For a year there was a teacher in Caplin Bight who took real pleasure in dispensing scraps of information on every subject in the universe. She scattered facts like candy at a picnic, and Eli stuck to her like a March lamb to its ewe. It was she who told him that the "horse stinger," as people called the dragonfly, had no sting, and could not bite him, even though Melinda Pike, the wife of Eli's father's shareman, Eleazer Pike, was ready to swear to a swelling as big as an apple, following a brush with one of the creatures, and could still show the scar, which had healed twenty years ago.

But the oddest thing about Eli was his manner of speech. The people of Caplin Bight, when addressing a stranger from the mainland, could use almost accentless English, learned from listening to the radio, but in conversation among themselves there lingered the broad twang of ancient British dialects that the fishermen of Devon and Cornwall and the Isle of Guernsey had brought to the coast three and four centuries before. Eli never spoke with a "bayman's" accent, but always like a schoolteacher, and mostly with the grave manner of an adult. This pleased his mother, who hoped to see him become a clerk or a shopkeeper, but made his father suspect him of putting on airs.

Eli was never very close to his parents. He called them "Father" and "Mother" or "sir" and "ma'am." They supplied his physical wants as best they could, but showed him no tenderness and seemed not to realize that he might have emotional needs. He could not remember when either of them had kissed him—not that he wanted them to. He respected them but was a little afraid of them, and disliked the strong smell of sweat that often clung to them, and their carelessness about washing.

It was part of his parents' religion to despise the body and regard it as unclean. Neither of them ever undressed in the children's presence. Eli could remember being taught, at the age of four, to turn his face to the wall when dressing by the kitchen fire in winter, lest the eyes of his family be offended by his nakedness. (If thine eye offend thee, pluck it out.) He recalled wondering, at the time, why his front should be any more offensive than his behind.

He was told that he must love his father and mother and, to a lesser extent, his small brother Timmy, but was not shown how to do it, and didn't really know the meaning of love or any of the strong emotions connected with it, until he began to turn, after his twelfth birthday, toward people outside his immediate family.

Because of this lack of love in the home Eli was never able to accept physical discipline from his parents without hatred and revolt. On the rare occasions when his father whipped him he suffered a deep sense of personal violation, as though he had been raped. It wasn't the whipping itself that he resented so much as the feeling that Elias was making a claim upon him to which he had no right. But punishment held some sort of horrible fascination for the boy, just the same. He found himself roused when a horse was whipped or another child was beaten. He linked this shameful pleasure in cruelty with the taboo against sex to produce a deep and abiding sense of guilt.

The moral code of Caplin Bight was simple and easily stated: sex was sin (except between husband and wife, in bed with their clothes on, and avoiding anything "unnatural"). Swearing or using "vulgar language" was sin. Sloth and sensual pleasure were sins. These were all sins against God.

There were also sins against man—to wit, murder, stealing, and lying.

This about summed up the primitive, negative moral code in which Eli was raised. So long as you didn't kill, steal, lie, or blaspheme, and so long as you kept yourself "pure"—that is, sexless—you walked perfect before the Lord. The only positive commandment was that of hard work.

Eli's strongest attachment in early childhood was to Timmy, whom he had been required to mind from infancy and for whom he developed a protective, nurturing instinct, like a hen with a chick. Timmy responded by regarding Eli as his ultimate authority—a response aided by the gap of four years between their ages—his shield against life's harshness, his mediator with the monumental figures of Elias and Martha, who moved through his world like the dim fathers of the gods through Grecian mythology.

Caplin Bight had a cove with a crescent of sand, and a landlocked harbor whose entrance was crowded with towering hills. Spruce forests stretched inland from the edges of old fields that had been cleared by the first settlers for the pasturing of a few cows and goats and sheep. Most of the fields were now deserted except for the buttercups, the everlasting daisies, and the children, who went there on summer afternoons to fish in the silver threads of trout streams that laced the forest, to lie in the sun, speculating about the universe, or to race barefooted along the broad cliff top, while the daisy stems flicked their ankles and the wind from the sea ruffled their hair.

They often traced the broad furrows in the grass where potato beds had been dug by a former generation, sometimes the vague line of a fence, long since fallen into decay, or the square hollow that had been a root cellar when Caplin Bight was in its prime, a century earlier and every foot of cleared land was in use.

The foreshore of the harbor—or landwash, as it was called, was crowded with stages—rickety wharves just big enough for a trap boat to tie up and discharge its cargo of codfish. Each stage had its attached store, where the fish was split and salted and later piled for shipment. A little farther back from the sea, with a road separating them from the stores, were the tall, spindly fish flakes, platforms built of spruce poles decked with small round sticks called longers, and topped with boughs, where the fish was spread to dry in the cool sunshine of late August and September.

A few small sailing vessels, with one-lung engines buried in their after holds, swung at anchor in the harbor. How these engines worked, Eli and his friends never knew, but the men professed to understand their innermost secrets. Anyway, they talked about magnetoes and jump sparks and make-and-breaks with a convincing show of knowledge. Thinking back afterward, Eli was sure that these little coasters were ridiculously underpowered, even though their main propulsion was sail. A single-cylindered, eight-horse-

power hunk of rusty iron, which you started by giving one
mighty heave on the flywheel, was required to propel a
sixty-ton ship. Some vessel owners boasted that their ships
could do six knots under power, but if you actually timed
them from port to port you would find their speed closer to
three or four.

But nobody timed them. Time was one thing that Caplin
Bight had to spare. The vessels reached port sooner or later,
and that was all that mattered. They made regular trips to
St. John's for supplies, and distributed small cargoes of
freight all up and down the coast. The bigger ones, over
thirty tons, even took fish to Spain and Portugal and Greece,
or down through the trade winds to Jamaica and Barbados
and Brazil, or into the steaming rivers of British Guiana, at
such times as the merchants of St. John's had more orders
than they could fill by using their own bottoms.

Mainly the harbor was filled with trap skiffs and small mo-
torboats. Some Caplin Bight people had been shipbuilders
for six generations or more, and prided themselves on having the best trap boats in the bay. Most of these boats were
twenty-five to thirty feet long, with maybe a nine-foot beam
and a great sheer forward. They were all very low in the
waist, and with rounded, undercut sterns that prevented
them absolutely from shipping a following sea. A small engine box, just abaft amidships, sheltered a tiny inboard engine. But the rest of the boat was one vast fish hold, except
for a tiny cuddy in the bows, where they stored the black
teakettle and the bread bag for boil-ups at sea. When the
fish were running, an iron pot, a small bag of salt, and a few
potatoes also were kept in the cuddy, for making fish chowder. There was nothing fancy about the steaming stew that
came out of the iron pot, but to sea-sharpened appetites it
tasted like the very manna from heaven.

No one could explain just why trap boats were built to
this pattern. The builders certainly knew nothing about the
laws that naval architects profess to follow. They just
"knew" that it was the right way to build a boat, from knowledge passed down to them, and the boats that they built

were most seaworthy. A trap skiff might drive away, or be caught on a lee shore and be smashed to matchwood, but nobody ever heard of one swamping or smashing in a sea, unless it was overloaded. So long as you could keep the boat's head to the wind she would ride out almost anything, including a hurricane.

Shipbuilders, as well as boatbuilders, worked without plans. Eli's grandfather, and all his forefathers before him, had built ships without ever seeing a plan. But the elder Pallisher had built his last ship when Eli was a baby. The chief shipbuilder in Caplin Bight now was Thomas Gilmore of Matthew, the mill owner. His first cousin, Thomas Gilmore of Thomas, also built ships, but never with the same flair as that shown by the older man.

Eli often watched Thomas Gilmore of Matthew sitting in a net loft throughout a long winter afternoon, while a circle of men knit twine into nets or traps, or just lounged about, "chewing the fat." The man would have a small ship model in his hands, built up plank by plank, carved with a pocket-knife from solid slabs of pine. He would pat it and squint along its lines. From time to time he would pick up his knife and delicately peel a tiny shaving from the flare of the bow. This would be his plan for the ship he would build in the spring. The ship would reproduce the model exactly, point by point, on a scale of twelve to one—a foot to the inch.

Once or twice Eli saw the shipbuilder hand his model over to Joshua Markady, the great, retired patriarch of the foreign-going trade, who wore a heavy gold watch chain across his belly and was one of the two people in Caplin Bight sometimes called "Mr."

"What do 'e think, Josh?" Thomas Gilmore of Matthew would ask, as the keen blue eyes under the overhanging fringe of white eyebrow peered monocularly along the model's lines.

Mr. Markady might deliberate a full minute. Then: "Believe she'd be a mite tender in a cross sea, Tom," he'd say. "Fast, though."

"Ay," Thomas Gilmore of Matthew would agree. "Thought that too." Then he would go back to pondering his model. He might even scrap it and start a new one, sacrificing just a trifle of her speed to make her stiffer, so she wouldn't roll you under when the going got rough.

That was the way the ships were born. Haphazard, you might think. But in capable hands they were good ships. Eli's grandfather had sailed them to fifteen foreign countries, and Mr. Markady to many more, without the help of radar or radio or storm warnings. Mr. Markady had sailed to all the continents, through every kind of weather known on earth. He had been dismasted and had seen his ships shot out from under him by submarines, but he had never lost one by wind or tide or error of navigation.

The small coasters came and went at all times between the treacherous rock shoals known as the sunkers, where the sea broke at the harbor mouth. The sunkers were treacherous in calm weather, when the sea did not break, for they could rip the bottom out of any boat, even small ones; but during storms they sent spray towering hundreds of feet into the air. The small iron steamer that was Caplin Bight's main and regular link with the world outside called only once a week, spring through autumn. It was a "one-way port of call" that the steamer skipped during her return voyage to St. John's. She sometimes took lumber from Gilmore's water-powered mill, and once or twice a year she would load cases of salmon put up in pink-labeled cans by Solomon Marks, the merchant, who owned the big store by the government wharf and held the destinies of Caplin Bight firmly in his hands.

When the steamer tied up to the wharf every man and boy in the harbor was there to meet her, to catch her lines, to help unload cargo, to swap the latest news with crew and passengers, to take barrels of flour and chests of tea and tubs of margarine from the side of the ship, lugging them on hand barrows to the big shed beside Solomon Marks's store. And sometimes there were colorful boxes of store clothes, and a few cases of canned milk and meat. They never once thought of asking pay for this longshore labor. Indeed, there was competition to see who could be smartest in lending a hand. They thought of it as something that had to be done for the good of all. If anyone had told them that they were giving free labor to Solomon Marks, who, even though he was the chief elder of the church, was privately regarded as a rich old pirate with more money than heart, it would have been thought a great joke. No one would give free labor to Solomon Marks even if he *did* rely on the merchant to tell him how to vote in an election.

The fishermen reasoned about it thus: Solomon Marks was smarter and better educated than they, and so better equipped to make important decisions. They might fight with him about their accounts, but deferred to him in matters that concerned the world outside. And although it was certain that he would rob everyone blind, it was equally certain that he wouldn't do anything to affect the welfare of the community adversely. Solomon Marks was short, stout, red-faced, and balding, with spatulate fingers and soft hands. He was cordially disliked by all the men who sold him their fish and took their spring outfits from him, but if he had stood for election himself every man in Caplin Bight would have voted for him—or, anyway, everyone except Mr. Markady, and perhaps the other "Mr."—Peter Simms, the retired magistrate, who lived on the nearest thing to a real farm: a five-acre lot three miles from the main settlement.

A single line of houses, all painted white, stretched around the shore of Caplin Bight, set well back from the water behind their white picket fences, which enclosed minute cabbage gardens and slightly larger potato plots. The last house out on the Point, next to the graveyard, was that of Mr. Markady, with nothing beyond it except the cliffs. He had a great gallery, like the poop deck of a ship, overhanging the breakers far below, and on that gallery Eli did a lot of his

dreaming—mostly of places with names like Pernambuco
and Oporto and San Salvador, for Mr. Markady never tired
of talking about them to anyone who would listen, and Eli
was among the best listeners he had ever met.

At the other end of the settlement was the path to the
Cove, which was just past the Head. No one could say why
one headland was called the Point and the other the Head,
but that was the way it had always been. The Cove was wide
and shallow with a sand beach where the fishermen spread
their nets to dry and boys went swimming in late summer,
when the sea had warmed up enough so it wouldn't actually kill them. They would dash naked into the icy surf,
which never warmed much above forty degrees, take a few
dozen strokes, then dash back to shore, to roll in the sand
and bake luxuriously in the sun until the sand dried and
could be brushed off, when they would be ready to start the
process all over again.

By this hit-and-run method they all learned to swim, more
or less. But an unwritten law, designed, no doubt, to preserve the decencies, forbade the little girls of Caplin Bight
to go near the Cove, so there were no girl swimmers in the
settlement, except for Virginia Marks, the merchant's daughter, who had been away to school and been taught to swim
in a class by an instructor. After her return Virginia had
made a few lonely trips into the water, but all her female
relatives frowned on the practice as unladylike, contrary to
the laws of nature, and liable to turn her blood. So she gave
it up and learned to do fancywork, as embroidery was
called.

Virginia was slender and dark and supple as a willow
switch. She looked to Eli like one of those paintings of Ruth
or Pharaoh's daughter out of the big Bible in his father's
living room. And she walked as the women in the Bible
walked—straight, and with a liquid rhythm, as though she
might be carrying on her head a stone pitcher of water from
the pools of Bethesda.

Four years older than Eli, she seemed to him almost to belong to another generation, and when she spoke to him, sometimes a little teasingly, he found it hard to answer her. It was strange, he thought, that Virginia should be the one person in Caplin Bight in whose presence he felt shy, for she often helped in her father's store and had an easy way with all the customers who came and went.

"Eli," she'd say as he stood at the counter, waiting for his molasses jar to be filled by her little brother, "maybe ye wouldn't mind taking a message to your mother?"

"Oh, sure," he'd promise.

"We've a new shipment of dress goods in this week—voile and merino and lawn, real good materials. I know your mother's been wanting a length for a meeting dress. You tell her for sure, won't you. And Eli—" her voice dropping slightly and taking on a conspiratorial tone—"we've a bolt and a half of London smoke."

"London smoke?" he'd echo uncertainly.

"Yes, that stuff with the dark flecks—you know." And almost in a whisper she'd add, "The ladies use it to make their bloomers." Then her eyes would dance and her voice would tinkle with laughter as she saw his embarrassment.

There was no one remotely like Virginia in Caplin Bight, and already at the age of twelve Eli had felt her stir his blood with desires that, he was certain, were both disgusting and sinful. He could not see her breasts move under her dress without wondering what it would be like to explore them with his lips, or her thighs make sweeping curves in her skirt without imagining that he might caress them, naked, with his hands. When he thought of this as he lay in the sun on the beach he had to turn over and lie on his belly in the sand, lest he become a laughingstock to the other boys.

The Cove, which flanked Caplin Bight on the side opposite the islands, was uninhabited except for the small house where Jehu Gilmore, who was thin, redheaded, and near-

sighted, lived alone with his lobster pots and his three sheep.
Jehu was the most God-fearing person in Caplin Bight. Even
some of the more conscientious churchgoers were ready to
admit that Jehu was just a little "touched" on the subject of
religion. In the midst of lambing he was likely to stop and
sing a hymn. He was a great Bible reader, strong on faith
healing, and had gained a reputation for putting away warts
with the proper incantation from the Book of Job. For some
years before Eli could remember him he had been urging
his neighbors to prepare for the coming of the Lord. His
saintliness was scarcely in doubt, but some of the less charitable people were inclined to accuse him of practising faith
without works.

Jehu had a small, leaky boat tied up at a stage that, if
appearances were to be trusted, was always ready to fall
down. The flake where he dried his few fish was built from
the thinnest longers in the settlement. He lived, Elias Pallisher used to say, on government relief six months a year
and on the grace of God the other six.

The boys who swam at the Cove didn't especially like
Jehu, and he didn't especially like them. He was the sort
of man whom boys everywhere try to victimize, and when
they could think of a mean prank to play on him they went
at it with glee. One night they tarred his windows, so that he
spent most of the next day in bed, waiting for a dawn that
never came. Another time, after he had been preaching
about a great hail that was to fall from heaven, every stone
about the weight of a talent, they climbed the cliff above
the beach and rolled stones down on Jehu's roof. When this
happened Jehu, indoors, fell on his knees and began praying
in a loud voice, and it wasn't until one of the stones, somewhat larger than a talent, broke through his thin shingles
and landed on the stove that he ceased praying and rushed
outside to call the wrath of God down upon his tormentors.
However, the only wrath that descended upon the children
was the wrath of their fathers, which, however, was quite
sufficient to meet the case. Eli got "tanned good" with a

switch, and knew that he deserved it, but some of his friends whose fathers retained the naval tradition of the rope's end suffered a great deal more.

There were three miles of local road connecting the chief points of the settlement—the government wharf with the Marks's general store attached, the church, the school, and the graveyard. Once every four years or so a public meeting was called to share out the road money sent from the government at St. John's. This usually amounted to something like a hundred dollars, and all able-bodied men were expected to contribute their labor day for day putting gravel on the surface or mending bridges. How it all worked out was a bit of a mystery, for there never seemed to be any gravel on the road.

The road into the woods—sometimes called the Country Road—was the only other one within Eli's horizon, and it hardly counted as a road. It ran upcountry past Peter Simms's farm, and on for six or seven miles, gradually turning into a trail and petering out. The old people called it a cart track, and it never occurred to anybody to straighten it or widen it or gravel its surface. It had started as a caribou trail, long before the first man set foot in Caplin Bight, was in use by the first settlers, when they plodded up to the highlands to trap fur or to hunt Indians, was enlarged by the first horse, and since then had remained unchanged, except as increasing traffic had denuded and hardened its surface. It was good for hauling firewood or shooting a deer or snaring rabbits—all jobs that were done after the snow had formed its own smooth pavement, and the bogholes had frozen hard.

In winter Eli made trips over that road with his father, traveling on the big catamaran—a heavy wooden sled with iron-shod runners. It was just a skeleton of a sled, really: a massive set of runners with two heavy crossbeams and four uprights for holding logs. Sometimes a pair of shafts might be attached so a horse could haul it, but the black, curly-coated Newfoundland dogs, some of which were almost as big as small ponies, hauled catamarans without shafts, relying on their masters to see that the heavy vehicles did not run over them when going downhill. Some improvident people, who did not own so much as a big dog, would haul the catamarans by hand, but their woodpiles were always on the point of being exhausted.

After the spring thaw the road to the woods remained unused. It never crossed anyone's mind that it might, one day, connect Caplin Bight with Lattice Harbor, up the bay, and thence, by another road, with highways stretching to the Pacific Ocean in the west and the palm-shaded lands of the Gulf of Mexico in the south. Such a suggestion would have seemed as wild as the notion that men might travel to the moon.

They cut, not firewood alone, but also saw logs from the public forest. In theory there was a "three-mile limit" along the shore where wood was reserved for the fishermen, but much of the three-mile limit had already passed into private hands from greased public paws, and in practice everyone cut wood where he wished. Most families produced their own lumber, hauling logs from the forest and sawing them on the halves at the Gilmore mill. The half that went to the mill provided most of the wood that the Gilmores exported. When trimmed lumber was needed it was planed by hand. The big mill saw, driven by a great, undershot waterwheel, had been operated by a Gilmore as long as anyone could remember, but before its coming the fishermen had sawed their own lumber by hand with monstrous pit saws. The wheel churned around in the spring freshet with a suggestion of tremendous power, and must have developed vast reserves of energy, for it never faltered or slowed, even when biting its way through a thirty-inch saw log of black spruce.

That great wheel creaked its way through Eli's boyhood, and might have been turning yet, had not the art of the wheelwright fallen into decay. Anyone can build a waterwheel, but it takes a skillful artisan to build a pit wheel, with its intricate wooden gears for transferring the power of the bigger wheel to the spinning saw inside the mill. Old Jabez Pike, who was thin and bent and feeble-looking when Eli could first remember him, had been the last wheelwright in Caplin Bight—indeed, the last on that whole coast. He was making pit gears and other wheel parts the summer before he died. But he had left no son or nephew to carry on the mysteries of his art, and with his death all the great water-wheels along the coast began to fall into disrepair. The mill owners mended them as best they could, and one or two of them, somehow, have been kept going even to this day, but most have been replaced by small gasoline engines that cough and break down and allow the saw to stick in the wood.

CHAPTER TWO

❧ ⁂ ❧

The bitterest memory of Eli's boyhood was the year of the
fish failure. He was twelve years old that year, would be
thirteen by mid-winter—half a man by Newfoundland
standards, and expected to do half a man's work. The year is
still remembered in Caplin Bight as one of "hard, hard
times." The Pallisher family, with only two children, and
with the best fisherman in the harbor at its head, was among
the few that did not "go on the dole" that winter, as they
used to say of those who had to apply for government relief.

Solomon Marks the merchant carried bigger accounts that
year than his suppliers in St. John's would have sanctioned,
and smaller stocks than any year since the war ended in
1918. Nevertheless, the specter of bankruptcy must have
haunted his sleep. He confided to Thomas Gilmore of Matthew that he might not be able to supply for the fishery,
come April, since he might not be able to get the stocks of
food and gear that would be needed to carry the fishermen
on credit until square-up time in the fall. Thomas Gilmore of
Matthew mentioned this conversation to his wife, and by the
next day everyone in the harbor knew that there might be
no supplies for the fishery that spring.

The dogberries hung heavy on the bough that fall, and
grandparents shook their heads, predicting a "real old-time
winter." Frosts came early. A week before Christmas snow lay
a foot deep on the ground, and the pre-dawn temperature
dropped almost to zero. A feeling of fear pervaded the set-

tlement. For in Newfoundland, in those hungry 1930s, people occasionally starved to death. Doctors visiting remote settlements sometimes wrote out death certificates with the stark word "starvation" scrawled above their signatures. In Caplin Bight they spoke only in whispers of the fate of Hezekiah Pike, the father of twelve children, who two winters before had been found frozen to death on his way to the dole office in Lattice Harbor, a pair of leaky sea boots and a suit of white overalls made from flour sacks covering his naked body in the snow drifts.

A fish failure such as that which hit the bay shore that year is one of the regular hazards faced by inshore fishermen who can travel in their small boats only to the nearby fishing grounds. The ocean currents and the climate vary greatly from year to year. The bait fish—caplin and squid and herring—come and go with the currents, seeking waters where their own food, the tiny plankton, can multiply. When the waters happen to be right the bait fish crowd toward shore in countless billions, some coming to feed, some to spawn, and the codfish crowd toward shore behind them until they are "eating the rocks" and the net traps at the headland berths are full to bursting every morning. But some years the water is too cold, or a titanic disaster overtakes the bait fish offshore, or the squid reach the bottom of their eight-year cycle. And some years—once or twice in each generation—all these things happen at once. Those are the years of famine for the men and women and children who live out of the cod traps. Day after day they rise before dawn, eat bread and tea by lamplight, don oilskins, and coax tiny engines into life, heading out through the murk to their trap berths, hoping that the fish may have struck in. Day after day they haul the huge, box-shaped hempen traps, only to find them empty save for the strings of kelp and rockweed tangled in their leaders by the force of the tide.

Elias Pallisher was, year after year, the most successful fisherman in the Bight. A tall, thin man, very dark, his hair showing a touch of gray, his face sharply cut and unemotional, but deeply lined from squinting into sun and wind, he was a trap owner with a big investment in gear and four sharemen working with him. Though most years he cured hundreds of quintals of fish (each quintal representing a hundred and twelve pounds dry weight) as shares for himself and his traps, he cured only twenty-eight—a little over three thousand pounds—the year of the fish failure. Even at that, he was more fortunate than the other fishermen. Some had five or six quintals, some literally nothing.

Elias was inclined to blame those who had nothing—the weak and the improvident among his neighbors.

"Warn't never a year a man couldn' scrape enough to feed hisself and 'e's family, do 'e work at it," he said to his wife and sons. "I 'lows anyone kin get fish enough fer 'e's own use, with a jigger if 'e got nought else, no matter how bad it be. An' 'e can raise spuds too, in the gaps betwix the rock, allowin' 'e've a mind. Ain't never knowed a year when ye couldn' pick berries neither, bein' as ye ain't too lazy t' bend yer back. But o' course there be those as expects God's gifts to drop straight into their hands."

"Hush, Elias," Martha Pallisher scolded. "It ain't fer we to judge. If some poor 'angshore be brought low be 'is own foolishness, maybe that be a cross an' affliction 'e can't help. An' it ain't the fault of 'e's wife an' children, surely."

"'Tis God's law," Elias stated flatly, "that a man suffer fer 'e's sins, kin 'e help 'em or no—an' that 'e's wife an' children suffer along with 'im. It be written that way, an' ye can't get around it."

But Martha was not among the improvident with whom she sympathized. She filled her root cellar with cabbage and turnips and blue potatoes grown in her garden, and her shelves with hundreds of bottles of jam made from berries that she and the children picked on the broad hills behind the settlement. Though Eli and Timmy were conscripted for berry picking, they went without reluctance, gathering the wild fruit throughout September and part of October. Since there was no teacher for the little school that year, and it remained closed until after Christmas, they had ample time for berry picking.

They gathered the kinds of berries that you eat straight from the bush, as well as the kinds that you take home in buckets. Among the former were the purple chuckly pears (beloved of the rose-colored pine grosbeaks that sang to them on the berry grounds), fat red crackerberries, which snapped and cracked between your teeth, and delicate little maidner teaberries, greenish-white and hidden securely from prying eyes by glossy leaves tasting faintly of wintergreen.

The berries for taking home were the plump yellow cloudberries, which were always called bakeapples and prized as the choicest fruit of the earth—also raspberries that hung in red clusters, juicy squashberries with flat disks for seeds, growing in clusters on small trees, and, above all, the plentiful blueberries that blanketed the hills until they glinted with the color of sunlight on sea water. A woman and two boys, eating their meals of bread and boiled tea on the barrens, could pick a hundred pounds of berries in a day. In bed with Timmy after such a day, and too exhausted to sleep for maybe the first half hour or so, Eli would close his eyes in the darkness and see, without thinking about them, great bunches of blue fruit among waxy red and green leaves.

The greatest treat of the fall, so delicious that it set mouths watering at the sight of the first ripe berry, was blueberry pudding, loaded with luscious fruit, boiled in a cloth, and popped open, fresh from the pot and dripping with purple juice, on the kitchen table. Mr. Markady called it "berry duff"—a term that he had brought home from his lifetime at sea, where duff, made plain or with raisins and laced with molasses coady (a sort of boiled sauce), was the daily dessert, which no ship's boy was allowed to touch until he had learned to box the compass, fore and aft, without a mistake. There was no danger of Eli's ever missing his duff. He had been taught the compass before he could read.

Elias Pallisher squared up his account at the store, bought his winter supply of flour and molasses, salt beef, butter and tea, rolled oats and sack peas without going into debt; but it was a close nick, and most of the men of the bight were being carried on the books over the winter, their credit limit exhausted. With the coming of the snow in late November bleak misery settled on the little harbor.

In normal years those on the dole could supplement their six cents a day, which they were allowed by the government, with some tiny income of their own. They could cut and sell a load of wood to those better off than themselves. Maybe a shipowner would purchase a thousand rinds of spruce bark, stripped out of the forest, to line the fish holds of his vessel. Maybe they could build a punt and use it for credit at the store. But in the bleak winter of the fish failure all those auxiliary sources of income dried up. No one could buy anything. Those reduced to desperation tried to live on blue mussels and kelp scraped from the rocks beyond the harbor mouth and boiled in sea water. Those who had nothing sought help from those who did not have enough. In Caplin Bight no one refused a neighbor who came to borrow, and so privation spread from door to door.

The people met in the little church on Sundays to sing and pray—all of them, that is, except Mr. Markady and his wife and family, and Mr. Simms, who were unbelievers and headed straight for the second death, as the pastor assured his flock, not mentioning anyone by name, but feigning great horror at their adjudged fate. They prayed throughout that bleak winter, albeit with less noise than formerly. But few in their distress had faith enough to pray for bread, as did Sister Esther Pike the widow, believing literally in the Lord's promise, "Your bread shall be given, and your water sure."

She prayed kneeling in her ancient kitchen beside the old stone fireplace with its dog-ironed hearth, too poor now to have a fire, with three days left before she could get a relief order and not a crumb in the house. She prayed for bread, reminding the Lord of His promise. Perhaps remembering the importunate woman in the parable, she prayed often, in a loud voice—or, anyway, in as loud a voice as her feeble strength could command. Now Sister Pike was everybody's aunt. Eli and Timmy had often called upon her in happier days when she had currant cookies to offer. Every child in the settlement had the free run of her house, but as the brothers approached her door one day that winter they stopped on the threshold, for they could hear her voice ringing through the old walls.

"Send bread, Lord!" she pleaded. "Send bread! Ye fed the Prophet Elijah when he were lost in the desert. Ye fed the five thousand be the Sea of Galilee. Ye promised to feed all yer children. Send bread, Lord!"

Eli always afterward felt a little ashamed of what he did then.

"Let's get some bread," he whispered to Timmy. "Let's play a joke on her, and make believe the Lord sent it."

When they went dashing into their own kitchen with the request, "Mother, we want two loaves of bread," Martha Pallisher was not surprised in the least, for she never made a baking these days without giving away some of it, to tide some neighbor over until a relief order came in.

"Who for?" she inquired, starting for the pantry.

"Aunt Esther," said Timmy. "She don't got a thing to eat."

"Poor Sister Pike." Martha sighed. "It be a hard winter indeed fer she, bein' as there's no provider in the house, and her brother's family accordin' to the flesh as bad off as herself."

From the tub in the pantry she scooped out about a quarter of a pound of margarine and wrapped it up. She wrapped and tied the bread, and hustled the boys on their errand of mercy.

Their plan was simple and direct. Aunt Esther's huge, old-fashioned hearth led through a straight stone chimney to the roof, which, like all roofs in Caplin Bight, had a fifteen-foot ladder against its eave at the back, in case of fire. It was a matter of the greatest ease for the boys to gain the roof and tiptoe softly across to the chimney, through which they could hear the old woman below, still praying for bread.

They could only imagine her reactions when the bread arrived with a thud on her stone-cold hearth, wrapped in brown paper and tied with shop string, for they heard only her voice, after a few seconds of startled silence, going up in a chant.

"Oh! Thank ye, Lord! Thank ye! I knew ye'd answer me prayer. Oh, thank ye Lord! Praised be Thy holy name!—and butter too!" She had evidently found the margarine.

At this point Eli, leaning on the lip of the chimney, burst out laughing. "It wasn't the Lord, Aunt Esther!" he called down. "It's us!"

The old woman still probably had no idea who might have been the human instrument of the miracle, for any child in the village might have called her "Aunt Esther." She didn't bother to find out, either. Going over to the fireplace she called up, tartly, "I don't care if He sent the devil with it! This bread is from the Lord. Praise His holy name!"

Just then it occurred to Eli that what she said might be true. He stopped laughing, and he and Timmy climbed down off the roof, feeling rather unworthy instruments of divine providence.

"Next time we hear someone praying for bread," Eli said to Timmy, "we'll go in the front door and offer it like Christians, instead of playing Santa Claus like a couple of fools."

Solomon Marks, who had prudently cut his stocks to the bone that winter, soon began "running short" of one thing and another. Among the first luxuries to disappear from his shelves was canned milk. It was rumored that he kept enough to supply his own needs stored away in his cellar, but no one knew this for sure. Mothers with weaned babies became desperate, for fresh milk was almost unheard of in a Newfoundland outport in winter, and it was very difficult, once the regular freight service stopped in the fall, to get anything in from the outside. Some families mixed flour and water into a thin gruel and put it into the babies' bottles instead of milk. The starchy liquid did not satisfy the children. They grew sallow, large-eyed, big-bellied, and cried weakly all the time from unsatisfied hunger. That winter, as Eli saw his own young cousins practically dying a slow death from malnutrition, he began having doubts about the goodness of God, which was so loudly proclaimed in the little church, but since he didn't want to be "skinned alive" he prudently kept these doubts to himself.

It was during the milk crisis that the settlement's unbelievers proved charity not to be a Christian monopoly. Aside from the local scrub cattle, the functions of which were to produce calves and to go dry every winter, the only cow in Caplin Bight belonged to Peter Simms, the retired magistrate. Like all Newfoundland cows, she was of uncertain ancestry, but with a well-developed talent for living off the land most of the year and subsisting on a small ration of hay during the hardest months of winter, but even in December she managed to give a little more than a gallon of milk a day. For years past, this gallon of milk had been taken by Mr. Simms's housekeeper to the kitchen every evening, where it was brought gently to a boil on the stove, to make thick, crusty Devonshire cream for Mr. Simms's porridge and jam. But the thought of babies without milk made him choke on his porridge. So one morning, pushing it aside unfinished, he donned his overcoat, hitched up his little bay mare, and drove the four miles to Solomon Marks's store, intent on sacrificing the eating habits of a lifetime to the common good.

"Tell everyone that has children under three years of age," he said to the group of men idling around the potbellied stove, "that if they'll send to my place every day I'll share the fresh milk equally among them."

It came to little more than half a pint of milk for each baby, but it helped to ward off starvation.

Then Joshua Markady, hearing of Mr. Simms's sacrifice, decided to follow his example.

"Mother," he said to his wife Anne, "we kin do without milk. David," he said to his youngest son, a boy a couple of years older than Eli, "take our three cases out of the cellar and load 'em on a slide. Put 'em on a counter in the store an' tell Sol Marks to share 'em out even among all the small children."

Again it was only a little—eight cans of milk for each child—but it helped to keep them going for another couple of weeks.

The thought must have occurred to more than one that there was something very odd about two of the unsaved, who were headed straight for the second death, coming to the rescue of Christian children whom the Lord had promised to feed, but so far as Eli was aware he was the only one who said anything about it, and even he said it only into the ear of Timmy as they lay in bed, waiting for sleep.

"Mr. Markady and Mr. Simms are both on their way to the second death," he said, "and Elder Solomon Marks the merchant is going to heaven with the elect, even though he keeps milk hidden away in his basement for his own tea, while Mr. Markady and Mr. Simms give all the milk they have to feed other people's children. You know, Timmy, if I were God I'd ask Mr. Markady and Mr. Simms to come to heaven and send Elder Marks to the second death."

"If I was God," said Timmy, "I'd have dumplings every day for dinner, and candy afterward, and gandies with lassy coady whenever I liked, and there'd be no salt fish or onions or turnips, ever. An' there'd be no Sunday school either," he added as an afterthought.

CHAPTER THREE

❧ ❧

Hard on the heels of famine came disease. First it was the flu, which visited Caplin Bight every winter and carried off only the very old or the very young. Then pneumonia appeared. Last of all the angel of death visited the stricken village in the guise of a strange pestilence.

It was the settled conviction of most of the people that all diseases came from God and could be cured by faith. They made an exception in the case of colds, which they looked upon as a seasonal nuisance akin to menstruation. And they made an exception in the case of infant enteritis, which hit all the children each year as soon as the house flies began to swarm, this disease being known as "summer complaint," and, like colds, blamed upon the weather. Sometimes children died of enteritis, but their parents never guessed the reason, looking on the dysentery as a symptom rather than a cause of their decline.

The youngest child of Sister Melinda and Brother Eleazar Pike, a little girl of a year and a half, became so ill in early December that they had to call a special prayer meeting to pray her back to health. Brother Eleazar was something of a backslider, who blew neither hot nor cold, but Sister Melinda was strong in the faith and had spoken in an unknown tongue at a prayer meeting in late November. So the duty of the congregation was clear.

When the little girl got the flu her mother rubbed on a big gob of goose grease from a crock kept for that very purpose and put a bit of Epsom salts in her milk to open her bowels, but otherwise thought little about it. All the children got the flu and most of them got over it. However, when pneumonia fastened bars of iron about the baby's little chest, and choked her breathing, and she appeared to be dying, Eleazar wanted to take her in a trap skiff to the nurse at Lattice Harbor. But Melinda wouldn't hear of it. What did he want to do, she asked, kill the child? They must have faith in God, she said, and call on Pastor Tishrite for advice.

Pastor Tishrite never had any doubts in these matters. He advised a séance. He didn't call it that, but that was the pattern it followed. All those strongest in the faith were invited to meet at Sister Melinda's house, where they would pray most fervently, and wrestle with the Lord, and bring down healing from on high. Taken along by his father and mother to see faith healing in action for the first time, Eli was not allowed actually to participate in the communal prayer service, since he was not yet "converted" and hence was not in a state of grace.

They gathered at the home of the Pikes at eight P.M. Pastor Tishrite and Sister Tishrite were there, and Brother Solomon and Sister Mary Marks, and Brother Elias and Sister Martha Pallisher, and Brother Thomas Gilmore of Matthew and Brother Thomas Gilmore of Thomas with their spouses, and Brother Jabez Penchley, and Sister Esther Pike, and Brother Jehu Gilmore from the Cove, and young Sister Christina Marks, the merchant's niece, who had been converted only three months before, and a number of others. They sat by the light of oil lamps in the Pikes' chilly big front room, which was reserved for funerals and visits of strangers and other rare occasions such as this. And there they prepared themselves for the solemn invocation of the supernatural.

There was a prayer, and a hymn, "When Mothers of Salem Their Children Brought to Jesus." Then Sister Tessie Tishrite, the pastor's wife, moved by the Holy Ghost, spoke of the power of faith, and how the Lord at His first advent had healed lepers, creating a type and shadow of the Great Healing that should come to all the righteous at His appearing. Then she spoke further of the Great Sore that should fall upon the ungodly, quoting from the Book of Revelation, and contrasting this with the leaves of the Tree of Life that were to heal those who walked by the pure river of water of life without sin.

Next Pastor Tishrite read from the Epistle of St. James, where it is explained about praying over the sick. Then he offered a long prayer and benediction, and the séance began.

The baby was laid in the middle of the room, rigid, with blue lips and almost in a coma, but still able to cry weakly, between fits of choking for breath. The people then gathered in a circle and held hands, so as to form an unbroken shield of faith about the child, and so that the virtue might pass from one to another until they all should become exalted. They sang another hymn, and then the wrestling with God began.

First one prayed in a loud voice, and then another, as the Holy Ghost moved them. And as one prayed, the rest kept up an obbligato of ejaculations: "Amen!" "Yes, Lord, yes!" "Hear us, Lord Jesus!" "Yes, God!" "Amen, Lord!" and similar remarks.

Sitting outside the circle with several other children who had been brought along to witness the miracle, Eli found himself caught up in the hypnosis of the prayer and carried along in a current of feeling not his own. This was the first time he had experienced the way a prayer meeting can bend the individual will to its collective purpose, and it frightened him a little. In an effort to break the spell he tried reciting the multiplication table to himself, but it didn't work. The parade of numbers slipped by unnoticed while the main part of his mind was occupied with a passionate plea to the Creator of the universe to come this instant to Caplin Bight and pinch hit for a registered nurse.

More concentration was needed, he decided. Now, suppose six men and a boy on half shares had a thousand quintals of fish, and the owner took an extra share for his trap. . . . It took him almost two minutes to solve the problem of the boy's share, and he found that in the process the trance was totally dispelled. No longer frightened by the feeling of possession, he decided to try, experimentally, allowing the hypnosis of the prayer to seize him once more. Then he broke it a second time, with a shorter effort of will. It came far easier than before, he noticed, and before long he was slipping in and out of the trance like a seal popping in and out of a spout hole between the rocks.

Since each person in the circle was allowed his turn at praying, and since some of them rather fancied themselves in the field of prayer oratory, the séance seemed in some danger of going on forever. It finally broke up, though, shortly before eleven P.M., with everyone in a state of emotional exhaustion and its mission accomplished. The baby had sunk into a fitful sleep, her breathing much easier, and a wisp of color had returned to her white face. Sister Melinda put the child back into her cot with tears of thankfulness in her eyes. Pastor Tishrite offered an exalted prayer of praise, drawing heavily on the Psalms for his phraseology, and the whole group, children and all, joined in singing the hymn, "High in the Heavens Eternal God." Then everyone went home in a glow of righteousness.

In the morning when Sister Melinda went to see whether the baby was well enough to want her breakfast she found the child dead, lying in the cot stiff and cold, just as she had left her there the night before. Sister Melinda screamed, and called upon the name of the Lord Jesus, who had raised the dead, as well as healing lepers. But this time the dead was not raised.

The death of the Pike baby posed no theological problem to the pastor. He pronounced flatly that the child had died because of lack of faith on the part of her father. This explanation gained such immediate currency among the congregation, being accepted even by Sister Melinda, that Eleazar refused to allow the pastor to bury his child. He persisted in this shocking apostasy even in the face of his wife's screams and tears.

He dug the grave himself, working all day in the frozen soil, and on his own shoulders he carried the little spruce box of planed boards with the body to the graveyard on the Point, where all the people of Caplin Bight lay buried, those who had died in Christ side by side with those who had died in sin. And there with his older children beside him, shedding tears upon the snow, he lowered the box into the grave and sprinkled clay over it, repeating in his ancient Devon accents the time-honored formula, "Earth to earth, ashes to ashes, dust to dust."

And then, because he could not read or write, he had his eldest daughter read from the Bible the traditional passages: "I am the resurrection and the life . . . this mortal shall put on immortality. . . . O death, where is thy sting?" And he shoveled the clay back into the grave, and tramped it down, and walked home, his children following.

Being too poor to buy a chiseled stone from St. John's, he planed a slab of pine and burned the baby's name upon it, as it was traced there by his daughter, with the day and year of its birth and the months and days of its life, and set the slab at the head of the grave, and went back to the net loft, where he sat by himself, knitting a leader for a cod trap, in the firm faith that the fish would return another year.

Sister Melinda went dumbly about her work, her own faith unshaken, a little proud, perhaps, that the Lord had seen fit to lay upon her such a heavy burden. But her eldest son, Pleman, a boy of Eli's age, stood firmly with his father in a house now divided by unspoken hostility.

Though prayers for the Pike baby proved useless, the same could not be said of all such cures. They were often very effective, especially if the patient was old enough to

believe in them himself. A second séance, held shortly after
the first, for the benefit of old Sister Miriam Marks, the
merchant's mother, whose flu had turned to pleurisy and
who was not responding to mustard plasters as she should,
justified itself in a most spectacular manner, for the old
woman not only sat up and asked for tea, but within the
hour got out of bed, declared herself completely cured, and
next day was helping her daughter-in-law with the house-
work as usual.

But the settlement was soon to be visited by a malady
that no faith could heal. The week before Christmas young
Samuel Gilmore, the seven-year-old son of Thomas Gilmore
of Thomas, was stricken suddenly by a disease that sent him
into a raging fever and killed him in three days. Before the
boy died five other children and two women had come
down with the same symptoms. Soon half the houses in
the settlement had someone desperately sick. Thomas Gilmore's second child died, and so did his cousin, the nine-
year-old daughter of Thomas Gilmore of Matthew.

By this time people were thoroughly frightened. Every
third child and every fifth adult seemed marked for death.
Everyone had the unspoken thought that he might be next.
By December 22 it was obvious that they would have to
seek help from Lattice Harbor.

Snow came first by the inch, then by the foot, driving before the wind for three days, then sifting down out of a
silent sky, burying everything and softening the world into
rounded white mounds. Up to that time, despite all the
prayers, no one who fell sick had recovered, and there was
a widespread belief that the village was suffering a "visitation," like that which afflicted the children of Israel because
of the sin of their king. Christmas came without aid from the
settlements along the coast. The world outside was white
with snow, and the world inside was black with despair.
The people of Caplin Bight went about as though waiting

for a deadly monster to pounce upon them from a dark corner.

It was the day after Christmas that nine-year-old Timmy woke in the morning, his eyes bright with fever, head spinning so he couldn't stand, and "pains inside," as he piteously told his mother. Eli watched his father eat breakfast and hurry outdoors. The snow, which had stopped during the night, was falling again, fitfully. The wind had gone down, but a big sea was running, and the boom of surf on the sunkers at the harbor mouth sounded like continuous thunder threatening death.

As Eli and Elias watched from their gallery, two great black and white birds came over the Head and banked seaward and separated and spiraled in opposite directions, as though flirting with the sky-spouting surf from the sunken rocks beyond the cliffs.

"Look at the eagles, Father!" Eli exclaimed.

"Ay, lad! Birds of ill omen, they be!" Elias told him. "Seed 'em more'n once when death was nigh. Cot one on a baited hook, I did, when ye was a babe in arms, but 'tweren't possible to tame the craiture. Jabez Pike's dog fought it to the death. 'Twas some sight, I'll tell 'e. The dog were tore somethin' pitiful, an' 'e warn't no use after, but 'e killed the eagle fair an' square."

"I think that's terrible!" Eli exclaimed. "Why didn't somebody stop it?"

"An' why should they?" Elias asked. "What good be an eagle, boy?—one o' the devil's birds, I'll be bound. Even hissed like a snake, it did, till the dog tore out its windpipe."

"I don't know," Eli said doubtfully. He looked at the great birds soaring above the storm and his heart lifted a little. To him they were not birds of ill omen, but free spirits, full of power and glory. The thought of one of them being worried to death by a dog made him shudder.

Elias dropped his hand roughly on his son's shoulder.

"Got worse than eagles to worry about, boy," he said. "Le's go find yer mother."

They went inside, where Martha was stoking the fire absent-mindedly.

"Woman," said Elias, "pack a lunch and git the teakettle ready. I'll want me heaviest clothes an' oilskins. I be goin' to Lattice Harbor fer the nurse."

"Elias!" Martha exclaimed. "Ye'll drown. Don't go, Elias, till the sea goes down. Ye'd be crazy to put out in this."

It was quite an outburst for a Caplin Bight woman, none of whom ever thought of questioning a man's decisions about the man's world of the outdoors.

"I been out in worse—an' fer worse reasons too," Elias said shortly. "Anyhow, somebody's bound to go fer the nurse if we ain't all to die in our beds, one after t'other."

Martha looked at him and her mouth set itself in the line of resignation that was becoming fixed with the years. "Who'll ye take?" she asked, peering out the window at the roaring ocean. She recoiled from the sight. "Elias!" she exclaimed. "Ye can't take a trap skiff out in that!"

"Some as couldn't," he admitted, "but me new skiff's good fer it. Pity she's hauled up. Take most o' the mornin' to git away."

"I'll go, Father," Eli volunteered, with twelve-year-old confidence in himself and his father's seamanship.

"An' indeed ye won't!" Martha snapped. "I don't aim to lose me whole family the same day. Ye are stayin' home."

"Could go alone, I s'pose," Elias mused, "but two men be more'n twice the worth o' one, any day. . . . I'll want a man as knows what he be about. . . . Eleazar Pike, I 'low. He been shareman with me six year runnin' an' as good a hand in a boat as I ever see."

Elias collected half a dozen men to help him get his twenty-six-foot skiff into the water. They hauled it to the simple log slipway that had served Caplin Bight well for generations. There, using capstan and cable, they let it slide backward into the water, greasing the slipway with cod-liver oil from a barrel of rotted liver whenever the keel began to burn into the logs. Elias had closed the boat's drain plugs, primed and oiled the engine, hooked up the little dry-cell battery, tested the magneto and filled it with the aromatic mixture of oil and purple gasoline on which it ran. He put lines on board, fetched the small hand-powered bilge pump from his net loft, and selected a pair of the small, multiple-hooked fishing anchors called graplins, for he might have to lie up in some open cove to weather a blow. He rigged a heavy tarpaulin over the forepart of the boat for shelter, forming a sort of cabin where they could remain dry, and even sleep if they had to. Last of all he put on board food, tea, water, firewood, two lanterns, and a small compass.

Lattice Harbor—in sight on a fine day—required three hours' running for the fastest trap skiffs when the weather was fair, but it might take six hours in rough water, or even longer if the boat was forced to heave to in the Reach or the lee of Lattice Harbor Island. It was almost noon by the time the boat was ready, and by then the sea was showing signs of dropping a little.

Eli went, with the group of men who had helped launch and provision the skiff, to the cliff top on the Head, where he and Pleman Pike stood together to watch their fathers make the dangerous run through the breakers at the narrows. It was a frightening but inspiring sight. The boat tossed and wallowed on her way out the run. They watched fearfully as she approached the tricky stretch of water between the sunkers, which were breaking white with every wave and sending up spouts of spray like twin cataracts.

Eli saw his father, far below, wave to the other man to cut the engine and allow the boat to coast, waiting his chance to run the short channel on a slack wave. Then he saw Eleazar connect the wires again, and the engine, still spinning slowly, at once barked into life. As it made its first few coughs, the boat was picked up by a swelling sea, right between the sunkers, and sent skidding sideways down the far slope. There was a thunder of surf, and the skidding boat was smothered in white spray. She seemed for an instant to be out of control, her small propeller out of water, her rudder scarcely biting the tip of the foam that snarled under her stern, and she began to slip toward the maelstrom of white water that swirled about the sunker on the port side of the channel. Eli's heart stopped, and he felt Pleman grab his arm in a tense grip. But the boat staggered in the trough and recovered, lifted her bluff bows to the next wave, climbed it, and headed triumphantly down the great green hill of water into a snow squall.

All through the group there was the sound of sharply drawn breath, for during the space of ten or fifteen seconds every man on the Head had stopped breathing.

"A nigh close call," one of them remarked.

"Mighty nigh," another agreed, "but they be through the worst of it now. Wind'll be offshore at Lattice Harbor, allowin' it don't chop or veer, but holds from this quarter."

"Ay," said another. "Have to see about a beacon, I 'low."

The harbor light at Lattice Harbor was maintained throughout the year, but the tiny gas-fed flame that guided ships into Caplin Bight was a seasonal affair, allowed to die in the fall when official coastal navigation ceased. It would be pitch-black when Elias returned, and maybe thick with snow as well. Nobody could be sure that so much as a single light from the houses would be visible. The problem was solved by getting two tar barrels from Solomon Marks's store. Empty and discarded, they still had enough tar about them to create a blaze that would be visible across the bay. They set one barrel on the Head, the other on the Point, on the cliff at the near side of the harbor, a hundred yards or so from Joshua Markady's house; then they agreed to stand watch after nightfall, and to light the beacons at the first sound of a boat engine or sight of an approaching light.

These preparations finished, they went home, some to work distractedly in their net lofts, some to sit hopelessly at the bedsides of wives or children who hovered between life and death. And Eli went home to listen to his mother's prayers for Timmy's life and for Elias's safety, and to watch from time to time beside his beloved little brother, who tossed and turned with eyes closed, or babbled deliriously, with eyes glassy and unseeing, throughout the long day.

The wind died, the snow stopped, and a watery shaft of sunlight lit the harbor in late afternoon. The sea continued to go down, and it was evident that, assuming Elias had succeeded in reaching Lattice Harbor, he would have no real trouble about the return trip, though the roar of breakers still echoed along the shore and came in a deep and continuous growl from distant parts of the bay.

Darkness fell at four-thirty, and small fires were seen on the Head and the Point, where some of the men were standing watch. Eli spent most of that evening at the window, waiting for the blaze of the first tar barrel to flare out redly against the darkness. It was around eight-thirty when he saw the blaze of light on the Head, and a moment later the answering flare from the Point, as first one beacon, then the other, sent smoke and flame licking into the sky.

"They're coming!" he cried to his mother, and raced outside into the deepening frost, Martha following him, her apron wrapped about her hands.

He strained his ears through the booming of the sea, but could hear nothing. Ten minutes may have passed before he heard, or fancied that he heard, the faint, far-off chugging of an engine. Then, as he watched, the tiny star of his father's lantern shone at the edge of the cliff, separated itself from the blackness of the rock, moved into mid-channel. As Eli raced through the snow down to his family stage on the central part of the waterfront, windows came alight all around the harbor.

That part of the population of Caplin Bight which wasn't prostrate on its back collected around the Pallisher stage that night to meet the young nurse. She was a scrap of a girl who had obviously endured agonies of seasickness during the trip across the Reach and up the windward shore.

But she stepped ashore bravely, clutching her bag, reeled, and had to be supported for the first few minutes as she followed Elias's lantern to his house.

She went straight to Timmy's bedside, spent a few minutes with the little boy, came out looking scared, and said the word "typhoid" almost in a whisper. Then she packed her kit like a country doctor, commandeered Eli as a guide, and set out to visit every home where there was a sick person.

For Eli, that night seemed to last forever. He catnapped on a dozen kitchen settles and was given cups of very weak tea by a dozen kindly women. By dawn he had almost passed out on his feet, but by breakfasttime the young nurse was still driving ahead with as much energy as ever. She seemed to have worked off both her seasickness and her fatigue.

"You must go home now," she told Eli. "I can't leave here, and I can't stop. But please tell your father that he must go back to Lattice Harbor at once, and send a message to St. John's. Here. This is it." And she wrote the message in pencil on the back of an envelope. Two of her patients had already died.

It took a day and a half for help to arrive from St. John's. When it came, it was in the form of a miracle that Caplin Bight had known only by hearsay. A little airplane on floats —a Gypsy Moth byplane—came humming through the air, circled gracefully around the cup of the hills, and settled down on the harbor, sending up twin plumes of spray as it taxied up to the government wharf. Even some of the sick got out of bed and plastered their faces to windows.

No man from Mars could have been treated with more awe and respect than the young "aviator" who climbed down from the marvelous open cockpit of that plane and helped the doctor down from its only other seat. But the people on the wharf almost ignored the doctor. The flier was dressed as befitted a superman: not in pants, but in knee breeches, with heavy boots and leather leggings. He wore a black leather jacket, a leather cap that buckled down over his ears, and pushed up on his forehead was a pair of goggles. He even wore long black leather gloves, completing the illusion of belonging to another species. Eli decided on the instant that aviation would be his career, and it is likely that most of the other boys of Caplin Bight reached the same decision simultaneously.

By the time they got around to thinking about the doctor he had his trunk unloaded and packed on a horse slide and was on his way to set up a temporary lab in the empty school, which the nurse had prepared against his arrival. He quickly confirmed the nurse's findings and turned the school into an isolation hospital. Then he sent the plane back for more emergency supplies, to help him deal with the epidemic.

The nurse, questioning the people about their water supply, already suspected that the source of infection was the brook that ran into the Bottom and powered Gilmore's mill. Most of the houses where the fever had struck first—including the two Gilmore families—secured their water from this brook, she found. The doctor lost no time in testing it and issuing orders against its use. He also found the source of the infection—a leak from a privy near the little pond at the brook's estuary, and ordered it removed. Ironically, if people had gone upstream twenty or thirty yards for their water, there never would have been any epidemic.

The doctor told the people that he had found approximately a hundred and fifty thousand live organisms to the cubic centimeter in some samples of water that he tested, and though nobody seemed to know what he was talking about, it sounded frightfully ominous. So, as he directed, they stopped drinking the water, and tore down the privy, and took the purges and intestinal disinfectants that he prescribed. Within three weeks the last of the patients from the temporary hospital was moved back to his home, the school disinfected with sulfur candles, and the doctor returned by the way he had come.

Apart from stopping the epidemic, his visit had another

important effect. He made a report to the Department of
Public Health and Welfare on the state of infant nutrition
in Caplin Bight. The result was that the milk crisis was
solved early in February, when a large supply of canned
milk, cod-liver oil (refined, for drinking, unlike the local,
inedible product), and orange juice was sent in from the
government by chartered schooner. These three items, the
public nutritionists said, were essential for the normal development of all children, born or unborn, and must be fed
not only to babies but to expectant mothers as well. The millions who had grown up without them must, they felt sure,
be mentally and physically deficient, with no teeth, soft
bones, and short life expectancy.

The visit of the angel of death had little effect upon the
basic religious convictions of the settlement. Though Pastor
Tishrite admitted that modern medicine might be one of
the instruments of divine mercy, he gave it a place far below
faith and holiness. Only the ungodly, he suggested, really
needed its ministrations, and his flock should learn from the
epidemic to mend their hell-bent ways before a worse disaster overtook them.

Many of his flock, however, had other views. Apart from
those who, like Elias Pallisher, considered it man's duty to
do everything possible for himself before casting his all
upon the Lord, there were others who began openly doubting Pastor Tishrite's effectiveness as a mediator with the
heavenly powers. His intercession for the divine grace of
healing had produced a few triumphs but a far greater number of failures. What about his personal standing with God?
Was he as strong in faith and prayer as he ought to be? Such
murmurings went the rounds of the congregation, and
though the pastor still had his loyal friends and supporters,
his authority was weakened and the way prepared for his
eventual fall.

But, at the time, Eli was not much concerned with these
theological speculations. That winter he went regularly into
the woods with his father and began to enjoy the feeling of

physical strength and well-being that only men who labor
ever know. He had worked about the yard, on the flake,
and intermittently in the trap boat, but this was the first
regular, organized work that he had done. For the first and
only time the boy and man began to draw together in a
sort of partnership. Elias was delighted with the way Eli
stuck to his work and improved and became skillful. He was
so pleased that he promised to take him on as a regular
shareman with his trap crew the next summer, on half shares.
It was not unusual for a boy to hire on as shareman at twelve
or thirteen, drawing half a man's share from the trap voyages until the age of fifteen or sixteen, when he could demand a full share like any other man.

Cutting and hauling firewood and saw logs by catamaran
that winter, Eli, without noticing it, passed through the
first of several doors into manhood. His father opened the
door for him, and he slipped through gently. Later that
year he found the second door.

CHAPTER FOUR

❦

Joshua Markady, onetime merchant, shipowner, and world-wide trader, was "still a young man," as they say on the coast of Newfoundland of vigorous men in their early sixties. For outport Newfoundlanders, if they do not die in childhood, and if they are not killed or lost at sea, usually remain healthy until their eighties, are often still working at ninety, and sometimes live more than a century. Mr. Markady had retired at the prime of life, now worked only when he cared to do so and only at jobs that took his fancy. He had made large profits in fish and trade goods during the Great War, and was regarded in Caplin Bight as sinfully wealthy.

"It is easier for a camel . . ." Thomas Gilmore of Matthew quoted and shook his head sadly, for he had a high personal regard for Mr. Markady. The mill owner was himself regarded as a rich man by the fishermen who hauled their logs to his mill to be sawed on the halves, but he saw no prospect of retiring at sixty, and he regarded such early retirement as the dividing line between virtuous thrift and the mortal sin of avarice.

Mr. Markady had been a skipper in his teens, and ship-owner in his twenties. His first vessel, a smart little eighty-ton fore-and-after built like a yacht, but laid out for cargo, he had sailed to half the lands of the civilized world. Later, as his business expanded, he sent other ships under other captains over the same routes he had sailed himself, losing two of them, during the war, to German submarines that, disdaining to waste torpedoes on such small game, had surfaced and sunk the wooden ships by shellfire, allowing the crews to escape in their boats.

In the palmy days of sail one of the greatest trading fleets in the world operated out of Newfoundland, and the island —one of the world's smallest countries—was hard put to find enough men to serve as crews. Ports such as Carbonear and Harbor Grace—then the island's second city—flourished on this world-girdling trade, sending big, old-fashioned square-riggers, and the smaller, newer tern schooners, to all the ports of Europe and the Mediterranean, to Africa, South America, and the Orient. Mr. Markady had got in on the tail end of this trade in time to reap some of its last and biggest profits and see it die. As Newfoundland's great sailing fleet was gradually forced off the seas by iron-hulled steamships he had turned bit by bit to coastal trade, sending his shallow-draft vessels into every cove and hamlet along the island's thousands of miles of shoreline, carrying fish and lumber to the trading centers, returning to the little coves with general supplies.

But that trade, too, dwindled. The iron ships began to follow the little coasters into the small ports, and soon monopolized the trade with all the major centers. The home-grown outport merchant, with his accounts of the fish trade going back five or six generations in big ledgers written in copperplate script, was displaced by the branch store of the Water Street firm, as the St. John's trader was called.

Mr. Markady, drawing on the experience of thirty years' shrewd trading, could see all these trends before they were fully developed. He realized that the great merchant traders of the past were fated soon to become mere peddlers of canned meat and marmalade, pushing other men's goods, and he found the prospect little to his taste. So he sold his store to Solomon Marks, one of his skippers who had done well and developed a wish to be in business for himself.

Then he sold all but two of his vessels at sacrifice prices in Nova Scotia.

He retired to his big house on the Point, for with all his wandering he had found no place he loved as he loved Caplin Bight, in spite of all its faults. In the big house his wife moved quietly about, like a wren in its nest, and the last of his sons, David, grew to manhood. Mr. Markady now appeared wherever life and work were on the simmer, a forceful, stocky man with a white mustache, a gold chain, and a teak walking stick, which he carried about the village as a badge of his position. He had a glint of good humor in his eyes, and a passion for hunting, both by land and sea.

He owned the only ten-gauge shotgun in Caplin Bight— a massive, double-barreled fowling piece with a report like a cannon. Unlike most of the fishermen's swile guns, which were used for all purposes, from hunting little bullbirds to celebrating elections and marriages, and which were loaded by pouring powder and shot into the barrel, Mr. Markady's ten-gauge was a breech-loader, which took shells that he filled himself at his kitchen table with coarse black powder and lead pellets.

He was granted a large measure of respect in Caplin Bight, as befitted a man who had owned great wealth, had visited fabled lands on the other side of the world, and wore a heavy gold watch chain. But he was also regarded as a great sinner, an unbeliever, a blasphemer, and irrevocably lost.

Through an accident that nearly cost Mr. Markady his life, but proved a piece of rare good fortune for Eli, this great sinner became the boy's spiritual father and started him on a greater journey than any he himself had made in the days of high adventure when he had sailed to Demerara and Santa Lucia, and beat on double tacks out of the Bight of Benin.

Slob ice (small, thick pans, packed closely together) formed in the harbor that winter, and in the Cove and along the inlets of the bay. As the year advanced it was joined by

northern slob, brought down on the Labrador Current and
by the outriders of the field ice from the Arctic in the early
days of March. Frosts came, and cemented solidly together
this conglomeration of ice pans, and soon it became possible to walk over the sea all the way from Caplin Bight to
Lattice Harbor, or to travel across the Reach by dog team,
or even with a horse and slide.

This was the way it was when Easter came, and April with
it, and Mr. Markady took his horse, Prince, tackled to a
fine side sleigh, across the Reach to Lattice Harbor to fetch
home for the holidays his son David, who, for want of a
school in Caplin Bight that winter, had been sent to the
larger settlement to board. David was expected to go up to
St. John's to school the following year, so his winter schooling was considered vital.

Now it so happened that the annual Feast of the Lord's
Supper, which coincides more or less with Easter, and is
celebrated with great fervor and solemnity in Caplin Bight,
fell on the day of Mr. Markady's trip to Lattice Harbor.
There was much fasting and watching and reading of Scriptures that day, in preparation for the solemn rite that was
to be enacted in the church after sunset. Children who had
not yet experienced the mystical rebirth of conversion, and
were therefore not in a state of grace, took no part in the
feast. Indeed, they were solemnly warned not to touch so
much as a crumb of the bread that might fall from the Lord's
table, for, "He that eateth or drinketh unworthily, eateth or
drinketh to himself damnation."

And so it chanced that, having been told to go about his
own affairs and not to bother his parents in the midst of
their meditations, Eli, having shed Timmy for once, wandered down by Jehu Gilmore's shack in the Cove, with a
very old and very rusty muzzle-loading gun, thinking he
might find a duck or two, or perhaps a few bullbirds, in an
open lead of water along the shore.

Besides the old gun, he had a wooden dog—a cross made
out of wood, with rows of large fish hooks fastened to both

sides of its beam and a light heaving line attached to the
upright. You spin a wooden dog around your head until it
achieves a great velocity, then let it go so that the line flies
out before you. You can throw it pretty well the distance
a normal gunshot travels, and use it to retrieve birds from
open water.

There were no ducks or bullbirds to be seen that day, and
Eli was practising retrieving ice pans from the open lead
with the wooden dog when the little black horse with Mr.
Markady and David came into sight along shore and started
across the Cove toward the Bight. They were moving slowly
and cautiously, the little horse picking his steps over rotten
ice that had been loosened by a gentle offshore wind.

They were skirting close to the beach when they ran into
real trouble, striking soft ice and an open lead at the same
time. The sleigh tilted sideways and backward, and Mr.
Markady shouted and jumped for it. He landed on his feet,
but skidded on the ice and went into the water with a re-
sounding curse that echoed off the cliffs. David jumped
at the same instant and splashed through soft ice. The
sleigh went down. It all happened in a fraction of a second.
The horse wallowed in the water, clawing with ineffective
hoofs at the loose ice pans and screaming in fear. Then the
harness dragged him under, his staring eyes and open mouth
pointing at the sky for one horrible moment while he gave
a shrill cry of despair before the slob ice closed over him
and the scream turned to a bubbling gurgle. David and Mr.
Markady were left by themselves in the water, clinging to
the edge of the rotten ice, which broke off in their hands as
they struggled toward shore.

Jehu Gilmore, who had been taking the spring sunshine
on the doorstep of his ramshackle home and dipping into
the Word of God from time to time as it lay open on his
knees, heard Mr. Markady's loud blast of profanity, awoke
from his holy meditations, and rushed down to the landwash, waving his Bible as he went.

"Have faith in God!" he cried. "Repent! Repent! Fer the

hour be at hand an' the wrath of God be great and very turrible upon all the heathen!" He opened the Book to select a passage for the exhortation of the struggling men in the water.

"Jehu," Josh Markady roared, "fetch us a rope here! Hurry, you fool!"

"It is appointed to men once to die," Jehu read back in a loud voice, "an' after death the jedgment!"

"Jehu Gilmore!" Mr. Markady shouted. "If ye don't fetch us a rope here this instant, be the bleeding Christ when I *do* get ashore I'll ram that Goddamn Bible down yer fuckin' throat!"

All this happened in the few seconds while Eli was wondering what to do. The heaving line of his wooden dog, he quickly concluded, would do the men no good. Where to get a rope around Jehu's ramshackle establishment? Suddenly he remembered the ladder at the back. It wasn't much, as ladders go, being made of two thin strips of scantling with palings nailed across, but it would serve. Eli might have had trouble toting a real ladder, but the flimsy thing of Jehu's was well within his strength. He dropped his gun, ran for the ladder, and brought it to the landwash before either of the Markadys had begun to sink.

Jehu was still prophesying from the shore. "Behold," he was declaiming, "the hour cometh that shall burn as an oven!"

But Eli didn't wait to listen. Dragging the ladder behind, he started for the edge of the ice.

"Get back, boy!" Mr. Markady yelled. "Ye'll fall through an' be no use to yerself or us. Lay down flat on yer belly an' push the thing in front of ye, end first."

His voice was weaker, and he looked as though he might soon lose his grip on the edge of the ice. As quickly as possible Eli did as he was told, worming his way like a seal over the ice until the end of the ladder was within a few feet of the men in the water.

"Toward David," Mr. Markady gasped. "He be lighter—

get out easier—help ye give me a hand, after." He was getting short of breath as the icy water drained the vital heat away from his body.

David grabbed the end of the ladder and hung on, then slowly dragged himself over the end of it. The ice broke again, and he sagged back, but he inched forward until he was lying flat along the scantlings. Eli then backed up, dragging him away from the edge until he was on solid ice.

When they tried the same thing with Mr. Markady they found he was too near to exhaustion to drag himself out of the water.

"Try haulin' me in," he directed. "I'll smash the ice as I go."

So they dragged the ladder toward shore, Mr. Markady hanging desperately to the end, the ice splitting and crunching before him as he came, until he hit a solid ice pan, lost his grip, and went under. For a terrible moment they thought he had gone down for good, perhaps drifted under the ice, but the tough old sea captain, who had survived many brushes with death in his time, came up blowing like a porpoise, coughed, grabbed the edge of the ice, and held on.

"Drag me over," he almost whispered. "Can't make it meself."

David, who was blue and stiff with cold, got down on his belly and crawled quickly to the edge. "It'll hold. It's thicker!" he called back to Eli. "Come here and grab me be the feet. We'll have to hoist him up on the ice."

So Eli held David to keep him from slipping in, while the older boy exerted his last ounce of strength, hauling the two-hundred-pound man over the ragged edge of the ice until he lay like a shapeless sack of old clothes, waterlogged but safe from drowning. Once on the ice, he managed to crawl ashore under his own power, where he sat up with a shuddering breath and began to beat his arms feebly to start the blood circulating again.

But that very moment he caught sight of Jehu, still standing by with his open Bible in his hand. The sight must have summoned up some hidden reserve of strength. "By God!" he said in a terrible, quiet voice, and lurched to his feet.

Jehu yelped like a kicked pup and lit out for his door, Mr. Markady shambling along in his wake like a great bear dripping from a swim. Before Mr. Markady reached the door (which was innocent of any lock or bar) Jehu had it barricaded with a chair, but door, chair and all, splintered and gave way before the violence of Mr. Markady's assault and Jehu fled out the back, calling on God as he went.

Once inside the Gilmore abode, the two boys following close behind, Mr. Markady's rage departed and he dropped to the rough wooden settle in the kitchen and started to laugh.

"Well, here we be!" he said. "David, lad, get off yer wet duds. We'll wring 'em out an' hang 'em be the stovepipe to dry. We can use a blanket fer the time bein' if Jehu got such a thing in the other room." He turned to Eli. "Boy," he said, "will ye use the pieces of that chair to heat up the stove a bit? An' see can ye get the door to shut again. This draft is goin' to be bad fer me rheumatism."

Mr. Markady, who had been dropping wet clothes like sods on the kitchen floor, now went padding into Jehu's other room, returning with two threadbare and moth-eaten blankets that looked suspiciously like government issue.

"Beggars can't be choosers, David," he said, tossing one to his shivering son. "'Tis sort of a rough homecoming for ye, lad, but think how lucky ye are to be alive."

"If it hadn't been for Eli—" David said.

"Ay," Mr. Markady agreed. "Never thought I'd owe me life to a bedlemer the size o' ye! But David's right, lad. Ye did exactly the right thing. A trained seaman couldn't've been more prompt or showed a better knack fer doin' exactly what was needed. Ye've got good stuff in ye, boy."

Eli couldn't do much except feel embarrassed under such extravagant praise. "'Twasn't nothing, sir," he mumbled.

"Nothin', eh?" said Mr. Markady. "And how old are ye?"

"Just turned thirteen," Eli said.

"Hmm," Mr. Markady mused. "I owe ye a big debt, boy, and I be not the sort as shirks me obligations. It'll be at least two, maybe three years before ye are ready to decide where ye want to go—what ye want to do. Maybe then . . ." A thought seemed to strike him suddenly. "What was that hunk o' rusty iron I saw ye luggin' along the shore?"

"A gun, sir," Eli said. "Belonged to my uncle Sam, but 'tis not much account now. Father lets me use it whenever I want."

"Like to shoot, do ye?" The twinkle had returned to Mr. Markady's eye. "Tell ye what. Soon as the ice moves off I'll take ye gunnin' over to Lattice Harbor Island, and I'll warrant ye'll come home with all the turrs ye can carry."

"Thank you, sir," Eli said.

"'Tis me owes the thanks," Mr. Markady said. "Let's see if there be the makings of a cup o' tea."

The room was heating up, filling with steam, and he was poking about with the blanket draped over his shoulders like a Roman senator in a toga. He had taken full charge of Jehu's little house, and where the owner had gone he neither knew nor cared.

For Eli, who had known the Markadys only casually before, this was the beginning of one of the great friendships of his life. Up to that time he had been, to Mr. Markady, just another one of the village boys, albeit one who liked more than most to listen to stories of the sea. He had sat for hours, listening to the old captain and occasionally sampling Anne Markady's excellent cooking. But now there was a sense of reciprocation, of a relationship to which he contributed his full share.

Mr. Markady was even better than his word. The ice went out at the end of April and he took Eli on an all-day bird-shooting trip (the first of many) to the big offshore island that lay on the far side of the Reach, about halfway between Caplin Bight and Lattice Harbor, where the duck-sized black and white sea birds known as murres—or turrs, as the fishermen called them—gathered to feed by the hundreds, and often by the thousands. Not only that. There was a new gun in the boat. It was a single-shot, twelve-gauge breech-loader that Mr. Markady had gone all the way to Broadport, far up the bay, to secure. With it there was a box of shells. The name "Eli Pallisher" was burned neatly into the stock.

Eli loved that gun more dearly than a boy loves his dog or his horse. No youth in Caplin Bight had anything like it, for the boys of the settlement were almost naked of personal possessions, and treasured even a trout hook as a great prize. Years later, when Eli owned his first sporting rifle, it gave him nothing like the same thrill. That gun is still in service today—old now, and battered, with many scars and many turrs to its credit—but still treasured, not so much for itself as for the wonderful old man who opened for Eli the second door into manhood.

CHAPTER FIVE

That year was one which Eli, and the other people of his little home town, could never forget. Looking back on it afterward, he often thought that it seemed too fantastic to be believed. But the things that happened—as well as the things that did not happen—left lasting marks on the people who lived through them.

It was the year after the fish failure, and the snow went early. Already by early May there was continuous sunshine, the forest floor was carpeted with moss, and only in the pools of deepest shade was there a little old, hard snow left for the melting. Offshore the sun glared with a piercing blue-white flame over the strings of field ice that floated far out, past the remote headlands that formed the mouth of the bay, traveling with the swift-flowing Labrador Current, seeking its destiny in the warm waters of the Gulf Stream to the south.

The gloom and despair of the hungry, disease-ridden winter quickly gave way to optimism as the first salmon were brought to shore from the nets beyond the sunkers— big twenty-pounders, gleaming like tarnished silver in the light and auguring plenty for the year ahead. They had salmon that spring by May 10, a week earlier than usual in Caplin Bight. Everyone believed that it was going to be an exceptionally good year.

Solomon Marks, catching the general enthusiasm, discovered that by stretching matters to the limit he would be able to supply for the fishery after all. Everyone was in debt to him, but he rather liked to have it that way, so long as the total debts were not greater than the total net worth of the settlement. For even if a man in Caplin Bight died in debt to the merchant with a load of obligations far greater than the value of his estate, his sons and grandsons would assume the burden and would work for a decade, or two if necessary, in order to clear the family from the assumed debt.

Eli and Timmy and their parents ate all the fresh salmon that they could hold, salted much more of it, and smoked about five hundred pounds in a little black smokehouse, which had a tight-fitting door and no windows, but a ventilator in the top, like a young chimney, and another near the dirt floor, to keep the air and smoke moving. Elias and Eli worked together splitting and cleaning the beautiful fish, then hung them by their tails in the smokehouse over a smudge fire of blackberry brush and turf, dampened down with peat moss as needed, to keep it from burning too freely. It was believed that blackberry smoke gave the finest flavor to salmon. As the fish were cured in the smoke they turned from bright pink to a deep, rich red with tints of brown, and took on an aroma that made every mouth water expectantly with the first whiff. All over Caplin Bight that month there hung an evanescent bluish haze and the tantalizing smell of blackberry smoke, making noses twitch and eyes water.

The boy went to the nets with his father each day at five o'clock in the morning, when the sky was red and green and gold. Every dawn Eli saw the sun rise over the sea in a flood of splendor, while they hitched their little punt to one end of the net and hauled the other end into the big trap boat, seeing, far down in the blue-green water, the silver-blue fish, caught by the gills but struggling nobly to free themselves as they came, arching with great power in their muscular tails over the side of the skiff. The fish were exceedingly strong and hard to handle, even after many hours in a net. Eli clouted them to death as they came aboard, thinking it strange that a fish with such vitality should die almost without a wriggle when you gave it one sharp rap on the snout. Eli loved the beautiful fish, but felt no pangs of remorse about killing them, as he did when the birds he had shot were picked up alive and had to be dispatched by twisting their necks. He was always horrified by the kicking feet of a turr or a duck when it was picked out of the water, awaiting the mercy of death.

Elias sometimes visited his fleet of salmon nets a second time, in the afternoon, but if so, he went alone. After helping his father to put away the morning's catch Eli would be free for the day—or, at least, almost free. At most he might be expected to poke his nose into the smokehouse once or twice to see that the chips hadn't started to blaze, or the smoldering twigs die out. From ten in the morning until nightfall he had freedom for expeditions through the forest, for lowering baited lines into trout pools, or maybe for a clandestine and forbidden dip into the chill waters of the mill brook.

The afternoon of May 12 was so warm that Eli and Timmy spent the whole time between noon and sunset exploring the nearby forest. They went first along the country road from the Bottom, then along a woods path, and finally by way of a secret trail to the little falls high above the mill.

"Let's go barefoot," Eli suggested to Timmy as they entered the woods.

"Ain't allowed, this early," Timmy said, but he said it in a questioning tone of voice that revealed his eagerness.

"Aw, there's nobody to see," Eli said, "and the ground's sure warm enough."

So off came their boots and socks, and they trod delicately, with feet sensitive from a winter spent in boots, through the venturesome litter of needle mold and the twigs and roots of the forest.

"'Tis more fun the first day or two," Timmy observed.

"'Tis more fun when you aren't allowed, too," Eli said,

"and if someone does see us 'twill make no difference so long as they don't tell Mother."

The boys weren't usually allowed to go barefoot until school was out in June. They were always required to wear boots to school, "for respectability," and as an all-day Sunday penance. But this year there was no school. The women, who laid down the rules about boots and things like that, had little authority over boys of Eli's age, while the men, who continued to be their lords and masters, were exceedingly indulgent about such matters, believing that exposure to cold and ice water, far from harming a boy, would make him strong and hardy.

As they explored more deeply into the myrrh-scented woods the magic of their surroundings began to tell on Eli and Timmy. They spoke only in whispers, fearful of breaking the spell that had settled over the green and brown aisles of the trees, with the golden shafts of sunlight falling through and luminous patches of gloom on every side.

May was the most exciting time to be in the woods, when you could walk through beds of moss warmed by the sun, and through others still wet and chill with melt water. Your prints would be deep and black in the sodden leaf mold as you passed through a clump of birches, just showing the first tiny trace of green in the tips of their buds, though the hedges of wild red currants already flaunted a bright myriad of star-shaped leaves against the dark purple of the spruces.

"Dare you to walk in the snow," Eli said to Timmy, and both boys laughed and went chasing ankle deep through the melting snow, crisscrossing the white bank of drift with their prints, coming out on dry, warm turf a moment later.

Then they trod, cat-footed, along a mossy path, making no sound. Not a twig snapped, not a leaf rustled. A chickadee came out on the end of a branch, and Eli signaled with his hand to Timmy to be still, as the little bird cocked its head at them and sang. Eli chirruped gently at it, drawing it closer. Attracted by the small squeaking sound that he made with his lips, a tiny kinglet, glorious in a hood of orange and gold, popped out of the bush, perched on the top branch of a little spruce, and inspected him with its beady black eyes.

"Ti-ti-ti," sang the kinglet in a voice like a cricket with the flu.

"Twee-twee," went Eli, sounding like air escaping spasmodically from the neck of a toy balloon.

"A-dee-dee-dee-dee," said the chickadee, adding its thin baritone to the chorus of song.

"I never knowed ye could talk to 'em that way," Timmy whispered.

Eli squeezed his little brother's hand and laughed, half expecting the small birds to flee at this human sound, but they, already aware of the boys' identity, batted not an eyelid at his laughter. The kinglet lost interest in them and delicately ate an aphid from a leaf. The chickadee, driven by the insatiable curiosity of its race, came closer, until it was no more than three feet from Timmy's nose, and marveled at the pools of bright blue in his freckled face, as a boy might marvel at the two-foot eyes of a dinosaur. Then the little bird came close to Eli, and he wondered if it could be observing the great difference between the bright, fair face of the little boy and his own olive skin and black eyes. But at last the chickadee, like the kinglet, lost interest and disappeared into the bush.

Timmy was beginning to fidget at Eli's side. "Let's go over to the brook," he suggested.

"Sure," said Eli. "Maybe it's warm enough to swim."

He wriggled his feet in the moss and enjoyed the mild tickling sensation of the tiny twigs between his toes. They walked on, stepping on dry sticks, and among the stiff, sharp needles of the blue-green ground juniper. He decided that he liked the sharp prickling of the juniper needles even more than the soft caress of the moss. Why? he wondered. As they walked along he picked a small switch from a young swamp maple and skinned it out and flicked at his feet.

"Whatcha doin'?" Timmy inquired, puzzled.

"I dunno," Eli admitted. "Feels good, that's all."

"Never knowed a durn fool use a switch on hisself," Timmy said.

Eli laughed. "'Tisn't hard enough to hurt," he said and flicked his little brother's legs lightly.

"Ouch!" said Timmy. "You stop now!"

Eli laughed again, still feeling the light sting of the switch on his own skin. It was pleasant, and somehow exciting. Why? he wondered. He thought of the switchings he had got a few times from his father, and flinched at the recollection. Could it be that pain was only a matter of degree? Could all pain be nothing but a sort of pleasure carried too far?

He was still wondering about it when they came out on the bank of the mill brook and dipped their toes into its swollen waters.

"Not too cold," he reported. Without another word he shed his clothes and began to wade out into the turbulent water.

"We ain't allowed, you know," Timmy said. But he was already shucking off his shorts, prepared to follow Eli in the pursuit of this forbidden pleasure.

The boys were not supposed to go swimming before the first of July, because up to that date fresh water was believed to have some harmful essence in it. The poison was believed to return on the fifteenth of August, and they were solemnly warned against venturing into fresh water after that day. Salt water was thought to be clean and free from witchcraft all year around, though cold enough to stop your heart if you stayed in it for more than a few minutes, except, perhaps, toward the end of summer.

They splashed one another and squealed as the cold water struck their bodies, and chased one another around the pool, and swam a few strokes, then got out of the water, teeth chattering, for rivulets of melting snow were still entering the stream from both banks.

"Bet we're the first in for the year," Eli told Timmy. "I'll race you to the top of that tree over there."

So they climbed trees and played tag in the sun, like two wild animals, whooping with high spirits, and when they were dry they dressed and went back to recover their boots near the mill.

In the settlement itself afternoons were the best time. Then a boy could make himself inconspicuous in the shady parts of the general store, listening to the wonderful talk of the men gathered about the central aisle, or he could go to the forge and make a place for himself on an overturned bucket in a corner, and listen to more talk on all kinds of esoteric subjects as the blacksmith, hammering white-hot sparks from his anvil, discoursed with two or three friends or customers while he made shoes for a horse or deck hardware for a coasting vessel.

But Eli's favorite spot on a warm afternoon was the end of the government wharf. There he could sit, dangling his toes over the clear green water and pretending to fish for the small tom cods that darted between the mossy timbers of the wharf piling, listening all the while, with pricked-up ears, to the chatter of the group of men who lounged about, quite unaffectedly doing nothing but chew the fat.

Eli spent a great deal of his boyhood eavesdropping on adult conversations.

He was doing it on the afternoon following the year's first swim when he learned that Pastor Tishrite had been recalled, and that there was something a trifle mysterious about his going. Determined to find out more about this, he became more omnipresent, but more inconspicuous, wherever men gathered to talk. But even among themselves the talk was guarded, and it took Eli a week of assiduous eavesdropping to learn that the pastor had fathered a child in a quarter forbidden by canon law: to wit, in the person of young Sister Bertha Penchley, whom, so they said, he had "deflowered."

Eli had to ask Joshua Markady the meaning of the word "deflowered."

The old sea captain laughed heartily, guessing at once that Eli had overheard the talk. "Why, ye young rake!" he said. "There'll be time enough fer ye to become interested in such matters. It just means that the bugger took her maidenhead, that's all. He was the first man between her legs."

"Oh!" said Eli, a little taken aback by this frankness. He wondered if he should ask what a maidenhead was, but decided against it. There were times when even a boy blushed to confess his innocence.

"Ye know now," Mr. Markady went on teasingly, "why so many o' the faith cures turned out wrong last winter. 'Twas the fault o' the pastor, ye see. He was nought but a wolf in sheep's clothing all along."

"Well," said Eli challengingly, "if you're going to make fun of faith healing, how do you explain the times that it works? Mrs. Marks, for instance?"

Mr. Markady laughed gruffly. "I seen sicker women than Miriam Marks ever was standin' to the pumps in a fall gale off Labrador," he growled. "All ye need is to convince 'em that they be better off on their feet than on their backs, and 'twould surprise ye how many o' the sick and lame can pick up their heads an' walk."

The recall of the pastor was conducted with tight-lipped discretion and prim propriety. Elder Solomon Marks the merchant carried on at the little church, and things were almost completely normal, except that the sermons were read out of an old book, in the elder's halting style, instead of being declaimed with free-flowing oratory full of exhortations to sinners to repent and seek the Lord. A new pastor was being sent out, ordered from some small northern charge by the church's St. John's office, and reports said that he was a man with God's hand upon him in a most exceptional way—a man full of zeal and holy fire, who spoke with tongues and saw visions of spiritual things not given to ordinary mortals to witness. So there was a good deal of anticipation even before the people laid eyes on him.

Eli was sitting on the end of the wharf, with shop-line fishing gear and a periwinkle for bait, when the coastal boat blew her whistle and slipped between the sunkers at the harbor mouth, bringing Brother John McKim, the new pastor, to his destiny in Caplin Bight.

He impressed everyone deeply the moment he stepped ashore, for he had a magnificent head, with deep, piercing eyes, and a trimmed beard, set on a lean, angular, and very tall frame. In fact, Eli thought at once, he looked like the Prophet Elijah in the back of the big family Bible at home, except that Elijah's beard was longer, but Brother John's beard was undeniably neater and more purposeful. And when the pastor spoke, the impression was even deeper. His voice rolled like the thunders on Mount Sinai—or anyway, as Eli imagined the thunders must have rolled when Moses spoke with God. The rumor that Brother John talked with God also, even as Moses, had received wide currency in Caplin Bight before his coming, and the moment Eli saw him he was willing to give it credence. If not God, then some other supernatural power seemed to possess the man.

Even the typhoid epidemic of the winter before had had less impact on Caplin Bight than had the advent of this strange, handsome, bearded prophet. Everyone expected that he would preach repentance and the imminence of hell-fire, as his predecessors had done. Instead he came preaching the time of the end of the world—proclaiming the hour and the day and the month and the year. From the moment that he stepped into the small pulpit in the little church on his first Sunday morning in the Bight he had everyone on the edge of the pews. He kept them there for months. He raised a state of jitters, followed by a state of hypnotic exaltation, such as only a man with his extraordinary personality could inspire.

Eli could remember Brother John's first sermon vividly. The preliminary hymns and prayers being intoned, and the decks cleared, so to speak, for action, the tall pastor towered over his inadequate little lectern and paused for a few seconds as though deep in thought, or gathering inspiration. Then his rich voice began to roll out over the waiting people.

"Behold the Lord cometh from afar," he intoned, "burning with anger. His lips are full of indignation, and His tongue a devouring fire."

This was his text, and it was not too different from the threats of doom and everlasting punishment that they had all heard before. But he infused a sense of urgency into the words that seemed to give them a fresh meaning.

"The Lord cometh," he said, "not in some far-off future time, but now, here, in *this* place and time. That is the message that I bring ye—the imminent coming of the Day of the Lord!"

There was a slight stir in the congregation. Those who were used to settling down for a Sunday-morning nap while the flames of hell crackled overhead pricked up their ears and forgot somnolence as Brother John went on to elaborate upon his text.

"God in the form of the awful shape of Justice," he thundered, "come to judge the earth, His eyes burning with coals of fire, His tongue a river of flame, licking over the forests and the mountains and the isles of the sea!"

While preaching Brother John seldom lapsed into the vernacular, as he did in conversation, and even in prayer, but spoke on an exalted plane, in the language of the Old Testament, which he knew almost by heart, and in the rolling phrases of the Book of Revelation, which he knew absolutely by heart, being able to quote it literally, from end to end, without glancing at a page.

The big church Bible lay open before him now, and he flicked its pages with practised fingers but never deigned to glance at a verse while his voice flowed on, his eyes riveting his hearers to their seats.

"For behold the day cometh when the mountains shall flow down like wax . . . and the slain of the Lord shall be at that day from one end of the earth even unto the other end of the earth. They shall not be lamented, neither gathered nor buried. They shall be dung upon the ground. And the stink shall come up out of their carcasses, and the mountains shall be melted with their blood, and the heavens shall be rolled together as a scroll, and the stars fall from their places." The voice rose and fell, describing this scene of appalling horror. It was powerful, hypnotic, yet liquid and flexible.

"Amen!" came booming from the back of the church. "Even so, come, Lord Jesus!" Jehu Gilmore had begun the obbligato of ejaculations that would continue as a minor theme throughout the course of the sermon. As it progressed, others began to feel the Power also, and to join in the surge of brief comment that ran like a crosscurrent under Brother John's words. Eli found himself, for a few moments, listening to the comments instead of to the preacher, but the latter was too smart to allow the control of his sermon to be taken out of his hands. Eli was brought back sharply by Brother John's voice, which had changed from its liquid roll and was now cracking out like a whip.

"For these things are to happen here upon the earth," he snapped. "Not in some far-off day of judgment beyond the grave, but right here, in the land that we know, and in our own day. Look!" And he pointed through the church window. "Think of the day when *these* mountains shall melt, and *this* forest shall go up in a puff of smoke like a feather dropped in a fire!" He paused, and his voice changed again. "Yea, as I shall show you, the year and the hour is upon us when the Lord shall descend from heaven with a shout and with the voice of the archangel and the great sound of a trumpet, for I am sent unto you even as was John the Baptist, to the lost sheep of the House of Israel, to proclaim the coming of the great and terrible day of the Lord!"

The echoes of his words rumbled among the high beams at the back of the little church where Jehu was now moaning softly while a subdued mutter of "Amens" and "Yes, Lords" rose on all sides.

In the pause that followed this announcement of Brother John's mission Brother Thomas Gilmore of Thomas, one of the lesser elders, rose in the aisle and began to speak in a low voice, prophesying in an unknown tongue, and Brother John was silent, allowing everyone to hear this cryptic prophecy, a sure sign and seal that the Holy Ghost was personally present in the room and taking possession of the willing bodies of the faithful.

But Brother John paused only long enough for the unknown tongue to lend its stamp of authenticity to his own prophecy. Then his voice rose again, covering the scattered voices of the congregation as a thick blanket covers and subdues a small fire.

"For in those days," he thundered, "men shall seek death and shall not find it, and shall desire to die and death shall flee from them, for there shall be a great earthquake, such as was not since men were upon the earth, so mighty an earthquake and so great, and the sun shall be black as sackcloth of hair, and the moon shall be as blood, and the stars of heaven shall fall unto the earth.

"Then all they that are drunken with the blood of the martyrs of Jesus—all the kings and the captains and the mighty men, shall hide themselves in the dens and the rocks of the mountains, and shall say unto the mountains, 'Fall on us, and hide us from the face of Him that sitteth upon the throne, for the great day of His wrath is come, and who shall be able to stand?'"

The thin windows rattled in the sudden silence, and a shudder passed through the congregation.

"Yes. How many of you will be able to stand?" Brother John asked, almost in a whisper.

Eli could see the whiteness of his mother's face as she
stared fixedly at the black figure in the pulpit, and hear his
father's whispered voice in hushed and anguished prayer.
Yet he himself was not swept up in the tide of the sermon.
The power of the words, the dark and thunderous poetry,
moved him with admiration, but he felt none of the terror
and glory that seemed to be shaking the congregation as a
forest is shaken by the gusts of a summer storm. The infection of the unknown tongues had spread, he noted, and
gibberish was pouring up toward heaven from three or four
separate points in the church. That it really *was* gibberish,
and not some foreign language such as Spanish or Chinese, he had been assured with absolute finality by Joshua
Markady.

"No nation on earth speaks so," the far-traveled old captain had told him, "only fools carried away be their own
folly." Eli half accepted this and half rejected it. While he
was willing to concede that the unknown tongues might
bear no resemblance to any language spoken on earth, he
was convinced, since it was impossible to believe that they
were faking, that something marvelous really happened to
the people who prophesied in this way. Even if what they
said was gibberish, it seemed clear that the Holy Ghost, or
some other invisible power, took control of them. Could it
be the devil? he wondered with a shudder, or one of the
evil spirits that his mother was always warning him against.
His mother lived in a world crowded with spirits, many
of them "fallen angels" that had, through some incredible
piece of stupidity, taken sides with Lucifer in his absurd
rebellion against the infinite power of God, and who now
prowled the air, attempting to gain residence in any human
mind that could be tempted from the paths of righteousness. Such spirits often caused madness or mania, his
mother had assured him, as well as lending their occult
powers to witches, mediums, and other adepts of the black
arts.

But there was little time for such reflections. The voice

of Brother John was still flowing down from the pulpit, sweeping his hearers along with it.

"Nation shall rise against nation," he proclaimed, "and kingdom against kingdom—as ye have seen it come to pass, even in our own day—and there shall be famines and pestilences and earthquakes in divers places—and have ye not seen them, even here? Have ye not felt the sting of God's wrath in both famine and pestilence?

"And then He shall send His angels with a great trumpet to gather together the elect from the four winds.

"But when, ye ask, shall these things be? Lo! The time is at hand! Even at the doors! I shall show ye later how we stand, today, in the very dawn of the great antitypical sabbath. The six thousand years of sorrow and weeping that began with Adam's fall be now at an end. The thousand years of Christ's reign be about to begin. Ye shall see it fer yourselves. I shall show ye, when I open the Lord's prophecies and reveal the times and the seasons that be still hidden in His Word, how He now stands without, ready to enter into His house. Verily, verily I say unto you, that the times be fulfilled, and the hour be upon us! And not another year shall pass, not another winter shall descend upon this earth until all these things be fulfilled, and the Lord Himself is revealed in the awful blaze of His glory!"

Brother John's deep voice trembled with emotion.

"Are ye ready, my brethren?" he pleaded. "Have ye washed yer robes an' made them white in the blood of the Lamb? For He shall appear all in a moment, at the sounding of the last trump. In a moment, ye understand! In the twinkling of an eye! For the trumpet shall sound, and the dead shall be raised incorruptible, and we shall be changed, cot up into the air to meet the Lord in glory, even while the mountains flow down on every hand, and the heavens blaze with the fires of the Last Judgment.

"Then those that have watched, and kept their robes spotless, shall rise with the Lord, as the stars come down on every hand, blazing and going out, and swallowed into everlasting darkness, and the awful sound of the trumpet ripping the sky apart, while sinners and unbelievers, left behind, shall writhe and scream in the ocean of flame that shall wrap the earth from pole to pole—a mere foretaste of the tortures of hell-fire that shall be their lot from henceforth even forever and ever!"

They were back on more familiar ground, and it was there that the sermon ended. He had not yet revealed the hour of the Lord's coming, but he had made an enormous first impression, and there was general confidence that he did, indeed, hold the "times and the seasons" in his keeping.

"The Lord's hand be upon 'im sure enough," Elias Pallisher pronounced as they walked home from church that morning. "Warn't no mistakin' that 'e spoke with the power o' the Holy Ghost."

But the sermon was just the beginning. It was followed by others, and time and again the elders were called together to discuss the prophecies and to pray for light, and little by little Brother John opened for them the seven seals with which the Book was sealed, and showed them the meaning of the prophecies as clearly as if they had been written in an almanac or a book of tide tables. These meetings were held in the homes of the elders, at night, where they pored over the ancient writings and deciphered the mysteries. Eli was privileged to sit as a silent observer at one or two of the meetings that were held in his own kitchen.

The elders sat around the table, with oil lamps burning and their Bibles open to the cryptic chapters that they had never understood—the measuring of Ezekiel's temple, the time and times and half a time foretold by the Prophet Daniel, the number of the name of the Beast, and similar recondite matters.

"Ye see it, do ye not?" Brother John would ask urgently, as an elder, painfully adding up the dates with his stub of lead pencil, labored, puzzled over the figures. "From the time of the Abomination of Desolation . . . an' now ye take forty years, and add that . . ."

Eli, quicker and surer with figures than anyone else in Caplin Bight, child or adult, was called upon by Elias to subtract the years between Adam's creation and the crowning of King David, from those between Noah's flood and the birth of Christ. When he was finished Elias stared at the figures in awe, for they pointed unmistakably to the year of the antitypical flood, the great Time of Trouble that should overwhelm the world, and to the crowning of the antitypical David, the Lord in glory.

"'Tis so indeed!" Elias would declare. "There be no gettin' around it."

"Ay, brother, the Lord have opened yer eyes. Now see this other prophecy, pointin' the same way." And they would begin computing the years from the Babylonian captivity, when the Lord's favor was withdrawn from the House of Israel according to the flesh, to the date when all things should be fulfilled in the consummation of Israel according to the spirit.

"Ye see, brethren!" Brother John would announce triumphantly when all the lead pencils were finished with their work. "Comes out to the same date, do it not?"

"Ay, it do!" Elias would agree. "There be no gettin' around it!"

So it went, one line of evidence after another, the Hebrew calendar painfully explained and translated into the calendar of anti-Christian Rome, such lunar months as Nisan and Ab related to the familiar solar months of March and April, June and July. Evenings that should have been spent repairing their boats and preparing for the trap voyage that would start in late June they sat around their lamps, comparing, with mounting excitement, the types and shadows of the Old Testament with the cryptic prophecies of the New, until the matter was settled beyond all argument. Dozens of different lines of figuring all worked out to the same date—indeed, to the same day of the same month—

the nineteenth day of the month Tishri, in that very year—which, being interpreted, was the twenty-fourth of October, or the twenty-fifth, sometime between sunset and dawn.

Having opened the eyes of the elders, Brother John's battle was all but won. And indeed there was little that the ordinary members of the congregation, many of them illiterate, could do other than follow the elders' reasoning from afar, seeing, as they confessed, in part, and as through a glass darkly. Their faith in the times and the seasons might have a shaky foundation, but their faith in Brother John's inspiration was more solidly based—they could see with their own eyes and hear with their own ears the miracle of his preaching and the cloud of small miracles that followed along as witnesses.

CHAPTER SIX

Eli's father, who had a lot of influence among the fishermen, contributed substantially to Brother John's success. Many of those with no gift for interpreting scriptural parallels, or measuring time from the date of the flood to the date of the last trump, were quite willing to trust Elias's judgment when he stood up in prayer meeting to announce that he had "proved all things" as the Scriptures directed and found Brother John's reckoning to be without flaw. No man who could set a cod trap with such uncanny judgment, or calculate to an inch the angle at which the leader of a salmon net would take the most salmon in any combination of wind and tide, would be likely to go astray on the computation of a date, the fishermen agreed.

After that the signs and the wonders began to multiply quickly. The little radio in Solomon Marks's store, where those without radios, or those whose batteries had gone dead, gathered to hear the news bulletins from St. John's, told of an earthquake in Peru. There were rumors of wars in the Holy Land, and persecutions of Christians in Turkish Armenia. A tidal wave swept away most of the fish stages in Notre Dame Bay. One of Jehu Gilmore's ewes gave birth to twin lambs three months out of season.

Brother John next informed his congregation that henceforth they must cease calling themselves a church, and using the sectarian names that belonged to Babylon. The time had come for the purification of the Sons of Levi, and they must be known as the Church of the Firstborn, which, indeed, was the church of all true Christians everywhere, while the little flock in Caplin Bight would be "an ecclesia of saints gathered together in the name of the Lord Jesus."

John McKim dominated every gathering of which he was a part. Though he spoke in the same uncultured phrases as the fishermen, he spoke with authority, and even when he kept silent his presence made itself felt. Outside the pulpit he was a slow-moving, humorless man, but seemed kindly, and when he first spoke to Eli it was with words of grave gentleness.

It was at one of the meetings called for the study of prophecy, and Eli had been called upon to confirm one more double or parallel out of the Old Testament, converting the Jewish chronology to that of the more recent revelation of Bishop Usher. Eli could do the simple arithmetic involved even without writing down the figures, he found, and after running through it twice to check, he confidently announced the result.

"Ye be sure, lad?" Brother John asked.

"Yes, sir," Eli said. "I did it two different ways, to check."

The tall man laid his hand gently on the boy's shoulder, patronizingly, smiling a little. "Ye seem to be a very likely lad, Eli," he said, "smarter than any I've seen fer quite a spell. Ye have more'n yer share o' talents from the Lord, seems to me. Pray that ye use 'em wisely, boy, fer the Lord will demand an accountin' of every gift. Ye be pretty nigh old enough fer conversion, I'd say. Ye should think earnestly about seekin' the Lord."

The big hand tightened for an instant on Eli's shoulder before Brother John turned back to the group of elders, seeming to forget the boy. But Eli noticed the black, prophetic eyes following him thoughtfully from time to time, with a look that made him vaguely uneasy.

The pastor's conquest of Caplin Bight was swift and almost complete. Everyone in the settlement "came out of Babylon" with scarcely a look behind. Everyone, that is, except the Markadys and Mr. Simms, who remained just as stubbornly unenlightened as they had in the days of Brother John's predecessors. In the fervor of this new conversion a short-lived movement grew up to run the unbelievers out of town—to "purge out from among ourselves the Mammon of unrighteousness," as Brother John expressed it. But for once he had overstepped the bounds of his leadership. Some of the elders went along with him, but public opinion was not on their side. Mr. Markady and Mr. Simms were deeply entrenched institutions in Caplin Bight, beyond the touch even of religious fanaticism, far too eminently respectable to be purged. So those two pillars of ungodliness, with their godless households, remained as a witness to Satan in the midst of the surrounding piety.

The aroused elders contented themselves by purging, instead, the town drunk, a little man named Peter Fitzroy who had arrived in Caplin Bight some twenty years before on a trading vessel and become stranded there like a jellyfish on a beach in the fall. Peter was brought to the mercy seat in a suitable state of repentance and tears, forgiven, and taken into the fold. After his conversion he began to wonder if his wife, who had left him long ago for a life of prostitution in St. John's, might not also be reached and saved—but this remained a private dream about which he did nothing except talk.

As for the two unbelievers with their unbelieving dependents, Brother John, failing in his efforts to banish them, pointed out that they were unwittingly fulfilling the prophecy. At the time of the harvest there must be a few tares left to be gathered together for the burning, while the Lord's wheat was gathered into the barn. They should be thankful, he said, that there were so few tares in Caplin Bight. In many places the tares far outnumbered the wheat.

But all was not perfect peace even within the bosom of the ecclesia. There came a day when Elias was in dispute with the majority, and the world for the Pallisher household looked black and threatening. Already the shadow of doom hung over the early summer, but this increased it.

The dispute, it appeared, rested on the early Christian practice of "having all things in common." Brother John was strongly in favor of this, and most of the elders agreed, but Solomon Marks, Thomas Gilmore of Matthew, and Elias all took a firm stand against him. The fact that they were, respectively, the merchant, the mill owner, and the most successful fisherman, who had most to lose by such a move, stood out plainly, and they were accused of being turned from God by the love of life and the pride of the flesh. The dispute ended in a sort of deadlock. The three recalcitrant elders were voted down, but refused to bow to the will of the majority. There was talk of taking their elderships from them, but between them they had far too much influence for this, so they were bidden to pray fervently and seek guidance from the Lord, while the dispute continued unresolved.

The night they took the vote and came so close to expelling Elias from the ecclesia, the boys were sent to bed early while their parents discussed the matter in the kitchen. But they could hear the voices of their parents through the floor grating, arranged to help heat the upstairs bedroom in winter. The voice of Elias kept repeating, with variations, that the Lord hadn't given him children to be made into beggars through the shiftlessness of his neighbors, while the voice of Martha kept saying in a worried sort of voice that she hoped they were doing the right thing.

Eli wondered if his father might be among the lost, like Mr. Markady and Mr. Simms. Then he wondered if he might be among the lost himself. He looked into his heart to ask if he loved the Lord, and knew that he did not. Indeed, he found such an unrepentant sinner as Joshua Markady far more to his liking than the Biblical heroes he was supposed to venerate. He tried to talk to Timmy about it, but Timmy wasn't a bit interested. The little boy mumbled and put his nose under the pillow, turning away from his brother. Eli then lay awake, with a gradually deepening feeling of being deserted by God and man. Perhaps, after all, he would *choose* to go into the second death with Mr. Markady rather than into eternal life with Brother John. There might be something rather fine, he thought, about a man's turning his back, scornfully, on God's offer of everlasting bliss. He felt a tear trickle down his cheek into the corner of his mouth. It was strange, he thought, that this feeling of noble damnation should make him want to cry. But that is what he did, nonetheless—something that no boy of his age in Caplin Bight would ever have admitted—he cried himself to sleep.

Timmy woke him at dawn. The sun was pouring with red splendor across the window, and the shadow of doom had lifted more than a little. They wrestled together on the bed, and made so much noise that Elias came in to order them to dress and go with him to the nets.

Their father had built a roaring fire in the kitchen stove, and made a "mug-up": a kettle of strong tea, and piles of toast. Eli and Timmy had been drinking tea since they were weaned. If it was bad for them, it didn't show. The mug-up wasn't supposed to count as breakfast. That would come later, prepared by their mother, and would include big bowls of porridge. The mug-up was just to "stay your stomach" for the trip to the nets.

"Eat hearty," Elias told them. "If ye are ever goin' to be worth yer keep ye've got to learn to eat and act like men. Every man as is any good eats hearty an' works hard."

It was the sort of simple philosophy that had carried him through thirty-three years of work, since he had entered the fishing boat full time at the age of twelve. It had given him his share of the world's goods, or perhaps just a little bit better than his share. He hoped to be able to pass along to his children the attitudes toward life that had served him so well. They would be quite good enough for this world and the next, he was convinced, if they turned out to be men like their father. The belief that children should surpass their parents, should seek higher and nobler ends, the conception that the world's salvation lay in its evolution toward some distant and shining horizon, had not yet touched Caplin Bight. Such beliefs belonged to the cultural pattern of far-off places, where skyscrapers raked the clouds and men dreamed dreams of walking in their carnal bodies across the dust plains of the moon.

Elias saw no contradiction in computing the end of the world by lamplight, and then, in the morning, passing out worldly advice to his sons. His mind worked in compartments, each safely sealed off so that the others could not impinge upon it and upset its convictions. But Eli was sharp enough to catch the logical implication that his father might not be fully convinced, after all, that the present evil world was to pass away with a great noise on the twenty-fifth of October coming. Naturally he said nothing about his discovery. But he grinned happily to himself over his toast and tea. It was far better, he decided, to have an inconsistent father who could sometimes be made to see a boy's point of view, rather than a logical one who never said or did anything foolish and licked you every time you did something not quite sensible yourself.

Considering the happenings of the night before, Eli was surprised at his father's good humor, which continued throughout the morning, as they hauled the nets and cleaned the salmon and rubbed it with salt, until Martha called them to breakfast at eight o'clock.

But the important events of the summer were not much connected with trap boats and the curing of fish. They all centered about the little church, where dire revelations were taking place almost every Sunday, and sometimes on prayer-meeting nights as well.

It was just about the time of the caplin scull that Brother John's projector, which was called a magic lantern, arrived from the outside world on the coastal steamer. This instrument was almost considered a sign and wonder in itself. It took the light from a flat-wick oil flame—wider than any wick seen before—and concentrated it into a narrow beam that was projected with dazzling whiteness on a white screen. When colored slides were inserted into the magic lantern, pictures appeared on the screen, glowing with living light, in colors more wonderful than anything in real life.

The slides were mostly illustrations of the end of the world, and there were a few that stood out with such vividly real horror as to make Eli shudder and to send chills chasing down his spine. There was one purporting to show the Great Sore that would fall upon men—a colored photograph of a dreadfully advanced case of cancer of the tongue and lower lip. This, Brother John explained, would happen to vast numbers of the ungodly—indeed, was already happening— as prophesied in Revelation, chapter 16, verse 2. There was another showing the wicked lying about naked in twisted heaps on the smoking earth, while the great sword of the Lord dominated the sky. And it didn't look as though the wicked had passed peacefully away, either.

Brother John had other slides showing the saints being caught up to meet the Lord in the air, as the Lord Himself had ascended and vanished out of sight while His disciples looked on and marveled. He fully expected to be one of the first to be caught up to sit on the Lord's right hand, while the faithful from Caplin Bight, and from other places that had little groups of Wise Virgins, would follow along closely behind to the Marriage Supper of the Lamb. While the truer-than-life slides gave to his words the impact of a personal experience, Brother John could explain all this with flowing eloquence and a fine flair for a well-mixed metaphor. The slides were not really needed to convince the congregation of the imminence of the Second Coming, but they did much to settle it firmly into the pattern of their daily thought.

When the pastor was established at Caplin Bight, and had secured a house of his own, he sent north for his spouse, Sister Leah, who arrived on the next trip of the coast boat. She was a childless, spinsterish woman who from the day of her arrival in the Bight rode herd ruthlessly on its morals, ferreting out sin wherever it might hide its primrose head and holding up her own rigidly perfect life as an example unto the community.

Sin, in her view, was just another word for carnal pleasure, the greatest of all sins being the rapture of the lovers' embrace. Though she admitted the value of such forbidden fruits as a means of testing the faithful, whether they be pure gold, tried as by fire, she nevertheless doubted the wisdom of the Lord in mixing up the stern duty of replenishing the earth with the sensual pleasures that seemed to be inescapable from it. If sex could have been all duty and no pleasure it would, she felt, have been a much more fitting arrangement.

Eli gained sharp and ruthless thirteen-year-old insight into the workings of Sister Leah's mind from the fact that he was forced, much against his natural inclinations, to sit in a Sunday-school class over which she presided. Warning the children against sex in language that was nothing if not obscure was her specialty. As with all healthy thirteen-year-olds, sex was, to Eli, a most fascinating subject, and one with which he had recently begun to experiment. Because of the surrounding atmosphere of repression, the experiments were carried out alone and in secret. Up to the time of her coming he hadn't worried a great deal about it, but Sister Leah promptly plunged him into a great maelstrom of doubt. It was obvious from her teaching that God demanded of Eli that he remain sexless; equally obvious, from the demands of his own nature, that he could not do it. For some weeks he struggled through the valley of indecision: heaven without sex on the one side, the second death with it on the other. In the end, sex and the second death won the day.

Sister Leah's appearance matched her personality. She had a plain, long, rather horselike face, a thin mouth, eyes set a bit too closely together, and straight, graying hair twisted into a tight knot at the back of her head. Though this grim woman might have been capable of doing vast harm to a class of boys and girls to whom she professed to teach the rudiments of morals, she had certain qualities that everyone admired. She was quite tireless. Her time was available to anyone who needed assistance. And no one could question her physical or moral courage. Report had it that down the coast the previous year she had caught a black bear stealing fish from a flake one day when all the men were away. While all the other women barred themselves indoors Sister Leah, armed with nothing deadlier than a broom, had advanced upon the beast and driven him off.

When Eli mentioned this story to Mr. Markady, the old man chuckled. "I can well believe it, boy," he said. "When that woman's righteous wrath be roused, 'twould take more'n a bear to face her down. Ye mark my words—if that bitch ever gets into heaven the Lord God will either have to mend His ways or move out."

He promptly christened her "Sister Leah the Pure" and succeeded in giving to her purity more than a hint of corruption.

"Don't ye pay too much mind to that dried-up old stick," he counseled Eli. "If the world was ruled be those born blind the pleasure of sight would be counted a mortal sin."

Eli thought this over for a minute. "Do you mean that it's all nonsense about purity and so on?" he asked.

"Oh no," Mr. Markady disclaimed, "not at all, boy. Ye go ahead an' be jest as pure as ye can manage, but if ye find yerself slippin' into a small sin o' the flesh now and then don't let it prey on yer mind. Many a saint have sinned that way without losin' 'e's immortal soul."

Mr. Markady and Eli were now on intimate terms, though theirs were mostly one-way conversations, with the talkative old captain lecturing and Eli listening. Eli could not discuss openly such a personal problem as sex with the old man, but in spite of that Mr. Markady's forthright and worldly attitude helped substantially in the boy's lonely pilgrimage, and certainly hastened his choice for the second death.

Sister Leah, of course, hated Mr. Markady, and Peter Simms too, with the sort of bitter, unforgiving hatred that is reserved for the deeply religious, and that, in other ages, launched massacres and civil wars. She looked forward with relish to the twenty-fifth of October when sinners such as they should begin to wail, "The harvest is past, the summer is ended, and we are not saved." She would be the first to reject their plea. She looked forward to the day with grim satisfaction—a day when they would crawl on their bellies on the burning earth, seeking mercy and finding it not. She explained it all to the children in Sunday school in language almost as graphic as Brother John's magic-lantern slides.

Not all the young people of the Bight fell under her sway. Eli had to keep his doubts to himself, but Virginia Marks was almost openly contemptuous. She went to church duti- fully, but she rebelled at going to prayer meetings and would take no part whatever in the women's works over which Sister Leah presided. At seventeen, Virginia should have been high on the list for conversion, but the Lord thus far had not touched her heart in the slightest.

"I'm surprised ye can stand it," she said to Eli when they met in her father's store. "That woman is a nasty old hypo- crite with an evil mind, and I'll be blessed if I'll bow and scrape to her."

"'Tis all right for *you* to get on your high horse," Eli said. "You're a girl."

"And what's that got to do with it?" she demanded.

"You don't have your father standing over you to belt you into line," he replied sullenly.

"Ha!" she scoffed. "Ye don't know Elder Marks so well as ye think, me lad! He mightn't belt me, as ye put it, but he'd lock me up and feed me on bread and water till I crawled on my belly if he wasn't afraid I'd be more than his match in the end. Even when I was younger'n you are now I knew that ye can let people shove ye just so far before ye've got to dig in your toes and refuse to budge another inch. You'll come to it too, Eli, and when ye do, they'll stop shoving."

"I don't know," Eli replied, "it seems we might all be in the Kingdom before I've much to say about it."

"The Kingdom!" Virginia scoffed. "Why, you don't really believe that nonsense about the end of the world, do you, Eli?"

"Yes," he said, somewhat reluctantly, "yes, I think I do. They got me to add up the dates for them, you know, and it really does work out—six or seven different ways too."

"Ha!" Virginia scoffed. "Ye can't be as smart as I thought —it only works out because— Ssh! here comes Father. . . . Anything else I can do for ye, Eli?"

So Eli never did hear her opinions on why the chronology could be made to do such tricks, and though Virginia was not yet judged among the lost she was clearly among the doubtful—one to be prayed for in prayer meeting, that she might yet be snatched as a brand from the burning toward which she seemed to be headed with all the fascination of a moth for a flame.

As that summer melted into autumn and they began to make their fish, washing it and spreading it on the flakes in the cool September sun, most of the people of the Bight had the distinct and urgent feeling that time was running down toward a full stop. Indeed there were some who refused to make fish at all, carrying their faith to its logical conclusion and regarding such worldly labor as a sign of backsliding and want of conviction. In mid-July there had been a shower of shooting stars, and in August a comet, which could be seen without the aid of a spyglass, following the sun down the evening sky. These signs and wonders were taken as confirmations of faith, and some of the fishermen had taken in their traps even before the caplin scull was finished, declaring it to be the Lord's will that they should spend the last days of this present evil world in prayer, rather than making fish, which would be of no use to man or mortal in the Kingdom.

As if the Lord wished to be ironical, or perhaps to test their faith, the fishery turned out to be a bumper one that year. Elias's trap crew, of which Eli was now a member, landed and salted and made over five hundred quintals— some fifty-eight thousand pounds, dry weight. The gross value was thirty-five hundred dollars—a tremendous amount of money in the years between the wars. Eli would never forget the credit totals at squaring-up time, because it was the first time his name appeared in the books of a merchant. His half share was reckoned at $194.44, the other sharemen's at $388.88. His father squared up and paid off the small debt that he had incurred the spring before, and put away over a thousand dollars, but Elias didn't talk about it, nor did Solomon Marks, who knew his financial secrets, as he did those of all the fishermen in the Bight. But say what you might about the old merchants, they regarded their dealers' accounts as a sacred confidence. No lawyer treated his clients' revelations, no doctor his patients' secrets, with such close-mouthed discretion as the outport merchant did the accounts of the men whom he outfitted. If Solomon Marks had been called into court and ordered to place his balance sheets in evidence, he would have done so without a moment's hesitation. But if ordered to put his account book on the table, he would have gone to jail for contempt, the account book still locked in his safe.

As the otherworldly members of the ecclesia saw Elias's flakes white with fish his status was more than ever in question. But they made no further efforts to stop his profane activities, and he made up for them by joining most heartily with the rest in the chorus of praise that went up day and night, mounting, at summer's end, toward an almost frenzied pitch.

Around mid-September, at Sister Leah's suggestion, the women of the settlement started work on white, ankle-length robes, to be worn on the night of the Lord's appearing. They were symbols, she said, of the true bridal garments that the saints wore inwardly upon their hearts. Solomon

Marks quickly ran out of white dress materials, and had to send off hastily to St. John's for more. Elias looked upon the gambit as a bit foolish, but did not say so to Martha, who was working upon one of the bridal robes—as they were called—like the rest.

The women also considered making little white surplices for the children to wear when they went out to meet the Lord, but they never got around to it. There was even some talk about making bridal robes for the men, but at such a suggestion even the elders of the Church of the Firstborn balked. The only one who could see any merit at all in it was Solomon Marks, and when he saw the opposition of the others he did not press the matter. The majority of the men were horrified. The idea of dressing like brides, of parading around in what looked like white nightgowns, even on the day of the Lord's appearing, shocked their conventional souls to the core. They said firmly that they would go to meet the Lord in their Sunday best, with white collars and ties and an extra lick of polish on their shore boots. Thomas Gilmore of Matthew, most outspoken of the elders, even said that a man could go to meet the Lord in his oilskins, if he had nothing better. Many a good man of Caplin Bight had been married in his oilskins, he pointed out, and every Christian marriage was symbolic of the eventual union of Christ with His church. That clinched the matter, so the symbolic preparations for the Marriage Supper of the Lamb were left strictly to the ladies.

Meanwhile prayer meetings were held every night of the week, and almost all day on Sundays. Jehu Gilmore testified from house to house, sometimes in English and sometimes in less profane tongues, but in either case made a point of staying for dinner. There hadn't been such an epidemic of general righteousness at Caplin Bight in many a long day, and Jehu, for the nonce, was in his glory.

Brother John, who had started it all, stroked his beard and sighed with holy pleasure. He felt sure, he said, that his little flock was readied, one and all, to receive the sign of the House of Levi in their foreheads. He had determined from Scriptural types and shadows that the House of Levi was the branch of the elect to which he and his followers belonged.

So he sat back with humble pride and meek self-satisfaction to await the coming of the great and terrible Day of the Lord.

CHAPTER SEVEN

❧ ❧

Eli remembered the day itself with great clarity and in a multitude of detail, from the moment he awoke in the morning and gazed on the plaster-of-Paris angel with its huge outspread wings decorating the wall at the foot of his bed, until the terrible events of the following night. The angel was old, and its gilt paint was peeling, and its wings were beginning to show cracks. But it was still an impressive figure, though the seraphic smile now looked just a little like a sneer to the boy who was preparing to meet the end of the world with such misgivings about his own salvation.

Since they still hadn't been able to get a teacher for Caplin Bight, there was no school to prepare for, and nobody really cared anyway, since earthly book learning would be of no use to the translated jewels of the Kingdom. But the extended holiday wasn't much fun either, for the weather had turned cold, long winter underwear had been dug out of drawers, and the children were dressed in bay wool socks, rubber boots, wool cuffs, and stocking caps almost every time they went outdoors.

This being the last day of the present evil world, Elias and Martha, like most of the other adults of the village, were attending all-day services in the little church. But such a vigil was considered too great an ordeal for the children, so they were turned loose, with strict orders against any kind of mischief or profane activity, until the afternoon, when they were expected to put in an appearance with

their elders for the final service before the watch in the
night, during which the Lord was to appear. During the
morning and noon hours the children practically had the
settlement to themselves.

As Eli fed the cat that morning he gave her an extra helping, reflecting that it might be her last meal on earth and
wondering what would happen to cats in the coming cata-
clysm. He had heard of no place for them in the world of
the spirit, though he seemed to remember having heard
that lions and oxen and other such beasts were to be led
about on a string by little children. He stroked the cat's
mottled gray fur and listened to her loud and grateful purring, hoping all the while that the Lord in His infinite mercy
might find a place for cats when He snatched the saints
from the burning earth.

He and Timmy got their own breakfast from the big boiler
of porridge that Martha had left on the back of the stove,
then went down to the Bottom, where the mill brook emp-
tied into the harbor, to sail Timmy's new boat, a fine,
schooner-rigged model, copied exactly from one carved by a
shipbuilder and rigged and ballasted by his father so that
it would tack, or reach, or run free, like a full-sized ship.
Timmy dug the beautiful boat out of the locker under the
settle, where it was lodged to be safe from all accident, and
followed Eli along the back path, past the empty schoolhouse, and down to the mill, where the great, ponderous
waterwheel creaked and groaned and kept turning and
spitting white spray.

As they walked Caplin Bight seemed to be deserted, and
there was a nip of frost in the morning air, clearing away the
haze of Indian summer, which had hung like a gentle benediction over the settlement and the bay beyond for several
weeks past.

Just below the bridge, where the millrace joined the
brook and formed a sort of tidewater estuary—or *"barachois,"* as it is called—they found conditions ideal for sailing
the new boat: a small current, a steady breeze, water with

just a ripple of waves. They were busy making it tack against the wind, and admiring its sailing qualities, when the stillness was broken by two sets of footsteps tramping the planks of the bridge above. Looking up, they saw Mr. Markady and David, just come down from the big house on the Point and armed to the teeth, like a pair of bandits.

"It's surprised I am to find the two of ye engaged in such a worldly pursuit this day," Mr. Markady greeted them. "Been banished from the church up yonder, have ye?"

"We're just sailing Timmy's boat," Eli said, rather irrelevantly. "See—isn't she a tidy one?"

"Ay, ye have a point there," Mr. Markady conceded, coming down off the bridge for a closer look and leaning his big moose rifle carefully against the bank as he came. "Boat sailin' be a sight more sensible than hymn singin', no doubt about that."

"You going hunting, Mr. Markady?" Timmy asked.

"No, boy," said the old captain, "just goin' as far as Peter Simms's farm." He turned to Eli. "Not gunnin' for 'im either, mind ye. But seein' as this is such a special day, with the end o' the world expected, us unbelievers thought as how we should have a little meetin' of our own tonight, out at Mr. Simms's place."

"A meeting?" Eli asked. Mr. Markady hadn't been known to attend a meeting since the last days of the traveling Anglican missionaries, when there were still some Caplin Bight people who adhered to orthodox Christianity. And of course Mr. Simms had never been known to attend a meeting in his life. "You don't mean to wait for the coming of the Lord?"

"In a manner o' speakin', yes, ye might say," Mr. Markady replied. "We'll not be expectin' Him to call in person, ye understand. But there's a chance that some o' His brethren, or brides, or whatever they call theirselves might pay us a visit later on."

Eli must have looked puzzled, for Mr. Markady explained further. "I hear on reliable authority that just about every hangshore in the harbor be plannin' to meet out in the grave-

yard tonight, practically under me windows, to pray an' sing
psalms while waitin' fer the Lord to descend an' the graves
to be opened, or to be cot up into the air, or whatever it is
that's to happen. I'd as soon not be home fer the blessed
event. Ain't worried about the house, mind ye. It be insured
against fire, flood, riot, an' act o' God—everything, in fact,
includin' the Second Coming. The Simms place isn't."

Mr. Markady had been half joking, but his face became
suddenly serious as he proceeded. "Boy," he said, "the hangshores in this bight be bloody fools, but they been neighbors
o' mine since we sucked our mothers' tits. I wouldn't do any
of 'em an ill turn, an' in the ordinary way I'd trust 'em with
me life. But I was never one to take chances with a mad dog,
even if he was me own. We'll be back later for some other
things we'll need, and for Mrs. Markady, an' we'll be prepared fer a siege, if need be."

"A siege?" Eli repeated. "But nobody's going to go gun-
ning for you, Mr. Markady."

"Most likely not," Mr. Markady agreed, "but ye see that
ye tell yer father where we'll be tonight. An' tell 'im we
don't aim to be disturbed, either. There be a good hundred
and fifty feet of clear space every side of Simms's house. Ye
tell yer father that any man as sets foot on the Simms place
betwix now an' tomorrow noon is liable to be shot like a
swile on the whelpin' ice. We got no mind to be blamed fer
it if it should just happen that the Lord changes 'E's mind
about comin' tonight."

He stopped to let this sink in, then repeated, "Ye tell him,
mind!"

"Yes, sir," Eli promised.

Mr. Markady could see that the boy was somewhat taken
by the wind, and softened a little. "Look boy," he said, "I'm
sorry about all this, but we can't take chances when our
neighbors have gone out o' their minds. I've half a mind to
make ye come with us, but 'twould likely start a row right
an' proper." He turned to the boat. "I'm surprised ye can't
trim sails better'n that," he said. "But then, another genera-

tion, give or take a few years, an' not a man on this coast'll know a sail from a mainsheet. 'Tis a bloody shame, the way seamanship be dyin' out. Here . . ."

He took the boat, tightened a halyard and a sheet, altered the rudder lashing a bit, then sent her shooting out into the wind. "Sails real pretty, don't she," he said. "I mind well the year Tom Gilmore built that hull. I'm surprised to see Tom mixed up so deep in this Second Comin' nonsense. See how much closer she'll sail now, when the falls be tight an' the sheets set fair an' proper—stops air spillin' off the luff o' the sail, ye see."

He picked up his gun and climbed the bank. "Good luck to ye, boy—an' to you, Timmy," he said. "Come see me tomorrow when this foolishness be over and done with. I've a mind to let ye help me build a real sailboat this winter."

"What do you make of all that?" Eli said to Timmy when the Markadys had disappeared up the country road. But Timmy just looked at him and shrugged, uninterested. It was his fixed habit to shut out of his mind such grown-up prattle as failed to make sense. Timmy had a settled conviction that everyone went somewhat wrong in the head as he got older.

The sun climbed and killed the frost in the air. The Markadys made another trip to the Point, returning with Mrs. Markady dressed in her best walking-out clothes, which included rustling black silk and buttoned kid boots. She stopped and rustled beside Eli and Timmy, and gave them peppermints from her snakeskin bag that had come uncounted years before from the workshop of an artisan on the Río de la Plata. After the Markadys had passed on, out of sight, the boys found a fall salmon in the brook, and Timmy went tearing back to his father's store for a net, but the fish escaped back to sea, much to their disgust, and before they knew it midday was upon them.

That day seemed to Eli the most unreal experience of his life, with all the twisted logic of a dream. The very landscape looked queer—the deserted settlement, hymns floating out from the church, sunlight glittering bright on white walls, the coming and going of the Markadys preparing for a very unlikely gun battle up in the valley.

Eventually the boys grew tired of sailing the boat and exploring the brook and wandered home, hungry for dinner.

"Father," Eli remembered to report as they sat at table to eat their half-cured fish and potatoes, "we met Mr. Markady down at the Bottom this morning—going to the Simms farm."

"Ay," Elias said, half absently, "a good man he be, accordin' to the flesh. 'Tis sorry I am, make no mistake, that 'e be numbered with Satan's host in this hour o' testin'.""

"David and Mrs. Markady went with him," Eli continued. "They had their guns, and he gave me a message for you."

"A message?" Elias asked, paying full attention for the first time.

"That's right, sir. He said to tell you they'll be at the Simms place tonight, and—these were his exact words—they 'don't aim to be disturbed.' He said to tell you anyone who set foot on the Simms place before tomorrow noon would be liable to be shot like a seal on the spring ice."

Elias stared at his son with a puzzled frown, half angry. "Shot?" he said. "Ye be makin' it up, ye whelp!"

"No, sir, that's what he said," Eli protested.

"Why," said Elias, pondering, "do 'e think . . . 'e mus' be afeared we'd do 'im an injury. Sure, there's nar soul in this harbor'd do a thing like that! Josh Markady have set 'e's face agin the Lord, an' the Lord will be 'e's jedge—not we, as have swore to be blameless before the throne!"

"He said something about taking no chances with a mad dog," Eli reported.

"Ye pay 'em no mind," Elias counseled. "'E be led astray be the devil."

"The poor man!" Martha Pallisher mourned. "An' poor Anne Markady too! 'Tis her I really feel for!"

"What about David?" Timmy asked. "Will he be burned up too when the Lord comes?"

"Ye hush!" Martha commanded sharply. "'Tain't fer we to jedge. The Lord sees the heart, an' will do justly, like the Book says."

The simple meal finished, the boys were whisked off to church, where they listened to endless hymns and prayers and testifyings. The service, like the other events of the day, had for Eli an air of unreality, but he could feel the mounting sense of excitement as the tempo of the various outpourings increased and reached almost a state of frenzy.

Until mid-afternoon it continued. Then the marathon prayer meeting, which had been running since dawn, was finally recessed. Some of the young women had fainted, some had spoken in tongues, and others had seen visions before they called the break and dispersed to their homes for final preparations before going out to meet the Lord.

The women brought their freshly ironed bridal robes from the closets where they had been laid away, and draped themselves in white from neck to ankle, looking very saintly indeed. Those of the men who owned a good pair of boots gave them a greasing to make them shine, and everyone who had a special suit, "To be married and buried in," as a few of them did, got it out of its moth balls in trunk or sea chest and put it on.

Eli and Timmy took advantage of the interruption to wander over to the Cove, perhaps with some vague plan of seeing this place where they had spent so many happy hours just once more before the world ended, though they didn't express any such thought consciously. In fact, up to this time the boys had scarcely talked between themselves at all about the subject of the Second Coming.

As they breasted the brow of the Head, where the path dipped down into the valley that formed the Cove, a great hammering and banging assaulted their ears. And there, perched astride the ridgepole of his little ramshackle house, was Jehu Gilmore, building what looked for all the world

like a small fish flake right on top of his roof. This seemed
like such a crazy thing to do, even for Jehu, that the boys
hurried over to investigate. As they hove alongside, Jehu
paused briefly in his labors and gazed down at them.

"Evening, Mr. Gilmore!" Eli called up politely. "Is that a
fish flake you're building on your roof?"

"Praise God!" Jehu called down in thunderous tones.
"Blessed be His name!" And he lifted his loud, if not tune-
ful, voice in a familiar hymn: "When the Lord from heaven
ap-pear-ears . . ."

He resumed his hammering in time to the music, Eli
and Timmy looking on in wonder while he finished the
hymn and the flake. Satisfied at last, he descended the
rickety ladder at the back and went through the door into
his kitchen. In Caplin Bight it was quite in order for the boys
to follow him in, so that is what they did.

A great fire was blazing in Jehu's little flat stove, and
roaring up the tin-pipe chimney like a line gale. A pot was
bubbling and fuming on the red-hot stove lid. Jehu stirred
it with great glee.

"That's the stuff, boys!" he shouted. "Praised be His name!
Dumplings and pork fat! Amen, Lord! Give me a hand here,
Eli. Even so, come, Lord Jesus!"

Eli had to admit to himself that he was overawed and a
little frightened by this esctasy, but he timidly helped Jehu
with the pot of dumplings and boiled pork fat.

"That's the ticket, boy!" Jehu shouted. "Praise God! Now,
outside with it, boy! Steady there! If ye spill so much as an
half an ell ye call down damnation upon yerself from God
out of heaven. Even so, Lord! Now, boy, hand it up the
ladder here. That's it. Accept, O Lord, this offering from the
hand of Thy servant for Thy first meal upon earth. Blessed
be His name!"

The boys had backed off and observed Jehu from a safe
distance as he placed the pot reverently on the little log
platform that he had built astride the ridgepole. Then he
burst forth with another hymn: "O hail! happy day, that

speaks our trials ended! The Lord has come, to take us home.
O hail! happy day."

While Jehu was preoccupied with his singing, sitting
astride the ridgepole and waving his arms at the sky, Eli
and Timmy beat a rather hasty retreat. They were used
enough to prophesying and preaching and speaking in unknown tongues, and other like manifestations of the Holy
Ghost, but even to their highly educated tastes Jehu Gilmore and his pot of dumplings seemed a trifle extreme.

They paused on the brow of the hill and looked back, but
Jehu was still on the roof, only now he seemed to be praying, his hands clasped, his face tilted toward the setting sun,
his voice going up like a fountain out of the evening shadows
that filled the Cove.

The boys went home thinking about supper, but it was a
journey accomplished in easy stages, for the way led past
Aunt Esther Pike's door, and she called them into her dim
old kitchen with its hand-hewn beams overhead, and its
huge old fireplace with a chair inside, and gave them the
last of her currant cookies, reflecting, no doubt, that the
homely art of baking might have no place in the Kingdom
that the Lord, in His infinite wisdom, was establishing that
night.

CHAPTER EIGHT

❧ ☙

Even within earshot of the last trump the force of habit
remains strong. That evening Elias dismantled the glass
chimneys of his kerosene oil lamps and polished them with
paper, inside and out, just as though this had been any other
autumn evening in the fourteen years since his marriage.
One wick that was slightly charred he trimmed and straightened. Then he lit the lamps and turned them up until a
beautiful golden glow flooded the house and the incense of
burning oil made the air heavy with the scent of home.

Martha fed her small family and banked the fire in the
kitchen stove, using ashes from the grate to preserve it
through the early hours of this last night of the present evil
world. She stacked the dishes in her tin dishpan, and, since
she had to hurry off to the open-air service in the graveyard
on the Point, and hadn't time to wash them, she left the pan
perched on the edge of the dresser, as the big, built-in sideboard was called. She even set the pot of porridge on the
back of the stove for the next day's breakfast, just as she had
done five thousand and some-odd times before.

Eli and Timmy were sent to bed. Some of the people were
taking their children with them to the vigil in the graveyard,
but Elias, who mixed his faith with a strong dash of horse
sense, pointed out that the fine weather of the afternoon was
rapidly worsening—it was overcast, close to freezing, and
threatening rain or snow. Moreover, he said, there was a
falling glass, and he didn't aim to have his youngsters trans-

lated into the Kingdom each with a case of double pneumonia. Pneumonia, he admitted, might be caused by lack of faith, but in his experience it was often aggravated by standing around in wet clothes in October.

Eli wished that he could protest against this decision, since if there were any chance of its really happening he wanted to see the graves open, and the sleeping saints arise, as the Lord descended, wrapped in a cloud, with His feet like pillars of brass mingled with fire, as he had heard Brother John describe the event in church.

In fact, ever afterward he regretted that he was not allowed to go with the faithful to the graveyard that night. He had to rely on secondhand descriptions, some of them related years afterward, and on the scraps and pits of information that he could glean from others at the time. He would much rather have seen it for himself. But he knew the futility of arguing with Elias, so he and Timmy went to bed in a mood of high excitement.

Martha left lights burning in the halls, upstairs and down. Then she and Elias took their two Bibles and their two hymnbooks and their heavy coats and mitts, and set out for the meeting. Elias had insisted that she wear a winter coat over her bridal robe. She could shed it later, he pointed out, in the warmth of the fire that would be kindled to light the outdoor service. Eli heard the door close behind his parents with a gentle click, and he and Timmy were left alone.

As the boys lay together in the darkness they began to discuss, in whispers and for the first time, the things that had been prophesied for this night. Until now it had seemed unreal, or at least a long way off. But now the night was here, and though some section of their minds refused to believe, some other part was excited and terrified with the certainty of great and horrible events impending. The darkness seemed sinister, and the comfort of sleep was long in coming. At last they heard the big clock in the hall strike nine times. Shortly afterward Timmy's whispers became drowsy and dispersed, and he gradually dozed off. Then Eli lay awake for a further time by himself, listening to the silence, before his thoughts, little by little, drifted into the fantasy that heralds sleep.

He was on a ship at sea. He heard the creaking of the rigging, and gulls called through his dream. The captain, who, he could see, was Brother John, came stumping along the deck in sea boots, and Eli cowered down in a corner with his back against the fo'c'sle head as the big black feet went past. He looked up. On the rigging of the mast a figure was suspended—like Christ on His cross. He was not at all surprised to see that the figure had the face of Virginia Marks. . . .

Eli groaned and half woke, and found himself in darkness between iron walls. He could feel paving stones with masonry between them under the soles of his feet, like the stones in the yard of the big general store that belonged to Elder Solomon Marks. He stooped down and picked up the stones, and they turned to music in his hands, to the rippling notes of a piano, and the sweet chords of strings—such music as came out of the gramophone in Mr. Markady's front room on Sunday evenings. But he heard a great voice crying, "These stones shall be made bread! Touch them not!"

He was awakened from his dream by a great crash that could only be caused by the end of the world. The crash and the succeeding clatter jerked him bolt upright in bed. Timmy, also sitting upright, grabbed him and held on tightly, rigid with fright. For the moment neither boy had the slightest doubt that this was *it*. The foundations of the earth were crumbling, and the imagination balked at the prospect of the next instant.

The next instant, however, went thus: there was a ringing note, as of a gong, or tocsin—or, even more, as of a large tin pan spinning on its rim, settling gradually to the horizontal. There was a tinkle as of broken glass or china. There was a plaintive mewing, as of a cat in distress. All the sounds came from downstairs. Then there was silence.

"Timmy," Eli said when his nerves had steadied a little, "I'm going down to see what happened."

"D-d-don't go," Timmy pleaded, his teeth chattering. "Don't l-l-leave me alone! I'm scared!"

"Gotta go down," Eli said as matter-of-factly as he could. "Fool cat might have upset a lamp."

"I'm c-coming too," Timmy said, bounding out of bed.

They tiptoed downstairs, picked up the lamp from the hall table, and peered cautiously around the kitchen door. There on the floor was a litter of spilled and broken dishes, the pan off to itself by one side. And there, under the stove, was the cat, tail fluffed out, hair stiff along her spine, ready to fight off the fiends from hell that she had loosed upon the world while prowling on the dresser.

The boys picked up the dishes that had survived the disaster, swept up the broken pieces, and cussed out the tabby. But they were so relieved that they took her back to bed with them and petted her until she lay still between them and purred.

It still wasn't late. The big clock in the hall tolled ten times as they again lay waiting for sleep, stroking by turns the big cat, which lay on the pillow catnapping, quite unaware that the sands in the glass of time were running out. Her purring grew broken, intermittent, then ceased altogether. And first the cat, then Timmy, and lastly Eli, drifted off into slumber.

This time Eli was on a vast plain with a sky of red brass overhead and red sand burning underfoot, and he ran and ran and ran toward the sea, and a black shadow ran behind him. . . .

And then he was in the shadow, and flew, with arms outstretched, swooping down over the piles of fish faggots that lay whitening beneath him, mounting toward the far rafters of the church, with the big, plumy branches of the trees going up on either side, waving, and bats flitting around his head. He rose in a wide spiral, then swooped low again, his white robes fluttering, listening to the deep, booming notes of the organ, which was played by Sister Mary Marks. . . .

"Come along, Timmy," he called, "to the Marriage Supper of the Lamb!" And he steered, banking, through a window into a blue mist, turning from side to side in sheer delight at the wonderful power of flight.

He started to do the crawl stroke, which David Markady had been teaching him that summer, and he was surprised how easy it seemed. He cut through the water like a speedboat, sending up a bow wave and a great feather of spray. The water was warm and caressing around his naked body, and his prow overhung the clear depths, where the little fish played. But he saw two hands that filled the sky pick up a mountain burning with fire and throw it down, and the mountain hit the water and hissed and sputtered and went out, and the water became blood. He struggled and panted, but the red, tarlike substance stuck to his limbs, and he sank down . . . down . . . down . . . landing with a jolt on the mercy seat in front of Brother John.

"Lift up thine eyes," Brother John chanted, "lift thine eyes to heaven and look. Behold! The elements do melt with fervent heat! The earth being on fire is dissolved! The heavens are rolled together as a scroll and the sea is no more. . . ."

This time Eli was all the way out of bed; Timmy was rolled into a tight ball under the covers, and the cat was up on the bedpost, hissing and spitting at the surrounding shadows. There was a windstorm outside, and the house was trembling with its gusts. But that wasn't all. There had certainly been a very terrible crash, as if the house itself were falling in around their ears. And *something* had landed right in the room itself—in fact, had hit the bed. Eli stood, petrified with fright, in the faint light of the lamp that fell through the door from the hall. He stared into the darkness that filled the corners of the room, trying to see, and mortally afraid of what he might see, and afraid of not seeing, all at the same time.

He didn't know how long he stood there, with his pounding heart gradually slowing to a steady thump in his chest, before he looked up at the plaster angel in the dim light and saw that it was as bare as a mooring post. He dashed out into the hall and came tiptoeing back with the lamp, and by its light he could see at the foot of the bed the wings of the angel smashed to fragments, the scales of gilt paint scattered like autumn leaves across the floor.

Timmy, under the clothes, had started to whimper. Eli began to laugh, but his laugh grew shaky and turned to a sob in his throat. He set the lamp on the table beside the bed and screwed the wick very low. Then he climbed in beside his brother. He was laughing and crying all at once, and he couldn't stop. He realized that something very peculiar was happening to him, and he lay back, still laughing uncontrollably. He had never heard of the word "hysterics."

The cat came and licked his face. At first this struck him as the funniest thing in the world, and he had another fit of laughing. But gradually he grew calm. Timmy was still crying hopelessly under the covers, so Eli dug him out and put his arms around him.

"Hush!" he said. "There's nothing to be scared about."

But Timmy refused to be comforted. "I w-w-want my mother!" he wailed, boring down into the pillow until it muffled his sobs.

"Don't be a crybaby," said Eli rather crossly. "It was only the old angel."

He put his arm around Timmy's shoulders again, and after a moment the little boy, lacking more adult comfort, hunched over close to him and buried his nose in Eli's nightgown, his crying petering out, gradually, to a few shuddering sniffles.

The great clock in the hall struck midnight, and presently they had all dropped off to sleep again—Eli and Timmy and

the cat. Truly the nervous systems of children and cats are
wonderfully elastic things.

Half awake from time to time, Eli heard the sounds of the
night. First the wind shook the eaves, then came the faint
brush of autumn rain against the roof. Then the clock struck
once, then once again, then twice. The rain returned again,
with delicate feet, pattering like a child across the tarred
felt of the eaves. The clock struck once more, and the rain
came in a downpour, prancing in a frenzy on the panes,
blowing in gusts and sheets against the clapboard walls, but
the boys slept on, while the lamp burned even lower, drinking ever so slowly from its bowl of amber oil, casting a halo
of dim light over the dark head and the golden head on the
pillow, and over the faint stripes of the drowsy cat, removed
as she was so far from the ancient tracks of her jungle to the
caressing fingers of a sleeping child.

But while the children slept, the night beyond was loud
with emotion. Over two hundred of the people of Caplin
Bight, led in procession by their prophet, had paraded
through the chill of the evening shadows to the graveyard
on the Point. Oil-soaked bundles of rags tied to poles, borne
aloft by the leaders of the procession, served as torches,
casting a ruddy light over the rugged faces of the men and
the white robes worn by the women.

At the graveyard a great quantity of wood had been collected for a fire. The founders of Caplin Bight, who had laid
out and blessed this piece of consecrated ground, had
planned not for their own generation but for eternity, so
that the graveyard still held only a scattering of graves at
one end, many of them bearing the dates of the epidemic
years when the death angel had visited almost every house.
Most of them were the graves of children.

At the other end, away from the graves, several acres of
open space had been cleared to receive the bodies of the
next generation, and the next, and the generations of them
begotten. It was here that the people had prepared their

huge fire for light and heat, and perhaps also with some thought of its use as a beacon, to guide the Lord to His own. It was here that they collected in ranks, white-robed women and black-robed men and children in motley, to pray and sing and testify until the Lord should descend with a shout as He had promised, and the earth should be cleft and the dead arise.

It started well enough. The fervor that had been building up for weeks made the night a great occasion. There was much speaking in tongues, neither speakers nor hearers understanding a word of what was said. More than one person saw visions of spirit bodies ascending and descending between heaven and earth, and a chariot of fire, like a comet, roaring across the sky.

Toward midnight they even achieved a sort of mass hallucination: the weeping and the testifying had by now reached an almost incoherent pitch; Brother John was leading them in a hoarse chant from the Book of Revelation, and the whole assembly was rocking to the cadence of the great, dark-tinted prose of the Apocalypse, when, looking up, he pointed and cried out, and there above their heads was a massive cross of fire in the sky.

At least Brother Thomas Gilmore of Matthew described it as a cross of fire. Nearly all the congregation saw it, and fell on its collective face, weeping and praising God. And if there were a few whose eyes were not opened to this vision they were too ashamed of their lack of grace to admit it to the rest. But there can be no doubt that the great majority either saw it, or distinctly remembered having seen it, afterward.

This was taken as the imminent sign of the End, which was now expected momentarily, and they joined in singing the great Hymn of the Ascension, punctuated frequently by ejaculations from the more leather-lunged and iron-throated members of the assembly: "Praise God!" "Come, Jesus, Come!" "Amen!" The singing droned on.

But instead of the End, came the rain.

It started as little more than a drizzle around midnight. But it didn't take long for it to dampen the hottest passions. There was an immediate cooling of the ecstasy that had shaken the congregation like the winds of a tropical storm.

Nevertheless Brother John prayed, and thanked God for this test of faith—for that, he was convinced, was what it was, a test—and afterward Sister Mary Marks spoke of how we must mortify this vile body of death, and while she was speaking the rain held up, and new wood was thrust into the fire, and it was felt that the little flock had passed the test with flying colors.

But the bonfire committee had misjudged the wood supply. Toward one A.M. it started to run low. Toward two A.M. it became evident that the greatest test of faith still lay ahead, and there were parallels drawn between this anti-typical army of the saved and the army of Gideon's host, when the fainthearted, and those who stooped, were dropped out of the legions of the Lord. By this time the fire had burned down to a big heap of red embers and the first large drops of a real rainstorm were hissing into its pulsing heart.

By two-thirty everyone was drenched to the skin, the assembly was in total darkness, a few of those on the outskirts, whose faith was weak, had already started for home, telling themselves that they would come back after fetching their oilskins, and Brother John was praying in a voice ringing with desperation, pleading with the Lord to put in an appearance at once.

The rain increased to a downpour, and the white robes, faintly visible in the thick darkness, showed the miserable little company of the saints huddled together as if for protection, all of them shivering and some of them wailing at the sky. None of those who had started for home came back. The wind rose, howling, driving the rain in cutting blasts before it. Brother John's voice rose with it, going up like a cataract, still dominating the huddled and miserable company of his followers. He shouted to be heard and as though he would shout down the noise of the increasing storm, to which the thunder of nearby surf began to add its deep undertone. He pleaded with God to stop the downpour and to still the wind. He commanded the elements to be quiet, as Jesus had commanded the waves on the Sea of Galilee. And he pleaded with the saints to have faith. This, he said, was the last great test. When they had endured it the Lord would appear. Only those who had come through great tribulation and washed their robes and made them white could enter in.

But it was a losing cause. The inexorable logic of the rain cut like a splitting knife through the fabric of madness that he had woven over Caplin Bight. A few of his followers remained, it is true, until dawn broke, leaden-gray, over the heaving and foam-flecked sea, and Brother John, his hopes, his confidence, even his faith, gone, threw himself down by the sodden ashes of the fire in a fit of uncontrollable weeping. It was Sister Leah, her hard face streaming with rain but not with tears, who lifted him out of the ashes and led him away, thus putting an end to the agony of that terrible vigil.

Elias and Martha were not among those who remained to the last. Shortly after the downpour started in earnest, Elias put an arm around his wife's wet shoulders and steered her quietly out of the group toward the invisible cemetery gate. They walked unseeing along the familiar path across the bridge, where the mill brook flowed into the Bottom, and back the front road toward home. They could hear other footsteps on the road behind them, but they made no greeting as they went. The returning people walked in silence, each keeping to himself, sullen and ashamed.

Eli was awakened by his mother and father as they entered the house. He lay for a minute, listening to the uproar of the storm. Then he left Timmy and the cat sleeping while he crept softly down to the kitchen to occupy a corner of the settle, as far out of the way as possible, while his mother built a big fire in the stove and made a badly needed pot of tea. She poured tea for Elias and Eli and herself. Then she hung the wet top clothes on the backs of chairs turned toward the heat.

Elias sat in silence for a long time, his sock-covered feet in the oven, a gentle haze of steam rising around him. Eli was surprised that he was not ordered back to bed, but his father seemed hardly to notice that the boy was there. He looked, Eli thought, like a man just getting over a bad dose of the flu.

At last he spoke. "We can thank God we made that fish after all," he said. And then, much later: "We must've bin mistook in the chronology." And, after another long silence: "Martha, maid, let's all go to bed."

CHAPTER NINE

❦ ❧

The few days that followed the vigil in the graveyard were unusually quiet. The fishermen moved about silently, picking up the worldly tasks that they had neglected. Many of them looked forward bleakly to a winter that would find them inadequately prepared. But, being practical and capable people, they awoke from their dreams of the Kingdom determined to do whatever was possible to repair their neglect.

They pulled the community together and began laying in stocks of wood and meat, working from the pre-dawn twilight until long past sunset. Many of them tried hand-line fishing throughout the last days of October and on through November and early December, proving, for the first time in their bay, that you could actually catch fish in those months —not in the quantities taken by traps during the caplin scull of June and July, it was true, but enough to insure a good supply for the winter.

The fish they caught that fall were the biggest, on the average, that they had ever seen. Split and cleaned and put into salt bulk, they ran to fifteen or twenty pounds each, and might dry out at eight or ten fish to the quintal. They were the best "eating fish" that had ever been landed in the Bight —an eating fish being one that you saved for your own table, far superior to the stuff that was made for export, which no self-respecting fisherman would put before his family.

Following the fiasco of the vigil in the graveyard the reli-

gious faith of the community wavered. Brother John himself
spent long hours by day and night in prayer and heart
searching, and, with his books of Bible helps, looking for new
light. Eli often saw his light burning in the window when
he arose before dawn to get ready for a day of hand-line
fishing, and knew that the pastor must have been poring
over his books all night. It was, he realized, a lonely agony
that Brother John suffered.

Even among the elders there were waverings, and those
who had time for such matters were summoned to sit with
Brother John, searching the prophecies and their own hearts
for inspiration. There was general agreement, though, that a
mistake had been made, somehow, in computing the chronology. A year, or perhaps a few years, had somehow been
mislaid, and they would have to wait a little longer for
Christ's return, remaining faithfully on the watch and sur-
viving this great test of their faith like Wise Virgins. The
proof that they really were living in the last days was altogether too strong to be put aside, and few of them even
thought about doubting it.

Meanwhile Brother John sweated over the prophecies and
reported the results of his labors in his Sunday-morning sermons. On the Sunday after the vigil he returned directly to
the attack, preaching on the words of Jesus as reported by
St. John: "Behold I come as a thief. Blessed is he that
watcheth and keepeth his garments." It was, by the pastor's
standards, a quiet and reasonable sermon, and though it did
not bring forth the chorus of ejaculations that had supported him in earlier times, or move anyone to prophesy in
an unknown tongue, his hearers were attentive as he
pleaded with them to trust the Lord and to have faith that
even this present trial should be turned, at last, into a blessing.

Late in November the local school board, with the help
of the church board in St. John's, succeeded in getting a
teacher, so Eli was sent back to his lessons, almost two years
behind. At thirteen and fourteen he did grades six and

seven and started grade eight. Even so, he was far ahead
of most of the children in Caplin Bight. Some of the boys
of his age were struggling with grade four. Some gave up,
then or a year later. But Eli had little trouble with his lessons. Whenever there was a teacher in the school he soaked
up whatever she had to offer at more than twice the rate
prescribed by the curriculum.

That was the winter that Aunt Esther died, and it was Eli's
first really close approach to death, for Aunt Esther, though
she had blood relatives on her brother's side, was really
closer to the Pallisher family than to anyone else in the village. She received her widow's mite—the government pit-
tance of ten dollars a quarter—and paid it over to Martha,
and went to live with the Pallishers.

It was generally understood that she wished to spend her
last days with them—in fact, that she had gone to them to
die, because she was getting too old to live alone and there
might be danger that she would die suddenly, unattended.

Aunt Esther had a sharp tongue and a heart of gold. She
commented caustically on the folly of all young people, but
spent her time knitting caps and mitts and scarves for them,
or baking cakes and cookies in the big stove in the Pallisher
kitchen. Her face was creased with many lines—cynical ones
around the mouth, but lines of laughter and kindliness
around the eyes.

She often spoke of death quite without fear, but made
Elias promise that he would bury her in a dry spot in the
graveyard, where there would be no danger of water seep-
ing into the pine box in which she would be laid to rest. She
had a great horror of being buried in wet ground.

Eli was Aunt Esther's favorite "nephew." The wizened
old woman with the sharp nose, sunken mouth, and pale
blue eyes made a strange companion for the warm, dark,
vital-looking youth. They would often sit together on the
settle in the evening, she wrapped in a large shawl of purple
wool, he with his lesson books laid aside while she told

about her childhood, and memories of times even farther back, when her mother was a girl. It pleased her greatly to find someone really interested in stories out of the forgotten past. She seemed to feel that she was handing on some precious tradition, weaving together the separate generations, helping to make Eli's world a part of her own, the fruit of a people who were not just a haphazard collection of individuals.

She would smile in a wistful, wintry way and tell him how sweet her mother's voice was, and how she sang in the church, before there was any instrument to carry the tune.

"She'd stand up before all the people an' sing the first notes, an' the others would join in an' follow along. Had a voice like a bird, she did. She be dead now, nigh on forty year, cut down in her prime one summer with the rapid decline."

Her mother, she told Eli, was afraid of Indians when she was a little child, even though the last of the wild red Indians had been killed by the white trappers and the Micmac hunters at least a full generation before that time.

"'Twas fair barbarous how they treated they poor 'angshores," she'd say of the Indian killings. "Shot 'em like wild beasts, they did. The last ones as I heared about was trapped out on the ice, just across the bay here. An' they was all killed except two women. An' the two women come up to the fishermen an' kneeled down an' bared their breasts, askin' be signs to be killed too, givin' theirselves up to death. An' there, kneelin' on the ice in front o' the fishermen, they took the musket balls through their hearts. . . .

"Muskets they used in them days, not rifles or shotguns, like now. . . . Father had a musket so tall I never could reach the tip o' the barrel as it stood in the corner, even when I was a woman full growed. They loaded 'em with black powder an' swan shot, an' they said a full load could cut a man in two, or bring down a deer. But they used balls too, fer deer an' seals an' Indians. . . .

"Never did see anyone killed with them guns, but Uncle Cy's boy Amos shot hisself out in the boat one winter, an' he were brung home dead to the world, an' white as snow. Had to help take off 'e's leg, I did, bein' the midwife. 'Twas fair turrible. We had nothin' to use except a ax an' a splittin' knife, an' nought to give the poor mortal to aise the pain. I can still hear 'e's screams. Had to put a rope's end in 'e's mouth to gnaw on, but he thanked us after. We dipped the stump in tar, but it festered fer all that, an' he suffered like a martyr until spring. But he got well, an' carved hisself a wooden leg an' went to the Labrador after, an' made good voyages too. . . ."

Aunt Esther would continue thus until she dozed in her big shawl by the head of the settle behind the hob of the kitchen stove, and would then dream, with a look of great peace, while Eli returned quietly to his books, reading history less colorful than Aunt Esther's, and geography less thrilling than Mr. Markady's.

She was a frail old lady with a courageous spirit that remained firm to the end, but she lost her appetite and gradually starved herself to death. She lived for months on nothing but tea and a little bread or buttered toast, and nobody could coax her to eat meat. She wouldn't be bullied or bossed either. She was stubborn and strong-willed, even when she became too weak to leave her bed.

They sat with her by turns for long periods, as she spoke less and less, always of the old days, and slept more and more. It was hard to believe that anyone could die so slowly or so peacefully. She sank by imperceptible degrees, without suffering and without struggle.

Even her terminal coma lasted for a long time. No one could say when it began or predict when it would end. Eli and his father and mother sat through it in relays, day after day, night after night, as her breath became slower and more labored, and began to rattle gently in her throat.

All one afternoon the slow, gentle death rattle continued.

Far into the night, slowing gradually to one or two times a minute, they could still hear it. There were long periods of silence between breaths; her face was cold to the touch; her hand no longer responded to pressure. A week had passed since she had opened her eyes.

Eli was standing watch when she died, sitting on the edge of the bed with his arm under her head. He fancied she was restless in her coma, and anxious for his touch, for the last faint contact with the world of men, that she might not be alone in her dying. But he could not be sure. Everyone else in the house was asleep. He could not tell when death came, if it can be said to come at all in such a case.

The clock in the hall had struck four A.M. and the old lady had drawn one or two shallow breaths with eternities between them. Slowly Eli became convinced that the long wait for her next breath would go on forever—that, in fact, she was dead in his arms. He experienced none of the violent emotions that people so often report in the presence of death. He straightened her wispy gray hair a little, remembered with affection how she had fed him cookies when he was a little child and told him stories of her girlhood during the last months of her life. Then he withdrew his arm as though fearful of waking her, kissed the cold forehead, and went to call his father, hearing, as he went, the clock strike the half hour. The first light preceding the March dawn would be coming over the snow before it struck again and the long ceremonial that follows death would have to begin.

Elias awoke and took charge at home while Eli was sent to fetch the women for the laying out. Elias's first cousin, Myrtle Pallisher, a middle-aged spinster who acted as midwife for the village, was the one he was sent to "roust out" first. While Myrtle was putting the pins in her hair, she sent him on to fetch Sister Leah, with the message that she had best look smart.

"We'll want to get the corp washed an' laid out afore rigor mortar sots in," Eli was told, "so do be quick. An' ask Sister

Leah to bring any old linen she have that do be wore out an' can be spared."

By six A.M. the women were at work, and spent hours with pans of hot water and soap, scissors, cloth, and piles of old rags. Elias and Eli and Timmy were rigidly excluded from the indecencies of the laying out, but the remarks of the women, as they came and went, were revealing.

"Weighs no more'n a small child," Myrtle said as she came to the kitchen for more hot water. "Baits me how sich a bag o' bones could hold the breath o' life so long."

But Sister Leah was the one who impressed Eli with the horror of death when she conscripted him to go on a hunt for more old cloth. "She be all gone abroad, poor dear," Sister Leah declared. "We'll need a tablecloth or a bed sheet to stuff her up properly, an' see can ye git a little waddin' fer the mouth an' nose."

Eli went as he was bidden, numb with the horror of it. But on the way he sat down and bawled. He didn't understand just why. He had loved Aunt Esther, but had long accepted the idea of her death, and her dying hadn't affected him. But for some reason or other the sudden ghastly realization that she was being stuffed like a duck for the pot— that this was what the euphemism "laying out" really meant—completely unmanned him.

The grave was dug that day in the frozen earth on the Point, near the fence on the high side of the graveyard where the ground would be always dry. The gravediggers worked without fee or hope of reward, hacking their way through three feet of frozen soil, and another two feet of subsoil and rock, before the earth was ready to receive Aunt Esther.

Elias made the pine box in his work loft over the woodshed, Eli holding the end for him as needed. It was the same place where he built small skiffs and punts, fashioned doors, window boxes and hand barrows, or sometimes did a bit of coopering with a stave knife, split birch boards and bands of willow, making the small barrels known as drums in

which fish would be packed for export. They lavished great
care on the coffin, trimming and planing the fine old sea-
soned boards of white pine that had been laid aside for
years for this very purpose. Every carpenter in Caplin Bight
kept a few coffin boards on hand in his net loft or workshop.

Aunt Esther, dressed in a pair of patent-leather shoes that
had not been worn before and a dark blue dress with white
lace collar that she had been saving for years to be buried
in, was laid in the pine box, and the box was set on chairs
in the Pallishers' chilly front room, where the curtains were
drawn so as to create perpetual twilight, and then the whole
population of Caplin Bight came to view the remains.

After the burying Martha attended to the distribution of
Aunt Esther's few personal effects in the way the old lady
had requested. An amber necklace that had lain wrapped in
a bit of velvet for half a lifetime went to one of the women
who had laid her out; a shawl pin, which seemed to have a
picture under its crystal front, and was most likely a piece
of moss agate, went to the other. She had directed that her
clothes were to be packed and sent to clothe the heathen at
some foreign mission station. Her house passed to her brother's family. She had remembered the children of the Pallisher household also. Timmy received a curious Chinese
toy made of ivory, which had come from the end of the
earth in a square-rigged ship out of Harbor Grace more than
a century before. Eli was given a watch that Aunt Esther's
father had brought from the States when she was a girl.

That watch was a revelation to Eli, and an amazing possession for an old woman so poor as Aunt Esther. A small,
delicate thing on a chain with a jeweled stud, it was covered front and back with a solid gold case delicately carved
by a goldsmith. Inside the outer case was another, also of
gold, but not ornamented. The chassis of the movement was
covered with very fine etched designs, and all the bearings
were jewels. A twenty-five-year service guarantee was
carved into the inside of the case and signed by the watchmaker. But the watch had already been keeping time for

well over fifty years when it was given to Eli. It is keeping time still, though it may now be nearly a century old, and has not been touched even once by a watchmaker since the day it left the goldsmith's shop so long ago.

CHAPTER TEN

❧ ☙

March melted imperceptibly into the long agony of the Newfoundland spring. The grass pushed up bravely into the fog. The rhubarb grew long in the little dooryard plots. Storms howled. The snow returned and buried the rhubarb. But at last it was June and school was out and the fish were running and the nightmare of April and May was soon forgotten.

It was the time of the caplin scull, when billions of the eight-inch bait fish appeared on the beach in a single night, and the sand of the shoreline, especially in the Cove, was spongy, like a carpet, with the spawn. Life in the Cove, for a brief period, became noisy and hectic, as the fishermen gathered there for the free harvest of the caplin, while life in the Bight hummed on its accustomed round, with hardship as general as the sea and joy as occasional as its foam.

Then into the quiet drone of the village Christopher came, and nothing was ever the same again. For Eli this was the great awakening, colored with hero worship and the strange excitement of a boy's first adventure of the mind and the heart. No one, before this, had touched him deeply and at once on every level of his being: emotional, intellectual, spiritual.

Eli should have been able to remember Christopher from his early childhood, for the young man was the son of Peter Simms, had grown up in Caplin Bight, leaving it when he was sixteen and Eli was six, to attend high school and the university. The boy tried but could not seem to form any picture of Christopher Simms at all. It was as though he had never seen him, even during his brief summer visits. With some curiosity, therefore, he stood at the foot of the gangplank with Mr. Simms and the little mare and trap from up in the valley, waiting for the coastal boat's passengers, Christopher among them.

In a moment Christopher walked down the plank—a lithe, athletic young man, with hands that looked restless and strong, even though they were not work-calloused like the hands of the people Eli knew. He had close-cropped blond hair, a ruddy skin, a face and voice that were strong and gentle, but a jaw that seemed stubborn and willful. He looked to Eli like the sort who would get his own way, if not by direct means, then by outlasting his opponent.

Mr. Simms must have introduced Eli and Christopher, for the old magistrate had the outside-world manners that would have made such an action natural to him, but Eli could never remember this either. He did recall helping to load the luggage into the small pony trap. There was a lot of it too—not just the small bags brought by the stewards from the cabin, but trunks and boxes that had to be hoisted out of the hold by the ship's deck winch and lowered to the wharf amidst the familiar melee of the baggage and freight that piled up there each time the steamer called. The promiscuous mixture was sorted out with the wildest kind of inefficiency, owners and agents bustling back and forth, hunting for their consignments, loading them on horse carts and wheelbarrows, while others helped to move the large shipment addressed to the general store into Solomon Marks's shed.

Even before his arrival Christopher had applied for the Caplin Bight school in the fall, and it was a foregone conclusion that the board would give him the job as teacher. The only thing that puzzled everyone was why a man with a college education—a degree, in fact, though few knew what a "degree" meant—would choose to teach in Caplin

Bight when he could have had his pick of dozens of larger
schools in other places, most likely as a principal with three
or four other teachers under him.

Some said that old Mr. Simms had demanded it, though
why any man would cramp his son's career in such a way
was hard to imagine—or why the son would heed such a demand, for that matter. Anyway, Christopher, twenty-four,
very much of an outsider, stuffed to the gills with book
learning, and seemingly with the magic world of the cities
open before him, came back to the dying village where he
was born, to the people whose minds, beside his, set them
almost in a lower species, and settled down to enjoy two
months of sunshine and loafing before the fish were spread
and the school was opened in the fall.

Eli met him for the second time on the day after his arrival, ambling along the foreshore in the late afternoon,
and was pleased and flattered to find that the young man
remembered him out of the hundreds of faces on the wharf
during the brief encounter of the day before.

"You not working either, Eli?" he asked.

"Well, no, sir, not today," the boy explained. "I'm on half
shares with my father's crew, but the fish have struck off
for a spell and none of us is doing much right now. Almost
nothing in any of the traps this morning, as a matter of fact."

"How's it going?" Christopher asked.

"The fish, sir? Not bad. We reckon we've got about two
hundred and thirty quintals dry weight in salt right now—a
third of a voyage, or thereabouts."

They walked on, skirting boats and stages, along the
sandy foreshore.

"My father was talking about you," Christopher continued. "Says you come to our house from time to time to do
some reading."

"Yes, sir," Eli admitted. "Mr. Simms has been very kind—
lets me use his library as much as I like. He has the only real

stock of books in the harbor, and I've almost taken charge of them, I'm afraid."

"Not many people here care a lot about reading," Christopher said. "How did you happen to take it up? What are you reading now?"

"I don't really know, sir," Eli said doubtfully. "I suppose Mr. Markady, talking about his foreign voyages, started it. I began reading about voyages and explorations, and the next thing I knew, I couldn't stop. Right now I'm reading the *Outline of History*."

"But Father says you never borrow any books, though he's offered to lend them. Why is that?"

"Well, sir—" Eli paused uncomfortably, not wanting to explain.

"Your parents think reading is wicked, maybe?" Christopher suggested.

"Oh, no!" Eli said hastily. "They want me to have all the schooling I can get. Mother even hopes I might get a shore job, working as a clerk. She never did like the sea. It's—well —it's the *kind* of books I've been reading in Mr. Simms's house. You know—like the *Outline of History*, for instance. Father can read too, you see, and if he found a book like that in the house he'd burn it, no matter who owned it."

"Ah—you mean it doesn't start off with the story of Adam and Eve and the serpent," Christopher said.

"It doesn't just leave it out," Eli explained. "It makes it look silly. But as long as I'm under Father's roof I daren't say so. If I said I doubted a single verse of the Old Testament he'd likely come for me with a boat hook."

"Then you've transferred your faith from the Bible to the *Outline*, is that it?" There was a curious expression of half amusement in Christopher's eyes that Eli couldn't interpret.

"No, sir," he said. "It isn't faith at all."

"What is it then?" Christopher was probing for something that Eli hadn't even considered up to that time. The boy had to stop and ponder for a minute.

"I suppose," he said at last, judiciously, "it must be the

difference between science and superstition. But faith isn't superstition, is it?"

"Good for you!" Christopher said, smiling. "You've come a long way." He paused for a moment, as though weighing the wisdom of his next statement. Then he plunged ahead. "Eli, I didn't tell you all my father said about you. He thinks you are rather special. He swears that you don't belong in a trap boat. He agrees with your mother to that extent, anyway. But her ambitions for you are much too narrow. It would be a crime for you to become a coastal skipper or a clerk, which is about as high as anyone here aspires to, nowadays. My father says you are not just the smartest boy in the Bight but the smartest he has ever seen here. What do you plan to do with yourself?"

"Well," Eli admitted, "I haven't thought about it much. I'm pretty good with figures, though. Maybe I could do something of that sort."

"Father talked to you about engineering, didn't he?"

"Yes, sir," Eli admitted, "but he said I'd need four years in the university, and I hardly see how that'd be possible."

"You know there are scholarships that can take you all the way through, don't you?"

"Yes, sir," Eli said, "but I'd be competing against people all over the island."

"You would," Christopher agreed, "but that shouldn't worry you. I've had a look at your school record, and even though you are still a grade behind what would be considered normal for your age in the city, it seems obvious that you can learn anything you set your mind to."

"I guess that's true," Eli agreed. "I didn't have much trouble doing two grades last winter. I might even have sat for the grade eight public exams if I'd known beforehand that I could do it."

"I don't know that you should aim at being an engineer, though," Christopher said. "Perhaps you should wait and see where your inclinations lie. There are other things besides being smart with figures, you know—more important things. My father seems to think that you could make a pretty big noise in the world if you got the chance, in the right profession."

It was the first time anybody had ever spoken to Eli like this. No one had ever suggested that he was anything more than a little bit odd. It was true that he had a growing conceit within himself, but until now no one had done anything to feed it. He groped for a reply, looking at the young man with a puzzled frown.

"I—I've never—" he began. "Sorry, sir, you're going too fast for me. I've never even thought much about leaving Caplin Bight."

"You'll have to think about it soon, though," Christopher said. He saw Eli's embarrassment and moved on lightly to other things. "Come," he said, "you can start conquering the world next fall. Let's go over to the Cove. We can talk on the way, if you want." As they left the settlement, breasting the rise of the Head, he stopped. "You know," he said, "I envy your bare feet. Do you think I could go barefoot too?"

"Sure," Eli said, astonished, "why not?"

Christopher laughed, took off his shoes, and kicked them under a bush beside the path. "Afraid I can't offer to race you," he said with a twinkle. "Not yet, anyway. But I bet I'll be able to do it before the summer is over."

It was the first time Eli had ever seen a full-grown man going barefoot just for fun, though some of the young men of the Bight had been forced to it during the hardest days of the depression—but he was to find out in the coming weeks that Christopher did hundreds of things that others never thought of doing, or else forbade themselves, out of mere custom.

It was too early for swimming, but they waded among the shoals of swarming caplin and watched the cast netters at work, taking the little fish by the ton. Then they climbed the hill above the Cove, and later found a sheltered nook on the beach, where they could lie in the sun and talk the rest of the afternoon to death.

Looking at the young man who had come so suddenly into his life, Eli felt a surge of almost magnetic attraction.

There was something a bit catlike about Christopher. It wasn't just that his blue eyes had a greenish tint to them, or that his face had a faintly smug look about it. He had a way of stretching lazily in the sunshine, of being luxuriously sensuous about bodily comfort, as though he were drinking in the world through his pores. He had a habit of pacing about with a prowling motion, restless and relaxed at the same time, like an animal stalking a shadow. And in spite of his seeming guilelessness, Eli found him enigmatic.

Exciting too. The young man not only represented the world outside, with its fabulous stores of knowledge and wealth and opportunity, but also opened Eli's eyes to a new level of human relations—a level where people met with complete honesty and trust and made no effort to hide their feelings from one another. Such relationships were almost undreamed-of in Caplin Bight, where all deep emotion was either repressed or sublimated into the transports of religious ecstasy.

Within a week Eli found his life revolving around Christopher's like a planet around its sun. As he worked in his father's trap boat he would find himself wondering what Christopher was doing, or looking forward hungrily to the evening in the Simms library, when they would share some small adventure of the mind. When they met, he always felt a great surge of joy and expectation. When they parted, his mind would leap forward to the next meeting.

Eli's infatuation must have been clearly visible to the discerning eye, for he had barely mentioned the new teacher's name to Virginia Marks when she turned on him sharply. "'Tis plain enough that you're in love with him," she said. "But ye might as well start getting over it right away, because that sort of puppy love never leads anywhere."

They were on the government wharf, where Eli had been taking a skiff load of salt from the shed, but he signaled Pleman Pike, who was with him, to take the boat over to his father's stage while he turned to confront Virginia, who stood beside him, her black hair blowing in the wind and her skirt rippling tantalizingly about her firm thighs.

"What on earth are you talking about?" he demanded.

Virginia tossed her head and spoke half teasingly. "Anyway, ye can't have him," she said, "for I mean to keep him for myself."

"You—you can't be s-serious," he stammered. "You don't really mean that you're jealous of me!"

"Jealous! Huh! Of a bedlemer like you!" she scoffed. But then, more seriously: "Yes, I suppose I am, a little. You see, I've been in love with Christopher from the moment he stepped ashore. That way he has of prowling about sends shivers all over me, like I was waiting for him to pounce. Does that make sense?"

"No," Eli said. "It doesn't."

"Well, anyway, he gives me the loveliest kind of chills, and I'm jealous of anybody who makes the slightest claim on him. If Christopher had a dog that he was very fond of I'd be jealous of the dog—and he likes you a good deal more than any dog."

"Why, that's absolute nonsense!" Eli exclaimed. "If you're so mad about Christopher then go ahead and marry him, if you can get him, but don't bring me into it."

Virginia regarded him coolly for an instant. "I do believe that ye are as innocent as ye look," she said. "What a baby you are!"

"I am not!" he said hotly. "I only wish—" But the wish was unspoken, for what he really wished, and had almost blurted out in his anger, was that he could be in Christopher's place, and have this flamelike girl burning with desire for him—a thought that, in a cool moment, he could no more have expressed in English than in Chinese.

She laughed, a merry, tinkling sound that made his heart flip in his chest. "Ye know, Eli," she said, "I like ye a little, especially when ye look like a lost calf, which is the way ye are looking now. But remember what I said about Christopher—he's mine."

"Aw, cut it out," Eli complained, "and be sensible."

"All right," she agreed, smiling again. "You get back to your fishing and I'll get back to minding shop. I only wish *I* could fish, instead of being stuck behind that damned counter. See you in church."

And she left with a self-conscious flick of the skirt that both provoked him and dared him to cross her.

With Christopher there was never any such two-sided encounter. Their relations were always simple and direct and uncomplicated. Indeed everything that Christopher did was uncomplicated, for he had shed the complexities of civilization, and viewed the world with the clear vision of a child.

Not only to Eli, but to the other children of the village as well, the new teacher was a revelation. For one thing he was gloriously lazy. Never before had they seen a man really idle in summer. Even such no-goods as Jehu Gilmore at least pretended to be busy from spring thaw until freeze-up. But Christopher would lie out in the sun on the Head for hours at a time, reading a book or just watching the gulls wheeling and dipping along the horizon. He went wading in the marsh, catching tadpoles and strange crawling things that he took home in bottles. And he went fishing for trout like a small boy. In fact the idea that a teacher, or teacher-to-be, might act rather like an enlarged edition of themselves had never occurred to the children. But Christopher seemed to have a gift for being a boy and a man at the same time.

CHAPTER ELEVEN

❧ ❧

One of the teacher's first acts was to acquire a boat—a thing his father had not owned since the day he retired from government service. It was a decked pleasure boat, a little smaller than a trap skiff but a great deal more comfortable and incomparably more beautiful. The boat was clinker built and double ended, with a mast taller than her overall length, a jib and a mainsail that dipped her lee rail into the water, and a small engine tucked into the stern, with a sailing clutch that would allow her screw to spin free when the engine was shut off.

The morning after Christopher sailed her home from Broadport he came looking for Eli to share the adventure of an all-day cruise, and since there was still a lull in the trap fishery the boy was able to go. As they rounded the stage head, and Eli caught sight of the little boat at anchor, he knew for the first time the love that a yachtsman feels, and the unreasonable conviction that a boat can have a life, a personality, and a soul. Eli had been used to work boats all his life, and in their stolid way they had a kind of beauty. But this was as different from a work boat as an Arab stallion from a dray horse. She sat, less like a boat than like a bird upon the water, tossing lightly to the tiny swells, seeming to sniff the salt breeze and to strain at her moorings in a desire to be off, tossing spray from her bows and dappling her deck with spindrift.

"My!" he breathed. "Oh my—she's beautiful!"

"Ah!" said Christopher. "I knew you'd say it. Now then—boarders to the main braces!"

They left their punt on the collar, jumped lightly aboard, and loosed the boat from her moorings. Then Eli hoisted the sails while Christopher took the tiller and sent her skimming over the waves between the sunkers straight into the rising sun. And when the first splash of spray struck his tawny cheek the boy laughed and tossed his black hair in the rising breeze and felt like a buccaneer of a younger day, coasting down through the glittering Spanish Main, seeking the isles that lie under the wind.

Then Christopher gave him the tiller and the mainsheet and told him to sail. So they headed up the Reach, with the wind baffling from quarter to beam, and the little boat lay over and spilled air from the great, taut bow of her sail, and recovered, as if she knew better how to manage herself than did the inexpert hands that guided her.

But soon the wind increased and Eli, not knowing the feel of a sailboat, almost sailed her under. His inborn sense of seamanship came to his rescue, however, and he saw Christopher, who refused to interfere, sitting by the jib halyard, laughing at him. He soon got the hang of handling the mainsail and tiller in combination, and by the time of the noon calm he was sailing her as if he had been handling small sailboats all his life.

They were now at the end of the harborless Reach where a tiny sandspit formed a pocket-sized *barachois,* and a thread of a waterfall dropped nearly a thousand feet, feathering out into a plume of spray long before it touched the sea. Here they dropped their small anchor in water so still and pellucid that they could see the spotted rock sculpins and the sand-colored flounders, almost crawling along the bottom, and the pink and purple starfish decorating the stones between the fronds of waving kelp.

Then Eli dipped his toes into the water over the side and said it wasn't so *very* cold, so they stripped and dived, going all the way under the boat, looking up at her strange blackness against the milky-blue surface of the air. Christopher even managed to reach bottom with the aid of the anchor rope, but it was an achievement scarcely worth the struggle, since he returned with nothing more worthy than a small green crab, which he made crawl around on deck for a while and finally dropped back into the sea.

Then they lay under the benison of the sun, chilled by the ice-cold water, until their skins dried and became chalky with salt, and Christopher disappeared into his cubbyhole of a cabin, emerging a few moments later with tea and sandwiches and biscuit and jam.

And as they ate they saw the eagles come home to their nest on the crag of the thousand-foot cliff, spiraling down out of the unimaginable depths of the firmament, black spots edged with fire in the burning sapphire of the sky, and they felt their hearts lift at the sight of the great birds soaring on motionless wings, claiming the remotest regions of the air as a part of the dominion of life.

Christopher lay on his back on the hot deck, looking up at them. "They tell me," he said, "that you are a pretty sharp lad with a gun."

"Well," Eli admitted, "'tis true I shoot a bit—mostly with Mr. Markady around the Lattice Harbor runs."

"Then you must make me a promise," said Christopher, "and swear to it on the *Outline of History,* that you will never shoot an eagle."

"Why," said Eli, shocked that his friend might imagine his doing such a thing, "of course I promise. But I wouldn't do it anyway. I have never in my life shot anything that I couldn't use for food."

"But eagles especially," Christopher insisted. "I love eagles. Think of how much grander the world would be if we had evolved from the eagle instead of the ape!"

"You take the theory of evolution for a fact, then," Eli said.

"It isn't a theory," Christopher said. "It is an established scientific law, like the law of gravity."

"But Brother John says it is a delusion of the devil, and that the evidence is all nonsense."

"Yes, I daresay," Christopher observed, "but Brother John, like all religious fanatics, speaks out of ignorance. Five hundred years ago he would have been ready to burn you at the stake for saying that the earth was round."

"Still, I wouldn't dare mention evolution at home."

"You don't have to. The laws of biology—and also the laws of physics and astronomy and chemistry that I intend to teach you—will forever remain closed to your parents, and to most of the other people here. You'll have to get used to belonging to a different order of life from that of your family and friends."

"I've always loved to watch eagles too," Eli said, looking up at the big birds, "but my father says they're sent from the devil."

The eagles were perched now, one beside the eyrie on the crag, the other on a lightning-blasted tree nearby, where the bolt had ripped the rock and killed the scanty vegetation.

"They are so different from us," Christopher mused. "What right do you suppose we have to call ourselves a higher species? They stand at the end of their line of evolution, two billion years of life leading up to them . . . and at last it may be proved—who can say not?—that eagles rather than men are the noblest work of God."

"Now you're talking nonsense," Eli accused him.

"Yes, maybe," Christopher admitted, and reached out to tousle Eli's hair. "You go right ahead and tell me whenever you think I am."

After that they swam to shore, the eagles watching, and by wading and diving in the shallow water they collected a heap of clams on the small bench of blue shingle at the foot of the skyscraping cliffs. Then Christopher swam back and brought the boat, her little engine purring, and they filled a bucket with the heavy dark brown shellfish.

And since a glasslike calm persisted through the afternoon they went chugging out the Reach, waiting for a breeze, but they caught a light air near Lattice Harbor Island, and cut off the engine, and sailed home through the iridescent evening, their hearts exalted and at peace.

Clearly the new teacher had kept something from childhood that most men and women lose. He had not forgotten how to play in the simple, absorbed, unaffected manner of a child. Nor had he lost his taste for the wonder and delight of the world. He went swimming with the boys at the Cove—the only man who had ever done it—and after a few minutes they got over the wonder and the strangeness of it and accepted him as one of themselves.

It was as a member of their circle that he started drawing them into conversations—pointing out the mysteries that lay all around them, overlooked, making them—many for the first time—think and ponder and ask questions. Indeed he taught the children as much, in the joyful, idle moments of that summer, as most other teachers had taught with chalk and strap in a winter of tears and frustration. And he did it effortlessly, without talking over their heads or seeming to push anything upon them. Actually he volunteered almost nothing but had them constantly appealing to him for information.

One day at the Cove they brought him into an argument about the tides, which they knew were caused, in some mysterious way, by the moon, then clustered around in a group and watched enthralled, for the best part of an hour, while he drew diagrams in the sand, explaining the universe according to Newton. And he went on from the tides to the seasons, while the world of Caplin Bight expanded outward through millions of miles of space, and the boys became, for the first time in their lives, residents of the solar system. No one's attention wandered, even for a second, and they kept pressing him to tell them more, while the golden afternoon melted into the blue of the evening.

Eli was the first of the boys to call him Chris, but before

long even the toddlers were doing it. The girls, shyer, more diffident, continued to say "Mr. Simms," but before the end of summer they too had come under his familiar spell, and his popularity in the school was guaranteed.

The oldsters expostulated about what they regarded as the children's lack of respect for the new teacher, and Solomon Marks, in his capacity as chairman of the school board, pressing his fat and spatulate fingers together, warned Christopher about "undue familiarity" with the children on whom he would be expected to ride herd that winter. "You're goin' to have trouble, Mr. Simms. Mark my words. Trouble." And he nodded his head in a knowing way.

But Christopher laughed it off. "I just can't imagine a child giving me any serious trouble, Mr. Marks," he said. "I've already taught for two full years, you know."

It was clear from the beginning that Eli's was to be a privileged relationship. Though Christopher was usually available to any child who wanted his attention, it was Eli whom he selected to share his pleasures—to go with him sea-trout fishing to Lattice Harbor Island, or to his father's house in the evening to sit by the open fireplace while they pursued their separate ways in Mr. Simms's books. He began to suggest things for Eli to read, to channel the haphazard and omnivorous appetite that the boy had developed for books, but always tentatively, never with overt direction.

"I'm not trying to set a course for you, Eli," he said as they sat together before the blazing logs in the stone fireplace. "No one ought to do that. You must develop your own tastes and preferences. But you might just take a look at this translation of the Greek dramatists. If you like it there's lots more in the same line."

And Eli would thank him and dip tentatively into the new volume, usually finding himself, shortly afterward, completely absorbed in some new adventure of the mind.

As the summer wore on Eli took to spending most of his time, when he wasn't in the trap boat, with Christopher. The teacher often pointed out to him subtle things that he did not mention to the other children: the way the light fell through a butterfly's wing, staining the whitewash of a paling fence with the color of primrose; how you could coax a dragonfly to perch on your knee, resting from its forays among the smaller insects. And he talked to Eli as an equal. Even Joshua Markady had never done that. Mr. Markady treated him as an adult when they stood together in his boat, stalking ducks between the long, oily swells of the Lattice Harbor runs, but the vast gap between their ages had forced him always to talk to Eli like a master to his apprentice, or a storyteller to his audience. With Christopher, Eli was always on equal terms, even if Christopher was a little more equal than he.

On the teacher's arrival the village had been bound by a most rigid set of clothing taboos. Except in the quarantined area of the Cove, everyone was expected to be "properly dressed" on all occasions. This meant that you scarcely dared to expose even an elbow to public view. Boys never went outdoors without their shirts, even on the hottest days; girls never exposed their legs above the calf. Even husbands and wives did not look upon one another's nudity: they mated in their clothes, and almost always in the dark.

Taboos of this sort have a way of crumbling when someone gives them a sharp push. The first time Christopher walked down to the government wharf and boarded his boat dressed in nothing more than a pair of slacks he was the object of many startled glances and a few "ohs" and "ahs." But before the end of summer various youths were working around the fish stages stripped to the waist without a second glance from anyone, and even a few of their little sisters were venturing outdoors with the vital spots where their breasts would later sprout exposed to the sensual sun. It was a silent revolution against a taboo that, so far as Caplin Bight was aware, had existed since Adam's eyes were opened in horror to his nakedness and he hid himself from the blushing face of Eve.

The revolution did not proceed without opposition. Sister Leah spoke out violently against it in prayer meeting and in Sunday school, declaring that this first laxity would lead on to all forms of lewdness. The matter was debated in meeting, but under examination the taboo simply failed to stand up. No one could advance any real argument in favor of the moral uncleanness of the male body—at least from the waist up.

But Christopher's most daring triumph in this respect was Virginia, who appeared one day in white shorts—the first ever seen on a sexually mature girl on that whole coast. The sight of a hand's-breadth of female thigh was such a novelty that Virginia actually interrupted work along the waterfront. Hoary-headed fishermen laid down their fish forks, and gawky youths forgot their barrows while they stared openmouthed at this vision of public indecency parading Jezebel-like (the phrase was Brother John's, delivered from the pulpit, inspired, no doubt, by Sister Leah) along the sun-baked pier.

There was some fulmination from the pious, who, though they might grudgingly admit some portions of the male anatomy to the light of day, unanimously regarded the female body as unclean, if not actually contrived by Satan for the furtherance of sin. Nevertheless, Virginia got away with it. She not only beat down her parents' opposition, and out-faced the tight-lipped females of her mother's generation, but won converts—rather hesitant ones at first—among the other girls of the settlement. In fact it became obvious that, no matter what might be said inside the church, this daring style of dress was going to become a fad among the teenagers, so that Solomon Marks himself, that pillar among the elders, was induced by considerations of trade if not of morality to place an order for girls' shorts in his fall checklist of next season's supplies.

This was the first revolt against authority ever to occur among the youth of Caplin Bight. But what was worse, from the elders' point of view, was the fact that the defiance of the clothing taboo seemed to be merely an outward symbol of an even deeper change within: a willingness to question, to demand reasons—even, it must be said, to doubt. It took them a long time to realize that this change was in progress, and to appreciate the threat to their power that it posed.

When Christopher was discovered painting his boat on Sunday this precipitated another prayerful debate in the ecclesia. The debate raged through two prayer meetings and came dangerously close to splitting the church. But in the end the liberals won the day. Work for profit was still taboo, it was decided, but work not connected in any way with earning a living might, according to the conscience of the individual, be classed as permissible relaxation. So a fisherman might not paint a trap skiff, but could perhaps get away with painting a small punt that was never used for any more serious purpose than birding off the Point. The distinction was a nice one, but the ecclesia regarded such nice distinctions as the very bread of spiritual life.

These changes in the social mores were the the first indications of what was to come. The next was Christopher's intimacy with Virginia. After he had been in the Bight a few weeks they not only began going about together but completely disregarded the taboo against young men and women being long alone in each other's company. After several trips with him in his boat, without another soul along to guard against the possibility of sex rearing its rosy head, Virginia's reputation was just about sealed, and the wise women of the village began watching her for signs of faintness, which might well be the heralds of a rising belly.

No one could blame Christopher for getting a little weak at the knees over Virginia. By all odds she was *the* girl of Caplin Bight in her time. Slim and dark, moving with supple, flowing ease, and with a smile that flashed into sudden life under long, heavy lashes, she seemed to hold all the gypsy's

promise of magic and passion. Moreover, her schooling in
the city had given her a touch of sophistication. She could
slip in and out of the local dialect as she chose. She knew
how to arrange her hair, how to sit, how to walk, how to
carry her head. She had learned, in spite of her sharp
tongue, the most difficult art of silence, and could make her
companion talk to her instead of chattering on endlessly
about nothing, as did most of the other girls of the Bight.

Virginia was well aware that she could have had her will
with any unmarried man of the bay, as well as with those
who didn't yet rank as men. She was the chief object of the
immature sex fantasies of the younger boys, as Eli could
tell by watching their eyes follow her, even though they
never talked of such things among themselves. Nothing
short of torture would have wrung from them a confession
that the image of Virginia followed them to bed, sent the
blood pounding through their loins and their hands guiltily
exploring the unmentionable region between their legs.

Virginia herself chose to ignore the fact that she was the
cause of much secret sin, or even to encourage the hunger
of her admirers. A wall of custom far higher than they could
scale prevented the boys of Caplin Bight from making any
approach to mature women. Virginia tripped about the village, accepting the admiring glances of the male population
as no more than her due tribute, and the dislike of woman-
kind as a sort of accolade.

Before Christopher's arrival she had been one of the lone-
liest people in the village, as shown by the way she had
sought out such a child as Eli on various occasions for her
confidences. For she was not only the outstanding beauty,
but also that unnatural rarity—a woman who took no trouble
to hide her brains. Thus her elders accused her of straying
from the fixed paths of revealed truth, and her contempo-
raries of flaunting her outland education. Even worse, she
had never experienced the emotional revolution of conversion, as every child of Caplin Bight was expected to do
sometime during the middle teens, if not earlier. Worse still,

she sometimes seemed to look upon the piety of her parents and her parents' friends with a trace of amused contempt. This gave her a somewhat witchlike reputation—a suspicion that she dealt with evil on fairly intimate terms.

It was inevitable that Christopher and Virginia should come together, and inevitable that they should act the way they did.

"I just can't be bothered with sham," she once declared in Eli's hearing. "Everyone here seems to live a special kind of public life patterned on the way he thinks people expect him to act. Well—I won't do it. If people won't take me the way I am, to hell with them."

So the heads wagged more profoundly as time went on. And Eli, if no one else, soon discovered that the suspicions of the wise women were well founded.

It was on the night of the August moon, which rose, full and red, like a globe of orange fire out of the bay, and then shrank ever so slowly to a small disk of pure silver, and Eli, because Christopher was walking out with Virginia, pursued his way alone along the cliff tops where he had played as a child, feeling somewhat neglected but happy nonetheless in the crystal beauty of the night.

He followed his nose through the mystery of the woods above the Cove, snuffing like a wild animal at the legion of scents that filled the warm darkness, in love with the quickness and the fecundity of the earth, feeling it breathe and stir under the gentle touch of his feet. There, to his right, a fox was hiding, or perhaps had just passed by, leaving its musk upon the bushes. Off to his left a clump of alders released their tarry balsam upon the air. Straight ahead he could smell the rank and earthy odor of swamp water. From time to time the tang of wood smoke reached his nostrils, and he could tell that it was wild-cherry wood, smoldering in Jehu Gilmore's little old-fashioned stove, in the small, ramshackle house on the grass flat far below.

He went out to the edge of the cliff top between the small

spears of the balsam firs, shuffling his way delicately along
among the shrubs and the berry bushes, feeling the first
touch of dew from the leaves and listening to the profound
silence of the northern night.

He had reached the coign of the cliff at the end of the
Cove where a little covelet was cut off by projecting boulders, and there he sat, listening to the soft murmur of the
sea, smelling the breath of the kelp beds from the rock pools
far beyond the beach, now exposed by the spring low tide,
when he noticed that the wake of the moon upon the water
was troubled as if by some creature of the deep approaching shore.

Then the monster touched the sand and reared up, and
was resolved into a pair of human figures—a grouping as
old as time: man lithe and strong and rugged, woman soft
and supple and full. They shook the water from their hair
and touched hands and stretched toward the sky, standing
in silhouette, outlined as if in cold fire, nude and incredibly
beautiful against the liquid silver of the moon.

Eli's heart reached out to their beauty, and contracted
with pain at the same time. He saw them walk up the sand
toward the shadow of the boulders, knowing that he had no
right to watch, that he should turn away, leave their secret
inviolate, but completely unable to follow these promptings
of his better nature. Instead he strained forward, watching,
suddenly torn by monstrous emotions, hating himself, and
hating the double-edged jealousy that filled his heart.

He saw them lie, and embrace in the shadows, and rise
and move to the shelter of the bushes, where the forest
spilled down through a cleft in the cliff and mingled its fore-
guard with the sand.

And there they lay, a world unto themselves, the man
whom he loved and the woman whom he desired, complete
in each other's arms, and he an exile from their paradise,
like a wolf on a rock, outcast and alone.

At length he tore himself away and walked until the chill
of the night cut through his scanty clothing and his feet

were numb with the dew, when he went at last to his home, to bed but not to sleep, until the moon set and he saw the bitterness of the dawn spilling like blood over the trackless plains of the bay.

As he dressed in the cheerless morning he knew what he must do, but he could not force himself to do it that day, or even the next. But finally, to ease the torture in his heart, he did it. He went to Christopher with the deep shame of his confession, and did dire penance as he forced himself to speak of what he had seen. And he was forgiven, and absolved, and sworn to secrecy. So for a time he made himself whole again, forswearing the desire of the flesh and gaining a bit of spiritual pride out of what he believed was a noble renunciation.

CHAPTER TWELVE

❧ ☙

The school was a fairly large building with a single classroom and two other small rooms, one of which was used for storage, the other being for wet boots and winter overcoats. The classroom had bare wooden floors, a long row of windows, desks where children sat in pairs, and a blackboard running the length of the end wall behind the teacher's desk. It had a permanent smell of dust, chalk, and unwashed clothing.

Into this drab and prison-like institution the children were herded rather unwillingly, even though they suffered from a sense of deprivation whenever the school was closed for lack of a teacher. No one had taught them that learning could take on the color of adventure, and for the great majority schooling was still drudgery to which they had to be driven, day after day, by the constant threat—and the frequent practice—of corporal punishment.

Everyone was curious, and Eli not the least, to see what would happen to this juvenile concentration camp when Christopher took charge of it. If betting had not been a sin against the Holy Ghost they might have wagered trout hooks against trade counters that he would, or would not, change from a pleasant, overgrown boy into a teacher, once the walls of the classroom closed around him.

He had over forty children to teach, their ages ranging from seven to sixteen and their nominal grades from one to nine. This might seem like a nearly impossible task, yet he managed to keep them all busy throughout the day, doing sums, writing answers to questions, correcting one another's work from the answers copied out on the board by the student who finished first.

If one of the older children did well he (or more often she) was favored with the privilege of teaching a lesson to one of the lower grades. If a bright child finished his lesson early he might eavesdrop on what was being done by the class above him. It was all very contrary to the methods taught in teachers' college. But such colleges were never designed to fit teachers for one-room schools. Anyway, Christopher's unorthodox methods worked well. The children learned even more from him in the classroom than they had on the beach and in the fields.

He devoted an hour or two each day to teaching the whole school, without respect to grade, things not found in the lesson books: such things as the names of the stars, the parts of a plant that was set to sprouting between a sheet of glass and a wet sheet of blotting paper, or the construction of a simple machine that would raise water from a bucket on the floor to a jar on the desk.

The children in the lowest grades, who absorbed all this in detail, could never have guessed that they were taking their first toddling steps in the sciences of astronomy, biology, and physics. These lessons had to be prepared with great care so that small children would understand them while big children would find them far enough outside ordinary experience not to be bored. Christopher regarded these lessons as the most important part of his teaching. He often sought Eli's opinion on them as they sat together in his father's home in the evenings, discussing his elementary science projects both before and after presenting them to the school.

His job was difficult but not exhausting, for he always seemed to be quite relaxed as he paced about the room, keeping half a dozen different lessons going all at once, and his task was eased by the fact that, almost without exception, the children worshiped the ground he walked on. As soon as they found that he wasn't going to beat their lessons into them they resolved to work harder to prove themselves worthy of such a novel dispensation—and he had his own little tricks for keeping the resolve alive.

Not that he didn't have problems. He did. And problem children too. But it was the end of the second week of the term before one of them pushed him a little too far.

Johnny Penchley had been the school's professional problem child since grade one, and the only boy in the Bight who had held somewhat aloof from Christopher during the summer. He was an orphan, living with his widowed grandmother, and had inherited a family reputation for shiftlessness, the Penchleys being regarded as the lowest cast among the families of the settlement. Eli had never paid any attention to Johnny, who was in Timmy's age group and sometimes played with the youngest Pallisher, but never very wholeheartedly; for Johnny was a freckled, redheaded imp of ten who had walled off his inner loneliness with high spirits and a show of belligerence, and didn't really get along too well with anybody.

He had been the despair of former teachers, and the object of dire prophecies (by some of the older, less charitable churchgoers) about those who are born to be hanged. Ever since school opened he had been leading up to a crisis, pushing the new teacher to see how far he could go, and Eli had begun to think that Johnny was going to get away with it, until the second Friday afternoon, when little Betty Gilmore came in from lunch, snuffling miserably, with a large wad of spruce gum—which the boys called "frankum"— chewed to a soft, stringy consistency and stuck in her hair.

Christopher, who had no trouble identifying the culprit, dispensed with all preliminaries. "Come up to my desk, Johnny," he ordered.

The boy got slowly out of his seat, looking as though he didn't really have to obey, and went forward with a suggestion of a swagger, expecting perhaps to be read a lecture, or to make amends. Instead Christopher, without a word, reached into his desk drawer and pulled out a strap— a heavy, three-foot strip of harness leather that nobody had guessed was there.

"Hold out your hand!" he ordered the surprised boy. The strap came down with a crack that made everyone in the room jump in his seat. "The other one," said Christopher.

This can't be happening, Eli told himself. He thought of Christopher playing with the children in the meadow above the cliffs, spending hours teaching them to cast a fly line or to do cartwheels and handstands. It simply didn't fit. But it *was* happening, just the same. And it was no mere token punishment either; he was giving Johnny a licking that the boy would remember all his life, swinging the strap so that the boy cringed and winced and uttered small, involuntary yelps of pain.

Eli realized about halfway through the whipping that he was unconsciously counting the blows. They didn't stop until Johnny had received a dozen on each palm. When the youngster turned to go back to his seat Eli could see that his hands were red and swollen, his breath was coming in tremulous sobs, and his freckled face was wet with tears.

The whole school was shocked into stillness, and after Johnny's sobbing died away there was an unnatural, almost deathly silence in the room—a silence that lasted until dismissal time.

As Eli walked home with Christopher that evening he felt a strangeness between himself and the teacher for the first time. Christopher must have felt it too, he realized— the iron curtain of the adult world had dropped between them—for he made an effort to tear the barrier down.

"There was nothing else I could do, Eli," he said. "I tried being reasonable with Johnny. There is such a thing as a boy's simply begging for a licking and not being content until he gets it."

"Maybe," said Eli, "but you didn't have to do it so *hard*.

Other teachers used to lick us. I got licked myself, lots of times. But nobody ever got licked as hard as that before— not in school, I mean. Besides, if you strap one boy it's just the start. You might strap me next."

Christopher permitted himself a short laugh. "Not much danger of that," he said, "and it's not 'just the start,' as you put it. You know perfectly well that my way of teaching children is to rule them by love and not by terror. I don't want to use the strap, and I don't *intend* to use it, except when there's absolutely nothing else for me to do."

He was silent for a minute, seeing that Eli wasn't convinced. "Look," he said, "if I gave Johnny the kind of licking he got dozens of times from other teachers—the kind he could laugh off—he'd be back looking for another one right away. I'd have to do it again next week and the week after. But the punishment he got today will last for a long time."

"Guess it should," Eli said. "'Twould make me feel awful mean if I got a licking like that."

"You know perfectly well that you are absolutely immune from any kind of punishment, so far as I'm concerned," Christopher said a trifle impatiently. "But you and Johnny are completely different types. You are not only three or four years older—almost a generation, at your age—but different in other ways too: you are sensitive, moody, responsive to subtle approaches. Johnny is what your mother would call 'hardened,' which only means that he has a shell, like a clam. And he's probably just as soft as a clam, underneath. Sometimes you have to use rough methods with people like that—not to control them, but just to get past their defenses."

This didn't seem at the time to make much sense, and Eli said so.

"Very well," said Christopher. "I'll bet you anything you like that within a week I'll have Johnny eating out of my hand. You wait and see."

As a matter of fact they didn't have nearly that long to wait.

It was the next morning—one of those beautiful, soft mornings of mid-September when the Newfoundland summer seems determined to go on forever—and they were setting out to try for one last sea trout in the rattle at Lattice Harbor Run when they saw a small figure approaching them rather shyly along the road. It was Johnny, with none of his usual bounce and noise and show of spirit. He walked up to Christopher and stopped, with head bent.

"Good morning, Teacher," he said, his eyes shaded by his lashes, a faint flush on his face. He looked up for an instant, then quickly down again, at his bare toes, which he shuffled self-consciously in the white dust of the road. "I—I want to say I'm sorry fer the way I been carryin' on," he blurted. "Gran says I oughter—an' I am, truly—" He stopped, embarrassed.

Christopher reached out, very gently, laid a hand on the boy's shoulder, and Johnny relaxed under his touch like a flower opening in the sun. He turned his face up to the teacher, his embarrassment melting, his features suddenly transfigured by an inner glow, his shyness swept away in what was perhaps the first flow of affection that he had felt for another human being. He moved in closer, and Christopher's hand slipped around his shoulders.

"You aren't mad at me," the boy said in wonder.

"Of course not," Christopher told him. "But aren't *you* mad at *me?*"

"Heck! No!" Johnny said, smiling warmly. "I deserved it. Gee, Teacher, that was sure some lickin' you gave me. I'm goin' to be a good boy from now on, you'll see. I wouldn't want a lickin' like that again, ever."

"You won't need it, Johnny," Christopher said gently, his arm tightening about the small shoulders. "We can be friends from now on, if you want it that way, and I won't ever have to punish you again." He winked at Eli over the little boy's head, but Eli guessed that the wink was to cover a lump in his throat. Abruptly, he changed the subject.

"Johnny," he said, "how'd you like to come trouting with Eli and me over to Lattice Harbor Island?"

"Gosh!" Johnny said, his high spirits returning on the instant. "Can I? Can I truly? Wait till I go ask Gran." And he dashed off, his supple brown feet like small wild animals scurrying along the road.

Christopher sat down on a puncheon tub near Solomon Marks's stage and looked at Eli with a faintly mocking smile. "Well, Mr. Psychologist," he said, "are you making any bets about who's feeling awful mean today?"

"Chris," the boy admitted, "I couldn't have believed it, only I saw it happen. I still find it hard to understand."

"Not so hard, really," the teacher said. "People are a lot alike, once you get close to them: lonely, mostly, and bewildered, and hungry to be loved. It's the getting close that's so difficult sometimes."

"You sure seem to have the knack," Eli said.

"It's not really a skill," Christopher told him, "it's just believing in people. If you believe in them the rest will usually follow. And I believe that all people—even the criminals in the jails—have compassion and kindness in their hearts, if only you can reach them."

In a moment Johnny came dashing back, bubbling with excitement. "Sure I can go!" he yelled. "Gran just said don't get drowned is all." He fell into step beside Christopher, shyly slipping his small hand into the teacher's restless one, and they walked hand in hand to the stage head, where they boarded the punt and rowed out to Christopher's sailboat.

It was a glorious day on Lattice Harbor Island. Eli did most of the fishing at the rattle, while Christopher took Johnny swimming on the beach at the other side of the island, and actually got him off the bottom, doing a dog paddle, face under water, for the first time in his life. When they returned to the rattle the little boy was full of his achievement.

"I can swim, Eli!" he yelled. "I can really swim."

Eli could see that Johnny was going to stick to the teacher like a leech, and he felt a small twinge of resentment. He knew that this was unreasonable and unjustified, especially since his own relations with Christopher were very nearly on an adult level, hardly to be compared with the father-son relationship that seemed to have sprung full grown between the teacher and the little boy, but the resentment was there just the same—irrational, evil, part of the Old Adam that Brother John assured him he carried in his breast.

He decided at once to put these unworthy feelings behind him and to treat Johnny with the consideration that Christopher would expect of him. In fact he did develop a sort of companionship with the little boy, very much like his relationship with Timmy. It began that day when Eli caught a sea trout that must have weighed all of five pounds, the biggest taken at Lattice Harbor Island that year, and gave it to Johnny to take home to his grandmother as an earnest token of his good intentions. He could see that Christopher was delighted by the gesture, and it also gave him a comfortable feeling of self-righteousness, far more rewarding than taking the trout home to his mother.

All day the little boy tagged worshipfully after the man who had thrashed him the day before, and when they left him at his grandmother's front gate at nightfall, lugging the big fish and half a dozen smaller ones, he turned back impulsively with a happy grin. "Thanks, Eli," he said. "Thanks, Teacher. . . . You're swell."

Christopher looked down at his reformed imp with tenderness. "Good night, Johnny," he said. "We think you're swell too."

As they climbed the hill in the dusk Eli found his own understanding of Christopher enlarged. Besides the well-established companionship that already existed between them, he found a new respect for Christopher's insight into the workings of the human heart. The time had come, he decided, to say something he had sometimes felt an urge to say before but had found difficult because of his age and the reticence that had been bred into him from infancy. He made the effort, and though the words sounded false and unnatural, they came out.

"Chris," he said, "I love you."

Christopher stopped and looked at the boy for a moment. "Thank you, Eli," he said. "Not for loving me, I mean, but for saying it. I know how difficult the word 'love' can be in the mouths of our people. We'd all be better for it, I think, if we could speak our hearts more freely. Maybe the hard life here, breeds hard exteriors." He paused, letting the moment reach maturity. "But I've got to leave you," he said. "I'll see you up at the house tomorrow. I'm going to see Virginia now. She gets off work when the store closes at nine. Her father and mother don't approve of me very much, but at least they haven't locked the door in my face as yet." He laughed a little as he said it.

"Chris," Eli asked, "why don't you go to church tomorrow?"

The teacher looked startled. "Why," he said, "you already know that I don't believe that crap which your Brother John preaches—"

"But why couldn't you pretend to?" Eli insisted. "You wouldn't be the only one. After all, there's some of it I don't believe either, but I've got to pretend to believe it, so long as I'm living with Father. If you'd just go to church regularly, and help out with the Christmas social and things, like other teachers always did, the Markses and the elders wouldn't have anything against you. They'd even let you marry Virginia, if you want."

"Eli, you young hypocrite!" Christopher exclaimed. Then he laughed. "Sometimes I forget that you're just a kid. It wasn't until I was a lot older than you that I realized a man can't live one way and believe another."

"But lots of people do," Eli insisted.

"Lots of people," Christopher rejoined, "don't really believe anything. . . . Matter of fact," he continued, "I *am* going to marry Virginia, and the Markses and the elders aren't going to stop me, but you can keep that under your hat for now. Solomon and Mary Marks would both make an awful fuss if she dared to talk about marrying a heathen like me, so we're putting off the row for a more convenient season. If it wasn't that the school is so important—and you and a few other youngsters particularly—I think we'd leave here and get married when school closes in June. But we talked it over and agreed that we just can't throw you to the wolves. We'll simply have to wait for a slack tide in the surrounding sea of righteousness, announce our engagement, and face the storm."

"But isn't Virginia more important to you than the school?" Eli asked.

"Well, yes," Christopher admitted, "in a way. But teaching is my work, you see. It's all I ever want to do. A man has to try the best he can to reconcile his work and his private life. He can't let one interfere with the other. You don't know the meaning of being a teacher, Eli. You can hardly begin to appreciate how anxious I am for you to keep this fire that has started to burn inside you right up to old age, instead of having it put out during childhood."

"Why, Chris," Eli said, perplexed, "I'd do anything you told me to. I'd go to the end of the world with you, you know that."

"Yes, I know," the teacher said gently, "but, you see, that isn't enough. You've got to be able to do the things that I *don't* tell you." He paused, reflecting a moment; then: "You've got to be able to go to the end of the world alone."

As they talked darkness had come and the stars were beginning to show. Christopher took the boy by the arm. "Come," he said, "up to the cliff top for a minute."

They climbed the footpath in silence and looked out over the sea toward the sky, now almost jet-black except in the north, where the glow of the sun still lingered. The great dome of the heavens was spangled with numberless stars, in chains and clusters and clouds of light.

Christopher stood behind the boy on the cliff top and turned his face to the heavens. "You've looked at these before, Eli," he said, "but perhaps you haven't thought much about them. That beautiful star that seems to change color and flicker like a candle is Capella. It is really two stars, and together they are a hundred and eighty times brighter than our sun. There, over the horizon, is the Taurus cluster. If you look for a while you may see why the Greeks called it a bull. Just to one side are the Pleiades, like a throne of light in the sky, with all the stars strung together by faint bands. There is the great star Aldebaran, and barely showing on the horizon is Betelgeuse. As you see, it is red, and in fact it is an enormous globe of the thinnest kind of gas, at least two hundred million miles in diameter. The earth would look like a speck of dust on its surface. Some of the light you see from those stars traveled six hundred years before reaching the earth.

"Men watched them for hundreds of centuries, and made up myths and stories about them, and measured their movements, and even set their calendars by them, before they even began to guess at what they were." He placed his hands gently on the boy's shoulders as he stood behind him in the starlight.

"And what are they," Eli asked, "apart from their size, and so on?"

"We still don't know, really. They are great furnaces blazing in the absolute cold of space, but we can still only guess about their beginning, or their end."

"Or our own, for that matter," Eli observed.

"It comes to the same thing," Christopher said. "We've got to go on asking those questions and trying to answer them."

"Why are questions so important?" Eli asked.

"Perhaps because asking questions is what makes us human," Christopher said. "No other animal that we know asks questions. And as time goes on we find the answers—at least some of them. Don't you think it's a wonderful thing to be part of that process?"

The teacher dropped his hands from the boy's shoulders and stood gazing into the depths of space. Eli turned and looked into his face, and could see his eyes glittering in the starlight—frosty, mysterious, filled with the awful cosmic mystery that he had just sought to touch and to point out to the boy. They walked down the path to the settlement.

"Good night again, Eli," Christopher said. "See you tomorrow."

As they parted, and Christopher turned along the path toward Solomon Marks's store, Brother John came up the road. He turned his head and looked after Christopher for a moment, then spoke to Eli. "Out late, ain't ye?" he asked. "Why do ye be hangin' around with that teacher so much?"

"Christopher and I are friends," Eli said rather loftily, his head still singing with the pride of their friendship, his heart exalted.

"I ain't so sure 'tis a good thing," Brother John declared. "Maybe that young Simms fella be all right in the classroom. They do say he have a knack as a teacher. But I ain't sure 'tis right fer a Christian boy to hang around with 'im in the evenin's. I must speak to yer father about it."

He moved off in the dusk, and Eli looked after him with sudden fear. It was the first time Brother John had offered him anything but platitudes out of a hymnbook.

Why, he wondered, would the preacher want to separate him from Christopher?

CHAPTER THIRTEEN

For some weeks after the chance meeting with Brother John there was no reaction from his threat. Eli didn't know whether he had spoken to Elias, as he had said he would, but if so the matter had ended there. Eli had done his work well that summer and fall, and this counted for more with his father than any vague fears about his fundamental faith. Besides, Elias was beginning to nurture commercial ambitions, and he saw in Eli the bright hope that his family might move up from the planter class to the merchant class, as the Markses had done half a generation before.

"Eli," he said one dark November evening as the boy sat by the broad-wicked oil lamp, doing one of his first algebra assignments with "Xs" and "Ys" that still seemed to have a strange will of their own, performing fascinating and almost unbelievable tricks, "ye be mighty sharp with figures, bain't ye?"

"Yes, Father," Eli said, looking up, "you know I've always been good with figures, but this here's algebra, where you use letters instead of figures."

"Letters?" Elias repeated. "What kind o' nonsense be that?"

"Well," Eli tried to explain, "it's really still sums that you're doing, but you don't know what they mean until you reach the end. This way you can do problems that are so difficult, you could never manage them with figures alone."

"An' be it of any martal use to anyone?" Elias asked.

"Oh, yes," said Eli. He groped around for a convincing illustration. "Suppose you wanted an eighty-gallon tank in a boat—to fit in the bows, say, where she begins to get sharp. 'Twould be kind of a queer shape, you see, and you could never figure out what size to make the different parts of it with figures, but with this you could do it."

Elias looked at his son as though he were some new kind of deep-water fish, brought up by accident on a trawl. "An' who do ye suppose," he asked, "would be sich a nincompoop as to put a tank in the for'ard end of a boat? Don't the tanks always go in the starn?" Then he laughed, because he felt he had scored off Eli and it put him in a good humor. "'Tis all right, lad," he said. "I be content ye kin do great things with yer larnin'. What I really aim to ask ye, though, is do ye think ye could do the bookkeepin' fer a store?"

"No," Eli said. "Not right now. 'Tis something I'd have to learn."

Elias looked disappointed. But he didn't give in. "Ye think that teacher could larn ye?" he asked.

"Well—I've never heard him mention bookkeeping, but I suppose he could," Eli said. "You want me to ask?"

"Mightn't do no harm," Elias said. He was silent a minute; then a thought seemed to strike him. "Look here," he said, "supposin' I was to get ye into Solomon Marks's business next summer—like ye were apprentice, say—even if ye had to take almost no pay fer it? 'Twould please yer mother, that's sartin. Maybe. We'll see." He mused a minute, then made up his mind to press the point further. "I'll tell ye, lad —though ye are to keep this quiet, mind—there be a few dollars put away—enough, I 'low, fer a small schooner an' a small store. An' I know fer sartin sure I could get credit up in St. John's. But o' course we'd need to be sot up right an' proper, with someone who knowed the bookkeepin' end o' the business. I been thinkin' about this a lot. Meantime, ye ask that young Simms fella do 'e know bookkeepin' an' will 'e larn ye. . . . But not a word to a martal soul about me goin' in business, mind!"

Eli promised, and Elias seemed content. For the moment
the boy returned to his problems and forgot about it. But
he got a stunning reaction when he broached the subject
to Christopher in Joshua Markady's kitchen the following
evening. Christopher and Mr. Markady had been drinking
hot rum toddies and arguing amiably about politics when,
during a lull in the argument, Eli asked if he could learn
bookkeeping.

"Bookkeeping?" Christopher asked, turning toward him
sharply. "What on earth for?"

"Well," said Eli, feeling, and probably looking, evasive,
"I'd like to know how to do it. Might help me get a job too."

Christopher eyed him suspiciously. "There'll be time
enough for you to worry about getting a job," he said. "And
besides, you'll never want that kind of a job. Now, tell me,
what do you really want to learn it for?"

"I'll tell ye what fer," Mr. Markady broke in. "That Bible-
readin' mother o' his wants to make him into a clark, that's
what. She sees a white collar the same way that imbecile
John McKim sees a halo." He looked at Eli shrewdly. "Moreover," he said, "unless I miss me guess, 'e's father be in on it
too. Wantin' to set up in business as like as not—been headin'
that way fer years if I read the signs right."

"Is this true, Eli?" Christopher demanded.

What could he say? What about his promise to his father?
Though he had resolved to be the very soul of discretion,
here they were, with his father's plans as good as posted in
the general store the very first time he had opened his
mouth.

"I—I c-can't talk about it, Chris," Eli stammered. "Please
don't ask. I promised. And please, Mr. Markady, don't go
around talking about my father's maybe going into business.
You could upset things something awful."

The old man grinned at him under his walrus mustache.
"Don't ye worry, boy," he said. "Elias's secrets be as safe as
the grave with me. There's some o' me own that I've kept

fer a long time—goin' on fifty year now." And he chuckled
with the enjoyment of a private joke.

But Christopher was pacing back and forth between the
table and the stove with a restless, predatory tread. "I'm not
going to teach you to keep books, Eli," he said suddenly.

"But why not?" the boy asked.

The teacher was still pacing, agitated. "Well," he said, "if
I had to make you into either a bookkeeper or a fisherman
I'd see you stay in the trap boat until your arse grew fast to
the taut!" He was speaking with more heat than Eli had
heard him use before.

"But what's wrong with being a bookkeeper?" he demanded.

"Nothing," Christopher admitted. "There's nothing wrong
with being a fisherman either, and you'd make a good fisherman, like your father. But you'd make a damned miserable
bookkeeper, no matter how clever you are with figures."

"But if it's what Father and Mother both want—" Eli said.

Christopher turned to Mr. Markady wrathfully. "Why in
God's name do children's parents have to try their best to
cripple them for life?" he demanded. "What makes people
such fools?"

"When ye have lived as long as I have," Mr. Markady said,
"ye'll be less astonished at men's foolishness. The man as
ain't a fool is generally a rogue, and 'tis rarely ye find one as
ain't either."

Christopher turned back to Eli. "Pleman Pike might make
a bookkeeper," he said. "'Tis certain he'll not make a good
fisherman. I'll teach *him* if he wants. I'll even do it nights
if necessary. But not you." He stopped his pacing in front
of Eli, looking as if he ought to have a tail to switch, or long
ears to pin back, and his stubborn jaw jutted forward a little.
"Why," he said, "rather than see that idiot of a father of
yours make you into a clerk in a shop I'd take him out in my
boat and run her under in a squall!"

Mr. Markady gave a great guffaw, breaking the tension.
"Spoke like a man, be God!" he said. "An' perfectly right too.

Look, boy, ye shouldn't need to be told this. Ye know ye are a cut above the hymn-singin' hangshores that ye are mixed up with in this bight. Ye've got to stay in school, and ye've got to go on to college, an' somewhere along the line ye can decide fer yerself what ye are goin' to do—which certainly won't be bookkeepin', or anything remotely like it. If ye wanted to sail to the Indies now—as maybe ye will—who knows?—I'd not raise a hand to stop ye. But writin' up ledgers in a store!"

Eli sighed. "Yes, I know. It's just that Father and Mother are so set on it."

"The time be comin'," Mr. Markady told him, "when ye will have to put Elias in 'e's place, same as if 'e was any other man. It won't be aisy, I know. 'E's a strong an' stubborn man. But ye won't have to do it alone, ye see. There's some o' the rest of us in this harbor as knows a trick or two."

"Certainly I can't just go tell Father that I'll have no part of his plans," Eli said.

"No," Mr. Markady agreed. "Take yer time, boy, an' don't cross Elias more'n he makes you. Ye are a fine lad, an' I owe ye a good deal. If yer father wants ye in the trap skiff another summer, go ahead. 'Twill do no harm. But let him understand, a little at a time, that when ye are a year or two older ye'll be makin' yer own way alone, not servin' 'e's penny-sized ambitions."

"It isn't going to be easy." Eli sighed. "Father has been used to getting his own way all his life."

"Well, don't be afraid to ask fer help when ye need it," the old captain said. "There's no man can do anything entirely alone, no one but needs the help of his neighbors sooner or later. If ye need help by an' by—in the form o' money, say, as ye most likely will—I'll see to it. An' ye may need help agin' yer family an' all their hymn-singin' friends. That's the kind that'll be harder to give."

"Of course it isn't going to be easy for you," Christopher put in, "but between myself and my father and Mr. Markady —all of us on your side—we can pull you through, I guess."

He laughed. "At least we have more brains, between us, than the lot of them."

"Now remember to go soft with Elias," Mr. Markady warned, "but don't tempt 'im to think that 'e kin make ye into 'e's storekeeper."

"Very well." Eli sighed. "I'll try."

He went home full of all this good advice and admitted to Elias that the teacher either knew nothing about book-keeping or thought it would be a waste of time teaching him.

"'E got time fer all sorts of other foolishness!" Elias exploded. "Fer books full o' heathen lies an' this algebra an' sich nonsense. We'll see will 'e teach plain honest figgerin' or not after the board have a talk to 'im!"

The board was only a synonym for the church elders, and they did indeed have a talk with Christopher. But he won a compromise. No one could deny that he was a good teacher or that the children were learning from him at an unheard-of rate. But he was forced to agree, angrily, to spend more time teaching the three Rs than he had been doing. Bookkeeping, however, was not his field. It had to be taught, he insisted, by special business schools, and if anyone wanted to learn it properly he'd have to go to St. John's. And since Elias was the only member of the board with a special ax to grind in this respect, there the matter rested. He muttered, but gave way.

"We'll see about gettin' ye into the general store," he told Eli. "I 'low ye should be able to larn business from Sol Marks a sight faster, anyhow, than from some fancy college fella who got 'e's head stuffed full o' foolishness an' thinks 'e knows a damn sight more'n 'e do."

Eli decided to postpone the inevitable fight about going to work with Solomon Marks until it could no longer be avoided and allowed his father to ramble on with his plans for opening a store and starting a coasting business, consenting, by silence, to his own part in it. But the first real blowup came far sooner than either Joshua Markady or Christopher expected.

It was during the Christmas holidays, while most of the boys and girls of his age were making the rounds of all the houses each night, dressed in borrowed plumes, with masked faces, dancing and playing jew's-harps and mouth organs, and getting their due of Christmas cheer as the mummers had done in Caplin Bight time out of mind.

Eli was now less interested in taking part in this rite than in tracing its origins. With Christopher's help he had run across a most fascinating set of books on Mr. Simms's shelf— a monumental work called *The Golden Bough*. Through its pages, with the help of index and cross references, he traced the growth of the Christmas customs of Caplin Bight. The mummers, he discovered, were servants and courtiers of the Lord of Misrule, who had been elevated to mock kingship for a few brief weeks at the old pagan fire festivals that were "Christmas" before the time of Christ; then, when his rule was ended, dragged to a cross or a stake to die as a sacrifice in place of the real king. There was more than a suggestion in the book that Jesus Himself had died as such a mock sacrifice—in fact, as King of the Mummers, in Jerusalem—a bit of sacrilege that Eli found terribly stimulating.

Eli was spending most of his time during the holidays in the place that he had come to love above every other on earth: Peter Simms's little library. He was there far oftener than he was at home, and took to staying, incautiously, all hours of the night. Often Christopher would be there too, his clear brow furrowed over some great tome, while Eli's dark thatch was bent over another, as they pursued their separate courses. Sometimes old Mr. Simms would be there too, his slippered feet perched on the rail of the fireplace as birch logs rustled in the flames, while his old eyes scanned the lines of leather-bound volumes that Eli, and even Christopher, could not read: such works as the *Critique of Pure Reason,* and the *Logic of Hegel,* some of them in foreign languages and even in foreign alphabets.

Often, however, Eli was left in the room alone. More than once he stayed there when everyone else in the house was sleeping—Mr. Simms, and his housekeeper, and Christopher. Then the boy would replenish the fire, or sometimes let it burn out unattended until the chill of the room disturbed him, when he would turn off the lamps as he left for the night, and walk home under the stars, his head singing with the dreams of dead men.

But unknown to him Brother John had been whispering in his father's ear, sowing suspicion. It was bad enough, said the preacher, that Eli might be soaking up doses of paganism from people like the Simmses, but who knew what else might be going on? At first Elias brushed this off. But the seed of suspicion grew. He ordered Eli to spend less time at Mr. Simms's house and to be home by bedtime. Eli agreed at once to this reasonable restriction, but within two or three days had slipped back, thoughtlessly, into his old routine. Once he got his nose into a book time simply ceased to exist. But if he could have foreseen what was going to happen he would have been more cautious.

It was one-fifteen in the morning on Old Christmas Day. The mummers had retired for the night, and the snow lay deep and crunchy under a frosty moon, when Elias rapped sharply on Peter Simms's front door. This, in a village where no one ever knocked, and the front door was seldom used, except for weddings and funerals, was most unusual.

It was a scandalous hour, as Elias had no doubt told himself many times along the way, in order to induce the proper mood of righteous indignation. Eli was sitting by the fire in the library at the time. Christopher had gone to bed. Mr. Simms was making himself a late-night cup of tea in the kitchen, and it was the old man who answered the knock.

"Come in, Elias," he said coolly, wondering at his mission. "No need to knock, you know. But kind of late for calling, isn't it? Is something wrong?"

Elias stood his ground on the stoop. "Be Eli here?" he blurted.

"Of course he's here," Mr. Simms said. "Didn't you *know* he was here?"

Elias ignored this and concentrated on his indignation, which was in danger of being suppressed by Mr. Simms's civility. "Where's 'e at?" he demanded. "What be 'e up to in yer house this hour o' the night?"

Mr. Simms showed no sign of losing his temper under this insulting provocation, but spoke placatingly. "You've no call to speak to me like that, Elias," he said. "Eli is in the library. As to what he's up to—I imagine he's reading. A while back he and I were discussing the merits of some of Spinoza's propositions. I'm sorry if you are losing sleep because of it, but the boy has amazing intelligence—"

"Fetch 'im out," Elias demanded, cutting him short. "'E's goin' home." He knew he was no match for Peter Simms in an argument, and had sense enough not to try it.

"You still don't sound very friendly, Elias," Mr. Simms said, "hardly civil, in fact, coming to a man's door and ordering him about like this. Go in and talk to the boy yourself if you wish."

"'E knows the rule about comin' home at a decent hour!" Elias exploded. "I've a mind to ferbid 'im yer house altogether."

Mr. Simms's patience finally was beginning to fray. "That's a pretty ugly thing to say, Elias," he snapped. "Drag Eli off home if it pleases your sense of righteousness. He'd be going in another half hour anyway, I imagine. Give him a tongue-lashing and try to make him feel like a criminal. It won't do any good. You'll just lose whatever respect he may have for you."

"'E be goin' home," Elias repeated, "an' 'e be not comin' back, an' if 'e do, 'twon't be a tongue-lashin' 'e'll get, but a lashin' as'll do 'em a sight more good."

"Elias," said Mr. Simms, "I'm an old man, and I'm not going to brawl with you like a rowdy on a wharf. In thirty years on the bench I got used enough to the sins and weaknesses of men, and I'm willing to overlook what you've said. But you must get this clear. Eli has as much right in this house as he has in yours. He has a mind of his own that you must let him use in his own way. Nobody is trying to lead him into evil—not here, anyway."

"Ye tellin' me what to do about raisin' me own son?" Elias demanded.

"The time for that is past, Elias," Mr. Simms said tiredly.

"We'll see about that!" Elias snapped, his voice rising. "'E ain't too big to be made to mind, even do I have to skin the young whelp with a horsewhip."

"Elias," said Mr. Simms quietly, "that's the second time you've made such a threat. If I thought you meant it I'd lock this door in your face. Just in case you do, I warn you that if you lay a finger on that youngster I'll make you sorry for it."

Strangely enough, this did not raise Elias to any new pitch of wrath but seemed to calm him somewhat. "Ye may have a grain o' right on yer side," he admitted. "I s'pose 'twould do no good to start knockin' the boy about, though 'e may desarve it, right enough. An' p'raps ye do mean well, though Brother John have declared ye be an agent o' the devil."

"I'm glad we are not going to part enemies," Mr. Simms said, "and I'm glad, Elias, that you've explained who's behind all this nonsense. Don't you pay too much heed to that Bible-thumper of yours. Let him save his advice for the pulpit. He's an ignorant man, though no doubt one with a lot of good in him. He might even have been a great man, if he had ever got the kind of chance that I'm asking you to give Eli."

"What do ye mean be that?" Elias demanded.

"I mean that John McKim is a back-country parson with almost no learning but a clever mind and a courageous heart. He's only a back-country parson because for some reason or other he was denied his rights when he was growing up. Thirty years ago he was a boy like Eli, with a mind like Eli's. But he was steered into a blind alley, cooped up in a little harbor with nothing but rocks and Bibles and hymnbooks to feed his mind. He never discovered the stored wis-

dom of mankind. That stored wisdom is what we are trying
to pass on to your son."

"Ye think the boy might really amount to something?"
Elias asked.

"He can amount to far more than anybody else who ever
grew up in this harbor," Mr. Simms said, "or perhaps even
in this whole bay. If he's given the chance he can be a far
bigger merchant than Solomon Marks, or a leader in the government, or a man who one way or another will speak for
thousands of his fellow men."

Elias was sobered by these words, by the opening of a
vista that he had never glimpsed before, and perhaps by
the renewed dream of family greatness. "Ye think so . . . ,"
he said, his voice soft, his eyes widening.

"I'm absolutely certain of it," Mr. Simms said.

Meanwhile Eli had come into the hallway. The raised
voices had brought his nose up out of his book, and he had
sat listening, in a cold sweat, to his father's wrath, shame,
and bafflement. He stood back from the doorway in the
shadows of the hall and watched these change to uncer-
tainty and hope. Only when the two men had reached a
sort of agreement did his father's eye fall upon Eli.

"I come to take ye home," he announced simply, without
heat or anger. "Do ye know 'tis half-past one in the morning?"

"No, Father," said Eli. "I'm sorry. I forgot all about the
time."

"Well—" Elias paused, continued with difficulty. "I'm
sorry, too . . . fer losin' me temper . . . always was me be-
settin' sin. Like ye said, Mr. Simms, I shouldn't talk to ye the
way I did. Come home, lad. I'm glad ye didn't come out
while we was arg'in'. I might've struck ye, an' then I'd be
sorry fer that."

"Good night, Elias," Mr. Simms said. "There's no hard feelings. Good night, Eli."

"Good night, sir."

The old man stood at the door, musing, as father and son

walked toward the gate. He seemed to be talking to himself. "Everything," he was saying, "everything of importance a man must do or discover for himself . . . one of the reasons the world is such a lonely place . . ." He was still standing at the door, talking to the darkness, with the golden light from the hallway spilling over his white hair, when Elias and Eli reached the gate and passed out of earshot into the still night.

"He says ye have it in ye to be a merchant even bigger than Solomon Marks," Elias told his son. "I wonder, now— do 'e know what 'e's talkin' about?"

CHAPTER FOURTEEN

❧ ❧

After Old Christmas Day school reopened and the ponds froze. Three days of hard frost and you could walk or skate on every lake in the country. Those with ponies began hauling wood on catamarans, taking a devious route across ponds and lakes for want of a regular slide path. The tough little horses, fat and frisky after the idle summer, quickly began the long winter process of thinning down to the bags of bones that would be turned out to nibble the first green shoots of spring.

Mr. Simms's cow had come home with a calf, fathered, no doubt, by a stray bull from Lattice Harbor, far back in the country. Rafts of eider ducks arrived from their nesting grounds in the north, and the caribou began moving toward the coast. Someone discovered that the deer were closer than usual that winter, so almost everyone who wasn't hauling wood went upcountry to try to shoot one. Most of them hunted with shotguns for caribou as well as for birds, using a musket ball, or rifled slug, to knock down the big animals, and many brought home bags of ptarmigan as well as deer carcasses.

Eli had already shot his first moose, on a trip with Mr. Markady in the fall, using a sporting rifle borrowed for the purpose. But it was Mr. Markady's moose. The boy now began thinking about making another trip, on his own, to get meat for his family's storehouse.

He broached the subject to Elias as they worked together

in the woodshed early one morning, sawing a big log of dry spruce into chunks to be cloven for stove wood. "Been thinking I might go for a moose or a deer," he said tentatively. "Maybe get a few brace of partridge too."

"Good idea," Elias agreed at once. "Bain't goin' alone, though, be ye?"

"I don't know," Eli said.

"Well," Elias said, "if ye went alone ye'd have to kill it mighty nigh the water where ye could get a boat, or nigh enough to the road to take the horse in. 'Course, a man *can* spell out a moose, even ten or fifteen mile, once 'e's quartered, but ye'd have to be force put, I 'low." Another thought seemed to strike him. "Yer mother wouldn't stand fer it, anyhow. She'd fret herself half to death. Wasn't thinkin' o' goin' with young Pleman Pike, was ye?"

"Pleman can't take the time off from school," Eli said. "Christopher says he mustn't miss a day if he expects to pass the public exams in June—he's trying for grade eight, you know."

"Ye'll have no trouble with grade nine, ye think?"

"Not a bit," Eli assured him.

"Can't go meself," Elias mused. "They do say the deer be scarce on the country right now, anyway. I heered tell three men from Lattice Harbor as come out be way o' the main brook yesterday seen no more'n five or six head. They still be a good ways in."

"I was thinking of going farther down the coast," Eli said. "I suppose I *could* go alone."

"I'd not stop ye, ye understand," Elias explained, "but ye've got to think o' yer mother. Why don't ye ask aroun', an' maybe ye'll hear o' someone who'd be glad to go with ye."

They fell silent, and the bucksaw bit cleanly through a thick circle of dry spruce. Then they moved to the next, and the big chunks fell in rhythm to the pale sawdust beneath. But ten minutes later whatever destiny it is that shapes our ends brought Brother John ambling to the door of the Pallisher woodshed, still looking every inch a prophet, even in mackinaw jacket and logan boots.

"Morning, Brother Elias. Morning, Eli," he greeted. "Fine wood ye be cuttin' there. Had to haul it a long way, I s'pose."

"'Twas dry on the stump," Elias told him. "Forty-odd sticks of it in a little draw just across the beaver pond. Not a long haul. Meself an' Eli cut an' trimmed three or four slide loads last week, an' now that the ponds is froze we're haulin' it. Be ye needin' a load o' dry, be any chance? Allowin' we gets a bit more snow, 'twill be child's play, bringin' it out."

"Thank ye kindly," said Brother John. "Maybe next month, if ye'd be so good. There be a fair bit in me shed right now, though." He paused, chewing a piece of bark. "To tell the truth, I was thinkin' I might go upcountry come Monday to see could I shoot a piece o' meat."

"Now ain't that curious," Elias said. "Eli an' meself was just talkin' about the same thing."

"Trouble is," said Brother John, "I ain't used to the country hereabouts. Wouldn't know where the deer'd likely be, or where to hang up fer the night. Ought to have a local man with me, be rights."

"Can't go meself," said Elias, "not while I got two share-men workin' on a new trap in me net loft. But maybe Eli could. He been all over the handy part o' the country with me, an' even farther with Josh Markady. All the way back to Wolf Pond, they was, October past. That's a fair piece in, ye know."

"What d'ye think, Eli?" Brother John asked. "Could ye make a trip with me up Wolf Pond way next week?"

"Yes, sure," Eli agreed. "I was thinking of going alone. We'd go by boat as far as the *barachois* at the mouth of Wolf Pond Brook, then walk about six miles to the place above the falls where Jonas Pike's little river boat is hauled up. There's an old tilt there. We can ask for the use of the boat, and 'tis no more than a day's journey from there to Wolf Pond. Mr. Markady has a big dory on the pond, but 'twould be frozen now and we'd have to walk three miles over the ice to the Markady cabin. It's a big cabin, and tight, and we could stay there a week if we needed to."

"Ye make it sound aisy," said Brother John. He looked searchingly at Eli with his prophetic eyes, that had darkness and light and mystery in them. "Be it settled then? Ye'll go with me Monday?"

"Monday," Eli said, "soon as 'tis daylight."

"Ye can take the small boat," Elias told them, "but mind ye don't take it too far up the barasway. Might freeze in this time o' year. Ye'll have to leave it nigh the gut."

"What about the river?" Brother John asked.

"There'll be current enough, I 'low, to stop 'en freezin' a while yet, but the barasway could be a sheet of ice be the time ye get back."

By Monday morning they were having the regular January mild. The sea was flat calm. The sky was hazy. The temperature had risen to well above the frost line.

"Only danger," Elias said as Martha packed a huge lunch in a bread bag and the pre-dawn light began to make the oil lamp look sickly, "is that ye'll get cot in a full thaw with rain that'll make the ponds break up. Allowin' that happens, ye'll have to walk back around Wolf Pond to the brook, an' ye'll never spell a moose aroun' that pond on yer backs."

"Do be careful, won't ye?" Martha pleaded. "'Tain't like ye had yer father or Mr. Markady to look out to ye. An' mind what ye do with that gun."

"Leave be, woman," Elias said. "The lad's been luggin' a gun aroun' since 'e were big enough to crawl, an' if 'e can't find 'e's way aroun' in the woods be now 'tis time 'e larned, or died tryin'."

Half an hour later Eli sat at the tiller of the little boat, cutting between the sunker and the rocks of the Point, aiming for the small-boat run inside the Offer Islands that led to Wolf Brook Barachois five miles out the coast, while Brother John sat with loaded gun in the bow, hoping for a shot at a sea bird.

"Perfect mornin' fer birds, Eli!" he called above the chug-chugging of the engine. "I think ye had best cut out between they two islands, though." He pointed. "Over there, where ye kin see they tickle-asses circlin' above the rocks. . . . Aise off when ye gets near the point o' the first island, though."

The little boat sputtered along the flat run through the stillness of the dawn until, sure enough, they could see a line of black dots on the water, near the place where the kitti-wakes—locally called tickle-asses—were circling.

"Turrs, all right," Brother John reported. "I'll get sot to shoot if ye'll cut the engine and coast in toward 'em."

Eli let the engine make a few more revolutions, until he saw the birds' heads coming up, turning. Then he discon-nected the switch to stop the spark and let the little boat glide silently toward the flock. Brother John held off until the last possible second, then fired just as the first of the birds started to dive. When the splash of shot settled, three of them floated, belly up, on the smooth water. Eli circled, waiting for other birds to come up. When they did, Brother John fired again, but they were scattered and he got only one more. Then Eli closed the switch, hove up the flywheel, and cut the engine in and out, running dead slow and jock-eying the boat carefully while Brother John picked up the four duck-sized black and white birds. Two were still kick-ing, and he twisted their necks before tossing them into the bottom of the boat.

"Plenty enough fer a scoff when we gets to the tilt," he remarked. "No need to try fer more. We'll be eatin' par-tridge, please God, be this time tomorrow."

"That was pretty nice shooting," Eli said, hoping to please him, though in fact the shots had been about as easy as you could ask.

"Good boat handlin' too," Brother John said. "How old be ye, Eli?—fifteen, is it?"

"Not quite, sir," the boy said. "I'll be fifteen this winter."

"Best age there is," Brother John said. "Wisht I could be fifteen again meself."

They ran along the shore for almost an hour, then headed through the gut into the protected waters of the *barachois*. Just inside, where the tide ran and there was no danger of ice, they hove out the graplin, made it fast to the stern, and took the painter ashore to a post.

There were heavy loads to be carried, but they shouldered them willingly—guns, shells, grub sacks, extra clothes, a can of oil, an ax, knives, an oilstone—everything, in fact, needed for a hunting trip, except for cooking pots, which they knew they would find in the tilt and the cabin.

Though it was easy enough walking around the *barachois* with its bleak sand dunes, it consumed another hour, for the semicircle of its bank stretched for three and a half miles. Fortunately Barachois Marsh was frozen, else this would have forced a detour of another half mile.

"Wisht we could boil up," said Brother John as they reached the mouth of the brook, "only we ain't got a kettle. Well—we kin stop an' eat some cold grub anyway."

The cold grub consisted of thick slices of homemade bread and butter and slabs of meat from the breasts of eider ducks, so it went down easily enough, even without the assistance of tea. Brother John, remembering his official station, even in the woods, said a rather long grace before they fell to and murmured a word of thanks when they had finished.

"Mighty good, Eli," he said. "Now if ye can find the trail from here we'll head into the country."

"'Tis not much of a trail," Eli admitted. "Pretty rough, and steep in spots too, but easy enough to follow."

It was about ten o'clock in the morning when they started up the brook, and though Brother John proved to be a good walker, it was the middle of the afternoon before they reached the big falls. The climb to the top was difficult, but once over the lip of the rocks they found that the character of the country had changed completely.

There, stretching away into the blue January evening, with gentle hills on either side, was a placid ribbon of water, unmarred by tide or ripple. The plain of the plateau—red-brown marshes of peat moss broken by islands of spruce—stretched off on either hand. An ancient esker, a bank of sand and rock left by the last great ice sheet, looking like a man-made dam, cut diagonally across the plain, ending at the lip of the canyon and there forming the bank of the river. On the flat top of the esker stood the little tilt, an eight-by-twelve-foot log hut with walls sloping to a high peak. A breathless, bluish peace hung over everything.

"It be beautiful!" Brother John exclaimed. "'Tis the way it must o' been on the sixth day o' creation, when God saw all 'E's work an' pronounced it good, an' rested from 'E's labor. Eli, lad, if all men could live in a place like this, breathe the air o' God's wilderness as we be doin' now, there'd be no evil in the world."

"None at all?" Eli asked innocently.

"Well"—Brother John peered at him, suspiciously—"except for original sin, o' course. . . . Eli, ye ain't sought the Lord yet. What be holdin' ye back?"

"I guess I just haven't been called," Eli lied. "I go regularly to Sunday services and weekly prayer meeting, as you know, but I've never felt the change of heart that leads to conversion. You wouldn't want me to pretend that I've had a change of heart when I haven't, would you?"

"No, boy, no—certainly not," Brother John said rather hastily. "There be some as do that, no doubt, but they do call down damnation on theirselves an' not blessin', fer the Lord reads the heart an' not the lips. If 'E don't speak to ye, 'twould be blasphemy to say 'E did—an' yet, I wonder—must be some reason in yer own soul, if 'E don't speak. Evil companionships keep many a soul from the Lord, ye know. That young Simms fella, now, that ye spends so much time with —I don't say he ain't a good teacher, but he don't know God, neither—and the Bible teaches us, ye know, that the devil often shows hisself as a angel o' light."

"If you're calling Christopher an agent of the devil you can just stop it," Eli said hotly. "He's the best friend I've ever had, and a good man too, even if he isn't the same kind of Christian that we are. I'm sure you couldn't help liking him if you knew him better."

"Ain't a case o' likin' or not likin'," Brother John argued. "I jest think the devil may be makin' use of 'im to lead ye away from God. All the worldly larnin' ye could ever get wouldn't be worth that, boy. Now if ye'd spend more time with me, an' less with an unbeliever, ye might hear the Lord speak to ye, as ye ought."

He was looking at Eli again with the same strange look that the boy had seen in the woodshed, and it frightened him a little. Here, he could see, was a man of extraordinary power and determination, used to getting his own way. In fact, Eli reflected, this was one thing that his father, Brother John, and Christopher all had in common. They were all stubborn men, and used to getting their way with others, though they used different methods to achieve their ends. He was oppressed, briefly, with the feeling of being trapped between these three strong, opposed forces.

"I'll tell ye the truth, Eli," Brother John said with a sudden smile that lit his features with almost angelic warmth, "I be mighty fond of ye, boy. It weren't no accident that I come pokin' in to yer woodshed Friday mornin'. I heered from young Pleman Pike that ye was talkin' about a trip upcountry, an' I thought as how this'd be a chance fer me to shoot some meat an' get to know ye better at the same time. I'd like to be yer friend, ye see. An' the Lord might work through our friendship, as He did with David an' Jonathan."

Eli was a little startled, but a little flattered too, that the most powerful man in the village should stoop to approach him like this. He could think of no answer that he wanted to make, so he allowed the silence to lengthen until Brother John changed the subject.

"We'll be spendin' the night here, I s'pose. Can ye cook?" the preacher asked.

"Not much," Eli admitted. "I can fry a piece of meat. But at home Mother does all the cooking, and Father cooks in

the woods and in the trap boat, so I haven't had much practice."

"Well then, I'll cook and ye can hunt," Brother John suggested. "I hear ye are a first-class shot with that fancy gun o'
yours. Why don't ye try them islands o' spruce across the
marsh yonder fer partridge while I sees what can be done
with the turrs?" He smiled warmly at the boy. "If ye'll be
back agin' dark I'll have a pot o' grub ready."

Eli hunted over the marsh methodically, taking the
nearby copses first. They were empty. But about half a mile
from the tilt he flushed a big snowshoe rabbit out of a patch
of rhododendrons, lined him up with the front bead of the
gun, and sent him somersaulting among the bakeapple
bushes. Even though the land was brown, the rabbit had lost
his summer coat and was now completely white. The echoes
of the shot were still returning from the hills when a covey
of ptarmigan exploded out of a copse. Eli ejected the shell
and jammed in another, knowing as he did so that it would
be too late. He swung the barrel, following the birds, but he
was too good a hunter to fire. They were already seventy or
eighty yards away. He watched them buzz low over the
marsh, cackling to one another like barnyard hens, and light
in a distant pocket of spruce trees. He had counted fifteen of
them, as white as the absent snow and fairly gleaming
against the dark landscape.

Slowly, with great caution, he approached the copse
where they had alighted. Once flushed, the birds would
flush again, more easily than before. He tiptoed around the
copse and crept down upon it from the windward side, for
he expected that the ptarmigan would have taken shelter
in its lee and would prefer to take off upwind, even in a
light air.

When Eli felt sure that he was within range he took out
a second shell and stuck it between his teeth, cocked the
gun, and walked confidently toward the trees. The explosion
of wings that occurred a moment later so astonished him

that he almost forgot to fire. Instead of the fifteen birds that he had seen alight, at least a hundred and fifty swarmed up out of the stunted spruces. He fired quickly just as they cleared the trees, jammed in the second shell, swung the barrel ahead of them, and fired again. The first shot had been too close for a good scatter, but five birds had fallen, flopping in the bushes. The second, longer shot brought down nine, some of them barely winged.

Eli dropped his gun and spent the next five minutes chasing wounded birds. In the end he had all of them—fourteen ptarmigan with two shots—not even close to the records you heard talked about in the net lofts, but just about as good as the personal claim made by any truthful man.

He was very proud of himself as he headed back toward the tilt, his kill in a burlap sack over his shoulder, his beautiful gun resting, empty, over his arm. He found Brother John sitting in the doorway, admiring the waning colors of the winter evening.

"Stewpot's boilin' somethin' furious inside," the pastor informed him. "Too hot to stand it in there. Smell it cookin'?"

"Sure do!" Eli said, sniffing.

"Say," Brother John observed, "I heered three shot. Did ye hit anything?"

For answer Eli unslung the sack, upended it, and dumped his collection of small game at the pastor's feet. At the sight of the rabbit and the fourteen ptarmigan the man's jaw dropped and he looked up at the boy with new respect.

"Eli, lad," he said, "if I was wearin' a hat I'd take it off. Ye must'a killed that rabbit with one shot an' they seven brace o' partridge with two. Boy, I'd hate to have ye gunnin' fer me!"

Warmed by his success, Eli grinned happily, but felt bound by the hunter's code to derogate his skill. "'Twas nothing, really," he said. "I saw a small covey go into a tuck of spruce, and then, when I flushed them out, the air was white with birds. You could hardly miss if you tried."

"'Twas great shootin' jest the same," Brother John said.

They set to work skinning and cleaning the rabbit, cutting it into pieces and storing it for the morning in a pan of salted water. Then they hung the sack of ptarmigan from a high limb where prowling animals could not reach it. By the time they had finished, the winter darkness had come and Brother John, sampling the contents of the stewpot, announced that it was done to a turn.

For years afterward Eli remembered that evening with a glow of nostalgia. The night pressed in with a wild yearning, speaking of man's beginning in the wilderness, and prophesying his end, while in the midst of the flux of time and the immensity of space was this solid human assertion of the present moment: the tilt, the lantern, the fire, holding all the elements of a magic rite. Not only was the stew fit to wake the dead, but there was a black kettle of strong tea with the smell of wood smoke in it, and *toutins*, which are pieces of bread dough fried golden-brown in fat. What a feast to remember! And the warmth of the fire in the mild night, and the feeling of companionship that went with it!

Eli discovered a new facet to Brother John that night as they sat together in the golden light of the smoky tin lamp and swapped stories, for Eli's stories were poor, prosaic, and factual, accounts of his hunting and birding trips told in bald narrative, but the pastor's were full of poetry, fancy, and strange imagery.

As the evening wore on, Eli began to feel himself deeply attracted to this formerly remote, dark, and powerful man, even though he feared him at the same time. There could be no doubt, he thought, about the truth of Peter Simms's assessment of the man: Brother John had been born with the seeds of greatness; only the invisible walls of the little fishing settlement where he had grown to manhood had turned him inward until he became the leader of a small, fundamentalist congregation in one of the backwaters of civilization.

Finally they sank into a companionable silence.

"Time we turned in, Eli," Brother John said. "'Tis been a long day, and there be another long one ahead of us tomorrow. Let's bow our heads and say a prayer.

"We thank thee, Lord, for all thy many blessings . . . for thy beautiful earth . . . for the birds an' beasts which thou hast put in subjection under us. We thank thee for each other, and for the love which thou hast put into our hearts. Fergive us our sins, and lead us into the light of thy holy countenance . . . for Jesus's sake."

It was a prayer to which Eli could say "Amen" without so much as a single twinge of conscience.

They stoked up the fire, closed the drafts to make sure it wouldn't get out of hand, then lay down on the floor under blankets in all their clothes, and fell instantly into a profound sleep.

When Eli stirred, and then woke, seeing the first gray light of dawn filtering into the little tilt, he realized that he was cold, and stiff from sleeping on hard boards. Brother John was still asleep, his face noble and peaceful, one arm pressed closely about Eli under the blankets. As he stirred, his hand, still in sleep, reached down to the region of the boy's groin. Eli sat up. Brother John's eyes opened, and he smiled.

"Good morning, Eli. I was having a beautiful dream. . . ."

Five minutes after waking, the pastor had the fire in the little wood stove roaring, a big kettle of water set to boil, and the pieces of rabbit sizzling merrily in the frying pan. He first fried, then simmered the bits of meat, and added potatoes that had been cooked the night before. Eli's nose twitched. The aroma of the rabbit sauté mixed with the essential perfume of boiling tea and spruce wood smoke made his mouth water as he set about the task of unearthing the Pikes' little river boat from its protective covering of brush and fir boughs.

The boat was of a peculiar design, locally invented, for navigating very shallow rivers. About fifteen feet long, it was as narrow as a canoe, to help it slip through tight spots between boulders, but had sloping sides, like a dory. It had a flat bottom of very thick plank, which, unlike a canoe, permitted it to thump along over rocks uninjured. It could be rowed by two pairs of oars, or paddled, or sculled from the stern, or, last, fitted with a small engine. There was also a pole for pushing it over shallows.

By the time Eli had hauled it down to the edge of the water, chopped out new thole pins for the oars, and repaired a broken thwart the rabbit chowder was ready, Brother John called to him from the tilt, and he went up to join the pastor in the enjoyment of what proved to be, truly, a delicious meal. They fell upon it like wolves. Then, after three cups of strong tea apiece, "To put the food to rest," they hung ten of the ptarmigan from a rooftree inside the tilt, packed four others into a grub bag, bundled their gear into the river boat, tidied up and barred the door, and started upstream with an orange-colored dawn banded with ribbons of apple-green following them.

It is eighteen miles from the big falls to Wolf Pond. If they could average two miles an hour, Eli calculated, they should reach it by four in the afternoon, while there would still be enough daylight to reconnoiter the pond comfortably. Then an hour's walk over the ice should take them to Mr. Markady's cabin before the fall of night.

The first two hours proved to be easy rowing, but after that there were spots where they had to pole, and even a few places where they had to haul the boat over the shallows. They stopped at midday in a long, wide steady, almost a little lake, where they saw the first signs of ice.

"After a hard freeze we might have to portage around this place, or haul the boat over the ice," Eli pointed out.

"Hardly worse than the bars we been over, though," Brother John observed. "Let's tie up here an' get some grub."

They moored the boat and had their lunch, three gray jays coming to share it and a flock of boreal chickadees chattering from the nearby trees, hoping the jays might leave a few scraps that they could quarrel over in their turn.

Then they pushed forward again. Brother John surprised his young companion. For a man who had made his living with a Bible for most of his life he proved remarkably strong and durable. He more than kept up his end of the rowing in the stern of the boat, and in fact pushed them along quite a bit faster than the two miles per hour, allowing for stops and delays, that Eli had counted on, so that they reached the rattle below Wolf Pond while the sun still stood well above the trees.

You could ride down through this rattle but not pole up over it, so they landed the boat and gear and made it up into packs, leaving the boat at the foot of the rattle for the return trip.

They came down on the ice of the pond about a hundred yards from the run-out, and there was a fox trotting along the edge of the water, where the current broke for the brook, peering into the riffle as he went. At the same time the expanse of Wolf Pond opened up and they could see, through the smoky blue of the January evening, the cleft in the wooded bank that marked the cove and the little stream where Joshua Markady had built his substantial cabin, with the red-gold of the barrens hanging above the cleft like a rich mantle. An hour of comfortable walking over the smooth ice brought them to their destination with plenty of daylight still in the sky and red-edged clouds promising fair weather for the morrow.

CHAPTER FIFTEEN

❧ ❦

The Markady cabin was big and comfortable, with two rooms, one having four double bunks and the other a waterloo stove—a large, flat, old-fashioned stove with two ovens and an immense firebox, designed for cooking a meal for twelve or fifteen people and heating a whole house at the same time. A woodshed built against one end of the cabin was filled with the dry firewood that Mr. Markady and Eli had cut in October. Since they might be spending the next several days here, Eli made use of the last hour of daylight to saw and cleave an additional supply of wood, while Brother John roasted the four ptarmigan in the oven and simmered a pot of vegetables on top of the stove.

When they had filled themselves once more with wild meat they sat back in the flickering red light of the fire and talked about plans for the hunt, but they were both tired and within a few minutes Brother John said, "Let's turn in. We'll bunk together."

"Why not?" Eli consented without a second thought. He lit a lamp and made up one of the bunks in the other room.

They undressed and crawled under the cold covers, shivering a little.

Then Brother John said, "Blow out the light," and they lay talking together in the darkness.

Finally they were silent, and Brother John rolled over and put his arm about Eli. Then, gradually, gently, his hand crept down to the boy's groin and began to caress his sex organs.

Eli lay rigid, in combined shock and revulsion, hating what was happening, hating the pastor, revolted in his heart and in his stomach, violated in all the taboos of his infancy and his Puritan upbringing. For though he had shaken off, already, many of the superstitions of his parents, the deep-seated sex taboos remained, as strong as ever. Apart from wet dreams, his sexual experience at this time was limited to solitary masturbation, carried out in dead secret and with a lingering sense of sin profoundly rooted in his soul. He had succeeded in getting rid of the notion that God would punish him, but the notion that sex was profoundly evil, and somehow must carry its own punishment, remained. As for sex play with a man—he was as horrified at the thought as he would have been at the thought of eating human flesh.

So far not a word had passed between Eli and Brother John, but now the pastor whispered, "Turn over this way."

It was the last word spoken that night.

Eli turned as he was bidden, and the man took his hand and placed it in his own groin, closing the fingers over his rigid penis and beginning the motions of the sex act. A shudder of disgust passed through Eli, but he continued performing his unwilling task in a cold sweat, while Brother John's heart pounded, and his breath came in deep gasps, and he struggled convulsively, and finally reached climax and emission.

As for the boy, throughout this passage he felt no sexual excitement at all, nothing but a cold hatred for the whole thing. And while Brother John dropped instantly into a deep slumber Eli lay awake, with a profound and bitter sense of violation. He cursed softly to himself, using the forbidden names of God, mouthing dark blasphemies that should have caused convulsions of nature, such as earthquakes or thunderbolts. But the night remained still. Nothing happened.

Near at hand in the forest a lynx screamed. Far off a fox barked. Both near and far Eli could hear the mournful hooting of two or three great horned owls. All the hunters of the wilderness were abroad, seeking the scanty meat of winter.

Eli thought of their lives of everlasting privation, and the sadness of all life upon earth was borne in on his mind. And he was still thinking of foxes and owls, and the great lean cats that prowled the forest, when they became confused, and mixed gradually into his dream.

When Eli awoke in the morning Brother John was already up and shaking him gently.

The pastor smiled engagingly. "Ye can lay in fer a while if ye like, Eli," he said. "I'll get the fire goin'. Daylight be comin' up fast."

Brother John whistled while he dressed and grinned at Eli as he left the room. But Eli did not share his good humor. He shuddered with revulsion when he thought about the night before, and a cold rage possessed him. How dare the pastor do a thing like that? he thought. But he was ashamed as well as angry—ashamed that he had allowed himself to go along with it. And he resolved at first that he would call off the trip and head for home. Then he thought what a disgrace it would be for a meat hunter to return with nothing more substantial than a bag of ptarmigan. It might be just as well, he decided, to continue the trip until they got an animal but to stay strictly by himself at night.

Still, in spite of it all, he had to admit that he rather liked Brother John. If only, Eli mused, he didn't want to do that awful thing in bed. . . . He lay in the bunk, trying to resolve this conflict of emotions, while he heard the pastor light up the fire in the other room and then go outside. He was gone only a moment when Eli heard him come back, quickly and softly, then go softly out again. A moment later there was a cannon-like report of a gun right beside the door.

Eli jumped out of bed, pulled on his pants, and ran outside, barefooted. As he reached the door Brother John fired again, and Eli saw a cow moose, not fifty yards away, collapse into the bushes at the mouth of the stream that, pouring out of the hills, entered the lake beside the cabin. The animal's big, clumsy feet were still kicking, and in a moment she dragged herself up on her front legs, her hindquarters seeming to be paralyzed. Brother John fired a third, then a fourth time, before the moose lay still, and they ran down the bank to look at her. A little pillar of steam, like incense from an altar, was rising toward heaven from a gaping hole in the animal's chest, where the last shot had collapsed the lungs and drowned the great beast in her own blood.

"'Fraid I ain't a crack shot like ye, boy," Brother John said, standing looking at the carcass. "I still gets buck fever every time a big animal is lined up in me sights. We can leave the butcherin' job till after breakfast, I 'low."

"Perhaps we should paunch it and fry the liver for breakfast," Eli suggested.

Brother John turned to look at him. "Heavens! Ye be half naked, boy! Ye'll catch yer death!"

"Nothing to catch, up here"—Eli laughed—"but I'll go dress now that the excitement is over."

They paunched the moose and fried about three pounds of the liver. Except for a slightly browsy flavor, it tasted like cow's liver—perhaps like a cow that had spent her life in the woods, grazing on trees, Eli decided. It had a slightly yellowish cast.

Then they set to work butchering the moose. As it turned out, Brother John knew exactly how to quarter an animal. First they skinned it and hung the hide in a tree. Then they separated the head and the hocks. Finally they cut the four clean quarters, using a saw along the neck and the back.

They were bloody and dirty when they finished, and enjoyed the luxury of washing in plenty of hot water and soap.

"Now," said Brother John as they cleaned up, "what do we do next? Do we start packin' the meat back to the boat or do ye want to try for another?"

"I think we should take a walk across the barrens," the boy said, "just to see what's up there."

So they hung the meat in the porch of the cabin, barred the door against the possibility of a prowling animal, and climbed the trail beside the little brook to the high barrens above. Here they found an outcropping of rock from the peak of which they could see a great stretch of country sweeping away for many miles to the north, west, and south. At first nothing seemed to be moving. Then, on a little marsh between patches of barrens far off to the north, they saw them—hundreds of gray and white animals huddled together, grazing on the marsh plants, which had turned white with the night's frost. Stragglers from the herd could be seen on either side of it, but none had strayed within about two miles of their lookout.

"Biggest bunch of caribou I ever did see," Brother John proclaimed. "Must be nigh on a thousand head."

"Should make it easy to get one," Eli said. "Mr. Markady says that the bigger a herd is, the safer they feel, so you can sometimes walk right in among a big bunch of them."

They climbed down off the rock and walked boldly toward the caribou, making no effort to conceal their movements. They walked rapidly, not caring if they made a noise. The caribou did not seem to notice them at all until they were about a quarter of a mile away. Then a few of the nearer animals, which had been lying down, got up but otherwise showed no sign of alarm.

"I'll let ye go in alone if ye like," Brother John murmured. "Have ye picked out the one ye intend to shoot?"

"Any one I can reach," Eli murmured in reply. "But a barren doe, if I can make sure of one. Both Father and Mr. Markady say that the stags aren't much good from the time they go into rut in October until well along in the winter. But a doe that's not carrying a calf is fat this time of year."

Brother John squatted quietly on his heels while Eli walked cautiously toward the alert caribou, moving a step at a time, then stopping, then moving ever so slowly again, until he was within a hundred yards of the nearest of them.

By now he had picked out his target—a large dark doe, a little to one side of the rest and looking as if she were on sentry duty. He judged that she was not carrying a fawn, and she seemed to be in excellent condition.

He cocked his gun quietly and began to walk briskly toward the doe. Her head came up sharply. She faced him for a second. Then she wheeled on her hind legs and began to bolt. She ran not away from him but off to one side, presenting a perfect running target. At the same instant the small group of caribou nearest the doe also took fright and began bounding away. Eli dropped to one knee, swung the gun so that the bead was just ahead of the animal and keeping pace with her. Then he raised it to the level of her antlers, for the heavy slug would drop a foot and a half at that range. Then he gently squeezed the trigger. The doe reared on her hind legs, fell in a half roll, rose as far as her knees, and collapsed.

Eli ran to where she lay, ready with another shell, but it wasn't needed. She was dead before he reached her, a hole in both sides of the rib cage, just above the heart.

"Perfect shot, Eli," Brother John said just behind him. "Lad, if ye keep on shootin' like that a box of slugs should last ye the rest o' yer natural life."

"I don't feel proud of it at all," Eli said, looking down at the doe. "I feel sorry, like I'd smashed a window or something. I felt the same way when I shot the moose last fall." He looked up at the tall man beside him. "Do you feel like that when you kill a deer?"

Brother John laughed. "Can't say as I do, boy. The Lord put the deer here fer meat. They be a sight prettier lyin' stretched on the moss like this than they be high-tailin' it fer the woods."

"It still seems wrong, somehow," Eli said, "to turn anything as beautiful as a deer into a hunk of meat. It isn't the same with birds, though I don't like picking them up half dead after a shot. I wonder, do all hunters feel this way?"

"I've heered tell as lots of 'em do," Brother John said, "but 'tis a passin' feelin', an' I never knowed it to stop a man from huntin' agin whenever he got the chance."

"Oh, I wouldn't stop hunting!" Eli exclaimed. "I like it.

And I know we've got to have meat. But meat seems like a miserable thing somehow, compared to a live animal."

They paunched and skinned the caribou, but had no ax or saw for quartering, so they turned it over to drain and headed back to camp. As they made a hasty kettle of tea and fried a rasher of moose Brother John remarked that it would be a long carry to get the caribou out to the ice of Wolf Pond.

"Still," Eli said, "we'll do it in two trips, with plenty of spells on the way. Hauling over the ice won't be much problem either, or getting the meat down to the big falls, but unless we can figure a better way to get it down the brook from there it's going to take us four days to spell it out to the *barachois.*"

They brought out half the carcass that evening, leaving two quarters for the next day. It had been a gruelling day's work, and as they shared the companionship of labor, Brother John doing a bit more than his fair portion of the hard work, Eli felt his unspoken resentment against the pastor ebbing little by little.

As he lay sprawled on the wooden bench beside the big stove in the cabin at bedtime, utterly exhausted, and Brother John, crouching before the fire, proposed, gently, deferentially, "We'll bunk together again, shall we?" he found that he didn't have the resolution to hurt the man's feelings with an outright refusal.

"I don't really want to," he said.

"Oh, come on," Brother John urged gently. "Why not?"

"Well—all right," Eli said, sighing. But the prospect left him with an icy unease. True, Brother John was the visible incarnation of divine law in Caplin Bight, but the boy's inbred taboos revolted, nevertheless, at what he suspected lay ahead.

But when they went to bed it wasn't as bad as he expected. He found the brief session of sexual play that was required of him certainly not enjoyable but a good deal more tolerable than it had been the night before, and once Brother John had collapsed into sleep he quickly dozed off himself, without suffering the violent emotions that had torn him the previous evening.

At daylight the next morning they brought out the last of their meat. At the cabin they knocked together a crude sled, loaded it with their gear and the eight quarters of meat, and hauled it, in less than an hour, to the run-out. There they debated hauling up the boat and running her, fully loaded, through the rattle.

"We might lose the whole works," Brother John pointed out.

"Yes," Eli agreed. "There must be six or seven feet of water in the steady below the rattle, and if we upset the boat everything would be carried to the bottom."

"Too risky," the pastor decided. "I s'pose we'll have to pack everything down to the landing."

So they took the safe but more difficult course, making five trips of it. Then they had to stow the caribou, the moose, their bags and shells and guns, all into the fifteen-foot boat, and step on board themselves, very carefully, so as not to sink her.

"Got about two inches of freeboard," Eli reported, peering cautiously over the side.

"Good thing 'tis flat calm," Brother John remarked, "or one of us would have to walk."

Dipping their oars with discretion, they began to descend toward the first shallows, where, they found, they had to fight and drag the heavily laden boat over the rocks.

It was the same all through that day until sunset—fifteen minutes of easy rowing followed by half an hour of struggling, sometimes even unloading and portaging part of the meat along the bank. Before they had struggled over the last ledge into the steady waters that stretched ahead six or seven miles to the lip of the big falls the sun had already set.

Darkness fell and it began to snow. It turned cold and the light wind chopped to the northwest.

"We can't stop now," Brother John said, "'less'n we be force put. There be no rocks or snags in this part o' the river that ye know fer, Eli?"

"River's safe enough, so I'm told," Eli said.

"If we was upsot here," Brother John continued, "we'd need the help o' the Lord to reach the tilt alive, in this weather an' wearin' wet clothes."

"'Tis all mud bottom, or sand," Eli said, "at least so far as I know. We should hear the falls about a mile before we reach them, if the wind holds light."

Actually they heard the falls long before that. The light wind died out. The night was pitch-black, and, except for the faint hiss of snowflakes in the water, silent. It was hard to say when, exactly, they began hearing the roar of the falls, for they mentioned it only after they had both been vaguely conscious of the sound for some time. The roar went on—and on—and on—getting louder, seeming to grow forever, gradually dominating the night, then reaching out to fill the very universe with its awful voice.

It now became a question of nerve not to land too soon, for the darkness had become nearly absolute and the cataract below them seemed to be sucking them forward toward destruction. There was no way to judge distance, and they began to have irrational visions of tilting, at any moment, over the lip of the falls into the murderous cascade beneath.

"There's really no danger, so long as we hug the left bank," Eli said, more to reassure himself than Brother John. "We ought to be able to see the end of the sand esker against the sky, even when 'tis as dark as this, and maybe the outline of the tilt too."

"I seem to remember a sand bar just below the landing," Brother John said.

"Yes," Eli replied, "there's a beach that shelves off to a bar. And below that there's a rock pile on this side of the river, just before the water breaks over the falls."

"I'm in yer hands," Brother John said lightly, "an' trustin' in the Lord."

Eli could tell by his tone that he really wasn't a bit afraid, and wished that he could say the same for himself—for if the truth must be admitted he had a feeling in his stomach that he had felt before only when lost in the woods or caught on a lee shore in a trap boat with a faltering engine.

They never did see the esker or the tilt. Instead they ran aground—hard aground—with the roar of the falls sounding like the crack of doom in their ears.

"Now," said Brother John judicially, "'tis a question of just where we be."

Eli reached cautiously over the side with an oar, probing, careful not to dislodge anything. He found water on both sides of the bows—also in front.

"We seem to be stuck in mid-channel," he reported, trying to keep a quaver out of his voice. "If we come off we'll likely go straight over the falls. How did we get this far off-shore anyhow?"

"Mighty poor guide ye be," said Brother John dryly. "Try reaching as far as ye can over the port side."

Eli probed again with the oar, as directed. "Sand beach," he reported, and promptly stepped overboard to lighten the boat and haul her in.

Brother John followed, taking more care not to get wet. "At my age ye have to think about rheumatism—or at least the chance ye'll get it," he explained. "Be the time ye are as old as me, Eli, ye'll have learned to trust the Lord better, and not get scairt so aisy."

"I wasn't really scared," Eli protested, "just a bit excited."

"Ay," said Brother John, "excited enough so when we grounded on the very spot we was makin' fer ye fergot we was drawin' a foot an' a half o' water an' thought we was on a bar in mid-channel." He chuckled. "Well, never mind. Ye are a good lad in the woods, an' ye'll get over it." He reached out and cuffed Eli affectionately.

"We'd better have a light," the boy said.

"Ay, fetch a lantern, will ye?"

Eli brought one from the tilt. They tied the boat securely, using a large rock at the stern to anchor her off, left the meat on board, and began to prepare for the night.

In short order they had a fire going, a meal cooking, and were as secure and comfortable as if they had never been groping through pitch-darkness in fear of sudden death. Eli hung his wet clothes behind the little stove and shortly was warming his toes as close to the glowing sheet metal as he could stand it.

"Goin' to blister yerself," Brother John warned him. "Here, let me rub yer feet."

He warmed Eli's feet in his hands, rubbing them briskly, then started tickling them, refusing to stop until the boy was in fits of laughter and had kicked him in the stomach. Then he grinned, let him go, and returned to his cooking.

"Figured out what we'll do tomorrow?" he asked.

"Yes," Eli said. "You head for home and bring my father's trap crew. They can spare one day from the net loft and the woodpiles. With their help we'll be able to lug this meat to the *barachois* in a single trip. If we give them a couple of quarters for their trouble we'll still have about three hundred pounds of meat each. And while you're gone I'll have another crack at the partridge."

That was Eli's fourth night with Brother John, and he was beginning to get over his initial revulsion at what happened after the light went out. In fact, he admitted to himself, a very small gleam of pleasure had started to shine on the mud. He still wasn't ready to let himself go—to enter wholeheartedly into the homosexual partnership that Brother John took for granted—but he was heading in that direction.

They still didn't talk about it. Indeed, up to now not a word on the subject had passed between them, and Eli suspected that Brother John wouldn't be able to discuss it at all. By day they were no more than any other two friends or companions. Only by night were they lovers. And there was no tenderness in this form of love. It was rough and sensual and exciting, and full of darkness—at the opposite pole from the tender, idealized relationship that Eli shared with Christopher.

But Brother John taught the boy the meaning of sensualism, the abandonment of the spirit to the crying demands of the flesh. Brother John, he could see, acted like two separate people. The Puritan Dr. Jekyll by day became the abandoned Mr. Hyde by night. But as yet Eli had not learned to divide himself into compartments. He took his respectable, daytime puritanical self into bed with him, so that—so far as Eli was concerned—Brother John and he shared a relationship highly colored with guilt.

Was it possible, Eli wondered, that the pastor carried on in this boisterously sensual manner with Sister Leah, his wife? But the moment the question crossed his mind he knew the answer. That bitter, monumental woman could respond to her husband's caresses no more than if carved from marble. If they had any sexual relations at all—which Eli doubted—it was a cold affair in which she submitted passively to a very tame embrace, radiating disapproval and spiritual pain while the pastor sought the rapture of the orgasm.

How lonely the man must be, how full of unsuccored wants, Eli thought, to have sought him out as he had done! For the first time he began to understand the feeling of compassion—a feeling that, he suddenly realized, Christopher had for the children whom he taught, for little Johnny Penchley, even for Virginia, whom he also loved in quite another fashion. It was curious, he realized, that he might have the same feeling for Brother John as Christopher had for the children—a strange paradox indeed, when one considered the relative positions of himself and the pastor.

He thought about this some more, and summoned up an extra bit of warmth when he responded to Brother John's advances that night.

As they prepared to part in the faint light of the morning Brother John spoke, for the first time and in a roundabout way, of their relationship. "I'll see ye tomorrow, Eli," he said. "In a manner o' speakin' our trip is over. 'Tis been a great pleasure to me, and I thank ye, boy, from the bottom o' me heart. I hope we's able to do this sort o' thing often in the future."

Eli smiled back at him and waved as he turned at the head of the trail. A strange man, he thought. Full of wonderful contradictions. The Prophet Elijah with a hard-on. He laughed aloud in the winter silence as he thought of the irreverent phrase.

Throughout that day as he hunted over the barrens, bringing in a large bag of ptarmigan and a couple of rabbits, Brother John kept haunting his thoughts, and the pastor's phantom lay beside him on the floor of the tilt that night. He actually began to feel lonely. The thought at first stuck in his gorge, but the teacher had drilled him in intellectual honesty. So he finally got it up out of the regions of repression into full consciousness. Though he had hated the sex play at first, he now missed the man who had lain beside him. He missed the hot hands exploring his body. The admission banished the phantom, and he allowed himself to lapse into a gently sensual phantasy as he drifted off to sleep.

CHAPTER SIXTEEN

It was a fine, cold winter, with crisp snow and a lot of sunshine. Eli spent much of the time outdoors, frequently with the teacher, but often with Brother John, and sometimes with Timmy tagging along.

The preacher had begun to treat the boy as his spiritual protégé, sitting often for half an hour at a time, explaining for Eli's sole benefit the myriad ways in which the Old Testament was reflected in the New. Eli already had a fair grasp of what was contained between the covers of the Bible, and Brother John was both pleased and surprised by the boy's display of Scriptural erudition. But none of this intellectual play with the prophecies and the types and shadows brought Eli any closer to that state of grace which the pastor so eagerly sought for him. As time went on, Brother John began to worry that some sinister force was holding his favorite in "the world."

"Ye have to reject the world, Eli," he said with assurance. "Ye have to seek the Lord with a pure heart, and them as seeks shall find."

More than once he hinted that as soon as Eli had found grace he would also find himself called to the Lord's ministry —an idea that Eli regarded with silent amusement.

Christopher viewed all this with ill-concealed impatience, though with a certain degree of forced tolerance. "If you want to make friends with the Mammon of Unrighteousness, I suppose that's your business," he told the boy. "It's not for me to choose your friends, though what you can see in that superstitious old preacher is beyond me."

Eli, outside of all reason, found himself jumping to Brother John's defense. "Even Mr. Simms says that he has some good in him," he pointed out. "Besides, he's not so ignorant and superstitious as you seem to think, Chris. It isn't his fault that he hasn't got a university education, like you."

"Oh," said Christopher, "don't get me wrong. I'd be glad enough to be friends with the man myself—though what we'd find to talk about, without arguing over every word, I can scarcely imagine."

"I don't argue with him," Eli said. "We hunt together, and cut wood, and things like that. He's a good man in the woods too, no matter how farfetched his interpretations of the Bible may be."

Christopher laughed. "I suppose I'm a bit jealous, if the truth must be told," he admitted.

"You shouldn't be, Chris," the boy said seriously. "You know how I feel about you, and you know how grateful I am for what you've been doing for me—you and your father both, but you especially."

"Yes," Christopher agreed, "but I have a little of the—what do you call it? the Old Adam?—too, you know. Jealousy is usually nonsense. Virginia is jealous of you, and I'm jealous of John McKim. Who are you jealous of?"

"Johnny," Eli admitted, "at least, I was at first."

"Johnny!" Christopher exclaimed and started to laugh again. "Why, you nut! Let's forget the whole thing, shall we?"

Joshua Markady, who still remembered with a trace of bitterness Brother John's attempt to oust him and his family from the village, was less tolerant than Christopher of Eli's new friendship. "Mark my words, Eli," he said, "no good can come of yer pallin' around with that black hypocrite. 'Tis natural, I s'pose, fer a boy of yer age to tag along after whoever'll look twice at 'im, but ye have enough friends, lad,

not to be in need of the likes o' John McKim. Next thing ye
know he'll be tryin' to get ye off to a Bible school, studyin' to
be a preacher."

Eli laughed at the old captain's acuteness. "Already hint-
ing at it," he said, "but he isn't making much headway."

"Well, I should hope not!" Mr. Markady rejoined.

Not to Joshua Markady, and not to Christopher either,
was he able to drop a hint of his real relationship with
Brother John. It was a secret so dark, so far beyond discus-
sion, that the thought of mentioning it to anyone else never
once crossed his mind.

His father and mother were pleased and flattered. Nothing could have made them prouder than the pastor's interest
in their son. Brother John, they were sure, saw in Eli one
marked from birth for great things, perhaps even with the
hand of the Lord upon him. They also viewed his association
with the pastor as a welcome antidote to his very question-
able friendship with the Markadys and the Simmses.

Eli even overheard his father reassuring his mother about
him. "There be a deal o' good in the lad," Elias said. "He
been flirtin' with the devil a little, 'tis true—exercisin' 'e's
mind, mostly, stretchin' 'e's wings, like. But ye'll see that
'twill all work out fer the best."

Eli smiled cynically to himself.

The effects of the relationship were by no means one-
sided, though. His affair with the boy worked a notable
change in Brother John. His towering sadness for the first
time took on a touch of joy. His sermons, still studded with
sin and damnation and the Second Coming, began to be
softened with frequent references to the Lord's all-embrac-
ing love for his people. One Sunday he preached on the
text: "He shall feed his flock like a shepherd, and gently lead
those that are with young." True, the Day of Wrath got into
it, and those that were not of his flock were chastised with

a rod of iron—but a small song of love was singing amid the thunder.

The very next week Brother John read out from the pulpit, "A new commandment I give unto you, that ye love one another, as I have loved you," then closed the Bible and expatiated on the meaning of the Greek words translated "love" and "charity" in the Authorized Version (information that seemed like very deep scholarship to his listeners, but, in fact, came straight out of his Bible helps). It was the first time in many years that the rough but kindly fisherfolk of Caplin Bight had heard the gospel of love preached within the walls of their little church. It sounded strange and somewhat upsetting to ears attuned to the gospel of hate, but on the whole they viewed with favor, if with a little mistrust, this newly revealed aspect of the Almighty.

Only Sister Leah regarded the change in her husband with the suspicion that it deserved. She must have suspected, in her heart, that her husband's relations with Eli were not all childlike innocence. But she said nothing about that. What she did say was that he was being lured from the stern duty of denouncing the sin with which they were surrounded and warning against the inevitable punishment to which it must lead. And she made a point of treating Eli with haughty disdain whenever, as often happened, he entered her home in her husband's company.

Meanwhile the homosexual alliance matured. Eli found himself looking forward, almost without pangs of conscience, to the rare nights when the pastor and he would sleep together. And in the months leading toward spring he learned some of the refinements of sex play—the physical techniques of giving, and receiving, pleasure. The sense of sin was repressed. But the guilt was there, festering underneath, haunting the background of his mind. He was able to live with it, however, since, for the moment at least, it was under control.

With Brother John the sense of sin took an altogether

different turn. Unable, consciously, to admit sin in himself, he transferred it to others, and specifically to Christopher, with whom Eli continued to spend even more time than he did with Brother John. The pastor began to make frequent and uneasy denunciations of the young teacher, even going so far as to assure Eli that Christopher was a personal agent of the devil, sent to Caplin Bight for the purpose of luring him away from the Lord—a fact which, it seemed, had been revealed to Brother John in a dream.

He assured Eli that he was praying for his salvation.

Meanwhile Sister Leah was praying for Brother John's salvation.

All this praying at cross-purposes created a somewhat heated and unpleasant atmosphere in the McKim household, and it continued unresolved as the winter wound up for its last and greatest assault on the unprotected bights and bays of that bleak shore.

At the end of February a howling storm swept up the bay, sending spray flying across the headlands, freezing to the rocks as it hit, forming great spires and domes of ice and frozen tapestries hanging down the sides of the cliffs.

The wind was down the bay, and as the sun set in the watery sky of late afternoon Eli saw a ship—a rare sight in their bay at that season—running before the wind, under sail, close inshore.

She came wallowing, with white spray frozen to her bowsprit and across her bows, dipping her nose into the waves as she swung in past the Offer Islands. She was a three-masted tern schooner, and as she arrived opposite the entrance to the harbor it could be seen that she was dangerously iced on deck and sheets. She sailed close past the sunkers, and they half expected her to tack and come about to enter the harbor, but perhaps her skipper was afraid he could not maneuver her in her clumsy state, through so narrow a channel in a storm, for she sailed on, into the outer part of the Reach, heading for Lattice Harbor Run. She was just about dead center in the Reach, with Lattice Harbor Island on her port bow, when the wind chopped and blew straight across the bay with even more force than before. They saw the ship heel over, then straighten, and start to sail laboriously on the port tack.

Elias and Eli stood on their gallery, watching the ship in the failing light.

"'E'll never make it," the man told his son. "On that tack 'e'll not clear Lattice Harbor Island, an' on t'other tack 'e'll not clear the rocks past the Cove there, not to speak o' the sunkers."

Indeed the ship was now in a classically hopeless position —caught on a lee shore in a gale with a harborless inlet behind her, her gear frozen, and so much ice that she was in danger of foundering even if she could be kept off the rocks. She was answering her helm only sluggishly, trying to tack out of the narrow Reach, which her skipper knew to be a death trap, ending, as it did, in great crags that rose sheer out of the water to the cloud-soaked rocks where the eagles nested.

She was so far away that they had trouble seeing her at all in the fading light, when Brother John came dashing up to the Pallisher gate with a spyglass under his arm, leading a party of men that included the two Thomas Gilmores, Eleazar Pike, young Pleman Pike, and half a dozen others.

"Her sails be goin'," he reported. "She'll be among the breakers o' Lattice Harbor Island inside an hour, allowin' she don't drive up the Reach—an' if she do that, then God help every man aboard."

"We'll need two or three boats," Thomas Gilmore of Matthew said. "No time fer trap boats. Punts'll have to sarve."

Elias took a long, careful look at the sea and the sky. "Ye could swamp a punt in this aisier'n fallin' off a greased log," he said. But he wasn't questioning the fact that the attempt had to be made—just stating the risks matter-of-factly. If the odds had been against keeping a punt afloat he would have said so and refused to go himself. But he regarded the odds as acceptable. "Ropes," he said. "We'll need heavy lines. Eli, fetch the moorin' lines from the net loft."

Other men collected, and darkness fell.

It was a bitter night as they launched the small boats in the howling darkness, with their oil lanterns shedding feeble, flickering light into the storm. Brother John proposed that he lead the men in his own punt, for it had a little more power than the others and could better be kept up into the seas.

"'Tain't likely anyone could live on they rocks," he said, "but there's a chance she'll strand on the beach an' they'll get off her alive. We got to go see. Jest a moment now, while we ask the Lord's help."

Every man knew that he was taking his life in his hands, on no more than the off chance that another man's life might be saved. But it never occurred to any of them to draw back. They stood on the foreshore for a moment, the wind driving freezing spray that hissed as it struck the fire glass of the lanterns, a circle of dark figures with bowed heads. Once again, in this group, Eli felt the solidarity of man against the blind forces of chaos, and the surging power of prayer uniting them in its dedication. He wished that Christopher were there with them, but the teacher, of course, was three miles up in the valley, wholly unaware of the emergency down at the shore.

"We go, O Lord, at thy command," Brother John intoned in his pulpit voice, so different from his daily speech. "If it be thy will to protect we, thy unprofitable servants, then bring us safe to harbor. And protect our brothers too, in their dire peril, and give 'em succor. Or if it be thy will to take 'em unto thyself then give 'em peace and extend to 'em thy grace. An' if we should not return, then let us know that we are in thy hands, an' doin' thy will, an' receive our souls into thy keepin' agin' the great day of judgment. For Jesus's sake."

And they murmured, "Amen," and followed him into the

punts and cast off into the storm. Eli was with Elias, and no abler man ever handled a small boat in bad weather. But though the boy was proud of his father, he felt even prouder of Brother John in the boat up ahead, for the preacher was not a seaman and might easily have sent the fishermen into the storm with his blessing, but chose instead to risk his life leading them to the wreck.

And Eli felt proud and exalted too. He knew perfectly well that he might not live even another hour, and he had none of the others' faith concerning the safekeeping of his soul in the Lord's hands. But he was not frightened. On the contrary, every nerve and muscle seemed twice as alive as before. He felt almost invincible. If this was the road to death, he decided, then it was worth the risk and worth the dying.

Fortunately only an hour or so had passed since the sudden chop in the wind, so that there had not been time enough to build up a very heavy cross swell. Otherwise the small boats might have had trouble getting through the narrows between the sunkers. As it was, they slipped out as easily as a hand from an oiled glove and found themselves with a cross wind and a following sea.

The boats heeled over and took a lot of freezing spray on board, but they were not in danger so long as they were handled skillfully, though a faltering engine or an unsure hand on the tiller could instantly swamp any of them. They had to be guided almost by feel rather than sight. The helmsman would bear down, to make the boat head up into the wind, then slack off, to allow her to run on course. Since he could see so little he had to know by the tilt of the planks under his feet, almost by instinct, when to heave down again, to keep the boat from swamping. Elias stood at the tiller, three other men in the thwarts, Eli in the bows, straining to see the whitecapped waves as they approached and to wave a signal to Elias if they looked more dangerous than the boat could stand while running on course.

The lanterns of the other punts repeatedly disappeared

into the troughs of the waves, sometimes being gone so long
that it looked as though they had gone under or gone out,
but each time this happened they reappeared, to bob triumphantly over the seas again, defiant in the howling blackness. And so it went on—and on—as they grew numb with
the cold and the boats grew slippery with ice, until they
could see the rocks of Lattice Harbor Island, a deeper black
against the blackness, and the awful white teeth of its
breakers, and hear the deeper boom of its surf coming
through the snarling noise of the storm.

They knew it would be impossible to land on the beach
without smashing every one of their boats to matchwood.
A landing would have to be made on the icy rocks of the
rattle, where the seas were sweeping alongshore, but they
would be in the lee of the wind.

As they ran into the narrow tickle between the island and
the point, the boats tossing, the seas sucking and gurgling at
the ice-covered rocks, they backed their engines and waited
while Brother John's boat ran in toward shore and he stood
with both feet planted firmly on the forward gunwales,
swaying like a mast in the lamplight, the storm tearing at his
beard and a coil of line in his hand. The boat plunged,
reared, started to slip toward the rocks, and he gave a great
cry and leaped, landed on the ice, slipped, clawed at it with
the fingers of one hand, held on as if by miracle, and somehow wriggled out of the reach of the surf.

They hove out a heavy graplin at the stern and he wrestled the line to the rocks above and secured it. Then the
men from his boat went ashore, and were followed by those
from the other boats, the men landing one at a time, making
use of the mooring lines for security, every man safe, with
their gear and their lanterns. It was a great act of daring and
skill, but on Brother John's part it was, above all, an act of
faith.

They now had to cross the island to the windward side,
for the ship would be either on the beach or on the rocks at
its point. They roped themselves together and climbed the

hump of the island, creeping slowly over the ice, feeling for footholds.

When they arrived at the beach they could see that it was empty, swept and bare, with a great line of boiling surf roaring and churning along its edge and flinging itself far up toward the frozen face of the rocks above. So they clambered up the steep incline toward the point, and from the top they could see, among the breakers and the ice below, the great hulk of the ship already beginning to disintegrate under the almighty pounding of the seas—the three spars tipped far over, the deck completely broken across, pieces of timber washing back and forth in the surge and suck of the water between the rocks.

At first it seemed as if men could not possibly have landed in the howling maelstrom of the little cove where the ship had struck the cliff, but they weighted a rope with a stone and lowered a lantern down the face of the rock, and there, huddled on a boulder, like statues carved in ice, were two men, still holding on, miraculously, with the seas breaking over them.

"You're to lower me down on a rope!" Brother John yelled to Eleazar Pike. "They'll not be able to move, if they still be alive a-tall."

So they rigged a stout line about Brother John's chest and shoulders, and he took another line in his hand, and three men planted themselves on the ice and lowered him down the face of the cliff into the frozen hell beneath. As the breaking waves drenched him, and spray froze to ice on his clothes, he bent the line about the ice-encrusted figures and gave a sharp tug, signaling to the men above to haul away.

It took all those on the cliff top to haul the three of them up to the safety of the ice-shrouded island, and even then they were not sure of their victory, for though the two castaways were still alive and still conscious, they were so encrusted with frozen spray, and so stiff with cold, that they could not move a muscle, and it seemed doubtful that they could survive even the trip back to the boats. Brother John had blood on his face and his hands, where the storm had dashed him against the rock, but he said it was nothing—a few small cuts, with no broken bones.

Then they inched their way back to the boats in the rattle and started the return journey to Caplin Bight.

The storm was no worse, but the sea was now building up from the new direction, so that they had to stand off carefully, choose their time, and then commit themselves to a dash through the breakers for the harbor entrance. There were beacons blazing on the Head and the Point to guide them home, and they blazed so furiously, even through the storm, that the men could see one another's faces, blood-red against the blackness, as they slid down the coiling seas through the narrows into the safety of the harbor.

There was no display of rejoicing as they landed—just a sense of dumb thankfulness for men, reunited on the stormy waterfront with waiting wives and children who might so easily have been left widows and orphans, returned from the maw of the sea. And there was also a deep, genuine sense of sorrow for the six men and the boy who, so the castaways told them, had disappeared when the ship struck. Every woman had the feeling that it might have been her own husband, her own son. They were strangers, it was true, but part of the worldwide community of those who risk their lives on the water, and hence part of the large family to which the people of Caplin Bight too belonged.

Each of the survivors was taken into a home, fed hot soup, given warm clothes and the comfort of a bed. The next day two of the bodies—that of a man in his sixties, and a boy of perhaps thirteen—washed ashore on the beach at the Cove and were taken and laid out in pine boxes. At that season there was no way to ship the bodies to their homes, short of a long and dangerous expedition through Broadport, so they were buried in the graveyard on the Point and the next summer stones were sent by the families, to be erected at the graves, the names of the man, Maher, and the boy, Walsh, standing there forever, strange and not at home among the Pikes and the Pallishers, the Markses and the Gilmores.

If Brother John had needed anything to solidify his position among the people of Caplin Bight his action on the night of the wreck was it. Nothing was said, directly, about his courage and leadership. Even mentioning such a thing would have made the people of the Bight squirm with embarrassment. But it was understood everywhere that he had risen a notch in public estimation, had proved himself to be more than a student of the prophecies and a shepherd of souls. Whenever the incident of the rescue was mentioned, his name was linked with it: "The night that Brother John and the men sove the two castaways on Lattice Harbor Island."

Eli jumped a grade that winter, and had to work to catch up with the class ahead—though "class" was hardly the word, since he had now left all the other students, even those older than himself, behind. Christopher, who expected him to do well in his grade-nine public exams, devoted a lot of time to tutoring, to keeping him at the pleasant task of digging into literature and general information, and teaching him the elements of composition.

"The first thing you need to be able to do to pass exams is to write," he assured the boy. "That's where so many first-year university students fail. No matter how much history or geography or science or French you know, you won't get credit for it unless you can put it down on paper." Those were the days before "objective" tests, when all examination questions, except in such subjects as math and physics, were to be answered in essay form.

Christopher's leisure was divided between Eli and Virginia. With time he had grown more careless about what he said and did before the people of the Bight, and in March, Solomon Marks laid down the law that the teacher was to stay away from his daughter or he'd see what could be done about it.

At first this made Christopher and Virginia a little more discreet. But during the Easter holidays Thomas Gilmore of Thomas, calling at the Simms home one evening unexpectedly, found the pair of them, not exactly in *flagrante delicto,* but in what he described as a compromising position.

He said nothing about it until the next weekly prayer meeting, when he raised the matter publicly, even going so far as to question the fitness of Brother Marks to serve as the chief elder of the church and quoting from the Epistle of Paul to Timothy to back up his words about those whose families were not properly in subjection under them. The ecclesia did not view the matter quite so seriously as Brother Gilmore had hoped, however. They exhorted Brother Marks, and prayed for him, that he might be given the strength to rule wisely in his own household.

Solomon Marks, of course, was furious. He was not used to being prayed over. Brother John privately agreed with him. The pastor and the chief elder, for the first time, found that they had a lot in common. Eli knew of their common cause and of their united hatred of Christopher. But he could never be sure which of them originated the plot to ruin the teacher.

It began with rumors. First there were dark hints about "goings-on" at the Simms house, a wagging of heads, words whispered behind hands. Pleman Pike brought the rumors back to Eli.

"There be stories around," he said, "that ye lets the teacher do with ye things that he oughtn't. I don't believe the talk, o' course, but there be lots as do. If I was you I'd mind me step—fer appearances' sake."

Mr. Markady next mentioned the matter. "Lad," he said, "there's word around the Bight about ye an' Christopher. 'Tis said ye are practisin' what the psalm-singin' 'angshores at the church calls 'unnatural sin.'"

"There's no truth in it," Eli said shortly.

"No, I never thought fer a minute there could be," Mr.

Markady said. "If that young Simms fella was the sort as went in fer that kind o' thing he'd hardly be chasin' the young Marks girl like a spring pup after a bitch in heat—would he now? But that ain't the point. There's goin' to be trouble, boy. I'm an old hand, used to trouble, an' can smell it comin'. Besides, I know what happens to them Old Testament Christians once they snuffs the smell o' what they thinks is sin—especially if there's a piece of ass mixed up in it. Makes 'em fair slaver at the jaws, ye know. In their language, as I s'pose ye've found out, sin is only a polite word fer fuckin'—it means nought else to 'em."

"How do stories like that begin?" Eli asked.

"Someone plants 'em," Mr. Markady said. "In this case, no doubt, yer fine friend John McKim."

"But why would he do that?" Eli asked, not believing it possible.

"Because he's jealous, an' because in 'e's heart 'e most likely hates ye, as well as Christopher, because 'e sees ye becomin' the man 'e might o' been if only 'e'd had the guts to try," Mr. Markady said.

CHAPTER SEVENTEEN

❦ ❧

No amount of talk, no matter how ugly, could hold back the swelling buds of April or the coming of the net-barking days, when traps and salmon twine and mooring lines were dipped into steaming pots of black essence to preserve them against the swarming, invisible life of the sea, whose encroaches they must endure for months to come. Then there were wood fires on the hills with figures moving around them like witches in some ancient rite, and the tarry smell from boiling caldrons drifted all over the Bight, making hearts sing and leap for the marching feet of summer.

In the midst of this natural rejoicing Eli went, in great distress, to Christopher, forcing himself to speak of a matter that all his inclinations forbade him to mention but that his misery no longer permitted him to keep to himself.

"You know what they're saying about us," he asked the teacher, "that we—that there's—that our friendship is *immoral!*"

But Christopher refused to take the matter seriously. He paced about restlessly but without unusual agitation. "Virginia mentioned it to me," he said. "It made me mad enough for a few minutes to want to go and choke anyone who repeated it. But then I calmed down. Suppose they talk? What harm will it do us? It might help to keep them out of worse mischief."

"But the talk will be believed," Eli insisted. "I'll be forbidden to have anything to do with you. And more than likely they won't let you teach here another year."

"Oh, I hardly think it could go as far as that," Christopher said. "After all, it's only a vicious rumor. You wouldn't expect your family to believe it, would you?"

"No," Eli admitted. "I suppose not."

"And as for me—well, teachers aren't all that easy to get, as you know. I've done my job well—better than the people who hired me could have expected. I don't think any of the students are going to fail the exams in June, and some of you are going to get high marks. Even the elders will be forced to cheer. How could they fire me, with a record like that?"

"Well, you may be right," Eli said. "I hope so, anyway, but it makes me feel terrible."

"Leave the matter alone, Eli, and in a short time 'twill die of itself, or, if you want to do anything about it, go and talk to your friend Brother John. He should be able to squash the talk if he believes in your innocence."

So Eli bearded Brother John in his den, but found the preacher in a stiff-necked and truculent mood. "Ye have brought it on yerself," he told the boy, "an' if ye are sufferin' 'tis fer yer sins. O' course there's talk. Why not? I have warned ye before to stay away from that Simms fella, but ye wouldn't heed me. He is an evil young man, an' ye are to leave 'im be, ye understand?"

"It isn't true!" Eli exclaimed with passion. "Christopher is far more of a real Christian than most of the people in your church—more than you are, as far as that goes."

Brother John's black eyes bored fiercely into the boy's. "Indeed," he said slowly. "Indeed, now." Then he went on, viciously: "An' who give ye leave to sit in jedgment?—ye who are not even among the saved? 'Tis fer ye to mind yer place an' seek the Lord humbly, askin' fergiveness fer sins before ye find yerself consigned to hell-fire! That teacher that ye be so fond of have brought evil to this place, settin' the hearts of the children agin' the fathers, as the Lord foretold. A false prophet he be, but the Lord will let'en go jest

so far before He'll cut 'en down—wickedness bein' permitted
to flourish fer a season, to try the elect, if they be pure gold
or dross!"

This was too much for Eli. "You're hardly the one to be
preaching about wickedness," he exploded, "seeing the
things they are saying about Christopher are true—about
you and me!"

It was the first time either of them had made any direct
reference to their relationship, and Brother John was frozen
into stillness for a minute. Then he spoke, with a terrible,
icy calm in his voice. "What are ye talkin' about?" he said.
"What do ye mean, 'you and me'? We ain't done nothin'
sinful, as I know fer. Ye watch yer tongue, boy, or 'twill get
ye into far more trouble than ye can handle."

Brother John turned away, refusing to discuss the matter
further, and Eli was left speechless at what seemed to be
his bland hypocrisy. Could it be that the preacher had managed, by some incredible piece of mental gymnastics, to convince himself that his relations with Eli were innocent?

The next time they met, Brother John had thawed to the
point of attempting a casual, friendly approach to the boy,
but Eli was having none of it. His alliance with Brother John,
he swore to himself, must be ended once and for all. So he
avoided the preacher, while the latter continued to make
excuses for meeting him, tried soft words, suggested that
they go fishing together. Then, as all these overtures were
rather rudely rejected, Eli saw the man begin to grow dark
and moody.

Meanwhile his friendship with Christopher reached its
most serene level. He had matured enough during the year
so that he could now approach the teacher almost as an
adult. Even though their minds ran in different paths, they
found frequent meeting places, for Eli, once his intellectual
horizon expanded beyond Caplin Bight and the Authorized
Version, showed a notable aptitude for absorbing many of
the main elements of human thought. In some directions he
quickly went outside Christopher's reading experience. In

others he lagged behind. But they had a common interest in the new directions being explored by science. For Eli it was a wholly intoxicating experience, as though he had suddenly discovered that, by spreading his arms, he could fly.

At the same time he shared with the teacher a pleasant physical companionship. In size and strength they were now more nearly matched, though Christopher could still better him in any physical contest except shooting—mainly, perhaps, because he enjoyed the self-confidence of a man, while Eli still suffered from the self-doubts of a boy.

But as June arrived, with its first warm days, Eli could feel the tensions of a coming crisis.

"I think you're just on edge because the exams are coming and the neighbors disapprove of you," Christopher said as they stood in the warm young sunshine, the school locked behind them for the day.

"I can't help the feeling that we are heading for some kind of disaster," Eli said. "It wasn't so bad when the rumors were flying and Brother John was denouncing you as the devil's disciple, but there's been a sort of uncanny quiet lately, as though they had made up their minds on some course of action."

"There's nothing to it," Christopher assured him, "just your imagination at work. Why don't we walk up through the woods by the mill brook, and enjoy what's left of the afternoon, and relax a bit?"

So they walked to the Gilmore mill and found the woods path that followed the bank of the brook, and there they shed their shoes and climbed the hill barefooted as they had done so often the summer before, reveling in the feeling of the warm, bare earth, now living and vital again after the long, sterile winter.

They mounted up as lightly as eagles on an ascending current of air, the feeling of trouble dropping away as they rose toward the sun-washed heights of the hill. There they came upon a small clearing in a place once occupied by an old log house, in the days before living memory. And they sat and looked through the trees at the village below, and at the summer sea, with just a tiny string of ice showing far off, near the mouth of the bay, floating southward from the remote Arctic toward the warm waters on the Banks of Newfoundland. Far out on the bay they could see the waters dappled by the rising of dolphins or small whales.

"Think the brook would be warm enough for swimming?" Christopher asked.

"Well, we could try," Eli said. "I suppose it wouldn't kill us, anyway."

So they explored the brook, and found that the sun-warmed water was pleasant enough for swimming, providing you didn't stay in for more than a few minutes. There was no place where they could really swim—just a pool between boulders, with a depth of three feet and a little fall splashing into its upper end.

They crawled out and sat, naked and shivering, on the grass.

"Feel better?" Christopher asked.

"Of course," Eli said. "Nobody could do much grieving or worrying up here—but down in the Bight—that's a different matter."

"Forget it for a few minutes," Christopher counseled. He got up and paced about the clearing with his restless, catlike tread. "I say—let's wrestle, shall we? Think maybe you're strong enough to throw me?"

Eli looked at his friend's tough, lithe body, muscles rippling under the skin, and felt a surge of physical desire rise inside him. Christopher always seemed to be holding him at arm's length, as though afraid of an intimate physical contact. What would happen, he wondered, if he probed past those defenses?

"Yes, I'd like to wrestle," he said. "Maybe I could throw you, at that. We don't have to dress, do we? I think I'd like to wrestle naked."

"Why—yes, sure," Christopher agreed. He stood against the dark fronds of the spruces, his skin fair and ruddy, almost like a flame against the dim, vegetative peace of the forest. He contrasted sharply, too, with his young friend, whose body was colored like buckwheat honey, presenting little apposition to the kingdom of the plants, blending into his surroundings like a wild animal, as though he had been born to run naked in the forest. His eyes were alive with a thousand black lights, while Christopher's flashed blue and green like sea water. Eli could see a faint tracery of blue veins here and there in his friend's transparent skin.

Christopher crouched, waiting for Eli to come to him; the boy approached warily, and they locked hands and began the struggle of trying to throw each other. They strained and panted, and began to sweat, and Eli seemed more than once on the point of tipping his rival, but Christopher always managed to twist out of his hold at the last moment, or to summon the extra strength needed to stay on his feet. Then he got his heel behind Eli's, and his arms locked behind his back, and in a moment the boy was flat on the ground with Christopher on top.

Eli struggled to rise, got a scissors hold on Christopher, rolled him over, but the greater stamina of the older man was beginning to tell: he broke the hold with one stiff contortion and pinned the boy firmly to the ground. Then he rolled free and lay on his back, sweating, waving Eli away.

"Enough," he said, "enough! You're getting pretty strong —no doubt about that. A pity, isn't it, that they've turned wrestling into ham acting?"

"I didn't know they had," Eli said, sitting up.

"Oh, yes—in the cities—a spectacle for fools. But it goes back, you know, past the dawn of history, one of the oldest and most vital forms of contest between men."

Eli, not interested for the moment in talking about anthropology, lay down beside Christopher and started tickling his ribs with a straw. Christopher laughed and grabbed him, and they tussled again, in play this time, not exerting their strength. The man had Eli on the ground, shaking him playfully, and the boy had begun to laugh, when there was a soft tread at the end of the little clearing, and Brother John emerged from the trees, like the angel Azrael come to judgment. As they heard his step they stopped their horseplay and sat up, and he came and stood above them, black against the sun, which still touched the edge of the mountain, some hours before its death.

Eli smiled up at the preacher guilelessly, but the prophetic face was filled with horror and wrath. He stood for a moment, saying nothing, allowing the chill of his condemnation to wither them like the breath of winter. Then he spoke, in his most compelling pulpit voice.

"Eli!" he thundered. "Have ye no shame, boy? Put on yer clothes this instant an' come with me!"

"Hold on!" snapped Christopher, jumping to his feet and pacing around the pastor like a panther with a deer at bay. "You've been spying on us, haven't you, you damned hypocrite? Who do you think you are anyway, coming around shouting orders like a troop sergeant?"

"I wonder at yer gall, Mr. Simms, I really do," Brother John said. "Ye are a blackhearted young villain, and a shameless agent o' the devil, leadin' this boy down the broad road o' vice that leads to destruction. The two o' ye, fer that matter," he continued, his voice rising, "walkin' with yer private parts nekked in the sight o' the Lord without shame! 'Tis whipped ye ought to be! And you, Simms! If I found ye like this in the days o' King Hezekiah ye'd be took out an' stoned!"

"We're not living in the days of King Hezekiah, whoever he was," Christopher said, "and as for you, McKim, you will kindly continue your walk and leave us alone. We have nothing whatever to discuss with you."

"How can ye do it, Eli?" said Brother John, turning to the boy, a note of pleading creeping into his voice.

"Do what?" Eli asked. "Is there something wrong with the two of us wrestling like this, here on the hill, far away from the harbor?"

"Wrong!" Brother John thundered, losing his temper and making a lunge toward the boy. But Christopher jumped between, grabbed the preacher by his black coat, and, using a reserve of strength that he certainly hadn't called upon while wrestling with Eli, gave him a violent shake and a sudden shove that sent him sprawling among the juniper bushes at the edge of the clearing.

"Get up and get going, McKim," Christopher said dispassionately. "I'm a peaceful man, not asking for trouble, but if you try to lay a hand on Eli I'll break that hooked nose of yours so it will never be straight again."

Brother John stood for a moment, irresolute, as though tempted to take up the challenge and do carnal battle with this agent of the Evil One. But he collected himself and delivered, instead, a verbal arrow. "The Lord says to turn the other cheek," he declared, "though it be a mighty hard thing to do at times. Ye've no cause to threaten me. I'd no intention o' touchin' the lad, but 'tis me Christian duty to admonish 'im when I sees 'im slidin' into the bottomless pit o' vice."

"We'll have no more talk about vice, either," Christopher said. "'Tis you, I can see, that's been spreading those God-damned lies about me and this boy. Well, I warn you, Mc-Kim, they'll either stop or you'll get a good deal more than a shove into the bushes next time I see you. Now get out."

Brother John went, but not exactly with his tail between his legs. As he turned into the path to descend the hill he looked back. "Ye'll be sorry fer this, Simms," he threatened.

"You know, Chris," Eli said when Brother John was out of earshot, "I'm scared of that man."

"Aw, what can he do?" Christopher shrugged. "You'll catch hell from your father, I suppose, but you're too big for Elias to thrash. Forget it. Wouldn't you like to go for another dip before we go home?"

"Maybe," Eli said, absently. "Don't try to put me off, Chris. I'm worried."

"Oh, come on," Christopher said. "Forget it."

They went back to the pool in the brook, stretched out beneath the falls and let it pour over them, doused each other with water, and chased about the shallows until their spirits were completely restored and their bodies refreshed and relaxed. Then they went back to the tiny meadow and lay in the warm evening, letting the air dry them, shivering slightly but filled with a sense of peace and well-being. At last they recovered their clothes, struggled into them, and started down toward the village in the gathering purple shadows of the spruces, with the softness of the dead fir needles and the sharp crunch of dry reindeer moss under their feet.

"I suppose I must tell you about the wedding," Christopher said as they descended the hill.

"Wedding?" Eli echoed.

"Yes. Virginia and I are going to slip up to Lattice Harbor and get married the week after exams. We only decided definitely on the date last night, and you are the first person I've mentioned it to."

"I'm glad, of course!" Eli exclaimed. And he was too, he told himself. He was convinced that he had conquered the rather silly pangs of jealousy that he had felt the summer before.

"No fancy wedding or anything," Christopher was explaining. "We don't want to stir things up around here more than necessary, so we just intend to have a private church wedding without any reception or announcement or anything else. It will be an elopement, if you like to call it that."

"But there'll be a few people from the Bight?" Eli asked.

"Well—you, of course, and my father—Mr. and Mrs. Markady if they should care to come, and Virginia's cousin, whom she says she'll swear to secrecy. But keep it quiet, won't you? If word of this got around, we'd have Solomon Marks and that ghastly wife of his down on our necks like harpies."

"I'll be as silent as the grave," Eli promised.

So they came down the hill, out of the forest, and the village lay on either hand, spread before them like two enormous white wings. And out over the sunkers they could see the eagles wheeling, soaring in effortless flight against the reflected pearl of the eastern sky. They stopped and watched the majestic birds soaring, and felt the mystery of the evening reaching out to touch them, to touch their minds and their hearts with the ultimate secret of life that united eagles and men and was far greater than them both —a secret that seemed to come very close, and to illuminate them from within, but still to elude their grasping.

Christopher sighed. "Things move so fast," he said. "About fifteen months from now you'll have to leave Caplin Bight, just as I had to leave it. But I hope you too will come back, Eli. You'll want to do something more than just go off to the university, of course—see a bit of the world, I suppose; maybe live for a while in big cities. Perhaps you'll even find your life's work there."

"Of course I want to see the big cities," Eli said, "New York, London, maybe even Calcutta and Tokyo—and the places where Mr. Markady sailed in the days of the traders —Barbados, Pernambuco, Naples—"

"But I hope you will come back," Christopher resumed. "Sooner or later, I believe, you'll find that life is better and fuller here than in any city. Having grown up here, and lived it, you couldn't forget—you wouldn't—"

"If I forget thee, O Jerusalem," Eli quoted.

"Yes," Christopher said softly. "Yes." He touched Eli's shoulder and finished the quotation: "If I forget thee, O Jerusalem, let my right hand forget her cunning . . . if I love not Jerusalem more than all the joys of the earth."

"I suppose I couldn't, even if I tried," Eli said.

"No," Christopher agreed. "When you grow up here you're a separate breed, forever. You may become a professor at a great university, or a research scientist, or something that I can't guess at, but I know one thing—you'll be a Newfoundlander, and a bayman, to the end of your days."

They walked together with a profound feeling of intellectual unity through a twilight that was deepening into night, until they parted by the store, with the sound of the landwash in front and that of the old green mill wheel creaking behind them. And as he walked home to cram for his exams Eli already half suspected that this evening would be remembered as one of the turning points of his life.

He waited for repercussions from their encounter on the hill with Brother John, but to his surprise the preacher said nothing more about it. The incident was not reported to his family, nor was it built into yet another rumor in the settlement. By the time the caplin run had started, and exams were being written, he had begun to hope that it might be forgotten altogether.

On the Monday exams began, the coastal boat was in, and the codfish were running to the traps, and there was great bustle and activity. Brother John left, with Sister Leah, for their annual pilgrimage to St. John's and consultation with their church's head office. Solomon Marks went at the same time, saying that he planned to place orders for his business with his suppliers on Water Street.

On the last Monday of June, when the exams were over, as Eli was starting to turn over plans for the long summer that lay ahead of him, and Virginia was packing a small bag for their trip to Lattice Harbor, the pastor and the chief elder returned together. With them was a policeman, and with the policeman a warrant, duly processed out of a court in St. John's, for the arrest of Christopher Simms, upon the complaint of John McKim and of Solomon Marks, that he had, on divers occasions, committed acts of gross indecency with a male person and a minor.

Christopher's arrest was the most stunning thing that had ever happened to Eli. It came so suddenly and unexpectedly that it was over almost before he realized what was happening, and he was left feeling shocked and numb.

As a rule the coastal boat lingered but a short time in Caplin Bight, especially at that time of year, where there was little or no outgoing freight. But on this particular day the ship was delayed an extra half hour to accommodate the policeman, and to allow his prisoner to pack. Word flew from house to house, small boys scurrying with the news and women passing the word across back fences that the teacher had been arrested. The result was that almost everyone who could walk was on the government wharf standing in shocked and respectful silence as Christopher and the constable walked through the crowd to the gangway.

As they drew near to the place where Eli was standing Christopher spoke a word to the policeman, the latter nodded, and they paused. The teacher managed a crooked smile. "Eli," he said, "you look like you'd just heard your own death sentence. Cheer up. This isn't quite as bad as everyone seems to think—I'm not on my way to jail, you know, just to answer a charge. This is all caused by malice or misunderstanding, and it should never get beyond the preliminary inquiry. It'll all be over in a week or two, and as soon as it is I'll be home. Have you seen Virginia?"

"No," Eli admitted. "She isn't on the wharf." He looked about, but the only member of Solomon Marks's household present was little Jesse, his nine-year-old son. Eli called the child over. "Jesse," he said, "why didn't Virginia come with you?"

"Pa wouldn' let 'er come," the boy replied. "Locked 'er in 'er room, 'e did, an' she be screamin' fit to be tied."

Christopher spoke again to the policeman. "We were to be married the day after tomorrow," he said. "Could you—do you think—"

"Sorry, sir." The policeman shook his head. "I would, you know, only the boat is delayed already."

Just then Johnny Penchley came shoving through the crowd, sobbing, hardly able to make himself understood. "Oh, Teacher," he wailed, "the boys say they be goin' to hang ye."

Christopher took the boy by the shoulders and shook

him gently. "Stop it, Johnny!" he said. "It isn't true"; then, to the policeman: "*You* tell him, Officer."

"That's right, son," the policeman said as kindly as he could. "Mr. Simms ain't goin' to be hanged. He got to go to St. John's for court work, but he'll be back again pretty soon."

Johnny accepted this, coming, as it did, from the awful majesty of the first city policeman he had ever seen, but refused to be comforted. He clung to Christopher, half hysterical, his face buried in the teacher's shirt front, so that Christopher, his eyes dark with pain, had to disengage the child and hand him over to Eli.

"Look after him," he whispered. "Try to do something for him—and Virginia—for God's sake try to talk to Virginia for me as soon as you get the chance. I'll write her by the next mail—"

"Yes," said Eli, "yes—I will—"

Christopher squeezed his hand and walked quietly up the gangplank, not glancing even once at the crowd that had gathered to witness his shame.

CHAPTER EIGHTEEN

That summer was the blackest and bitterest that Eli ever lived through. It was not enough that he had to suffer the raw wounds left by his friend's arrest; he was subjected to a subtle campaign of persecution and harassment, none the easier to bear because it was conducted with solicitation and for the salvation of his soul. Almost without exception the pious members of the ecclesia assumed that Christopher was guilty and looked upon Eli with mixed pity and contempt. Even Elias and Martha refused to accept his solemn oath that his relations with the teacher had been innocent.

"I'll grant ye that ye might've been led astray unbeknownst," Elias said bitterly, "but 'twas a terrible sin jest the same—a sin so black that the Lord won't name it in 'E's holy word—a sin agin' the Holy Ghost. If ye don't repent an' ask God's pardon ye'll suffer the second death."

"Maybe I deserve the second death," Eli retorted sharply, "but not for anything I did with Christopher, and I won't lie to God about it, just to please you or Brother John."

This, unfortunately, was interpreted as stubborn unrepentance, a condition all too familiar to those who must do battle with sin on a communal as well as a personal basis.

The Sunday after Christopher's arrest Brother John preached a triumphant sermon, taking his text from the First Epistle to the Corinthians: "If any man defile the temple of God, him will God destroy." He didn't mention Christopher by name, but he fairly crowed with righteousness triumphant over unspeakable sin, and, in a modest and roundabout way, took credit for having wrestled with the devil and overcome him.

Except for brief flashes of defiance, Eli was crushed. He was dragged to church with his parents to listen to the self-righteousness and the reproving and the admonishing and the praying, and he took it without protest and was bowed to the earth with misery. He refused, however, even to speak to Brother John. The pastor came to his home to pray for him, and singled him out in prayer meeting for the prayers of the congregation, and attempted to talk to him about a humble and a contrite heart, all without the slightest success. The most he could ever get out of Eli, when they found themselves for a moment alone together was: "I hate you, Brother John. I hate you! Every night I pray to God that you'll die."

Virginia, though, was openly rebellious and defiant. The story was spread about that when her father finally let her out of her locked room she tried to kill him with a meat hook from the storehouse—though it was hard to say how anyone could know this to be true, not having been there to see it. Certain it was that she appeared not once in church, and it was generally believed that she was lost beyond repentance or recall.

"I'm on the side of the sinners, and I intend to stay that way," she told Eli fiercely when they met in her father's store. "I love Christopher and I'm going to marry him, and they aren't going to stop me. I'm surprised you can still stand the inside of that stinking church after what's happened."

"Well," Eli said, realizing that he was making what sounded like a lame excuse, "I'm still under my father's roof, you know. I don't have much choice."

"Choice, is it?" Virginia said scornfully. "I wish I'd been born a boy. I'd show those sniveling hypocrites something!" She looked at Eli challengingly, her black eyes flashing, but he lacked the strength to meet her challenge.

His eyes dropped, and he felt ashamed. "I'm sorry, Virginia," he mumbled. "What do you want me to do?"

She sized him up for a moment. "You must be more of a child than I thought," she said. "If you don't know what you should do then what's the use of my trying to tell you? But *somebody's* got to stand up to them, even if it is a girl!"

It was no use. Eli felt small and helpless and frustrated, like some small animal that wanted to crawl into its small burrow, away from the world, and talking to Virginia, who should have been able to share and lighten his sorrow, only seemed to add to his misery. He wished desperately that he might be back in the recent days of his childhood, when life was secure and simple, and uncomplicated by the problems of love and hate and responsibility.

Virginia's father and mother both put on a show of great shame, Mary Marks even going to the extreme of wearing a black hat in church. But this symbol of mourning was doubtless in the main a play for attention. Mary Marks had always been a rather ineffective and simple-minded woman, her ineffectiveness underlined by her position as the merchant's wife. She made up for her shortcomings by being a poser. She stood up in prayer meeting and asked in a broken voice that the ecclesia pray for her poor lost daughter whom she loved so, even in the clutches of Satan, and they prayed for Virginia three weeks in a row before Brother John, prompted by Sister Leah, ruled that it would be an affront to God to pray any further. Virginia, then, was officially written off among the damned. The effect of all this was to harden her rebellion, to set her up as a permanent outcast in her own family, and to force her in self-defense to become what she, as well as her parents, regarded as a hardened sinner.

Johnny Penchley seemed to be even more miserable than Eli, whom he followed about like a lost puppy, seeking some sort of relief. For weeks on end Eli was his only contact with reality, but nothing that the older boy said or did served to raise him out of the limbo of his misery. More than anyone else, Johnny had become totally dependent upon Christopher, so that with the teacher's arrest the child's burgeoning world came to a violent end.

Eli's real friends stuck by him in his trouble. Joshua and Anne Markady, who had never lent ear to the slander that filled the village, believed it now no more than formerly. The boy began spending more time with them than he had before. Old Mr. Simms was, of course, linked with them in the alliance of the damned. He had called Eli into his study the very evening Christopher was arrested and put him on the carpet.

"Eli," he said sternly, "is there any truth at all behind this charge?"

"Not one word, Mr. Simms," Eli assured him.

"You and Christopher are very fond of each other," the ex-magistrate pursued. "You are quite sure that you never— ah—stepped beyond the bounds of propriety?"

"How can you think such a thing, Mr. Simms?" Eli wailed.

"I don't, boy," the old man assured him. "I just have to be sure. If anything of the kind *had* happened I'd be just as anxious to help you as I am now. I'm hardly a stranger to such matters, you know—but there's a big difference between helping someone who has slipped, however innocently, on the wrong side of the law and someone who's the victim of a misunderstanding."

Eli felt tears behind his eyes and tried to keep them back. "I swear to God, Mr. Simms," he said, his voice quavering, "that we never did anything wrong."

"You'd tell me if you did," Mr. Simms persisted.

"Yes," Eli whispered, no longer able to hide his tears, "I'd tell you if we did."

"Very well then," the white-haired old man said, patting his shoulder, "there's no need to be miserable. I'm sorry I had to ask you this, boy, but it clears the matter up. You can be sure that nothing more will come of it—at least so far as you and Christopher are concerned. Somewhere along the line the court will find out the truth and the charge will be dropped or dismissed. Then we'll see whether we have a case for action against those who laid the charge in the first place. It's a serious thing, you know, to accuse an innocent man of a felony."

Even a few of the church people, Eli found, refused to be swayed by the pressure of the majority. Young Pleman Pike went out of his way to make it clear that nothing had changed between himself and his former dory mate. "I don't believe the lies they spread about ye, Eli," he said, "or the teacher either, regards to that. But even allowin' 'twas true, 'twould make no difference to me."

Virginia's cousin Christina, a full member of the congregation who had seen the Lord in glory and received the Holy Ghost, had words of kindness and comfort. "I do feel sorry for ye, Eli," she said, "and for Mr. Simms too. He can't really be as bad as they think; he seemed such a nice man. But don't turn yer face away from the Lord, Eli, the way Virginia have done. . . . Poor Virginia! She be really bitter about it, an' impatient under affliction. It do make me feel terrible to see her lost, an' no hope for her, it seems, we being blood relations, an' almost like sisters an' all. . . ."

Then, as July burned hot and the still seas of summer became hazy, Brother John and Solomon Marks were off again, to testify at the preliminary inquiry—and Elder Thomas Gilmore of Matthew, next senior after Elder Marks, presided at the Sunday services and the weekly prayer meetings. They were gone only a few days when they returned, obviously pleased with the results of this pre-trial hearing. Christopher had not been freed by the grand jury as he had hoped. Instead they had returned a true bill, and his case had been set down for trial by the supreme court when its sittings were resumed in August. He was released on five thousand dollars' bail—an enormous figure in those days, but with his father's help bail was arranged through a trust company in St. John's, and he was set free late in July.

Unannounced, he arrived in Caplin Bight, accompanied by a young lawyer—a dark, dapper little man with a clipped mustache and sharp, alert eyes. The first lawyer seen in the Bight for many years, he was received with respect and curiosity, but with some suspicion. Joseph Lee was his name, and, since he was in a great hurry, he and Christopher came not by coastal boat but by train to Broadport and by chartered launch from there. They stayed in Caplin Bight only three days, investigating the circumstances of the charge and interviewing potential witnesses.

Most of the people, they found, refused to have anything whatever to do with the case. The fishermen, with one voice, declined to appear even as witnesses to Christopher's good character and reputation. This, the lawyer admitted, didn't surprise him, considering the nature of the charge. It was true that one or two of Christopher's older students, including Pleman Pike, would have been willing to appear on his behalf, but Mr. Lee ruled against it.

"We're not going to put a string of teen-age boys on the stand," he said. "Eli will be quite enough."

They interviewed Eli at home, with his father and mother present.

"We are going to call your son as a witness for the defense," Mr. Lee told Elias.

"Ye'll do no sich thing!" Elias declared emphatically.

"I'm afraid, sir, you can't do anything to stop it," the lawyer told him politely but firmly. "If you try to prevent the young man's appearance as a voluntary witness then we shall simply issue a summons and have him called anyway. This, as I suppose you realize, is a serious case, which, if badly handled, could result in a prison term for Mr. Simms."

"No more'n the bla'guard desarves!" Elias exploded. "In fact, if I had me way 'e'd get a good deal more."

"The court will decide that," Mr. Lee said suavely, "and, if necessary, the court will order Eli to appear as my witness."

Elias gave way. "Then I'll be there too," he said. "Not as a witness, mind ye, but to see that ye don't trap me son into any worse trouble than 'e be in already."

"You need have no fear for your son, sir," the lawyer assured him. "He is not accused of anything, and in fact couldn't be accused, legally, in a case of this kind. It is settled, then? You'll let him appear as a voluntary witness?"

"Ay," Elias agreed grudgingly. "Have to, I s'pose, since ye say the law can take 'im anyway."

Later that evening, at the Simms home, they began to sketch out for Eli the direction they thought the trial would take.

"What we want you to do," said the lawyer, "is to testify to Mr. Simms's good character, and the honesty and innocence of his relations with you. We can build the strongest sort of defense, I should judge, by putting on the witness stand the victim he is supposed to have seduced. I wouldn't dream of allowing you to testify if I wasn't firmly convinced that he is innocent of the charge. But if you go on the stand and explain the real nature of your relations with Mr. Simms, and if your story stands up under cross-examination, I don't see how a jury can help believing you. The most important part of your testimony may well be under cross-examination. That's when the prosecuting lawyer questions you. We are trusting you not to lose your head, and not to allow the Crown to break down your story or make you contradict yourself."

"What will you want me to say?" Eli asked.

"Just tell the truth, exactly," Mr. Lee said. "Answer only the questions that are put to you, in as simple and straightforward a manner as you can, never elaborating unless you are asked to do so.

"When the Crown prosecutor examines you he may try to trip you up and make you contradict yourself, or he may simply try to get you to elaborate on your story, hoping that you may be concealing certain damaging facts. He will be a smart and experienced lawyer, and you must think carefully before answering him. You must not allow him to hurry you, and you must not answer anything off the cuff, without thinking about it first. Tell him the strict truth and say nothing on your own—just answer his questions as simply and truthfully as you can."

"What other witnesses are you going to call?" Eli asked.

"Mr. Simms himself, and a Doctor Altonberg, a psychiatrist, an expert in mental and nervous diseases, who has interviewed Mr. Simms at length and believes that he would be quite incapable of committing the crime with which he is charged. This will be a new sort of evidence in a trial of this kind, and the Crown will try to have it ruled out, I expect, but we are hoping to get it in, just the same. If the court accepts it we'll be setting a precedent, but whether they do or not we'll try to see to it that the jury hears the doctor's opinion."

"What about Virginia?" Eli asked.

"You mean, about calling Miss Marks as a witness?"

"Yes."

"She has volunteered to appear," the lawyer said, "but I can't really see that there would be much point in calling her. She says that she would be willing to swear that Mr. Simms made love to her, and that they were to have been married. I'm afraid this might do more harm than good. It would have no real bearing on the case, except perhaps to prejudice some members of the jury against Mr. Simms. You see, there is abundant medical evidence that some homosexuals are fully potent with women, and the Crown would certainly make a point of this— Ah—you understand the terms I am using?"

Eli assured him that he did.

"Besides," Christopher interjected, "I'm against asking Virginia to go through the ordeal of appearing at the trial. There is a chance, you know, that we may be able to prove perjury against her father."

"Yes," the lawyer agreed, "Mr. Marks gave false evidence at the preliminary inquiry—evidence that I rather think he knows is false—and he is apparently willing to give more of it at the trial. I intend to try to show that he is lying on the stand. If I succeed in doing so, he might be arrested right there in the courtroom and tried for perjury."

"What sort of false evidence did he give?" Eli asked.

"His story," the lawyer said, "is not only that he saw you and Mr. Simms coming down from the mountain on the evening McKim swears he caught you in an unnatural act, as he puts it, but, further, that he saw you at other times and places in indecent situations." He held up his hand as Eli started to interject. He was smiling. "Yes, I know all this lying must sound shocking to you, but lying in court under oath is a lot commoner than you imagine. What I am hoping is that, given enough scope and encouraged to elaborate upon it, Mr. Marks's fable may develop contradictions that will help me to tear it down before judge and jury. Few people can make an outright lie so watertight that it will stand up to prolonged cross-examination.

"You see, we can perhaps convince the court that John McKim is honestly mistaken—that in his religious zeal and his Puritan horror he misinterpreted what he saw. Nothing could be more natural. Indeed, I feel that some such thing must really have happened. He was probably carried away by his shock at seeing a couple of undraped bodies, leaped to the conclusion that he was witnessing a sin against nature, and then built his suspicions into a dead certainty."

"I think he was determined to get Christopher long before that," said Eli.

"Yes, I'm certain of it," Mr. Lee agreed. "Mr. Simms represented a threat to his power here. All the more reason for believing that he was deceived. In any case, we could hardly make out a minister of the Gospel—even one of an extreme fundamentalist sect—to be a liar and a perjurer. But there can be no question about such misinterpretation with Solomon Marks. It is true that, being a merchant, he would be considered by the typical juror to be almost beyond reproach. But merchants occasionally turn out to be rogues, and some of them have gone to jail before this. I think we are going to have to paint him as a complete scoundrel, willing to go to almost any length to try to stop Mr. Simms's marriage to his daughter."

Suddenly Eli was struck by an appalling thought: perhaps he owed it to Christopher to reveal his own relations with Brother John. Might not this be just what was needed to cement together the pieces of the case for the defense? But almost as soon as the thought occurred to him he knew that he wasn't going to be able to follow through with it. Every habit of thought and speech that had been bred into him from the cradle onward recoiled and rebelled at the impossible confession.

Speak! his inner voices commanded. This is the time to tell it! Tell it now!

But he hung back for a bare instant, and in that instant was lost. An overpowering wave of shame and censorship and cowardice rose up inside him and constricted his throat so that he felt almost as if he were choking. He got so far as to open his mouth, but literally could not force the words out. And then other arguments came crowding in upon his mind. Perhaps such a confession would not really be needed after all. Mr. Lee thought he could prove Brother John honestly mistaken—maybe that would be the best line of defense? Suppose he confessed that he had committed unspeakable acts with the preacher, who would then believe him when he said that he was innocent of the same acts with others? Yet all the time he knew, with another part of his mind, that Brother John was Christopher's chief accuser and that a word from himself might be all that was needed to strike this accuser down. The emotional turmoil of the conflict was almost unbearable.

"What's wrong with you, Eli?" Christopher asked, seeing the violence of the passion that was shaking the boy. But Eli couldn't face him, as he had not been able to face Virginia on a lesser issue. Torn asunder by a feeling close to despair, he stumbled to his feet. "I—I'm afraid I'm not well—" he managed to say, then almost ran from the room and into the night air.

"It's been pretty hard on him, you know," he heard Christopher telling the lawyer as he left.

He walked among the balsam firs and let them talk to him, and heard the far-off grinding of the surf, but neither the sea nor the forest spoke peace to his soul. None of the old simplicities remained. The immemorial landmarks had been removed and he wandered in a formless country, near the edge of an abyss.

But above him the stars still marched, and as he walked the small sounds of the night came out around him. Above him stood the vastness of the galaxy, and the faint smudges of light that men were just beginning to guess must mark the nearby parts of a limitless universe beyond galactic borders. And he was central and alive in the murmuring world of small things and in the vast world of unimaginable silence that stretched outward and backward toward the moment of creation.

He walked a long time, and stopped beside the vocal waters of the stream. There he drank from a night-filled pool and watched the spears of the spruces, black against the wash of starlight. The short night notes of thrushes, awakened by his passage, spoke out of sleep. A small animal, prowling, rustled softly through the kalmia bush that overhung the water. Why, in this world where all things seem at home, is man alone an alien in his own house? He walked on, and came to his father's gate, and crept into the doorway and silently into bed.

Then the voice of Elias cut through his sickness. And the dawn had come, with its renewal of pain.

CHAPTER NINETEEN

❦ ❧

Summoned by telegram, they went up to St. John's on the coast boat in the hot days of August. They went together—the just and the unjust—Eli, Elias, Solomon Marks, and Brother John, with Sister Leah, who wished to be present at her husband's day in court and to profit from the spectacle of sin receiving its due reward.

Of all the company, only Eli kept to himself, speaking not at all to the McKims or to the merchant. In fact he spent most of his time on the bridge or in the chart room, where he found that the captain, a short, square but nevertheless intense man with a broad red face under his dark blue and gold braid, was delighted to have a young passenger with a keen interest in the techniques of coastal navigation.

No one in Caplin Bight, so far as Eli knew, had ever owned a detailed chart of the coast. Even Mr. Markady seemed to have only the general chart of Newfoundland with its ocean approaches. But this coastal ship was equipped with very large-scale charts that Eli found fascinating, as he did also the job of keeping track of the ship's position, laying off courses, and figuring distances from the log.

The captain allowed him to calculate the course to each port of call, and the likely routes through the channels, finally explaining why the ship would use one particular route rather than another—a choice not always dictated by distance alone, but sometimes influenced by tides and currents. The old man even began teaching the boy to "shoot the sun" at noon, though he explained that doing this was as much a matter of practice as theory, accuracy being a knack that took some time to acquire. In fact during that trip Eli never seemed to be able to get the sun within half a degree of its true position.

"Thirty miles off course!" the captain would growl. "Boy, ye'd have us on the rocks for sure! Why, accordin' to your figurin' we're just about on top of that mountain there to the sowthe!" And he would point out to Eli the place on the chart with the latitude and longitude that he had figured for the ship's position.

The captain knew, of course, why the boy was going to St. John's, just as he knew the business of all the other passengers on his ship—and that of most other people in the ports to which he sailed, for that matter. But he was far too tactful to mention the coming trial. He invited Eli to eat at his table—a courtesy that, through some oversight or other, he neglected to extend to the merchant or the preacher— gave him the run of the ship, and did as much as anyone could to help him forget the grim errand on which he was traveling. The nearest the captain came to mentioning the trial was when they parted on the bridge, after the ship had docked in St. John's.

"A pity it is ye can't spend the summer on board," he told the boy. "'Tis a seaman I'd make of ye, for sure. 'Twas a real pleasure having your company, and if ever ye should happen to want a job in the coastal service I'd be delighted to put in a word with me employers. But I'll be seeing ye on the return voyage, no doubt—under happier circumstances, I hope."

"I hope so too, sir," Eli said. "And thank you very much for being so kind."

"Not to mention it," said the captain, waving him down the companionway to the deck.

The day of the trial came, as all things do, in the fullness of time.

They were summoned to the century-old courthouse in downtown St. John's with its turrets and towers and high, narrow windows, which looked like something designed for defense by crossbowmen against the attacks of robber barons. It was a castle out of some Germanic story, except that, instead of the Rhine flowing past its portcullis, there was the noisy flow of traffic along Water Street and the screaming of gulls above the docks and the turgid waters of the harbor, just across the road.

Inside, all was dust and darkness, currents of air charged with decay moving sluggishly between the ranks of the cruel mahogany furniture, blackened with age and ugly with Victorian carving. Dim light fell through high, dusty windows, making beams like paths that slanted down through the impure atmosphere—three-dimensional roads where the motes danced.

"The King versus Christopher Simms" was the first case on the calendar, set down for Courtroom Number One with the chief justice presiding.

But since the matter at hand was considered too shocking for the public ear, the trial had been ordered to be held *in camera*. Nevertheless, a limited number of members of the press had been admitted under special privilege with the understanding that anything they reported must be in the most generalized terms, and inoffensive to public taste.

The morning papers had mentioned the case as that of "a teacher from a northern outport, charged with gross indecency involving a sixteen-year-old fisherman." The slight inaccuracy with respect to Eli's age did not matter. The item achieved its purpose: to tickle the public imagination without publishing anything that would seem improper to the narrow code of the day.

The wizened, round-faced old judge, wearing robes and circular gold-rimmed spectacles under his shining bald pate, paced slowly into court, preceded by the official crier. Present also was a collection of judges, magistrates, and lawyers not connected with the case. But only selected members of the public were admitted, so as to surround the trial, like other cases involving sex crimes, with an aura of mystery that made it seem, to the outside observer, even more monstrous than in fact it was.

By law every Newfoundland juror had to be a land-owner—therefore, in essence, those from whom the jury was selected all belonged to a single class. Mr. Lee clearly regarded this as a handicap for the defense, and tried to offset it by using his rights of pre-emptory and special challenge to weed out whatever fundamentalists he had discovered—thus insuring that there would be no religious prejudice against his client.

The trial began with the reading of the indictment: "That the said Christopher Simms did, on the fifth day of June last past, at the settlement of Caplin Bight, in the Dominion of Newfoundland, and at divers other times in and about the said place, feloniously seduce one Eli Pallisher, a male child of the age of fifteen years, and him the said Christopher Simms then and there wickedly, unlawfully, and feloniously did carnally know, contrary to nature and to the statutes of the said Dominion, and against the peace of our Sovereign Lord the King."

The Crown prosecutor was a Department of Justice lawyer named Biggs—a sandy-haired, lean man, with remarkably protruding nose and teeth and a meticulous, academic air. In his opening statement he went much further than the words of the indictment, expatiating at length upon the wickedness of the "sin of Sodom," as he called it, and upon the disgust and loathing that it must arouse in the hearts of all decent people. He called Christopher's alleged crime the darkest in the black calendar of vice.

Then he offered to introduce a sworn statement, made upon oath by one Jehu Gilmore, a fisherman of Caplin Bight, deposed at Lattice Harbor before a magistrate. It was a list of three dates with descriptions of compromising events that Jehu claimed to have witnessed at the Cove.

Mr. Lee promptly objected to this statement's being received unless Jehu Gilmore should be called to be cross-examined upon it, and proposed that the trial be postponed until this could be done. The judge ruled in his favor, and the Crown, without argument, offered to withdraw the statement. To this, also, Mr. Lee objected, but without success. The statement was withdrawn, and the jury instructed to ignore it.

Mr. Biggs then called his first witness. Brother John, looming impressively over the stand, identified himself as a minister of the Gospel serving the Caplin Bight charge, described his growing suspicions as Christopher Simms lured the young people of the settlement out of his church, and then told, under the careful questioning of the Crown, how he had found the defendant in the clearing on the mountain, naked, with the boy Eli in his embrace.

"And what were they doing?" Mr. Biggs asked.

"They was engaged in the act o' sodomy," he replied.

"And then what happened?"

"They jumped apart when they heered me approach, an' the prisoner jumped up an' threatened me, an' used violence."

"How much violence?"

"He struck me an' knocked me down."

"Did you strike back?"

Brother John drew himself up. "No," he said. "I be the servant o' the Lord, bound, as He commands, to turn the other cheek. 'Tis not fittin' that I lift me hand against any man, even in self-defense."

"And what threats did the prisoner use?"

"He said 'e'd—these be 'e's exact words—break me hooked nose so it'd never be straight again."

The answer provoked laughter—subdued, as befitted the professional status of the spectators—and the judge tapped gently for order.

There was more of the same sort of thing before Mr. Biggs turned the witness over to Mr. Lee.

Mr. Lee began slowly, and very deferentially, asking the pastor to describe in more detail the scene that he had witnessed on the hill.

Brother John generalized.

"But this 'act of sodomy,' as you call it," Mr. Lee insisted. "Please tell the court exactly what you saw—what they were doing, that is."

Brother John faltered. He was obviously embarrassed by the question. He was not a natural liar or fabricator. Nevertheless, he tried to rise to the occasion. "They was—embracin'—in an indecent way—ye know—like man an' wife!"

"Describe their positions exactly," Mr. Lee insisted firmly.

Brother John blushed. "They was—lyin' on the ground," he said, "with the prisoner on top—as ye might expect."

"And, the boy was—how?" Mr. Lee demanded. "Describe his position."

Brother John thought for a moment. "Face up," he said. " 'Twas he looked an' saw me first."

"Not face down," Mr. Lee insisted.

"No, sir," Brother John said.

Mr. Lee paused for a moment, consulted his notes. "Now, about the alleged assault the defendant made upon you. Did you threaten him in any way?"

"Most sartainly not!"

"Did you threaten the boy?"

"No, sir."

"Think a minute. Did you order the boy to go with you, and start toward him in a threatening manner?"

"I admonished 'im, as was me Christian duty, not to do the horrible thing 'e were doin', an' maybe I stepped for-'ard to plead with 'im."

"Did you raise your hand?"

"I don't remember."

"And it was then Mr. Simms pushed you?"

"Yes, maybe so."

The dialogue went on a long time, Brother John's story

being softened and modified, but essentially left intact. Mr. Lee managed, however, to convey the idea that the minister might have been mistaken, in his horror at the scene, about what Eli and Christopher were actually doing when he found them on the mountain. As he turned Brother John back to the Crown, Mr. Lee seemed well satisfied with the result.

Solomon Marks then told how he had seen them, descending together from the hill path, "Linked arm in arm like a pair o' lovers, long past the hour when Brother John McKim had left."

How did he know when McKim had left?

Because the pastor had gone to him at once, as the chief elder of the church, to discuss what steps ought to be taken in the matter.

Then he told how Christopher and Eli were often together in the otherwise empty schoolhouse long past closing time. He knew of this because the school was his special business, he being chairman of the school board.

He told how Eli was a constant visitor at the Simms house, staying half through the night.

Did he have personal knowledge of this?

Yes, for he was often out to receive freight consignments when the coastal boat arrived in the hours before dawn, and on two such occasions he had seen the boy come down the road from the Simms farm at two or three A.M. Besides, it was common knowledge. Everyone knew about it.

Last, Solomon Marks produced to be what seemed to be pure fabrication. He told how he had seen the teacher and the boy together behind his freight shed, late at night, "Indecently exposed and in a shameless embrace."

Mr. Lee spent fully half an hour trying to break down this damning story. But the merchant either believed it, or had it too well rehearsed. It was as though it had actually happened—though perhaps all in his head—so that he could now recall every detail with absolute perfection.

Finally the defense lawyer abandoned the scene behind the shed, rather worse off than if he had ignored it altogether.

"You have a daughter, Mr. Marks?" he asked.

"Yes, sir. Name of Virginia."

"She and Mr. Simms spent a lot of time together, did they not?"

"Well," Solomon Marks temporized, "not what ye'd call a lot. They gadded about some."

"Isn't it a fact that they planned to get married?"

"Not to me knowledge," Solomon Marks declared. Then, at the memory, his wrath got the better of him. "No, sir!" he shook his head with conviction. "They said nought to me about marryin', and I'd've moved heaven an' earth to stop 'em if they had!"

"Thank you," Mr. Lee said suavely. "That is what we wanted to know." He smiled at the jury, waved the witness off the stand, and the court recessed.

"Things aren't as bad as they might be," he told Eli during the recess. "True, we didn't manage to prove Marks a perjurer, though I'm convinced now, more than ever, that he is. But we shook McKim's story pretty badly and showed that Marks might have had a strong motive to injure Mr. Simms. The jury will be ready to see a new interpretation to all the evidence when you go on the stand."

When court reconvened Mr. Lee made a brief statement, saying he would show that the Crown's case consisted of misconceptions built upon rumor and prejudice. Then he called Christopher.

Apparently unworried, and dressed conservatively in gray sharkskin, the teacher looked as nearly as possible like a member of the middle-middle class—a junior of one of the better families of the jurors' social circle. Mr. Lee's first questions tended to confirm this impression—that he was a university graduate, and son of a retired magistrate who was the biggest landowner in Caplin Bight.

"You worked away from home for a number of years," Mr. Lee said. "What led you to return?"

"My father requested it because the school had been without a regular teacher for two years, and had actually been closed all one winter."

"It was a very small school, was it not?"

"One room."

"You had taught before?"

"Yes—first as a grade teacher, then as vice-principal for a year in a six-room school in St. John's."

"You resigned from the larger school because you felt you were needed in your home town?"

"Yes, and also because my father requested it."

"When do you recall first meeting Eli Pallisher?"

"On the day of my arrival. He was on intimate terms with Mr. Peter Simms, my father, who had mentioned him in letters to me as a brilliant youngster with the most promising prospects, provided he got proper instruction. They were together when the boat docked, and the boy helped me with my luggage."

"Describe your relations with the boy."

"They were very close, almost from the beginning. Aside from my father and Miss Marks, he was the only intellectual companion—perhaps I should say intellectual equal—whom I found in the settlement. We soon discovered that many of our tastes were similar and that we could share the private debate that most literate people seem to enjoy."

"Your relations were entirely intellectual?"

"Oh, no! We developed a deep emotional attachment. Before my arrival my father had already accepted Eli almost as a son. To me he was like a younger brother, companion and friend for whom I had the deepest affection and the highest hopes."

"What about your relations with your other pupils?"

"I had no trouble with any of the children. They worked hard and steadily. With one exception I never had to punish them."

"Did you have the same sort of—er—intimate relations with the others as with Eli Pallisher?"

"If you mean did I love them, yes, I did. And they knew it, and trusted me, and worked hard because of it. But none of the others had the brilliance of mind and spirit that I found in Eli, or the same emotional responsiveness."

"You and the boy spent a great deal of time together."

"Not as much as I would have wished, but all that I could spare from my work and my other friends."

"You mentioned a Miss Marks."

"Yes, my fiancée. We were to have been married two days after I was arrested. All the arrangements had been made. She is the daughter of the Mr. Marks who testified here this morning."

"How did her father feel about your alliance?"

"He tried to break it up, with threats and intimidation. And he forbade me to enter his house."

"Now," said Mr. Lee, "I believe that nearly all the people of Caplin Bight belong to a certain rather odd religion—the Church of—ah"—he paused, consulted a slip of paper—"the Church of the Firstborn. Is that not so?"

"Everyone in Caplin Bight belongs to it," Christopher said, "except for my father and me and Mr. Joshua Markady and his family."

"Would this explain the objections to your marriage with Miss Marks?"

"Mainly, I think. Virginia's father is the chief elder of the church."

"You yourself refused to join?"

"'Refused' is hardly the word. I wasn't asked. But in any case I would have considered joining such a sect a piece of pure hypocrisy."

"Now, sir," said Mr. Lee, "we will take a look at some of the evidence produced here this morning. You say you spent a lot of time with Eli Pallisher. What did you do besides talking about books?"

"All the things that young men do in an outport—we fished, hunted, swam, went sailing—"

"You recall the day Pastor McKim found you together on the hill?"

Christopher smiled crookedly. "How could I ever forget?"

"Will you describe it, please?"

"It was one of the first days of summer. A beautiful afternoon. We were both feeling tired and tense, preparing for the examinations that were due in a couple of weeks. After school we climbed the hill, seeking relaxation. We decided to take a swim in the brook. Afterward we sat in the clearing, and I asked him if he would like to wrestle me."

"Was this the first time that you had been undressed in each other's presence?"

"Heavens, no! Almost every day in summer we went swimming from the beach at the Cove, where all the youngsters—boys, that is—swim without clothes."

"So you saw nothing unusual about undressing together?"

"Of course not."

"Now this—er—trial of strength. You were wrestling when Mr. McKim came into the clearing?"

"Not seriously," said Christopher. "I had thrown Eli, and pinned him, and at that point I had him on the ground, sort of shaking him in fun, if I remember."

"There was no—ah—sexual feeling between you and the boy at all, was there?" Mr. Lee asked.

"I suppose all deep emotion has some sexual content," Christopher said. "In that sense my love for Eli, and his for me, could be called a sexual relationship. But neither of us ever made any kind of physical advance to the other. Nor did we ever attempt to perform any kind of sex act together."

"What about the evidence given by Mr. Marks?" the lawyer asked.

"It may be true that he saw us often together, sometimes late into the night, for Eli spent many night hours in my father's library. But of course Mr. Marks's interpretation of what he saw was completely wrong. I'm afraid he is one of those people who is bound to see something evil in anything pleasant and beautiful. And of course he was suspicious and mistrustful of me because of Virginia."

"But what about the night he says he saw you behind his shed?"

"I have never been behind Mr. Marks's shed in my life," Christopher said emphatically. "Either he saw someone else and, in the darkness of night, fastened upon me because he hates me so, or else the story is an outright lie."

The questioning continued until Mr. Lee was satisfied that the jury had gained a good insight into Christopher's motives, when he passed him over to the Crown.

Mr. Biggs's first question came like a shot. "Are you a Christian, Mr. Simms?"

"Objection!" came instantly from Mr. Lee.

"Sustained," said the judge.

"But, my lord," Mr. Biggs exclaimed, "my learned friend has already questioned the prisoner about religion."

"That," said the judge crisply, "was to establish that Mr. Simms did not belong to the same faith as the majority of the people in Caplin Bight. Beyond that, his religious beliefs are irrelevant. Objection sustained."

Nevertheless, Mr. Biggs had made his point—perhaps more sharply than if Christopher had been allowed to answer. The churchgoing landowners in the jury box were now looking at the young man with renewed interest and perhaps a new sort of suspicion.

"Well," said the Crown prosecutor, "Mr. Simms's religious faith—or lack of it—aside, his attitudes toward love—as he calls it—are certainly relevant. Mr. Simms, answer me this . . ."

And he continued for nearly an hour, first making it clear that Christopher regarded love, and the personal relations associated therewith, as a private matter, with which church and state had no business to interfere, then pursuing his relations with the children whom he taught. He kept substituting the word "boys" for children, and Christopher kept correcting him. The subject of "love" was mulled over until it assumed, in the lawyer's mouth, a nasty inflection, and its reappearance became almost sickening, sounding, at last, like something unfit to be mentioned in polite society.

"You wouldn't call this *Christian* love would you, Mr. Simms?"

"Yes," said Christopher, to everyone's surprise, "I would. What I'm talking about is precisely the circumambient compassion taught by Christ—to the denial of one's self-interest."

"But the lover—if you will pardon the expression—gets nothing out of it at all?"

"On the contrary," Christopher said, "the emotional dividends from this sort of investment are enormous."

"Ah," said Mr. Biggs, with a sarcastic inflection. "The emotional dividends. But of course there's no dirty sex mixed up with it? Or am I wrong? Did you admit earlier that there was?"

Christopher leaned forward, his eyes and his voice snapping. "Sex," he said, "is not dirty—except in your mouth, sir."

"You regard it as sacred, perhaps, beyond all human regulation?"

"If a sexual relationship has no love in it," said Christopher, "then it is entirely vicious, and it makes not the slightest difference whether it is blessed by some church or not."

Mr. Biggs drew a long breath. "Yes," he said. "I think the court has perhaps heard enough of your views on free love." He paused. "Now, about this—wrestling match of yours."

He led Christopher all through it again, trying to give it the color that it had received from Brother John. But Christopher stood up to the ordeal without losing his temper or altering his story in the least. Simple and unshakable, it had the ring of truth, even under the slanted questioning of the Crown. By the time he left the stand Mr. Lee looked like a man snuffing the perfume of victory.

The defense lawyer next called Dr. Altonberg, who testified that he had examined the defendant at length without detecting any mental or emotional abnormality. He described tests that ruled out faking, and by which an expert could get a complete picture of the emotional make-up of his subject. He called Christopher "A nervously restless but brilliant man, well balanced, emotionally and intellectually mature."

Mr. Biggs made his expected effort to stop this phase of the doctor's testimony, but the wizened old judge, peering over his gold spectacles in an apologetic manner, disagreed with the prosecutor. "I know that we have not been in the habit of receiving this sort of evidence as touching a case of this kind," he said, "but I have gone into the matter thoroughly, in advance. There is nothing whatever in the law to rule out expert evidence by doctors concerning the emotional condition of a prisoner. The rules affecting a plea of lunacy aside, I feel that it is time we began to recognize, in this court, the new science of psychology, and to make use of it in our deliberations. I propose to give a written decision on this later."

"You will permit me to register a protest against this precedent then, my lord," Mr. Biggs said.

"Oh, certainly. You are entitled to have a formal protest entered in the record."

Mr. Biggs was in an ugly mood by the time the next witness was called. It was late afternoon, and the courtroom was even dimmer than in the morning, when Eli came to the stand for the defense.

Mr. Lee had him repeat the story of his relations with Christopher from the time they first met the summer before, had him tell his version of the encounter on the mountain and deny that he had ever been with the teacher behind Solomon Marks's shed.

"And those nights in the Simms home, which my learned friend regards as so villainous. What did you do there?"

"We read books, often half through the night—history, science, literature—even some philosophy, toward the end."

"And what are your feelings toward Mr. Simms now?"

Eli had thought, long in advance, how he would answer

this question. "Christopher," he said, "is the grandest person I have ever met. I love him the way some people love God."

Mr. Lee turned to the bench and bowed slightly.

"Before learned counsel for the Crown begins to cross-examine, I have a few questions myself," the old judge stated.

Mr. Biggs looked surprised and pleased, and he too bowed slightly.

"Now, boy," said the judge, "you may be quite easy and informal with me. I want you to tell me a little about what you learned from your evenings in the Simms home."

"Well," Eli began, "old Mr. Simms, the magistrate, has a big room filled with books—oh, well over a thousand of them—"

"Indeed!" said the judge. "That would be most unusual, in a small outport."

"Yes, sir, he collected them during his many years as a magistrate."

"What kind of literature did you read?"

"Well," Eli admitted, "I started with what Mr. Simms calls 'modern trifles,' mostly popular novels of the nineteenth century. And then I read Bulfinch's *Mythology,* and some of the English historians—such as Gibbon, you know. Last year I got to the dramatists—Shakespeare, then Marlowe, and then Christopher put me on to some of the Greeks, in English translation."

"Did you form any opinion of the Greek dramatists?"

"Yes, sir," Eli said boldly, "I haven't read all the Greek plays, by any means, but among the few I have read I prefer those of Sophocles."

"Indeed!" said the judge. "The Oedipus cycle, perhaps? Hmm—you did mention philosophy?" He was now leaning forward eagerly.

"Yes, sir. We read and discussed the dialogues of Plato, and then some of the propositions out of Spinoza's *Ethics*—"

"A-ha," the judge broke in, "and how did you find the learned Jew?"

"Most interesting, sir. I liked the mathematical form of argument, in particular. Math has always been my strong point, ever since I did my first sums."

"Yes," said the judge. "Anything else?"

"This spring I read Schopenhauer's *World As Will and Idea.*"

"Huh!" the judge grunted. "A dangerous romantic. You want to be careful of branching off in that direction. Much better to stick to the main line of development."

"Yes, sir, Mr. Simms says so too. He says I must study Kant before I try to go too deeply into the modern sciences."

"Yes indeed," the judge agreed, "quite right—the necessary basis for modern thought. You are—fifteen, did you say? And what about your schoolwork?"

"I was away behind because our school was closed so much before Mr. Simms came, but I hope to do grades ten and eleven this year."

"Yes," the judge mused. "Mr. Simms is quite right about you, I'm sure. I too bespeak for you a great future. . . . The law, perhaps? Ahem!" He sighed wistfully. "Mustn't stray from the business in hand, I suppose." He turned to Mr. Biggs, who was standing, fidgeting, a look of pained surprise on his protrusive face. "You may cross-examine, counsel."

"Yes, my lord," said Mr. Biggs in a pained tone of voice. "I must admit that I hardly see the relevancy—"

"No, counsel," the judge interrupted. "No, indeed—though perhaps it tends to show that the boy learned something—but you must allow an old man his moment of diversion on the rare occasions when he finds something of personal interest in one of these sordid trials. . . . Continue, if you please."

Mr. Biggs continued, very put out indeed.

He tried to revive the technique that he had used with Christopher, but it had somehow lost its edge, and he noticed the jury beginning to fidget. He suggested that some of Eli's reading in the Simms library had been "contrary to established beliefs and morals." When Eli insisted that it wasn't, he switched back to Schopenhauer and asked had he read the philosopher's essay on sex—"The one in which he makes fun at the love between men and women."

"He didn't make fun of it," Eli said.

"I asked you a question," the lawyer snapped, "not for your opinion."

"Then you shouldn't volunteer such opinions yourself," Mr. Lee interjected sharply.

The judge tapped his gavel good-naturedly. "Learned counsel must not get into an argument," he said, his eyes still holding their friendly gleam.

Mr. Biggs, with ill-concealed savagery, turned back to Eli and switched his attack once more. "For a person of your age you seem to be unusually familiar with sexual matters," he said. "Where did you learn it?"

"The theoretical part I learned from Christopher and his father," Eli said.

Mr. Biggs leaped into what he thought was an opening. "Ah," he said, "the *theoretical* part! And what about the *practical* part? Where did you learn that?"

Eli drew a deep breath and forced his voice to be steady. "The practical part," he said, "I learned from Brother John McKim, the pastor of the Church of the Firstborn, who testified on this stand this morning."

There was a hush in the court, and out of the hush came the voice of the Crown prosecutor, seeking clarification. He spoke slowly, cautiously. "You mean," he said, "that your pastor gave you instruction in the practical affairs of life—leading toward marriage and so on."

Eli laughed a little unsteadily. "No," he said, "I don't mean that at all." The universe was crashing and spinning inside his head, but his voice was still under conscious control. "I mean I slept with him, more nights than I can count, and we did together the very things of which Christopher Simms is accused." He was breathing unsteadily, he realized, and his heart was pounding frightfully, but the truth was out, in all its horror and all its self-degradation, and the sky might fall where it would.

There was a sharp intake of breath all over the courtroom. Sister Leah, toward whom Eli had been looking as he said this, set her mouth in an even harder line than before and stared at her husband, who half rose, than sank back in his seat, a look of complete incredulity on his handsome face.

The judge again rapped for order—sharply this time, and addressed Eli sternly. "The Reverend Mr. McKim is not on trial," he said. "It is a very serious thing to accuse a man of such a crime, especially under oath, and without corroborative testimony."

"Nevertheless," said Eli, "it is true."

Christopher was staring at Eli with a sharp, penetrating gaze and a look of sudden revelation in his eyes, as though, for him, everything had fallen into place for the first time. Mr. Lee was scribbling furiously on his note pad. Mr. Biggs stared at Eli for a moment, as though making up his mind what to do. Then he turned his back with a shrug, as though the boy were some loathsome reptile that he wished to be rid of.

"I'm finished with you," he said in a tone of withering disgust, and sat down at the counsel table.

Mr. Lee waved Eli off the stand. It was the end of the evidence, and the court recessed until the evening, then met again, under lights, for the summing up by counsel and the judge's address.

The charge delivered by the chief justice to the jury was very nearly a résumé of the case for the defense. He had been impressed with Christopher's testimony, and with his teaching, as reflected in his student. He pointed out the sharp conflict in evidence, that the burden of proof lay with the Crown, and that any doubt should favor the defendant. He referred briefly to the new type of evidence introduced by the doctor, then went on to excuse Eli's "outburst" on the stand. Though he did not direct a verdict, he left no doubt about where his sympathies lay. Then he told the jury to retire, and recessed the court until the verdict should be in.

As they were filing out of the courtroom a messenger touched Eli on the arm and informed him that the judge wished to see him in chambers. He followed the messenger wonderingly to the big, dim, book-lined office with its enormous leather chairs, where the chief justice sat alone, waving him toward one of the overstuffed thrones near his mahogany desk.

"Sit down, my boy," he said. "The jury will take about half an hour, I expect, and you need have no doubt about their verdict. It will be 'not guilty.' I want to talk with you a little more about your studies, if you would be so kind—and Mr. Peter Simms. We were friends once, you know, though I couldn't say it in court. I knew him well when he was a magistrate on circuit. A fine man, a student. . . . Perhaps you could tell me a little about him, since his retirement?"

So they sat and talked until the half hour was long gone by. The judge ordered coffee and sandwiches, and they ate and talked some more. Two hours had passed, and the time was near midnight before the court messenger returned to say that the jury had reached a verdict.

A few moments later they sat and heard it: "Guilty as charged."

There was a feeling of shock among the professional spectators, and the judge stared at the jury foreman incredulously, taking no pains to hide his displeasure. "I heard aright?" he snapped. "Your verdict is 'guilty as charged?'"

"It is, my lord," said the foreman, a note of defiance creeping into his voice.

The judge sighed deeply. "Christopher Simms," he said, "stand, please. It is my painful duty to pass sentence upon you. Is there anything you wish to say?"

Christopher was silent for a moment, then spoke slowly, thoughtfully. "Just this, my lord," he said. "While I still have the opportunity, I wish to thank you for the way you have conducted this trial, and the witnesses who appeared for

me, for the fine manner in which they acquitted themselves.
I wish also to reaffirm my innocence. . . . The jury, I suppose, acted from honest prejudice, my accusers from pure
malice. I do not even offer them forgiveness. No gesture of
mine could do them any good.

"Time will show how wrong they are, and how impossible is their self-appointed task of suppressing the flame of
love and freedom in the human soul. It has been a long
time growing, and it never can be put out. Even though I
stand here waiting to be sentenced, I don't feel sorry for
myself. I feel sorry for them, and for the gentlemen of the
jury."

The old judge spoke humbly, apologetically. "I suppose,"
he said, "there are times when every judge feels like Pontius
Pilate. I am sorry to have to impose this sentence, but I
have no choice. It is the minimum that the law allows. No
doubt the case will be appealed," he said, looking toward
Mr. Lee.

"I sentence you, Christopher Simms, to serve two years at
hard labor in His Majesty's penitentiary in this city. I can
mitigate the sentence only a little. I direct that it shall be
served from the date of the prisoner's arrest. This sitting of
the court is adjourned." And he arose without waiting for
formalities and strode off toward his chambers.

Two policemen came for Christopher. There were a few
jeers and catcalls from the loafers who had assembled in the
hall outside the courtroom, but the disturbance was quelled
by the police, who set about the task of clearing the building
for the night. He was taken out a side door to the waiting
police van. He walked proudly, his head high, his step light.
And as he went he looked at Eli and smiled.

CHAPTER TWENTY

It was berry-picking time again, and the land was bright with sunshine and dark with hate.

Eli had learned hatred—not a child's hatred, but the deep, bitter, lasting hatred of a man—earlier than should be, for he would be sixteen that winter, and though he was man-size, his heart still held much of the simplicity of childhood, along with vast depths of wrath and despair.

He returned to Caplin Bight after the trial in a sort of numb stupor, nominally in his father's care, though already he had made up his mind that his relations with his family and with Brother John and the Church of the Firstborn must come to a sudden and immediate end. There could be no more pretense, no more sham, no more lying.

"A man cannot live one way and believe another," Christopher had said when they first met, and now, for Eli, it had worked out that way. A child might do it, or a fool—not a man.

The day they arrived on board the coast boat, chased into harbor by a mountainous following sea, and walked down the gang-plank amid the stares of the assembled people was as difficult for the boy as the day Christopher had walked out of the courtroom into prison. Nobody said anything. They just looked. Here were the righteous and the unrighteous, the victors and the vanquished, returning together, to be judged anew, rewarded and punished afresh, world without end. Or so the good people of the ecclesia supposed.

Brother John and Sister Leah, disembarking, were met by the church elders and the elders' wives, who murmured welcomes and moved off with them in a buzz of rumor. Many people nodded to Elias, and a whole group clustered around the merchant. But Eli was ignored. Though no full account of the closed trial had been published, it seemed that some faint hint of his unspeakable accusation against the pastor must somehow have gone ahead and made him an outcast. Of the few who had been in court only Sister Leah, apparently, believed him.

But as they turned into the street from the government wharf they met Virginia Marks, who had come, Eli was sure, on purpose to see him—certainly not to meet her returning father.

"Hello, Eli," she said. "Welcome home."

"Hello, Virginia. Christopher sends you his love."

This simple exchange, charged with feeling, lit a spark of anger in Eli's father. "Ye are not to talk to that girl, Eli," he said.

"But you can hardly stop me talking to *him*," Virginia retorted, tossing her black hair defiantly. "I'll see you later, Eli, when your father isn't around. I want you to tell me all about the trial."

Eli said nothing in reply but walked home with his father in silence, all the tears in the world pent up inside him.

His mother greeted him gently and distantly, but he was too chilled and heartbroken to make more than a perfunctory response to her greeting. Timmy said a timid "Hello," but regarded his big brother owlishly, his eyes following Eli about as though he were some strange creature he had never seen before. The child's companions had been talking to him, Eli supposed, asking him questions that he couldn't answer, repeating stories of Eli's intercourse with the devil.

And the evening being upon them the family sat together and broke the bread of affliction, but for the first time in Eli's memory he was unable to eat at his father's table.

It was prayer-meeting night, and they were all being hustled about by Martha, preparing for the midweek service, when Eli decided that this was to be his moment of truth. He felt sure that if he allowed himself to be taken to that service he would never make a stand on his own behalf again, but betray Christopher and himself, and all the things the teacher had worked for, and all the things in which he so passionately believed, whenever they might be challenged. Compromise, he decided, must stop short of betrayal, for one betrayal could only lead on to another, until life had lost its meaning and become a mere trap for the soul.

"I'll not go," he said.

There was a dead silence while the three members of his family took a long look at him.

"Ye'll—what?" Elias asked quietly.

"I'll not go to the prayer meeting. I don't believe in the God you worship and I won't pretend to pray to Him."

His mother, he noted, had turned white. Elias sat down slowly. He looked at Eli without speaking for a long time. Then: "Eli," he said, "if ye were a year or two younger I'd thrash the daylights out of ye."

This was exactly the sort of remark that Eli needed to put steel into his resolution. His heartbeat had picked up, and his breath was coming quickly, like that of a wild animal getting ready for mortal combat. "Try it," he bit out at his father. "Don't let my age stop you. Go ahead and thrash me if you think you can do it. But I warn you, I'll do my best to kill you."

He saw his father's jaw and hands clench, but Elias controlled himself. Then there was another long silence, broken when Martha got her breath back and could trust herself to speak. "Eli," she said, "ye be overwrought. P'raps 'tis best ye stay home tonight, son. Elias, ye leave 'un be, now! 'E been through a sight o' trouble, an' 'e bain't accountable. 'E'll think better o' this tomorrow. I'll stay home with ye, son, if ye've a mind?"

"Go on to the meeting," Eli said tensely. "Nothing makes any difference—nothing you can say or do. It's all been done."

"Maybe yer mother be right," Elias temporized. "Ye been through a lot, 'tis true. But I'll not shelter a blasphemer under me roof, ye understand. Ye can think it over fer tonight—ye needn't go to the meetin'—an' we'll talk of it tomorrow."

"All the talking's been done too," Eli said, much calmer now. "There's nothing more to talk about. I should have had this out with you at least a year ago, as Virginia told me. I'm never going to darken the door of that damned church of yours again so long as I live."

This was too much for Elias. He rose, started toward the boy, fury in his eyes. But Eli grabbed the heavy iron poker with its solid brass handle from the hob of the stove, reversed it, and raised it to strike, backing up a step as he did so. The weapon was quite capable of killing any man at a single blow. Elias recoiled, and Martha jumped between them.

"Leave be, Elias!" she screamed. "Eli, *ye sit down now!*" She gave him a gentle push. "Lord, Lord! Oh, what have I done to have me husband an' me son fightin' beside me hearth like a pair o' murderers?" She began to sob.

Eli kept his grip on the poker, feeling quite calm again. "Stop blubbering, Mother," he said. "All Father has to do is keep his temper and nothing will happen. I said if he laid a hand on me I'd kill him, and so I will. If he touches me I'll smash his head with no more thought about it than if he was a seal on the whelping ice." After a pause: "I'm leaving your house," he said.

"If ye do," said Elias, "ye'll not come back."

"No," said Eli, almost abstractedly, "I'd not mean to."

Martha was now crying uncontrollably, and Timmy too was sniffling, half in grief, half in fright. Eli walked to the wall and took down his gun, went to the drawer in the dresser and pocketed his box of shells. Then he went to the hall for his coat.

"Eli, come back!" his mother wailed in anguish. "Don't ye see?—yer father means it! He'll lock ye from the door!"

"Yes, Mother," said Eli, "Father means it. And I mean it too."

"Oh, son—" Martha began to moan.

But Eli's heart was already dead in his breast. It could not be touched further. He walked out the door and closed it very gently, then walked away into the storm. He rounded the harbor through the rising wind with the thunder of surf in his ears, not meeting a soul on the road. Then he climbed the rough path to the Point. As he opened the door into the Markady kitchen both Joshua and Anne Markady rose to meet him.

"How are ye, lad?" the old captain asked. "We've been expectin' ye. Mother—take Eli's coat."

Mrs. Markady, looking, Eli thought, more than ever like a small slip of a girl, somehow prematurely aged, came forward and laid a hand on his arm. She had never been a woman of many words, but her eyes were warm and full of kindness. "Welcome home, Eli," she said. "There's a bed ready fer ye."

"Ye see, lad," explained Mr. Markady, seeing Eli's look of surprise, "we talked about it, Anne and myself, an' we concluded that there was only one thing that ye could do."

"Ye've a home here, Eli," Mrs. Markady said, "so long as 'tis needed."

"Thanks," the boy murmured. "Thanks."

"Have ye eaten, lad?"

"No—but I don't think I could, either. . . . Would you mind if I just left my things here and went out and walked for a little while?"

"'Tis not a good night to be walkin', lad, but we understand how it is with ye. Go ahead if ye've a mind. Take as long as ye wish. We'll wait up if ye are not home early."

So Eli walked out into the gusty rain and felt his way blindly down toward the shore. He crossed the bridge over the mill creek in the Bottom and came to the waterfront, where the spray blew in stinging sheets over the short log breastwork that skirted the water between the creek and his father's stage. Rain and salt spray came blowing together in level gusts of violence, drowning the night and wedding into a single pattern of chaos the earth and the sea and the sky.

As he walked he thought a long while about Christopher and the curious fact that he had not seemed to be hurt when he was convicted and taken off to prison. Underneath his surface restlessness, Eli realized, the teacher had deep resources of peace that he held inviolate within himself and that the winds of fortune could not ruffle.

I am not like that at all, he decided. When I'm hurt, I want to rail against the world, to fight back, to destroy my enemies, or to die trying.

And as he walked many of the teacher's words came back to him. Some of them were hard sayings—especially much that he had said after his arrest, about not confusing suffering with punishment. He had called it a crude and primitive superstition to believe that when you suffered you were being punished—but that was exactly what Eli had been taught to believe from the day of his birth. And he remembered an earlier, happier time, when Christopher had tried to show him the way to the beginnings of courage. "You've got to be able to go to the end of the world alone."

He pictured Christopher's face in the darkness—the green, catlike eyes, the half-amused set to the mouth, the stubborn jaw; he thought of their carefree days together, and he could feel the tears rising in his throat. He could almost feel the clasp of his friend's strong hands upon his unstrong shoulders as they stood together on the hill and the universe flowed past—and the tears rose into his eyes and overflowed, mingling with the salt spray that wetted his face.

The world was dark. In all his life he had never really

seen black darkness before. And he crept along beside the sea wall with gusts of black storm blowing out of the night, cut off from the world as though it had ceased. Then, as the roar of water rose to fill the fathomless void, a moment of blind panic seized him. This, he thought, must be the way it felt to be suddenly sightless, to face forever the prospect of an empty abyss—falling forever into emptiness—falling, falling and waiting—waiting for the vague terror of death to pounce with icy talons.

Fragments of old passages from the Scriptures that he knew by rote and loved for their beauty and passion slipped across his memory like mocking ghosts out of his childhood.

"They that go down into death, to the sides of the pit . . . unto whom is reserved the blackness of darkness forever.

"All they that see thee shall narrowly look upon thee."

He stopped and lifted his face to the driving rain, with the wind of panic still blowing through his soul. He forced the irrational fear back into the pit of his stomach, and stared unseeing into the storm squalls. This was what King David of Judah had known so many centuries before.

"Thou shalt not be afraid of the terror by night . . . nor of the pestilence that walketh in darkness."

He started walking again, lost forever in the blindness and roar of the storm, wholly absorbed in its will, carried along like a chip in a spring freshet.

He knew that the old stage from which he had fished was on his left—the ancient waterfront fishing room of the family of the Pallishers that he had forsworn—the stage where his father had landed fish, and his grandfather before him, and generations that reached back into the fourth dimension of the darkness. It was as though the stage had become an extension of himself, or he of the generations of which it was a part, as though he could feel it, reaching out through the night, and back through the time of his forebeing, stretching out into the dark, warm waters of his ancestral harbor, into the friendly waters before birth.

"Oh, that thou wouldst hide me in the grave until thy wrath be past, that thou wouldst appoint me a set time, and remember me."

He found by instinct the familiar path where he had walked so often with the quick, instinctive feet of childhood.

"Thou shalt not be afraid . . ."

He groped his way toward the end of the stage, feeling for the mooring post, the chaos of nature rushing past him, the rain stinging like a switch on his face. He looked toward the sky where there were no stars, and toward the sea where there was no light, and felt the whole creation whirl into a vortex around him, with himself sinking, rapidly, inexorably, endlessly, into the center of a pool of emptiness. . . . This, then, was the end—the pit—the bottomless pit, the second death from which there was no returning.

Then there was a star, a single point of light, a tiny focus infinitely far, inside his head. He felt his whole body shaken by a sob from within, as though by a gust of the storm from without, and the tears still rising in his eyes, the ache of all his days and dreams clutching at his throat, and the night of the world pressing down. But suddenly in his soul there was no darkness—no darkness at all.

So Eli rose and retraced his steps through the night.

"I will arise, now, and go unto my father."

But the father he sought was Joshua Markady.

And Mr. Markady met him at the door with a smile. "Ye look better, lad, much better—like a drowned rat, to be sure —but human now."

And Anne Markady joined in, timidly. "Ye should have some tea, Eli, if nothing else—to keep off the pneumonie."

He thanked them and accepted their kindness, and went and changed his clothes, then sat at the ship's table by the wall and had tea, with thick slices of Mrs. Markady's bread and butter, and slabs of cold meat, and pickles.

And as he ate, Mr. Markady said, "Lad, ye must tell me about Christopher, and how it was at the trial. I don't love him as ye do, of course. But I always admired the young man, an' enjoyed talkin' with 'im, an' was nothing short of amazed at the way he had with children—believed he'd go far too. But that's all finished now, I s'pose. . . . Tell me, how was it when he went to prison?"

So they talked about Christopher. It was the first time that Eli had spoken at length to anyone about his love for the teacher. And for the first time he found that he could pour out his heart unhindered, and tell the extent of his grief and the blight of his hopes. And Mr. Markady, who, in his quiet way, also loved this dark, mercurial boy, but had up to this time always dominated their conversations with a sort of dreamy monologue, now listened silently, murmuring just a few words from time to time.

"Yes, lad. I never realized, fully, the depth of affection between ye. Yes, 'twas a great crime, indeed. And he walked out like a prince, ye say? Ah, yes, he would. Aren't ye proud, now?"

Yes, Eli realized, he was proud. Proud of Christopher, and proud of his own love for him—even, in a way, proud of the shame that they had been forced to share. In the midst of all the suffering there was a sort of shining glory that redeemed it out of pure horror and gave it a kind of unearthly beauty, like an aureole of light above crucifixion.

"I'm glad you've told me this," Mr. Markady was saying. "He wouldn't have wanted ye to give way to despair and bitterness, ye know."

"I know," said Eli. "I'll do my best. I can bear up, I think."

"Ye'll have all the help we can give ye, lad," Mr. Markady promised.

At last, worn out physically, and emotionally exhausted, he went to bed in one of the rooms long since left vacant by the growth and dispersal of Mr. Markady's numerous children. But he was not exhausted in the way that invites sleep. He lay restless for a long time, the lamp burning low on the table beside his bed.

Just after the clocks had chimed for two A.M. he heard the storm abate. Then the chaos of the world outside gradually died away into the majestic voice of the surf, rising to dominate the world, like the voice of God speaking across the clash of nations.

Eli lay listening to it, his soul like a coiled spring within him, sleep very far away. And he heard the clocks strike again, and the far-off moaning of an owl in the forest.

The night was growing old when Mr. Markady came into the room and stood looking down at him. "Eli," he said. "Ye can't sleep."

"No," the boy admitted, "I've been lying here just listening to the sounds of the night."

The old captain drew up a chair beside the bed, sat down, and leaned forward. "Lad," he said, "I think I know how it is. . . . If ye haven't done all yer weeping, then maybe ye are not too old to weep in me arms. I had seven sons, ye know, and nigh as many daughters, an' ye are the eighth, an' the only one I've never seen in tears."

And he stretched forth his hand and touched the boy on the cheek, and Eli wept with Mr. Markady's wrinkled hand on his head. And he slept. And in the morning he awoke with a sore heart, but refreshed.

CHAPTER TWENTY-ONE

◈

From the Markadys' big, decklike veranda, which was solidly braced into the sea-worn rocks beneath, you could
view a great sweep of the ocean on all sides, except for that
part cut off by the Caplin Bight peninsula. The morning
after the storm Eli walked out there, dressed only in a pair
of trousers, leaving black tracks across the pearl-gray of the
wet decking, chilling his feet, but feeling, in compensation,
the warm touch of the last sun of August as it rose across the
bay. The morning air, washed clean by the rain and the
spray, tasted like fresh water from a hill stream.

Surf came thundering in over the sunkers, spouting to
high heaven, then rolling on, to crash against the square
black rocks of the Point and dissolve into towering clouds
of spume. Now and then a few splashes came right over
the rails of the veranda, making the boy shiver deliciously
as they struck his bare skin.

Far away to his left—on the port quarter if you thought
of the house as the ship after which it was patterned—he
could see the blue domes of the numberless Offer Islands,
ringed with white on a purple sea, and the misty leads of
the narrow runs that led out the bay toward the far-off
capes and the life-laden waters of the Labrador Current.

On his right—the starboard beam—lay the Head, plumed
in tossing feathers of white. The Cove was invisible from
this position, but the land beyond it could be seen, and the
gap of the Reach that divided Caplin Bight so effectively

from the lands on the hither side of Lattice Harbor. Outside, beyond the point of the Reach, stood Lattice Harbor Island, gray and solid above the sand beaches and sheer cliffs, its feet hidden in a white haze of spindrift. Straight across the bay the land lay upon the horizon, barely visible, a smudge of red-purple under the furnace of the rising sun. The bay itself was ribbed with white-topped rollers streaked with a crosshatching of foam in narrow, parallel bands, as if laid down by a chalk line.

Mr. Markady came out and stood beside Eli, saying nothing, but, like him, absorbing his fill of the morning, and exalted by the splendor of this familiar world which, no matter how often you saw it, seemed like a fresh miracle every day.

And as they stood the eagles came, soaring on motionless wings above the breakers of the Head. They were on their morning patrol from their nest crags far up in the Reach. High in the sky they came, black against the white mare's tails that streaked the vault of blue. And they stopped and wheeled above the spouting sunkers, turning their heads to both sides, searching the foam with their telescopic eyes. The flashing white of their head and tail feathers could be seen as they wheeled against the sky, great wings straight and flat like the arms of crosses in the heavens.

Suddenly one of them dropped and flew in a fast glide along the foot of the cliffs, banking between the spouting pillars of the surf, and dipped and touched the water, and soared aloft again, riding the powerful updraft where the wind hit the cliff face, then pointing into the sky on wings that beat with slow, powerful strokes, the carcass of some dead bird, killed by the storm, clutched in its powerful talons.

"I always admired the eagles, Eli," Mr. Markady said. "I remember 'em when I was a boy, an' they were called 'grepes' hereabouts. There's been a pair of 'em comin' here since before I built this house, an' I see 'em over the sunkers as long as I can remember. Not the same ones, I suppose—

but they look the same. 'Tis as though they'd found that immortality ye was told so much about up in the church. In a manner o' speakin' I suppose ye might say that they *have* found it."

"Mr. Simms says that in this sense all creatures except man are immortal," Eli told him. "He says man is the only creature under the dominion of subjective time."

"I'm easy put out o' me depth be Peter Simms," Mr. Markady remarked, "but in this case I think I see what he means."

These musings were interrupted by Mrs. Markady, coming to the door to call them to breakfast. "Eli!" she exclaimed. "Ye'll catch cold, sure, out in the mornin' chill practically naked! An' no boots either! Boy, ye need a woman's watchful eye on ye."

Eli laughed pleasantly. It was comforting to be fussed over.

"Not that ye don't look handsome like that," she resumed with a sly smile, and with what was, for her, a good deal of daring. "Lord, but I wish I had a daughter about David's age that I could marry off to ye!"

"Hush yer nonsense, Mother," Mr. Markady said kindly. "Ye are too old for such thoughts. What do ye have fer breakfast?"

"Well—seein' this is a kind of homecomin' there's Sunday fare—fish and brewis and scruncheons—and watered roast rounders, which I know ye both have a likin' for. . . ." Then, softly, rather shyly, she added, "Ain't it fine, Josh, havin' a boy in the house again?"

As Eli slipped in through the door he put his arm around her thin shoulders and touched her faded cheek with his lips. She smiled at him out of eyes that were still clear and youthful, and patted his arm. "Yes," she said. "I'm most grateful—really I am."

Eli was indeed fond of fish and brewis—Newfoundland's national dish, consisting of watered salt cod of the amber-colored shore cure, cooked with watered sea biscuits—a tradition that Newfoundland families brought down from the

Royal Navy of the seventeenth and eighteenth centuries. The "scruncheons," tiny cubes of salt fat-back pork fried until they were brown and crisp, were the essential sauce for fish and brewis.

The rounders came smoking from the fireplace—small, cured fish, not split, but dried round, for roasting or broiling. Sometimes rounders were grilled over an open fire, sometimes wrapped in wet paper and laid right on the coals.

They were polishing off their breakfast with toast and jam and a big silver pot of tea, strong and black, when there came a most diffident tap on the door and young Timmy entered, looking embarrassed and rather as though he had been trapped into doing something he'd give his eyeteeth to avoid.

"Morning, ma'am," he said to Anne, "morning, Mr. Markady. Eli, Mother sent me. She says to tell you she'd have come herself, only Father says we're none of us to speak to you. He says ye have gone out to the Evil One like the scapegoat from the Children of Israel, and that we are to leave ye to Satan in the outer darkness."

He was interrupted by Mr. Markady's deep-throated laugh. "That'd make me the devil, I suppose!" He glowered under his white brows at Timmy, who looked shocked, not having thought of this interpretation.

"Oh, no, sir!"

" 'Tis all right, boy," Mr. Markady assured him. "I take it as a compliment, so ye can rest aisy. What'd yer mother send ye for?"

"With this," he said, and placed a parcel on the table. "Some of Eli's things." He swallowed, more embarrassed than ever, and looked down at his toes while he ran through the message in which he had been rehearsed in a rapid monotone. "An' she says to tell ye that she be prayin' fer ye, an' that she have asked Brother John, an' he be prayin' fer ye too, that ye may come back to the Lord, an' to yer family." Timmy, who only reverted to the broader style of dialect in moments of great stress, couldn't remember the rest of it. He faltered, looked up, and stammered out a message of his own. "Eli—I—I wish ye could come back. Can't ye? Mother cries, and Father stamps about, lookin' black. An'—oh, I can't tell ye how miserable it is in the house—" He paused, then added in a very small voice, "An' how lonely I be by meself in the big bed."

"Timmy," said Mrs. Markady gently, "sit down and have some tea." She firmly believed that one way to relieve any child's distress was to feed him.

"Thank ye, ma'am," Timmy said. He was always ready to eat, even when nervous or upset. In fact at such times he seemed to develop a sharper appetite than ever. He now began to stuff himself on bread and jam and tea while Eli opened the package he had brought, revealing Aunt Esther's gold watch, some socks and handkerchiefs, a couple of books that had been given to him by Peter and Christopher Simms, and a tiny, cheap Bible that had once been a Christmas present from his mother, "To My Dear Son Eli" traced upon the flyleaf in her uneven, semiliterate scrawl.

Eli closed the little Book quickly and looked away. Such trivia, he found, could affect him much too deeply. He forced himself to be calm. "Timmy," he said, "I can't go home. Not ever—at least, not to stay."

"Oh, Eli!" the youngster exclaimed. "Why?"

"I'm sorry, Timmy, I can't expect you to understand all that has happened, but if you did you'd know that I can't go home, no matter how hard it is for me to stay away. There'd be nothing easier for me than to say I'm sorry, and go with Father up to the mercy seat in the church, and confess I'm a sinner and ask forgiveness, and be taken back and prayed over. Only, you see, I can't do it."

"But why," the little boy demanded, puzzled, "if ye wanted to?"

Eli sighed heavily. "If I did I'd be committing the sin against the Holy Ghost. 'Twould be betraying Chris like Judas betraying Jesus—and not Him only, but myself too."

Timmy certainly didn't understand all this, and Eli didn't

expect him to, but the little boy understood the earnestness and sincerity in his brother's voice, and that was enough.

"You're the only brother I have, Timmy," Eli continued, "and I'm sorry to have to hurt you. It isn't that I choose to do it—you know that. Maybe when I'm older I'll be able to help you in the same way that Chris helped me. Meanwhile you'll just have to try to believe that I am doing what has got to be done."

"I believe you, Eli," the child said.

"Good. Then there's one more thing. Take a message back to Mother. Just say that I love her, that's all."

This wasn't exactly true, he reflected, except to the extent that he was beginning to learn to love all people who were hurt and defenseless in the hands of fate. What he really felt for his mother was a sort of weary pity, but this hardly seemed to be the kind thing to say. And if he didn't really love his mother—which must make him some sort of minor monster—then the least he could do was try to be kind to her.

Mrs. Markady went to the cupboard and got a fancy little iced sweetcake out of a jar and pressed it into Timmy's hand as he turned toward the door. "Don't feel that Eli has left ye, dear," she said. "Ye can see him here whenever ye've a mind—an' I'm sure yer father will not try to stop ye, once he've had the chance to cool off a bit."

Timmy smiled bleakly at her, sank his teeth into the cake, and padded down the steps and through the dew-wet garden to the road. Eli watched him go and went to the kitchen window, following the small figure with his eyes, the child who had demanded his care and protection so often from babyhood on. He felt a great loneliness inside him. But he noticed that Timmy finished the little cake in two or three bites, and he thought he heard him whistle as he set off down the hill toward the Bottom. His little brother was no longer a baby, he reflected, but was beginning to learn to take the world in his stride, the rough with the smooth. He turned back to the room, smiling slightly.

It was a day of visitors—and of violent contrasts. The next arrival was a most unexpected one—Brother John. He came striding up the path with every show of confidence, as though the Markady yard were a regular part of his dominion. His black hat was set squarely above his black brows, his pointed beard neat and bristling.

"Looks for all the world like a sheriff comin' to serve summons," Mr. Markady chuckled as he went out to meet the pastor on the veranda. He did not invite Brother John into the house, nor did he offer any word or sign of welcome. "McKim," he said without preliminaries, "ye've more brass than an old-time ship o' the line. What brings ye to me door?"

Brother John smiled slightly, quite unruffled. "Ye can save the civilities fer yer friends, Mr. Markady," he said, his voice cold and hostile. "I come to have a word with Eli."

Mr. Markady grunted, and was about to reply, when Eli spoke up. "Here I am then," he announced, appearing in the doorway.

"I want to talk to ye, lad," said Brother John, "alone."

"Anything you have to say to me can be said in front of Mr. Markady," Eli responded coldly. "And as for me—you should know perfectly well that I have nothing to say to you at all."

"Eli," said the pastor pleadingly, "we were friends once, remember? More than ever now I want to be yer friend. I prayed fer ye last night. The whole ecclesia prayed fer ye—"

"Yes," said Eli. "I had word of it. It was most thoughtful of you. I hope your prayers got as far as the ends of your noses."

Brother John was shocked by this piece of impudence. "Don't hate me, Eli," he pleaded. "I always treated ye with great favor an' believed the Lord would speak to ye through me. What I did was fer yer own good, boy—fer yer good, an' fer the greater glory o' the Lord. Ye was entrapped an' ensnared by the devil—a brand that had to be snatched from the burnin'—I did it from the Christian love that is in me heart, seekin' the sheep that be lost, like the Lord says in the parable."

Mr. Markady had heard about all of this sort of thing that he could stand. "McKim," he said, brushing past Eli and coming to the top of the steps, "ye are not just a confounded hypocrite—ye are something much worse. Ye are that rare kind of villain that can fool even himself." The old man paused for two heartbeats, to lend emphasis to what he was about to say, then continued. "I am goin' to have to shoot ye, McKim. 'Tis a pity that it got to be, because in a manner o' speakin' ye are an able man, an' in some other time or place ye might have turned out far different from what ye did. But ye are goin' to have to die, just the same, for what ye did to Christopher Simms, and young Virginia Marks, and this lad here."

Brother John started to speak, but Mr. Markady stopped him with a ponderous hand uplifted, like an old sea dog of a captain quelling a mutiny from the quarter-deck.

"I never killed a man in me life, McKim," he said, "an' I'm old to start, but the very first time I ketches ye in the woods, or out in a boat, or any other place where it can be made to look like a huntin' accident, I am goin' to shoot ye like the dog that ye are. The first time I get the chance I'll put a bullet through ye, or a load of shot into yer guts, or ram yer skiff an' drown ye. An' in case ye think I am makin' an idle threat, in the heat o' the moment, I swear it to ye on the blood of the Lord Jesus—so help me God, amen!"

This savage threat was uttered so calmly and matter-of-factly that even Brother John's great courage quailed before it. He looked at Mr. Markady uncertainly, and started to back down the steps. "Ye wouldn't!" he whispered.

"Oh, and indeed I would, and I will too," Mr. Markady declared. "Go yer way, McKim, an' leave this lad be. 'Tis evil enough that ye have done to 'im already. But watch where ye walk, McKim, and mind that death will never be more than just one jump behind ye."

Brother John stared for a moment into the old captain's face, as though seeking to read what lay behind his words. Then he turned on his heel and strode off down the path toward the mill. But from that day forward he hunted no more, nor did he go birding off the headlands in his motorboat. He was not even known to venture to the country for firewood. He stayed at home and read his Bible, and his Bible helps, and his tracts, and attempted to make a new computation of the chronology. He became sallow, and there began to be a slightly haunted look in his magnificent eyes. Eli thought, too, that he looked hungry and sad as he gazed after the boy, sometimes, during his walks about the settlement.

Just once more that summer the pastor approached him —humbly, as though goaded to it by a power he could not withstand. He was a proud and stiff-backed man, and it must have humbled him sorely to have to plead with a boy. But he did it. It was just past sunset, about a week after Eli's return to Caplin Bight. The boy had spent the late afternoon at the Cove, with Timmy and young Johnny Penchley, Pleman Pike, and several other younger boys, swimming from time to time in the sea, which, after the long and gradual warming of the summer, was now a little less icy than usual.

As the sun went down the younger boys had dressed to hurry home to their suppers, and Pleman, shortly thereafter, had bidden his friend good night and followed them. Then Eli, left alone, went in for one last dip under the spreading redness of the sky. As he emerged dripping and naked from the lapping surf and walked up the gently sloping sand toward the rocks at the far end of the Cove where he had left his clothes on the little bit of beach that was sheltered there by the coign of the cliff, the boy saw Brother John, his black hat laid beside him, sitting upon the spur of the bold outcrop of rock that divided the little private corner from the main beach. The pastor must have been watching from the woods above, he realized, waiting to catch him alone. He turned to face the man.

"Eli," said Brother John—just the one word, full of pleading.

The boy waited coldly, watching the black eyes, now lit with sharp red sparks from the fires in the sky, rove over his body, full of hunger and pain.

"Eli—come back to me. Ye ain't really a wicked boy—I know ye ain't. The Lord sent ye to me, as he'd not have done without a purpose. I be willin' to fergive ye, Eli—" He stopped, his eyes still pleading, and his next words came in a low voice, almost in a whisper, and with great effort. "An' ye fergive me too, Eli, if I've done ye wrong."

It was as far as he could go, as far as his terrible pride could humble itself. He reached out a hand, and saw the boy recoil from him, and for the first time Eli felt a small spasm of pity mingled with the hatred that was in his heart. He could see that the involuntary gesture of loathing had hurt the pastor far more deeply than any curse he could have uttered, but his anger still was not appeased.

"Ye can't really hate me, Eli—ye can't!" The man's eyes looked desperate in the failing light, the irises and pupils like night, the whites stained pink with the bleeding sky.

"No," said Eli, "perhaps not. You're too low down for me to hate."

This wasn't true, but he hoped, viciously, that it would wound Brother John still further. Now that he had the knife into him, he took pleasure in twisting it. He turned scornfully away toward his clothes where they lay on the sand against the wall of rock.

Brother John's voice followed him, very low. "Eli—ye wouldn't really let that terrible old man come after me with a gun? Ye'd not be party to murder?"

"It wouldn't be murder," the boy said icily, pulling on his trousers without turning around. "It wasn't murder, was it, when the Lord sent fire upon Sodom?"

This too was said not from conviction but in the hope that it might wound the pastor more deeply than anything else. Eli put on his shirt, tightened his belt, and started to walk away. "It isn't the Lord that speaks to you," he said. "It's the lust of the flesh, speaking out of your own evil heart."

Then he walked off and left Brother John sitting on the rocks, his head bent on his knees, the fire of heaven spilling over him as it had spilled of old upon the people of Gomorrah.

He was still sitting there—praying perhaps, or was he weeping?—when Eli reached the crest of the ridge and looked back into the blue bowl of twilight that was the Cove. Again the boy felt a twinge of pity for the lonely figure huddled on the rocks—but not enough to turn his heart to forgiveness. Then he thought how Christopher had walked with him along this same path, on his second day in Caplin Bight, fifteen months ago—and love and hate and despair welled up together in his heart and drowned out the little spark of compassion that had started to grow there.

CHAPTER TWENTY-TWO

During the second week of September the school opened again, presided over by a teacher well beyond the years of passion—Miss Marian Parslip, a woman originally from Broadport, her iron-gray hair twisted into a tight knot and fastened with pins, a thin, rather drawn face, with large, quick eyes, a thin covering to her temper, and nerves worn thin by half a lifetime of struggle against entrenched super- stition and the will to ignorance. Nonetheless, when Eli went to register for grade ten, she met him warmly, with a faded but sincere smile.

"You are the young man I have been hearing so much about," she said—and then, a little hastily, fearing she had said the wrong thing, she went on to explain: "Your school- work, I mean. You skipped a grade and still got honors last year, didn't you?"

"Yes, ma'am."

"And you are hoping to do the last *two* years of high school this winter?"

"That's right," Eli said, "but I'd better explain, ma'am, that I don't expect to spend a lot of time in school this year. Since I'd be the only student aiming at grade eleven, I'd be more in your way than anything, wouldn't I? And I'm sure I can study much better at home, where there aren't thirty or forty small children reciting their lessons. But you needn't be afraid I won't keep up. Just you set the work for me and don't worry about the rest."

"You are an exceptional student, and you may study any way you wish," she agreed. "Kindly say when you need help, and I'll give it to you—evenings or nights, when the children are off my hands, if necessary."

"Thank you, ma'am."

"There's just one other thing," she said a little awkwardly, but with the air of firm decision of one well used to meeting awkward situations. "I have heard, of course, about your, er—relations—with the last teacher. I want you to know that nothing of that kind will be held against you—not in this school, anyway, irrespective of what may happen outside."

"Thank you," said Eli somewhat dryly. "I've been taking care of that situation for myself."

"Yes," said Miss Parslip, "I'm sure you have."

"And also," Eli continued, "I want you to know that I'm proud of my relations with Christopher, the way you would be proud if you had a friend who was a saint."

"A saint?" she echoed.

"Well—not exactly. He was a very earthy sort of person, and he seemed to have more energy tied up inside him than he knew what to do with. He wasn't a mystic or a dreamer or anything like that. But there was a little of the saint in him."

She looked at him for a moment with a shrewd, penetrating glance. "I had heard that he was a very talented teacher," she said, "and that the chief justice, when he passed sentence, virtually ordered an appeal."

"It didn't do any good though," Eli said bitterly. "It seems an appeal would be heard only because of some irregularity in the trial, or new evidence or something of that kind."

"And the lawyers didn't find any grounds for a new trial?"

"Not yet, anyway. Everything about Christopher's conviction seems to have been quite right and proper, so far as the law is concerned. The only things wrong were the facts, and the way they were interpreted by the jury—and the determination of Brother John and Solomon Marks to get rid of him at any cost."

"Is it true, then, that he was a victim of religious persecution?" Miss Parslip asked.

"Not, perhaps, in the way you mean," Eli replied. "But it is true that he was sent to jail because he seemed to be a threat to the power of the church in Caplin Bight. His trial was a farce, the evidence trumped up by people who make a business out of a kind of bogus righteousness and use it to hold power over the people here."

"Is that so now?" she said, her eyes widening. "Such undercurrents of evil to exist in so small a place as this!"

"'Tis not evil so much as ignorance," Eli said wearily.

"Ah," she said, her eyes lighting up, "you know that already? My, you are an exceptional boy, indeed. But then, of course, you went through that trial. It must have been a frightful ordeal, was it not?"

"Bad enough," Eli said. "I'd face almost anything, I think, rather than go through it again."

"Is there anything else you would like to tell me?" she asked.

"No ma'am. Well, just one thing, perhaps. It isn't my place to tell you how to do your job—but the children here—the young ones—they got used to Christopher's ways, you see. You'll find that you won't have to be harsh with them."

She laughed—a little crystal, tinkling laugh, surprisingly like Virginia's, he noted, and sounding almost absurdly young in such an aging woman. "I'll remember," she promised. "I'll only beat them when they don't do their homework. I take it I have a lot to live up to, after Mr. Simms."

"Yes," Eli said, "but it will be easier because he was here."

As the boy was leaving she called him back. "I mean to be a good churchwoman," she said. "Nothing extravagant, you know, but I'll do as much as is expected of me. And I hear that you are a—well, a backslider. But you might visit me sometimes, at home, just to talk a bit. That would be proper enough, would it not? Even if you should need no assistance with your work, I should enjoy talking with you sometimes

—but I could hardly be seen going to Mr. Markady's house, could I?"

Eli grinned at her. "You've got the idea," he said. "You won't have any trouble here, the way Christopher did."

She smiled thinly. "I'm a lot older than Mr. Simms," she said, "and a bit more cunning, perhaps. Besides—I'm just a teacher, not a saint."

He wondered for a second if she might be laughing at him, and searching her face he still could not be sure. He liked her, he decided, even if there was a suspicion that she found him a little amusing. The interview had lasted hardly more than ten minutes, but they were friends already. Eli heard, afterward, that she took up the cudgels on his behalf among the people of the village whenever his name was mentioned.

It was the morning after school began and the sun was pouring in over the open deck of the Markady house where Eli lay, doing the assignment in math for the first week of the term. He was stretched out on the hot boards with his books, for he had found long since that he could study best while lying flat on his stomach. But he was not doing so well just now, for the sun, burning into his skin, filled him with a vague feeling of unrest. He hurried through the geometry and then through the algebra problems, dashing off his answers without checking, confident they were right, and picked up the book of world history whose first two chapters he had planned to absorb and pigeonhole that day.

It was no use. The Paleolithic and the Neolithic kept changing places, and the sun kept warming his blood and telling him that history would be better done by lamplight. He went indoors for his shirt, but the sun found its way through that too. Finally he closed his books, laid them neatly on the hall table beside the front door, and padded softly out into the golden September morning.

Anne Markady's late roses and garnet-colored hollyhocks in the little green square behind the house, where trees and walls sheltered them from salt spray, nodded to him, assuring him that there was a time for everything under the sun —a time to study, and a time to leave off studying, a time to work, and a time to ramble. This, past all question, was a morning for rambling. He sniffed the air and found it most intoxicating, filled, as it was, with the amber perfumes of late summer, the spicy, sensual scents of a world bursting with brown seed and swelling with sun-warmed fruit.

Eli cat-footed down the road in the gentle dust, watching the men and women on the flakes above the harbor busy making salt fish. It occurred to him suddenly that he might never make fish again, and he was not sure whether he should feel sorry about it or not. Sometimes it could be monotonous and back-breaking work. Later in the day, he reflected, the fish that was now being spread might be in danger of sunburn, and if so it would have to be picked up, collected into piles, and shaded. But this early in the morning the day had almost perfect "dryth." It had been a good year for the trap crews, and the flakes were white with fish.

Then, as Eli debated reverting to childhood and going paddling in the millpond below the big wheel in the Bottom, the bright sun seemed to grow yet brighter, the soft clouds softer, and he noticed for the first time that a late thrush was singing. For up the road came Virginia, swinging a pail, her head wrapped in a scarf and a scarlet kerchief knotted about her throat.

"Well," she said banteringly, "if it isn't Mr. Pallisher. And how do ye do?" looking at him all the while under her long black lashes.

"Hello, Virginia," he said gravely. "You're off to the barrens, I see."

"Why yes, sir," she said, still in her bantering tone. "I go a-berrying. But you of course must stay at home and study to be a lawyer, or prime minister, or whatever it is."

"I was doing exactly that," he said, "but the sun first drove me into the garden, and then the road kept coaxing my feet to leave the gate, and, as you know, I was never much good at resisting temptation—so here I am, foot-loose, fancy free, and ready to do your bidding."

"Then ye shall carry my pail," said Virginia, handing it to him and looking up with a little red smile that made his heart skip. For the first time he realized that he was taller than she, and that there was an appealing and defenseless quality in her beauty. This summer she had somehow ceased to be the remote, queenlike creature he had worshiped from afar the summer before.

"I'm proud of you, Eli," she said, dropping the bantering tone.

"Proud?" he asked, genuinely puzzled.

"That ye found the guts to stand up to your father and that black devil McKim," she explained.

"Oh, that!" he said. "I didn't have much choice. They drove me to it."

"But I was beginning to think that you never would. I tried before, you remember, to make you stand up to them."

"Yes," he laughed, "but then I was a child. Now I'm a man." It was the first time the thought had entered his mind that he had crossed the ultimate threshold. But it was true, he realized. The night he had walked out of his father's house he had left his boyhood behind forever.

"Ah yes," she said a little shyly, looking up at him, "ye are, aren't ye?"

They walked up the country road in the general direction of the Simms place, then took the path to the left, on the opposite side from the mill brook, toward the berry barrens. They ambled through the soft shade of the spruces with the sun on their backs, and they were silent for a long time, though it was not the silence of strangeness or embarrassment but of those so at home in each other's presence that no artificial tie—not even that of conversation—was needed.

As they emerged above the trees Virginia slipped her hand gently into Eli's, clasped his fingers, and said, "Talk to me, Eli. Tell me about Christopher—for you love him too. It was cruel that they would not let me be with him at the trial. It's been all over for a month now, and I still don't know what really happened."

Eli squeezed her fingers and looked down at her—a vivid, gypsy-like creature—almost, he thought, like some glowing red flower under a tropical sun, and yet so slight and grace-ful. She was no longer gay and carefree, he realized. Instead she looked wounded and lost, her black eyes like those of a doe in the forest about to flee at the approach of the hunter, or like those of a stray child who is afraid of the dark.

"Well," he began, "you knew him even better than I did. I saw the two of you at the Cove one night last summer, when you and he went swimming together—and you lay in his arms in the moonlight. I was a little bit jealous, you know, because I was sort of in love with you myself—like all the young boys in the Bight—"

As he called back the memory of the night on which she had given her virginity to Christopher her fingers clutched his convulsively. "Don't, Eli—don't," she whispered. "I can't bear it. Not yet, anyway—perhaps we could talk about those things another time. But right now tell me about the trial. You were there, and of course my father was there too, but he won't speak of it, naturally—and all the people here purse their lips as if the whole thing was a blasphemy too great to be talked about."

"Yes," Eli said. "So it was too—a blasphemy. St. Paul had a phrase for it—'crucifying Christ afresh.'"

"But tell me about it, Eli," she pressed. "Don't go wander-ing off with those Scriptural allusions of yours. You sound like that beast John McKim."

"They come naturally," he apologized. "They were bred into me. I sucked 'em with me mother's milk."

"The trial—" she insisted.

So they walked in the sunshine, up the barren hill, she scuffing in her brown sandals, he treading with unshod delicacy among the prickles of the berry bushes, while he began anew, reliving the agony of the trial.

But somehow as he went along, calling up the scenes of pain one after the other, with his hand still clasped in hers, the agony passed out of him, and only the glory remained, and he saw the thing in its symbolic beauty—the shining, truthful spirit of a man standing among dogs—and he thought of Mr. Markady's question, "Aren't ye proud of him, now?"

He had almost forgotten that he was speaking, or that he had a listener, until Virginia pressed his fingers again, exclaiming, "Oh, Eli! You make it sound so beautiful!"

"Yes," he said doubtfully, "somehow or other I suppose it *is* beautiful. It is beginning to turn out that way—though it didn't seem the least bit beautiful at the time. Even Christopher couldn't quite transfigure that dreadful, sordid courtroom."

"Eli," she declared, "I've been so full of hatred! I still am. When I think about it all I want to kill someone. And how I've cried! Oh, I cried myself sick, night after night—but that was long ago, when first they took him away. I cried until I hadn't any tears left. Until you came. But I almost feel like I could cry again now."

"Don't, Virginia," he said. "I wouldn't know what to do if you started to cry. And besides, it's too lovely a day for that."

"You wouldn't know what to do!" she exclaimed. "Why, you'd take me in your arms, silly, and stroke my hair, and comfort me—and maybe you could kiss me just a little—on the cheek, of course."

"Of course," he said. He looked at her and felt a great wave of tenderness well up in his heart.

But the day passed off quite innocently. They filled their pail with berries and went home through the golden afternoon like two children on an outing, parting where they had met in the morning, beside the little bridge over the millstream in the Bottom.

"Back to your books!" Virginia said. "I'm a bad influence on you, Eli. But don't think for a minute that I'm going to reform. You'll walk with me again soon?"

"Why—tomorrow of course!" he promised, wondering if tomorrow might not be too far off, then repenting at the call of duty. "In the afternoon," he said firmly, "after my poor books have had their turn. We can even take Christopher's boat if it's a fine day, and sail up the Reach and look for eagles."

"Eagles?" she asked, astonished.

"Of course," he laughed, "you wouldn't know about them, but Chris and Mr. Markady and I are all eagle lovers."

"Oh," she said. "I thought they just ate babies. Well—I'll be working in the store tomorrow, but I'll make Mother take over around four o'clock. See you then." And she tossed him a make-believe kiss.

So it began—the first great, tender, sinful passion of his life. The days of Indian summer remained quite lovely and peaceful, with soft sunlight pouring down through the blue haze of the valleys, as though nature herself were conspiring to set a seal upon this dangerous adventure. During their first two or three meetings Eli was easily able to rationalize himself into a state of contented innocence. This, he reasoned, was a classical case of Platonic love. What could be more natural than the development of such a tender affection between two of the people most deeply bereaved by Christopher's imprisonment?

"'A hand may first be kissed, then a cheek,'" he quoted blithely, humming happily in self-deception.

It was only later that the torture began.

Virginia, much more than he, was the aggressor in the affair, though Eli was not entirely innocent either. She kept edging him a little further, a little deeper, always a step nearer to the abyss that they knew, somewhere in the backs of their minds, lay waiting for them. Even so, it might have ended differently had he brought to her only the tender idealism that he had learned from Christopher. Unfortunately or otherwise, he brought also, sealed up inside him, the dark sensualism that he had learned from Brother John.

Virginia's gypsy-like appearance was deceptive and self-contradictory, he found, for she was a gypsy with a profound sense of sin. Raised with the same deep-seated taboos as Eli, in the same world of guilt and damnation, she had rebelled against it all much earlier than he, but was left with a profound conviction of being lost—indeed, had embraced this idea almost eagerly. No one raised as she had been raised, and turning away from the superstitions of the fathers, can ever escape a haunting sense of sin. But with her this sense had been brought gradually into full consciousness, until she accepted her damnation with a fierce passion, choosing of her own will to be numbered among those outcast and anathema and consigned to everlasting fire.

"I'm going to tell you just how I feel, Eli," she declared. "I could never talk like this to Christopher—my God! What am I saying?— But it's true, all the same." She turned to him, her eyes flashing. "Christopher is just too bloody good for me. I love him—I'd die for him, by God! But he's so naturally gentle, and so—so—confoundedly *perfect*, that I could never feel as free and natural with him as I do with you."

They were walking along the cliff top at the time, crossing the prints of the potato beds of long ago, kicking at the autumn dandelions that blossomed everywhere around them on slender stems.

"Eli—I never was the sweet young merchant's daughter waiting to be received into the church that Christopher supposed when he knew me first. Oh, yes—you saw us lying together; we were just like man and wife. That's not what I mean. . . ." She was silent a moment, then went on, fiercely, almost defiantly. "I never believed in any of it—not really —none of the things we were taught. From the day I started to grow up I was like a tiger in a cage. It was, 'Virginia, do this,' 'Virginia, don't do that.' 'Keep your knees covered, dear!' Wouldn't it make you want to spit? And what's the

use of them telling you about purity of heart when God
plants the apple of temptation right in your own belly? And
they talk about salvation and robes of righteousness and
stuff like that, while all the time you know that *your* kind
of salvation is down between your legs.

"All any real woman wants is a man, Eli—not the marriage
of the spirit, but a man. It doesn't make any difference if
you're churched and bedded or if you sneak off at night
to do it in the berry bushes, it's all the same thing. When a
man takes possession of you your soul may be damned to
hell, and good luck to it if it is, but your body is redeemed
forever and ever."

"Nothing very wicked about that, I should think," Eli said.

"No—but I haven't told you all of it—not half of it. I want
to tempt people—to coax them into sin. That gives me the
greatest pleasure of all. I can't stand the smell of righteousness in a man—it makes me sick. You don't have the least
trace of it, and that's one of the things I like about you.

"You see, I'm a natural-born temptress. I want to dance
like the Egyptians, with only gossamer to cover my body
and the hot, hungry eyes of men consuming my flesh.
I want to ride like Lady Godiva, naked on the back of a
coal-black stallion, while the eyes of the saved gleam from
behind their lace curtains. I'd like to tempt every one of
them into the most shameful lust and madness, so they'd
drool at the mouth and do sinful acts they couldn't help—
That's the kind of woman I am.

"And that isn't all. For years I've wished for my parents'
death, Eli. Not just since this thing with Christopher began,
but long before. I hate both of them deeply and terribly. I
hate all the things they stand for. I hate the God they worship. I hate—hate—hate!" She spat it out almost viciously.

Eli said nothing, and Virginia too fell silent, slowly growing calmer. Then, speaking more softly and sadly: "Well—
I've got it off my chest, anyway. You see, I'm already
damned, Eli. No one could be more certain of the second
death than I am—not even Lucifer himself. Nothing I might

do with you could sink me any deeper in hell. They used to tell us in church about the perfect liberty of the children of God. But it's the children of the devil who have the real liberty. Once you are damned past all salvation, then you are free."

They walked up through the grove into a little clearing where, years before, there had been a mill—its bed now overgrown with moss, the tower whose vanes had once reached for the winds of heaven now but a hexagonal depression in the turf.

"Look," she said. "I'll show you what I mean."

She kicked off her sandals and began to dance within the six-sided print, like a witch performing some rite out of the black arts. Slowly the dance began to take on meaning. Her movements were dreamy, languid, promising surcease from sorrow. But the dreamy, languid dance slowly changed and became sinister, with mocking invitations to evil. Then gradually it began to turn into an indecent burlesque—a strip tease.

One by one her light garments fell at her feet and were kicked outside the print of the magic hexagon, while Eli watched, fascinated, wishing she would stop but unable to say so or to tear his eyes away from her sinuously moving limbs.

Finally she stood before him, utterly and magnificently nude, her breasts firm and high, the muscles of her belly rippling like tiny animals scurrying under her tawny skin, her thighs long and smooth and golden, the most perfect image of female beauty that he had ever dreamed or imagined. She ran her fingers slowly down over her body in a caressing gesture, while his heart pounded uncontrollably, and his mouth turned bitter with salt, and his genitals swelled to bursting.

"Don't, Virginia, don't!" he cried in genuine pain.

"Why not, boy?" she said in a throaty, languid voice. But she turned quietly and picked up a single garment—her dress—and slipped into it, and came, as quietly, and sat down beside him, and buried her face in the folds of his sweat-stained shirt. "I know," she said. "It's not because I am damned that you have to be damned too. But I love you, Eli. There, I've said it, and I'm glad! I love you, and I want you, and as I'm a wicked woman it isn't likely that I'll let you go, is it?"

He kissed her then, tenderly, and she responded with tenderness, all the fire having drained out of her. But he could feel the tense desire underneath, like a beast in its lair, waiting to spring. And he could feel the same desire coiled within himself, also waiting.

CHAPTER TWENTY-THREE

It was the night of the full moon of September, and the sea lay outward from the Cove like a sheet of white silk. But it lived too, panting gently along the line of the sand like some great animal breathing in its sleep. And they walked, Virginia and Eli, along that breathing edge, touching both the water and the land, feeling within them and beneath them the life of the earth and the sea, spread, defenseless, under the enormous eyes of heaven.

So they came to the coign of the cliff where Eli had thrust the arrows of his words into Brother John a few weeks before, and there they paused.

"Let's swim, Virginia," he said.

And she answered simply, "Yes, Eli, let's."

So they stripped and stood in the moonlight. It was the first time that he had stood naked before a girl, but he felt neither excited nor ashamed—rather, he felt exalted as he took her hand and led her into the milk-white sea. The water, still untouched by the chill of autumn, rose caressingly between their thighs, and they lay down in its embrace and swam outward, toward the moon.

They circled and dived like seals, shattering the moonlight into thousands of jewels, which slowly grew and softened and united once more into a path of light leading to the edge of the earth. As they circled, Eli could see Virginia, like the image of evening and morning, first black against the moon, then white against the shore. And time seemed to become distorted in this mime of day and night, to stretch, and lose its meaning, until the moment merged into eternity and there was nothing in the universe but themselves, and the water, and the moonlight.

Then they returned, and touched the shore, and rolled in the dry sand, and brushed away the warm, clinging particles, drying themselves as the children did when they swam by sunlight in this same place. They walked up the beach and lay down in the shelter of the rock, out of the sight of the prying moon. Without a word she put her cheek against his, and he began to caress her beautiful body, tenderly.

And the coiled beast within him arose, and spoke with the voice of thunder. But she pushed him gently away, with a little sobbing noise in her throat. "No, Eli, no—not here," she said, "not in the sand."

And they rose and walked up the bank toward the line of the woods, where the carpet of tiny blackberry bushes began. She was crying a little as she turned toward him in the moonlight. "Oh damn!" she said. "Oh damn! Damn! Damn!" the tears wetting her face. "Come on and take me, Eli. I want you to. Life is such a bloody mess! Come on—I'll lie down in the bushes, and you can do whatever you want."

And he lay and entered her on that cry of despair. And they struggled together in great passion, and the night wind came softly and dried the sweat from their straining bodies.

And the seeds gathered and burst, and she lay weeping in the blackberry bushes while he touched her face tenderly and kissed her gently, as one would kiss a child. And in that moment, when the tenderness and the passion united and were made one, Eli knew that he had become, finally and utterly, a man.

He held her close to him, thinking for the moment that nothing else mattered—nothing but the two of them, and their love, and their perfect union, in a world unpeopled and apart.

"But why are you crying, Virginia?" he whispered in her ear.

And she whispered back, through her tears, "Don't you understand, Eli? For me it all happened before—in this same place, and step by step, the very same: it was just like this with Christopher."

And it was then the torture began, just a small worm at the beginning, gnawing in his heart.

At first he banished it, refused to face it, tried to fence off his mind into compartments. But as the days passed and he held Virginia almost nightly in his arms, the torture would not be laid. Instead it waxed, and became strong, and gnawed at his vitals until he could contain it no longer. All his life had been guilt-stained with the fundamentalism of his fathers. He had been assured from infancy that he was born in sin and shapen in iniquity. But now, for the first time, he felt that he really knew what the black old Bible-thumpers meant when they talked about the *conviction* of sin. True, even before meeting Virginia he was already tainted, having committed abominations with Brother John, and that perhaps was why he had slipped into this affair so easily, the slope being already well prepared. But this was quite a different matter from his escapades with the preacher. Here he was not just violating a taboo, but violating the things that he held most sacred of all: trust and friendship and the love he had received from the man he worshiped—or so he thought.

This, he decided, must be what was meant by the sin of adultery—not in the superficial, legal sense, but in the deep, moral sense—the spiritual sense. Yes—it was adultery that he and Virginia were enjoying. Even, in a sense, it might be called incest. If there was any such thing as a forbidden union between a man and a woman, this, he believed, must be it: a black pit of forbidden lust. He shuddered at the thought.

With Virginia it may have been easier—she who felt herself already damned. But to Eli the process of damnation was a prolonged agony, like a crucifixion. And he was convinced that she too carried her burden of guilt—maybe not so heavy as his—and fought against it with exhibitionism and the attempt to shock her neighbors. Certainly by the standards of the settlement Virginia's behavior was outrageous, for she flaunted her affair with Eli defiantly.

"I'm going walking with Eli," he heard her fling at her father once, "and you'll not stop me. Maybe you'll try to send *him* to jail too?"

She spoke to the merchant with bitterness, and to her mother with contempt, but with Eli she was always tender. In fact, underneath the fire and the passion she held a great depth of tenderness, an all-pervading quality that touched her sensualism and made it holy, so that their passion achieved some of the divine attributes of love.

None of this redeemed it for Eli, however, and at last, able to bear his inner conflicts no longer, he forced himself to seek counsel from Joshua Markady. The old captain was well aware that Virginia had been pledged to Christopher, and of course knew what was going on between her and the boy. Eli's first stumbling approach to the subject brought the familiar sparkle of inward mirth to the old eyes and the words of half a century's experience to the loquacious tongue.

"I can see well enough that ye are in misery, lad," he said. "And in transports of joy at the same time, I suppose. But don't ye know that 'tis the way with love at your age? If ye didn't have one thing to torture yourself with—why, ye'd find another."

"But I can't help feeling that what I'm doing is contemptible, and even dishonorable," Eli told him. "Here I've gone and stolen Christopher's woman, and he's in prison, where he has no defense at all. . . ."

"Yes, lad, I know," said Mr. Markady, his big brows beetling at the boy. "'Tis quite unforgivable what ye've done—quite!—but then, ye know, we all do unforgivable things. Every man born of woman does 'em. Some as faces the fact, the way ye are doin', an' some as don't. Them as don't—like yer former friend John McKim—sometimes poisons their whole lives with the sins that they'll never admit. Facin' the fact that ye are a rogue is half the battle. Not too many as can ever admit it to theirselves."

"Just the same, admitting that I'm a wretch doesn't seem to help matters in the least," Eli said.

"P'raps not, lad. P'raps nothing I could say would help. Love between man an' woman is a thing ye can do little about. It takes possession of ye, and there ye are. It just don't obey the rules the way it ought to. But I've a suggestion fer ye, jest the same. Why don't ye write to Christopher? He's allowed letters in prison, ye know. Tell 'im about yerself and Virginia."

Eli had never thought of this and at first wasn't sure that he approved of the idea, but gradually he brought himself around to it. For the burden of guilt, the relief of confession —an ancient formula that has never been improved upon.

He spent what seemed like endless hours on the letter without getting it right. How do you tell your dearest friend, whom you love more than your life, that you have stolen his betrothed? He began perhaps a hundred different ways before he gave up trying and simply poured out his guilt and his misery in three or four simple paragraphs, saying in the end that he couldn't ask Christopher to forgive him, and didn't want it, but that he simply had to tell him anyway.

Back came a note by the next coastal boat, written on the official letterhead of the prison. It lay a long time in his hands unopened, while the inner sickness knotted his bowels. But at last he grasped the envelope, tore it open savagely, unfolded the single sheet, and read:

"Dear Eli:—

"I hope you make the most of your affair with Virginia while it lasts, because as soon as I get out of here I'm going to steal her right back from you as fast as I can do it. Don't do anything foolish, like marrying her, because that won't stop me either.

"I can't blame you, you rogue, for making off with her as soon as my back was turned. In your place I'd likely have done the same. As for Virginia, if she wants a little amusement with you,

she's welcome—I don't believe any woman should be expected
to remain sexless for months and years at a time, any more than
a man. But don't get the idea that you can keep her.

"I've written her, and I've written my father. It's against regu-
lations for me to write all those letters so early in my career as
a jailbird, but I've become secretary to the warden (a kind and
sympathetic man), who says he'll make an exception 'by virtue
of the powers invested in [him],' whatever that means.

"I am glad to hear that you are living with the Markadys. I was
worried about how you would manage with Elias and Martha. But
who could ask for better parents than that magnificent old man
and his gentle little wife? I hope you continue to visit the old
farm sometimes. My poor old father must be awfully lonely, I
should think.

"For heaven's sake get rid of this nonsense about feeling guilty.
You can't help falling in love with Virginia, and you are just going to have to bear as best you can the suffering that it is going
to cause you. You're in for hard enough times without torturing
yourself with guilt as well. Stop letting the ghosts of your childhood rise up to haunt you.

"As I sit here in the warden's office with the prison silence
around me I have only to close my eyes and I see your faces
again—yours and Virginia's—and I love both of you, not less, but
more than before.

                                              "Christopher."

Knowing Christopher as he did, Eli should have expected
something of the kind—lighthearted and unconventional but
also generous and rational. Nevertheless, he found the letter's message both unexpected and puzzling. Obviously
Christopher did not grant this great, great passion of his the
seriousness that was its due. Eli felt sure that Virginia loved
him deeply. As for his own feelings for her—they were utterly beyond expression! Rarely in the course of the human
story had such a love as theirs come to full flower. There
could be no question of their separating—just let Christopher
try anything of the sort! But Christopher seemed to regard
the whole thing as a game—even talked of "a little amuse-

ment." Amusement indeed! If only he knew how far from amusement it all was!

And yet, he reflected, Christopher *must* know. There could be no mistaking what Eli had written. Well—at least the letter seemed to give his love affair with Virginia a sort of tentative and temporary blessing. He could be thankful, at least, that Christopher didn't feel that he was being stabbed in the back. Perhaps, after all, the teacher had never loved Virginia very deeply. Could that be the explanation?

He showed the letter to Mr. Markady, who read it through and grunted—but all he said was, "Calls me a 'magnificent old man,' do 'e? Sounds like a church ruin. Were 'e here now instead of in jail we'd see who's old and who isn't. Bet I could beat 'im in a standin' jump, or hand wrestle 'im to the ground, any day o' the week."

Eli's relief was great, though the burden of guilt remained. But now at least it had become bearable. Going up the path toward the hills that evening he and Virginia swapped letters and spent a long time talking about them. He found her letter even more puzzling than his own, and her attitude toward it baffling.

"I'm glad Christopher still loves me enough to want to steal me away from you," she said. "Of course I don't know that I shall ever see him again. You can't tell what prison will do to him, can you? He might never come back— But still, it makes me happy to know he wants me."

"I'm not going to give you up," Eli said, "not even to Christopher."

"Ah!" she said. "I can just see it—the two of you, swords flashing, fighting to the death for my lily-white hand!"

"Virginia! Be serious!"

"But I am! Not that it'll be my hand that you'll be thinking about of course. And not that you'll fight to the death, or anything silly like that. Indeed I'm sure you won't fight at all, in a physical way—but you've no idea, not being a girl, what it does for a woman to have two lovers contending over her like this!"

"Virginia, you're still making fun of me," he said, grieved. "Well, suppose you were to find out, one fine morning, that you were going to have a baby."

It was the first time that the subject had been mentioned between them. It was the first time that he had been *able* to mention it. And it had an immediate, sobering effect upon Virginia.

"Yes, it could easily happen," she said. "I've thought about it a lot, Eli. Don't think it hasn't been right on top of my mind. It's the only real cause for worry that there can be between us, isn't it? If it should happen it could be confoundedly awkward, couldn't it? We must try to be more careful in the future—"

"Careful!" Eli exclaimed. "That's a lot easier said than done. If I could have stopped myself by being careful I would never have fallen in love with you in the first place. But I don't think much about anything when you're in my arms. Nothing seems to matter, except the two of us—nothing that ever happened before, or is likely to happen afterward."

"Well," she reflected, "I suppose even if you *did* knock me up it wouldn't be the end of the world, exactly. Of course, 'twould be one more thing for my father and mother and the church elders to raise a great lamentation about, but after all I wouldn't be the first girl in the Bight to get a child from a man who wasn't her legal bedded husband."

"It scares me more than anything else, really," Eli said. "Not that I wouldn't be willing to have you in marriage, God knows, if you'd let me, in spite of all Christopher's warnings. He could hardly try to stop our marrying if we were having a child, could he?"

"I never said I'd marry you, Eli, even if we were having a child," Virginia said. "I'm not saying I wouldn't, mind you, but I'd have to think about it more than I have. Having a baby and getting married are two entirely different things, you know. Of course I'd want the child to have a legal father all right and proper. Who wouldn't? But if that didn't seem to be possible—and I certainly wouldn't let you give up your life and your career for it—then I'd go ahead and have it anyway, right here in the Bight, whatever might be said about it.

"And one thing I'll tell you for certain. If it comes to the worst, I'll not be like that poor simpleton Bertha Penchley, who got herself in trouble with that last pastor who was here before McKim and let them sneak her off to St. John's to an institution and take the baby away from her. If there's a baby we'll have it and we'll keep it and take it to Lattice Harbor to the old Anglican clergyman, to be baptized in the porch of the church, and call it Christopher."

CHAPTER TWENTY-FOUR

A second, minor storm broke upon the people of Caplin Bight that autumn. Eli heard its first faint rumblings from Miss Parslip. Though he had spent more time at home than in the classroom, he had become quite companionable with the new teacher, who, despite her spinsterhood, was sympathetic toward his affair with Virginia.

"'Gather ye rosebuds while ye may,'" she quoted blithely one afternoon as they sat in the empty schoolroom after classes, "but watch your step, my boy, and remember the old Greek belief that the gods exact payment for every pleasure. For heaven's sake don't go getting yourself *married*. There will be time enough for that after you have graduated from college. You *are* going to college, of course?"

"Mr. Markady says so," he told her. "I suppose it would be impossible for me to qualify for a scholarship this year—though I could pretty certainly do it next year. Anyway, he says he'd rather have me save the year and let him pay for it."

"Quite right too," she agreed.

"And don't worry about my going back fishing to support a baby," he continued. "We've talked about that too. Virginia and me, I mean."

"My!" she said with a little gasp. "You modern young people! Why, when I was a girl— But you don't want to hear about that, of course." She returned to the business in hand. "Here, I'll run through this theorem of the quadratic formula

just once. Since you don't seem to have any aptitude at all
for memorizing formulas, I suppose you will have to be able
to work out the steps leading to them, or visualize them—or
whatever it is you mathematical geniuses do—every time
you need them."

As she finished the neat, tight pyramid of equations Eli
flipped the paper over and on the reverse side ran off the
steps leading to the quadratic formula with a pencil. "Got
it!" he said.

She gave him a look in which admiration and amusement
seemed to be equally mixed. "Eli, in all my years as a teacher
I have never known a student who could do that—grasp a
whole page of mathematics almost in an instant, I mean.
You have an enormous gift for this sort of thing. I wonder,
now, if we were to move on to the binomial theorem? . . .
But no—later. After Christmas perhaps. Besides, the children
are really a trial, and I *am* tired."

"They've been giving you trouble?"

"Well, not really—just the usual things. There is only one
I could say I am having trouble with—that young Penchley
boy, the orphan. I have tried reasoning with him. I have
tried talking with the grandmother. I have even thrashed
him a couple of times. But none of it does any good. I cannot do a thing with him."

Eli laughed. "That's Johnny," he said, "the professional
rascal. Even Christopher thrashed Johnny—the only one he
ever did—but, oddly enough, from that day forward Johnny
practically worshiped the ground Christopher walked on."

"Well, it didn't work out that way with me," she said. "I
have had children before who tried to make a game out of
baiting the teacher. But this is much worse. If it were just
mischief I could put up with it, however great a nuisance
it might be, but I am afraid he really hates me. He is sullen
and withdrawn. I might almost call him bitter, if you could
say that of a small boy. It worries me. I am told that you
might have some influence with him. Do you think you
could try talking to him for me?"

"I'll try," Eli said doubtfully, "but if he hates you because you have replaced Christopher it may be hard to do much with him."

"Yes—that's what I am afraid of," she said.

Eli found Johnny almost totally unreceptive. When reminded of his resolution to reform, the boy wavered once or twice but clammed up again immediately afterward. He seemed to reason, and perhaps correctly, that what he was now enduring was no part of the compact that he had made with Christopher, and that he was absolved from his obligations.

"Johnny," Eli said, "I don't expect you to understand what happened to Chris, or why it happened. But I do expect you to remember your promise to him, and to live up to it. . . . You do remember, don't you?" he insisted.

"I remember," the child admitted in a very small voice.

"You seem like you're trying to hate the whole world. And all that can lead to, you know, is harm to yourself."

"I don't hate you, Eli."

"Very well then. You know it's not my fault that Christopher went to prison—or Miss Parslip's either. She's trying to help you—don't you know that?"

Johnny said nothing but nodded dumbly.

"Then why are you carrying on like this?" Eli demanded. "If Christopher were here to see what you are doing he'd be ashamed of you."

The child's lips quivered, and Eli thought for a moment he was going to cry. He wished to heaven he would. But instead Johnny turned and ran. Eli let him go, thinking that perhaps he would run off and cry by himself, and come back the next day to admit that he had been wrong, as he had done the summer before. But he did not come back, and Eli did not pursue the matter, for he had many things besides Johnny on his mind. He bitterly regretted, afterward, that he had not pushed the little boy harder.

If anything, Miss Parslip reported, her problem child was now worse than before. All she could do was try to keep him quiet and pretend that he wasn't there. And because of her sense of responsibility for overcoming ignorance in even the most stupid or the most willful she found this exceedingly hard to do.

"But I wouldn't mind so much except that he *isn't* stupid," she said. "It is the hardest thing of all to bear when you see a bright child gone bad."

"I'll have another talk with him," Eli promised.

But then, one morning, as a light rain was swishing the roof and Eli was stuffing himself with one of Mrs. Markady's breakfasts, Virginia came tripping up the steps, adorable in an olive-drab raincoat and carrying a black umbrella.

"Eli," she said without preliminaries, "they've arrested Johnny Penchley and are taking him to Broadport to the magistrate."

"What's he done?" Eli asked, putting down knife and fork and leaving his tea untouched.

"Broken into Father's store," she said, "and just about wrecked it."

"No!" he whispered.

"Oh yes, he has. And Father swears that he'll send him to jail and keep him there till he rots."

"Hey, jest a minute, girl," Mr. Markady interjected. "They don't send twelve-year-old children to jail—not fer breakin' into a store, anyway. Now, tell us exactly what happened— slow an' aisy, if ye please."

"'Twas last night," Virginia explained, "late—long after closing time, anyway. Father was already in bed when he heard a noise in the store. He rushed down in his nightshirt, wondering what could be going on—not thinking about robbers, of course, for who in Caplin Bight would rob a store? And there was Johnny, gone mad, it seemed, with heaps of stuff pulled off the shelves, cases broken, even the big front window smashed where he'd hurled a chamber pot through it. 'Twas that, no doubt, that woke Father."

"A chamber pot!" Mr. Markady exclaimed.

"Not just one," Virginia said. "Every chamber pot in the store was out in the road, smashed."

Mr. Markady started to laugh in big, deep guffaws, as he pictured in his mind this nemesis of the chamber pots.

"And then what happened?" Eli asked.

"Well, Father grabbed Johnny, who was swearing and trying to get at the ax that he had used on the cases, and Father says he'd no doubt have attacked him with the ax too if he hadn't grabbed the boy and shook him half senseless and clouted him quiet. Then he took him and locked him in a closet, where you could hear him bawling most of the night, and sent the boat to Lattice Harbor for the ranger. Ranger's boat is at the government wharf now, with Johnny on board, and he'll be up before the magistrate this afternoon."

Mr. Markady stopped laughing, and began cursing quietly to himself.

"Father!" Anne Markady exclaimed. "With a young girl listenin'!"

"She've heard worse—up in that temple, or whatever it is they calls it. Ye see, Eli, how 'tis all workin' out? Like fate, boy. Ye sow dragon's teeth an' ye reap monsters. Now the question is, what can we do to help the child? Sol Marks can have 'e's store repaired, aisy enough. I s'pose the boy's got to be punished fer what 'e's done, though if Sol haves 'e's way the punishment will be all out o' proportion to the crime— an' it don't seem just, somehow, knowin' what's back of it."

"For a start," Eli said, "we can go to Broadport and try to explain things to the magistrate."

"Ye are right, o' course," Mr. Markady agreed. "We'll take my boat an' be there in five hours or so—not too far behind the police boat, I expect."

"I'm going with you," Virginia said. "The store can be closed for the day."

"Why, of course, if you want to," Eli agreed.

The police boat had already pulled out of the harbor by the time they had reached the collar where Mr. Markady's boat was moored. And as they headed out across the Reach for the rattle at Lattice Harbor Island they could see it pulling away from them on the long run up the bay. Fortunately the day remained calm under the light drizzle of rain, so they had an easy time of it, pulling into the big roadstead at Broadport just after noon.

The men on the wharf who caught their lines told them that court would convene at two o'clock and invited the three of them to share their midday meal. But since the boat was equipped with a little galley, and provided with some food, they politely refused the invitation and boiled their own stewpot. Then they walked about, looking at the town and waiting for the court to open.

Broadport was one of the few Newfoundland fishing settlements with the dubious blessing of a courthouse. In most places court was held in the schoolhouse by a traveling magistrate. Here the magistrate was resident, presiding in an old wooden building topped by a brown clapboard tower that bore as decoration a clock that did not run. Scaling paint partly hid the building's shingle walls, while an ageless collection of dirt obscured its windows. Two or three times a year the magistrate left Broadport to make a visitation through his district, which included the whole bay. He then heard cases in the settlements as he traveled.

At two o'clock they presented themselves at the courthouse and followed a small straggle of local people inside. It seemed that nothing very interesting was on the blotter, for the proceedings were attended only by the professional loafers. Inside, they found the building fully in keeping with its decrepit exterior. It was unbelievably dark and pervaded by a musty smell of suffering and despair.

The bench was a sort of sideboard with a paneled front, painted dark brown, equipped with a dark brown gavel and a big black Bible for kissing when the oath was to be administered. Over the bench hung a faded and much-stained pic-

ture of Queen Victoria in her fat and regal old age. In front
was a small wooden enclosure for the prisoner or the dis-
putants; to one side a little platform with a chair and a single
step leading up to it was provided for the witness under examination. In the shadows were ten ancient wooden pews,
rescued from some long-deserted church, for spectators or
for witnesses waiting their turn to be heard. Eli and Mr.
Markady and Virginia sat with half a dozen other spectators
at the opposite side of the courtroom from Solomon Marks
and his wife, both of whom were obviously furious at the
sight of Virginia in the company of the opposing party.

The magistrate arrived and everyone stood, and sat again
as he took his place on the bench—or rather, behind it, in a
chair. He was a big, fattish man with a very square jaw, a
very broad face, pink jowls, balding gray hair, rimless spectacles, and a soft, sensual look. Eli had heard of his reputation, his love of imposing maximum sentences, his proverbial
harshness with first offenders.

Magistrate Prior sat down with ponderous dignity and
glowered at the room. The first case brought up was a civil
dispute involving land, and was quickly referred to a higher
court. The second involved a forlorn-looking little man who
pleaded guilty to being drunk and disorderly and was sentenced to "ten dollars or thirty days." The third dealt with
a man accused of assault. It seemed to be a simple case of a
quarrel and a fight over a bottle of rum. After consulting his
law books the magistrate sentenced the man to three months
in jail at St. John's, without the option of a fine.

Then the ranger came in with Johnny. Anyone could see
that the boy was scared half to death, but he managed to
look defiant in spite of his fright.

"This being a juvenile case, the court will be cleared of
spectators," the magistrate intoned, "only witnesses and
those otherwise involved in the case to remain."

The half-dozen loafers from Broadport got up and left.
Mr. Markady, Virginia, and Eli remained seated.

Solomon Marks jumped to his feet. "Please, Yer Honor,"

he said, "there's three people from Caplin Bight bidin' here
as are not connected with this case."

The magistrate consulted with the ranger, then turned
back to the room. "Those not appearing as witnesses must
leave," he said.

Eli, who now considered himself an old hand at this business of trials, stood up. "I wish to appear for the defense," he
said. "As a character witness."

"Are you related to the prisoner, or what?" the magistrate
asked.

"No, sir," Eli said. "We are not related. But I know his
background very well, and I think the court ought to hear
it, as it has a direct bearing on the case."

"Quite a sea lawyer, ain't you?" snapped the magistrate.
"Very well, you may stay. But those not appearing as witnesses must go."

"We'll wait fer ye outside," Mr. Markady whispered, and
he and Virginia left the courtroom.

Johnny was not asked to plead. Instead the ranger was
asked to state the charge and call witnesses.

"Breaking and entering, and malicious damage," were
the charges.

Solomon Marks was called and spent about fifteen minutes describing in minute detail what had happened in his
store the night before. However, he didn't mention keeping
Johnny locked in a closet all night.

Then Mary Marks went to the stand, and in her hesitant
and imprecise manner gave her version of the events.

As the enormity of Johnny's crime unfolded, the magistrate's little pig eyes began to widen and he started to view
the boy with the expression of a restaurateur sizing up a
steak.

The ranger briefly described the arrest and the deposition
made by Solomon Marks, which agreed in substance with
his statement under oath on the stand.

Last, Eli was permitted to sit in the witness chair, and to
kiss the big Bible as the sole deponent for the defense.

"Now then," said the magistrate with a hostile stare, "you say you know the prisoner's history, and that it has a bearing. You may make a statement, but be brief."

So Eli told how Johnny was an orphan, always in trouble at school, always rowdy among his playmates, until the year before, when Christopher had taken him in hand. He described the change that the teacher had brought about.

"Mr. Simms took the place of the boy's father, you see. Now, as you know, Mr. Simms was arrested and sent to prison earlier this year. Mr. Marks was one of the two men solely responsible for sending Mr. Simms to prison—on false evidence, I may add. Johnny knows this, and he is fighting back in the only way he can, at his age."

Eli could see that he had made little impression.

"You are just about as brazen a young liar as it has ever been my misfortune to have in this court," the magistrate told him, "and it is a good thing for you you're here as a witness instead of in another capacity. However, you are not on trial, I'm sorry to say. Do you have anything else to add concerning the history of the prisoner, aside from his association with a convicted sex criminal?"

Eli suppressed the urge to shout that Christopher was not a sex criminal. "Just to ask you to take the boy's history into account," he said. "No one denies that he broke into the store and did a lot of damage. But when you consider the strong motives of revenge, the suffering that he must have gone through because of Mr. Marks's actions, perhaps you might let him off with a suspended sentence. If he's released I'll undertake that the damage will be made good."

"That's enough!" the magistrate snapped. "Quite enough! You are not a lawyer pleading the prisoner's case. You may stand down."

He called Johnny before him and gave him a long lecture on the sanctity of property and the frightfulness of crimes committed against it. He impressed upon him that having no father or mother was pretty close to being a crime in itself. He told him that he was undoubtedly heading for a life of delinquency and conflict with the law, a life that would lead to long stretches in jail, and perhaps, in the end, to the gallows and the hangman's noose.

"Now," he said, "you have got to be punished, and I am going to impose sentence. Ten years ago, besides sending you to jail, I would have sentenced you to be birched. But unfortunately the law has become soft in its treatment of young toughs such as you. Much as you deserve it, I cannot have you whipped. But I can sentence you to two years in prison, and that is exactly what I am going to do—sentence to be served at the Boys' Home and Training School."

Throughout the lecture and the imposition of sentence Johnny had maintained his posture of defiance. He walked out now, the ranger holding his arm in the gesture of a police officer with a criminal, still defiant, his head high, his eyes mute, to face what must have seemed to a twelve-year-old boy an everlasting punishment, in exile and among strangers.

"More of that divine law we hear so much about," Eli reported bitterly to Virginia and Mr. Markady as he joined them on the rotting steps of the courthouse. "The innocent suffering for the guilty. They've sent him to the reform school for two years."

He began to curse, softly but intently, coupling obscenities with choice blasphemies.

"Don't, Eli," Virginia pleaded. "You're only hurting yourself."

"Nothing of the sort," he said. "I'm working off steam, and telling whoever arranges things up above just what kind of a son of a bitch I think he is. When Christopher went to jail I was so hurt I wished I could die. This time I'm not hurt— just angry—so mad, in fact, that I want to bite someone—that fat bastard of a magistrate, for first choice."

Solomon Marks came down the steps with his wife, chuckling as he came, highly pleased with the result of the trial, but his face turned black as he saw Virginia. "Girl," he said, "we've jest seen a sample o' the majesty o' the law in action. Now I'm warnin' ye. Ye are gettin' to be out o' hand and unmanageable, an' I've the law on me side, an' I'll call on it if need be."

"Father," Virginia said, "you've done enough wickedness already. You got a taste last night of what happens when you hurt even a child more than he can stand. Don't try to interfere between Eli and me, because I'll stop you, even if I've got to use poison to do it."

"Why, ye—" Solomon Marks began, turning livid at the awful threat and advancing on his daughter.

"That'll do, Mr. Marks," Eli said, stepping between them. "I'll back up every word Virginia says. If you want to get rough, just try it with me."

And because Solomon Marks was a coward, he backed down.

Then Virginia did something that must have taken a bit of nerve. Right there, on the broken-down steps of the courthouse, with the world looking on, she threw her arms about Eli and kissed him. No Caplin Bight girl had ever before been known to kiss a boy in public—nor even heard of its being done, most likely.

There was a shocked exclamation of "Virginia!" from her mother, a belly laugh from Joshua Markady, and a blush from Eli.

"The hell with them!" she whispered in his ear.

"All right," he whispered back. "The hell with them if you say so."

For the next few days Johnny's crime and punishment provided the small talk of Caplin Bight. No one could remember any boy from the settlement ever before having been sent to reform school, and there seemed to be no clear idea of just what a reform school was like, but that it must be something truly dreadful everyone, especially the youngsters, agreed. However, there was little sympathy expressed for Johnny, despite his long exile to this house of punishment. All the sympathy was for Elder Solomon Marks, who had suffered hundreds of dollars' worth of loss in broken and damaged property, and who, it was said, had acted with true Christian restraint, considering the circumstances.

Eli wasn't there, of course, but he heard from Timmy, who was, that they had offered a special prayer in church for Elder Marks, that he might be consoled in his loss and learn to bear it with patience and fortitude. Johnny's old grandmother was there too at the time, and prayed with the rest. Nobody thought, somehow, to pray for her, or seemed to suspect that she might be suffering just as much as the merchant. She received only a few perfunctory expressions of regret: "A pity young Johnny went to the bad, but ye could see it comin'." "Always wild, 'e were. 'Spect they'll knock it out of 'im though, where *he* be gone." And more of the same.

It was clearly understood and agreed by all concerned that the old woman by rights ought to be made pay for the damage. But since she had nothing to pay, except for her widow's mite of ten dollars a quarter, Solomon Marks stood up in prayer meeting and announced that he was forgiving her the debt, and Brother John preached a sermon on it, taking as his text the last verse but one of the Lord's Prayer, which, he pointed out, appeared in some versions thus: "Forgive us our debts, as we forgive our debtors." Brother John had a great variety of texts and translations available to him in his Bible helps, and was able to quote from the original Greek, or to use whichever version best fitted any particular occasion.

So it all ended to the greater glory of God.

But an imperceptible change in the power structure of the village was well under way. The authority of the church elders, which had gone unchallenged since the days of the Apostles, for all anyone in Caplin Bight could tell, was under attack and was shaken. First, the stubborn worldliness of the Markadys and the Simmses had persisted against all the best efforts of the faithful. Next had come Eli's open defiance of his father, a church elder, then Virginia's revolt, and finally Johnny's attack on Elder Marks.

To make it worse, Eli was beginning to collect a sort of following among the boys of the settlement, many of whom secretly wished that they could defy their fathers and carry on a torrid affair with an older girl and get away with it, as he was doing. Young Pleman Pike, who was Eli's age, and had fished with him, and was now studying to be a bookkeeper, began to pal around with him again, in defiance of the edict of ostracism issued by the church. Sometimes Pleman's younger brother and cousin came along with him. Timmy still worshiped Eli from afar and frequently sneaked into the forbidden Markady kitchen. And Eli was generally looked up to by the older students in school, who had a healthy respect for his brains as well as for his prowess with shotgun and rifle.

Once or twice Eli took Timmy with him on visits to Peter Simms, and before long the little boy began going there on his own. The old man, bowed as he was with age and grief, summoned up a hidden fund of humor and compassion and made a sort of pet out of the lonely youngster—and this in turn promised more trouble for the future. Eli simply didn't have time to make a project out of raising Timmy, but old Peter Simms had eternity for his portion. Aged men and children have an important thing in common—they are never pressed for time. So Peter sat and read to the boy by the hour—sometimes, perhaps, things that Timmy understood but dimly if at all. And Timmy became an expert liar, and an expert at not getting caught, so that he suffered less at Elias's hands than might have been supposed.

But for all his dissembling Elias could plainly see that his second son was in danger of being tempted by the devil, if not of actually joining the great company of the damned, as the elder son had done, so he bore down on him pretty hard and made him attend every church function of any sort whatsoever and beat him whenever he was caught in an indiscretion. Eli, who felt responsible for the hard life that Timmy was forced to lead at home, tried to make up for it as best he could. But Timmy, he was glad to see, didn't regard it as a hard life. He seemed to be able to bear the churchings and the birchings with unsuppressible cheerfulness.

CHAPTER TWENTY-FIVE

⤙ ⤚

By the time Christmas had arrived once again in a fine flurry
of snow the people of Caplin Bight had begun to accept the
wickedness in their midst with some show of resignation.
That is to say, they put up with it because there was nothing
they could do about it. The leaven of unrighteousness was
here to stay, it seemed, and showed more and more signs of
leavening the whole loaf. In a sermon by Brother John with
strong overtones from Sister Leah it was shown, however,
that the really important thing was to keep one's own robes
from being soiled with this leaven.

The report of this sermon, brought to him by Timmy and
Eli, almost cured old Mr. Simms of his melancholy. "Getting one's robes soiled with the leaven of unrighteousness!"
he exclaimed. "Why, Eli, 'tis a classic! One of the most beautifully mixed metaphors ever coined by man. How anyone
can hear it, and not laugh—"

But the ecclesia saw nothing funny in the phrase—it was
taken up, repeated, and widely used around the harbor.
The youth of Caplin Bight was already sadly infected with
this leaven, Brother John said. Indeed there was serious
reason to suspect that some of them might be past all hope
of salvation. But was not this also a fulfillment of the prophecy? Had not the Lord Himself said He would send not
peace but a sword?—setting the son against the father, the
daughter against the mother, the daughter-in-law against
the mother-in-law, so that a man's foes should be those of

his own household? The ones who were now following after unrighteousness were unwitting instruments for the fulfillment of the prophecy, he pointed out, increasing the signs of the Lord's Second Coming, and so adding to God's glory, even while they served their father the devil.

The only one who could not view sinners with the slightest degree of equanimity was Jehu Gilmore. Now that Eli had assumed the mantle of leadership among the unfaithful, the fanatic from the other side of the ridge could never meet him on the street without stopping to prophesy against him. As for Virginia, he denounced her to her face as a "Jezebel and a harlot," and assured her that he had seen, in a vision, the special niche that the devil was preparing for her, where the flesh that she flaunted would squirm and writhe in flames forever. He became quite carried away, she reported, as he pictured her private corner of hell.

But Christmas offered some slight antidote to the prevailing hatred that held the settlement in its grip. The general spirit of peace among men that spilled across the Christian world at this season moved even the most faithful church members halfway toward forgiveness of those against whom they had sinned. Martha Pallisher tried to persuade Elias to allow Eli to come home for Christmas Day, and through Timmy, who relayed the news, Eli sent back word that he would be glad to go. But Elias would not compromise to the point of permitting an apostate son inside his door—whose lintels, he pointed out, had been consecrated with the Blood of the Lamb. However, he relaxed his proscription so far as to allow Martha to give Eli a sweater she had knitted, and to deliver it herself to the Markady door, the lintels of which the Blood of the Lamb had never touched.

Among the apostates themselves the season was very gay. David Markady came home from his studies in St. John's. Miss Parslip left for her sister's home in Broadport, and the children began trooping through the settlement with catamarans and stocking caps and mitts knitted from black and white homespun. There was a concert in the school, and even a few sprays of evergreen in the church. A daring suggestion from some of the more liberal members of the ecclesia that it might be nice to put up a picture of the Nativity was squashed by Sister Leah, who pointed out that this would be just about the same thing as a graven image —an idolatry and an abomination in the sight of the Lord, and tending toward the whoredoms of Rome—so that was the end of that. The church remained as uncompromisingly free from any contamination by Art as it had been before.

But the old pagan customs of the yule log, the Christmas tree, and the wassail bowl (mostly without alcoholic content) and mummering—all flourished unchecked. Every child, and most adults, went about disguised with improvised masks, wearing clothes of the opposite sex, making the rounds from door to door and carrying on a perpetual party.

There were few musical instruments—sometimes a squeaky mouth organ, sometimes a jew's-harp, very rarely an ancient button accordion—but everyone could sing, and most could step dance to whatever tune was being played, or to the nasal humming and hand clapping of a caller. The singing was somewhat marred by the mummer's need to disguise his voice, lest he be recognized and unmasked, but the spirit of festivity was violently alive.

It was considered proper to offer mummers festive food and drink, and the Markadys had laid in a large stock of cake and sweet fruit-flavored syrup for this purpose. But Mr. Markady went through the ritual of offering every mummer, regardless of size or suspected sex, a drink of black Demerara rum. And in that settlement, where tasting liquor was regarded as "defiling the temple of the Holy Ghost," it was surprising how many accepted the sinful glass. Not only some of the men—singly or in pairs—but at least a dozen boys, and perhaps half as many girls, sipped their first choking jigger of damnation in the Markady kitchen that season. Eli knew for sure that Pleman Pike was among the young masked revelers who fell before the liquid temptation, and strongly suspected that another tippler, dressed in a pair of men's sea boots and a sou'wester, was none other than Sister Christina Marks, who had been convinced of sin and baptized into the Lord's death two years before.

Word of all this got around, of course, and there was a bit of a row, but not much, for it was the season of license, with racial memories of the Lords of Misrule and the Abbotts of Unreason and the old ceremonials of terror and glory that surrounded the dim ancestors of Saturn.

With the Christmas mail came letters from Christopher. Eli had written nothing about Johnny's committal, but Christopher had heard of it from his father and was indignant.

"I have asked the warden about springing the youngster [he wrote], and he says it can be done sometimes. The most promising method is to try to have him released into the custody of some responsible adult. I'm afraid they wouldn't release him to his grandmother, who is old, and evidently incompetent to keep him out of trouble, but if she could be persuaded to sign a document transferring guardianship—to my father, for instance—it might be possible to arrange it. The authorities would have to be satisfied that the custodial 'parent' was able to provide for the child and to exercise the authority and discipline necessary to keep him from another brush with the law.

"Please talk to my father about this and see if something can be arranged. I wish I were out of here. Even with the warden's help it is so difficult for me to do anything from prison."

The letter was long, and said a great deal about life in jail. Christopher was not only doing the warden's secretarial work, he reported, but was also back at his old job of teaching.

"I spend the whole of every afternoon conducting classes. My youngest student is sixteen, serving two years for theft. My oldest is sixty-six, a 'lifer,' serving 'at the King's pleasure' for rape. He'll probably never get out. They range from grade one to grade ten, but few of the prisoners got any further than grade three or four, and many cannot read or write at all. Some of them go to classes just for something to do (finding something to do is almost a full-time job for many people in jail) and have no intention of learning anything, but some of them are very good students. There's no way to tell, of course, whether I'm helping them to get jobs when they're released or only training them to be better criminals. Perhaps some of the ones who have learned to write so beautifully will be able to graduate from break-and-entry to forgery.

"Being in prison does a lot to a man. Here, more than anywhere I have been, I get the feeling that we are all going to sink or swim together—that if there is no salvation for men such as these, then there is no salvation for any of us."

Included was a short note from the warden.

"Dear Eli:
"I have heard so much about you from Mr. Simms that I seem to have known you for years. If you come to St. John's during the next few months you can visit him any time in my office. I want you to know that we are trying to make his stay here as painless as possible. He is helping us greatly with our rehabilitation program, and though I am trying to get him an early release, I wish we could keep him here permanently.

> "Your obt. servant
> "Raphael Mallalley."

It was the last day of the old year, and the snow lay round about, as the carolers kept reminding everybody *ad nauseum*, deep and crisp and even. Eli had been occupied for the first three days of the holidays with the construction of a bobsled, using runners from four pairs of old skates and a wheel from a discarded barrow. This dangerous vehicle could pick up a speed of perhaps forty miles per hour on any icy slope, making it the fastest thing on land or sea in that whole region. At a time when most joyriders still used the big, slow, clumsy catamarans Eli's bobsled was looked upon with the same fear, envy, and mistrust that were reserved, in other times and places, for the very hottest of hot rods.

Bobsleds are made not for one or two riders but for a whole party. So during the holidays when the snow had hardened Virginia and David and Eli never lacked com-

pany. In spite of motherly warnings that they were "going to their deaths," would-be riders came in such droves that the bobsled's patrons had to make the teen-agers, and some younger ones too, queue up for turns at the game of cata-pulting down the steep hills of Caplin Bight and taking sharp bends in great showers of snow that flew from the runners like spray from breaking sunkers in a winter gale.

They had spent the last day of December pursuing this breathtaking sport with energy worthy of a more serious purpose, and were as hungry as bears in April, when they guided the sled into the horseshoe of the Bottom and hauled it up to its hitching post at the Markady door. They could smell Christmas fare spilling its fragrance through the chinks of the windows, and they rushed indoors with mouths watering to find that there was company already seated around the board, feasting on the best of Mrs. Markady's cooking.

Peter Simms and old Sister Carrie Penchley, Johnny's grandmother, were breaking bread with Joshua and Anne Markady at the huge old ship's mess table that served the Markady kitchen.

"Ye be famished, no doubt," Mrs. Markady said as she hurried to set three more places.

"Turn to and try to catch up," Mr. Markady advised them. "There's a conference brewin' fer after supper."

It was an unspoken social law of the Bight that you never talked business at meals. But the conference started on the spot, immediately afterward. They sat back, and the men lit pipes, and Mrs. Markady produced a bottle of rum, from which Mr. Simms and Mr. Markady and David and Eli, but not Virginia, poured a small tot each. The latter would cer-tainly have had her "snort" too, had it not been for the presence of old Mrs. Penchley, but there were limits to how far she would go in outraging her neighbors' prejudices—one of which was that the taking of alcoholic liquors must remain an exclusively male vice.

"Now," said Mr. Markady, "'tis like this: Mr. Simms and Mrs. Penchley have come about young Johnny, as ye must have guessed. Mr. Simms have a letter from Christopher makin' a proposal similar to the one ye received in the last mail, Eli. He've talked the matter over with Mrs. Penchley already, and she's willin' to sign over guardianship."

"That's good," said Eli. "I'm very pleased you've agreed to do it, ma'am."

"It do seem to be fer the best," she said. "'Tisn't that I'm shirkin' me Christian duty, ye know, but there be nought I kin do with the young whelp meself, though the Lord knows I tried."

"The thing is," said Mr. Simms, "that even with the help of a housekeeper I feel I'm too old to take on full responsibility for a twelve-year-old boy, especially one who is likely to be more than a handful, as Johnny may easily prove to be. Anyway, I'm not a bit sure the commissioner would agree to the child's release on such terms. But if Mrs. Penchley were to appoint Joshua and Anne Markady as guardians, and they were to apply for Johnny's release, then I would say from what experience I have had in such matters that they would most likely get it."

"Mother an' me are quite willin'," Mr. Markady added. "What do ye think Christopher would have to say to it, Eli?"

"No doubt at all," Eli said. "He'd be delighted."

"It be very generous of ye, I'm sure, Mr. Markady," old Mrs. Penchley put in. "An' 'twere kind of ye all to go to Broadport an' try to help the young'un in the first place."

"Not a bit of it," Mr. Markady said. "Mother an' me've had a boy in the house—an' generally a gaggle of 'em—almost as long as we can mind. An' now with David up in St. John's most o' the year, an' Eli plannin' to join 'im inside o' twelvemonth, 'twouldn't seem natural not to have another youngster sproutin' up behind the kitchen table."

"Besides," Eli added, "he'll be where I can keep an eye on him, as I half promised both Christopher and Miss Parslip I'd do anyway, and then fell down on the job."

"Very well," said Mr. Simms. "I already have the papers made out for assignment of guardianship. They just need to be signed and witnessed—which we can do here and now.

"Then the next step in what Christopher describes as 'springing' young Johnny—some dreadful convict argot that he has picked up in prison, I suppose—is for the assigned guardians to write to the Commissioner for Public Health and Welfare, enclosing attested copies of the assignment and asking him to release the boy into their custody—which he can do under the authority of the Child Welfare Act. After that the whole matter is in the lap of the gods—or of the commissioner, rather."

"Ye'll draft the letter too, I take it," Mr. Markady said.

"Why, certainly, if you wish," Mr. Simms replied.

"Well," Mr. Markady said, "since ye've had as much experience with matters o' law as I've had raisin' youngsters, 'twould seem the best course, wouldn't ye say?"

"I'll bring it to you in the morning," Mr. Simms promised.

After which the bottle of Demerara was passed around again and Mrs. Markady was told that mummers might be admitted.

The appeal to the commissioner was sent by way of Lattice Harbor and Broadport, since the mail service by coastal boat had ended for the season. Then the long silence began.

The winter slipped whitely by, and the Arctic ice closed in, and Eli closed his grade-ten books for the last time and plunged into the grade-eleven studies, and a second letter was sent, taken by hand to Lattice Harbor, and Easter was upon them before the expected telegram arrived. It invited Mr. Markady to a meeting with the Director of Child Welfare, one of the officers serving under the commissioner, at his office in St. John's.

"Hell of a time o' year fer travelin'," the old captain grumbled as he packed his gold-headed cane and his best black suit. "But 'twill be an excuse to visit David, an' 'twill give Eli that chance to see Christopher that he been pinin' for.

Ye got the mare tackled, lad? . . . Good. I hope we has better luck than the time ye fished me out o' the Cove. Do ye mind that fool Jehu Gilmore callin' on me to repent, an' me strugglin' in the water an' goin' down fer the last time?" He chuckled contentedly as he packed the side sleigh with luggage and rugs against the long trip over the frozen sea.

To reach St. John's they first traveled along the shore ice to Broadport, then up an open stretch of the bay by boat to a large patch of local ice at the inner end, then over this on foot for three miles to a branch railway line, hauling their bags on a borrowed sled. They reached the grimy old capital on the twelfth of April, just as the first ships of the sealing fleet were butting their way into the harbor with loads of fat and pelts and meals of seal flippers for the waiting St. Johnsmen.

They registered at an ancient wooden hotel within sight of the railway station, and the next day Mr. Markady went off to visit his son while Eli hired a cab to take him to the prison beside Quidi Vidi Lake, just beyond the other end of town.

A policeman in a little sentry box at the gate sent Eli's name in to the warden, and moments later another policeman was sent to lead him through the vast stone canyon of the prison yard to the warden's office. There he was met by an aging, gray-faced man, whose natural cheerfulness came through his prison pallor and who revealed a broad streak of kindliness under his burden of worry.

He grinned at Eli and shook his hand and offered him a cigarette, which the boy accepted, though he had never tasted one before, and seated him in a big leather chair in front of his desk.

"Well, Eli," he said, "and how are ye, me b'y? 'Tis the Honorable Mr. Pallisher that I'll have to be callin' ye a few years from now, I'm told. Have to watch me step with ye, won't I?"

Eli was a little taken aback by all this exuberance. "How is Christopher?" he asked.

"Ah, now there's the sort o' man that ye meet but once in a lifetime! 'Tis seldom that we gets the likes of Mr. Simms in a place like this, I'll tell ye. I'm sorry ye'll have to wait a while, but he's out."

"Out?" Eli asked incredulously.

"Down to the customs house on Water Street, as a matter of fact, puttin' through a consignment for the penitentiary."

"You mean he goes out—into the town—on business for you?"

"An' why not, indeed? It wouldn't be runnin' off he'd be, like a criminal, ye don't suppose?" The warden laughed heartily. "Ah, 'tis lucky ye are, me b'y, to have the likes o' Mr. Simms for a friend. He was restless an' high-strung like, the first few days here, but he soon settled down, an' since then he's been the greatest thing that ever happened to this prison. I've made him a promise meself that if he can't get a job when he's released I'll be movin' heaven an' earth to get him back here, on the staff. 'Tis agin' the Act, ye know. But I think maybe I could get the Department o' Justice to put through a minute o' the Governor-in-Commission to make it legal just in this special case, if need be."

So he chatted, candidly, beguilingly, until Christopher arrived, with a police messenger at his elbow.

"The shipment is outside, sir," he reported, "and the bills of lading are in my office."

"Ah yes," said the warden. "I'll attend to it, so I can leave the two o' ye together. Spend as long as ye wish visitin'. Ye can have lunch with the staff, Eli, if ye should want to stay till then."

"Couldn't he have lunch with the prisoners?" Christopher asked.

"Well . . ." the warden considered. "I never heard of it bein' done by a visitor—not even by the members o' the grand jury on official tours—but I can't say as I know any specific regulation agin' it. Anyhow, if ye want it that way I'll arrange it." He chuckled, grinned roguishly. "'Tis ruinin' me prison discipline ye'll be, if I let ye have your way," he said.

Then he went out, closing the door very gently behind him, like a conspirator.

Christopher stood just inside the closed door, looking a little taller, gaunter, and older than when Eli had last seen him, eight months before. His face had taken on a slight cast of sadness, and his eyes a look of strain, as though he might be working too hard at too exacting a job. In spite of his lighthearted letters Eli suspected that prison must have hurt him deeply. Most of the old fun and restlessness and coiled energy seemed to have gone out of him. But beside these surface marks of suffering there was also an inexpressible calm, as though he had learned the secret of an inner peace that the accidents of fortune could not reach. His eyes were alight, now, with quiet pleasure.

"Eli," he said. And he put his arms about the boy, and they stood for a long time saying nothing, doing nothing, merely letting their loneliness be healed, each by the other's presence. And Eli was not ashamed of the tears on his face.

Then they sat, and Christopher's eyes were filled with the old green fire that Eli had always found so fascinating. "I'm proud of you, Eli," he said. "Not just at the trial—though you were wonderful there too—but the way you've acted since. I guess you were forced to grow up much quicker than you should have. And you're going on to become the man I looked forward to. I was afraid, you know, that you wouldn't be able to make it, alone."

"Well, not exactly alone, you know, Chris."

"But even with the help of that grand old man who's adopted you. It would have been awfully easy for you to give in."

"Yes, I know," the boy said humbly. "I almost did. I spent most of a night out in the rain, bawling my head off. And not only that—I might have drowned myself. It didn't seem like drowning at the time, but afterward I realized how awfully close I'd come to it. Or I might have gone crawling back to my father."

"But the thing is, you didn't, no matter how close you came."

"I don't think I could have done it alone, or even with Mr. Markady's backing," Eli said. "It was you, the year before, who made me go on. You remember the night on the cliffs? And the evenings in your father's study?"

"How is my father, by the way?"

"Well, but showing his age. Young Timmy has taken up with him."

"Elias allows it?"

"Oh no! It's a very clandestine affair. There'll be a frightful row if Father finds out."

"Well," Christopher said, "I'm glad Father has someone to keep him company, anyway. Now, tell me about Virginia."

So Eli told him. He told him everything. Even the bit about the coign in the cliff at the Cove where he and Virginia had had their first intercourse, and this, he could see, shook the older man. He ended with an awkward sort of half apology for himself.

"I couldn't help it, Chris. God knows I tried to stop. But I couldn't help myself any more than I could help drowning if I fell overboard in a winter gale. She was the first girl I ever loved—"

"Yes, I know. I know just how it is. I well remember the first I ever loved too. And the first is seldom the last, you know. It is something to remember, tenderly, all your life. But later, if you are lucky, there will be another love, perhaps several others, where you will reach greater emotional depths."

"But that's impossible—" Eli started to protest.

"Yes," said Christopher, "I know it seems impossible now, but that's how it will happen, just the same. You may never again know the airy ecstasies of passion's first flight, but you will know deeper and more abiding emotions later on."

"Maybe," said Eli, unconvinced, "if you say so."

"I'm glad you've told me all this," Christopher said. "You wouldn't tell it at all if your intentions weren't as pure as the daylight."

"Chris," said Eli, "don't get any wrong ideas. I'm not going to give her up—not even to you. If you can take her away from me fair and square, that's something else. But I won't step down—I—I just can't."

"I'm not asking you to give her up," Christopher said, "not yet, anyway. Later on, we'll see."

"Chris," Eli said, puzzled, "it's awfully strange, the way you've acted about this whole thing—"

Christopher cut him short. "I'm just not bedeviled by conventional stupidity, that's all. Do you think I'm fool enough to believe that a woman can love only one man, or only one at a time? Or that she should never open her legs for anyone except her ever-loving spouse? Virginia loves me as much as ever, Eli, or she will when I go back to her. Nothing is changed between us. If she loves you too, that's her business. I'm not going to tell her who she can love and who she can't. I never asked her to be 'faithful' to me, as they call it. I'd have no right to demand that she return to her childhood for two years while I served out a sentence in prison. And I've never been able to see why it should make a woman any less lovely or desirable to a man just because some other man has had a go at her. All that stuff is the rankest kind of bull shit out of the nineteenth century."

"Just the same—" Eli began.

"Just the same nothing," Christopher cut in. "If you and Virginia can get pleasure out of making love together, for God's sake try to do it without feeling guilty on my account."

"I still feel guilty about it," Eli said, "though I'd go on feeling guilty forever rather than give her up."

"Look, Eli, I tried to say this in my first letter, but maybe

I didn't make it clear. It isn't really me that you're feeling guilty about—it's simply that, deep down underneath, in spite of all the unlearning that you have done, you still feel that sex is sinful. You still act as if it ought to be fenced about with taboos. You still can't believe that it is something to be enjoyed with a carefree heart, like a picnic, or a swim in the ocean.

"Look—I'll bet you're still ashamed of masturbation—ashamed to hear it mentioned, ashamed to admit that you practised it regularly before you started having intercourse with Virginia."

Eli nodded dumbly.

"Well, it's nonsense. I do it here in prison, like most of the other prisoners who haven't formed sexual partnerships among themselves. I'd print the fact in the newspapers if it would do any good. All the messy nonsense that clutters up our sex lives from puberty to old age starts with the masturbation taboo, and goes on from that to all the higher forms of sexual activity.

"Now," he said, "you know where your guilt springs from. Face it. Think about it. In a little while you'll be able to get rid of it, along with all the other lumber that your ignorant parents piled on your young back when you were a baby."

Eli whistled, and laughed. "Gosh! What a speech!" he said.

"I know I sometimes make speeches," Christopher said. "But that's my job. Don't try to wriggle off by accusing me of speechifying."

"I'm sorry, Chris," said the boy. "I'll try."

"Try hard. Remember, next time you start feeling guilty because you and Virginia are doing what any two healthy youngsters ought to do, that the reason for your feelings is that your mother slapped your hands the first time she saw you start to play with your genitals when you were lying in the cradle before you could talk." Christopher grinned—the old, infectious, lovable grin that had helped to endear him from the time they had first met. "Feel better, Eli?"

"Yes." The boy grinned back at him.

"Good. Now we can move on to something else. What other news do you have?"

"Johnny."

"Oh, yes. How have you got along with your appeal to the commissioner?"

"We really came to St. John's just for that," Eli said. "We are here to try to spring him, as you suggested in your letters. His guardianship has been legally transferred to Mr. and Mrs. Markady, and the department has accepted the transfer and registered it. The Director of Child Welfare then invited Mr. Markady to come to his office for an interview, and we are to see him this afternoon."

"That sounds encouraging," said Christopher. "See whom, do you mean? Johnny, or the director?"

"The director."

"But you'll see Johnny too?"

"Yes. We'll be seeing Johnny too, either this evening or the first thing tomorrow morning."

"Poor Johnny," Christopher mused. "What happened to that poor child shouldn't have happened to a dog. It was hard enough on you and me and Virginia—the trial, I mean—but at least we could understand what was going on. Think how much harder it must have been for him, facing something completely beyond his understanding. Wouldn't it be shocking if Brother John and Solomon Marks, trying to destroy me, only succeeded in destroying a little boy?"

"I feel, myself, that I let Johnny down," Eli confessed.

"That's how it always is." Christopher sighed. "I've had the same sort of feeling, more than once. Even when we do our best it is never really enough. We just have to keep on, that's all. Why do you feel that you let Johnny down?"

"After your arrest I never really got through to him," Eli said. "But I never really tried as hard as I could have. I had other things to do, you see."

"There are never any other things so important as people," Christopher told him. "You'll just have to make another try with Johnny, and try harder this time."

"Yes," Eli promised, "I'll do it if they'll give me the chance."

CHAPTER TWENTY-SIX

So they talked until the forenoon was spent, and ate lunch with the prisoners in the mess hall, as Christopher had suggested. Then Joshua Markady arrived and took Eli with him to the office of the Director of Child Welfare.

The director turned out to be a wizened and careworn man with a face like the prunes of yesteryear, and a tired voice and a hopeless manner, as though from the beginning he had expected nothing at all out of life and had since found his expectations richly confirmed.

"Ah, Mr. Markady—" he said.

"This," said Joshua, "is me youngest boy, Eli."

"Ah," said the director, waving them toward chairs in his little, dim office. "You have come about the Penchley boy, of course." He pressed a button that was set into the edge of his desk, and a sunken-faced lady of middle years appeared from the adjoining office.

"Ah," he said, "Miss Template. Let me have the file on the Penchley boy, if you please—the one I asked about for this afternoon's appointment."

Miss Template, who had the file already in her hand, laid it gently on his desk and drifted out like thistledown in a zephyr.

"Ah—ah—difficult case, Mr. Markady," the director began, turning his spectacles on the old captain, "very difficult— most unresponsive. Frankly if the boy wasn't a first offender, and so young, I'd be inclined to keep him for a rather long spell of—ah—treatment. But there *is* a chance that he might respond to an—ah—change of environment."

"I'm sure I could keep the lad out o' trouble, if that's what ye mean," Mr. Markady told him.

"I don't doubt you, sir," the director said. "You impress me immediately as a most competent man. Besides, we have —ah—looked into your—ah—background, you know—always do in cases like this, of course." He smiled bleakly. "But you are taking on an—ah—difficult assignment, Mr. Markady— most difficult, it is only fair to warn you. Have you—by any chance—heard anything at all about the boy's record since we—ah—admitted him to the home?"

"Record?" Mr. Markady asked. "No."

"Well—ah—" The director consulted his file. "I do hope this doesn't make you change your mind. . . . Ah—let me see. First of all, we hadn't had custody of him for more than—ah—six weeks, apparently it was—before he ran away. No difficulty about running away, you know. There aren't any locks or bars or anything of that sort. He and two others —they were both older than he—disappeared, and were— ah—at large for—let me see—ten days, before we found them here in St. John's, being sheltered in—ah—well, I'm afraid it was a house of ill fame, to tell you the truth—in the lower part of the town, near the waterfront, you know." He pursed his lips and peered over his spectacles to see how Mr. Markady was taking all this, but Mr. Markady merely nodded and said nothing.

"After his return to the home there was a record of—ah —persistent hostility, I'm afraid. No progress in schoolwork, according to the teacher's report. Poor co-operation in work teams. That's on the farm, you know. The report of the superintendent mentions poor response to—ah—discipline.

"And then, last month, he was involved in—ah—a plot— to burn the home down, I'm afraid, according to the evidence."

"Burn it down!" Mr. Markady said incredulously.

"I'm afraid so, sir," said the director. "That's arson, you

know—a most serious crime. Almost succeeded too. Think of it! A public building worth a hundred thousand dollars!"

"Ye are not makin' much progress reformin' the lad," Mr. Markady observed.

"That would seem to be—ah—incontestable, I'm afraid," the director admitted. "Er—after hearing all this, do you—ah—still wish to assume the responsibility—"

"All the more reason the lad ought to be released, if ye ask me," Mr. Markady told him. "Looks as though he needs a home an' family in the worst kind o' way."

"I'm not sure that I agree with you entirely," the director said. "It happens sometimes, even in the most—ah—recalcitrant cases, that we begin to make progress after a year or so. And yet—I must admit—this boy seems to have an—ah—antipathy to institutional treatment. They are well cared for at the home, you know—ah—well fed—they all gain weight rapidly—comfortably housed, given just the right amount of firm discipline—and a good deal of freedom and responsibility. We expect co-operation from the boys, and as a rule, I'm glad to say, we get it. We try to impress upon them that they are there to be helped, not punished."

The director went on with his little lecture, which Eli guessed must be kept in a pigeonhole in his mind expressly for occasions such as this, but ended by telling them that they could drive out to the home the next morning in a government car, talk to the superintendent and to Johnny, and then, if the interviews were satisfactory, he would see about signing the release papers for the youngster.

He dismissed their protests of thanks with a wave of the hand and rang for Miss Template, who promptly materialized.

"Ah—Miss," he said. "Will you arrange for a car from the motor pool to pick up Mr.—ah—Markady and his son here, at ten tomorrow morning, and take them to the—ah—boys' home? Please call the superintendent in advance, and explain. Oh, and Miss Template, I'll want the file on that—ah—affiliation case—"

"It's already on your desk, sir," she said softly.

Miss Template picked up Johnny's dossier and drifted away with it, as the director began studying a thick sheaf of correspondence, a worried frown on his brow. Mr. Markady and Eli almost tiptoed as they followed Miss Template out the door into the corridor.

The superintendent who met them in his office at the Boys' Home and Training School the next morning was a square, brisk man with an urbane and charming manner. He insisted upon chatting at length, and on impressing them with the splendid record of his institution. He was a community man too, he let them know casually—member of the Red Cross and the Rotary Club, an organizer of rural councils, and of amateur concerts, and of football matches and the like.

They listened patiently through what they felt was far too much of this sort of thing before, at long last, the superintendent sent for Johnny. The boy came to the door and knocked rather timidly and stood at attention just inside, his eyes roving over the three of them, but saying nothing at all except, "Yes, sir," and, "No, sir," when the superintendent spoke to him. He was reserved, withdrawn, and watchful. Eli thought that he looked very strange in his black oxfords, long pants, white shirt, and tie—and with a haircut. Johnny had always had a mop of unmanageable red hair—now it was cropped short, and it was neat and slick. His eyes, which had always danced, were sober and cautious.

"How be ye, lad?" Mr. Markady asked.

"Fine, sir, thank you."

"Ye've grown a little, I see."

"Yes, sir."

"Like it here?"

There was a long pause. "No, sir."

Mr. Markady laughed and turned to the superintendent. "Tells the truth, anyway," he said.

But the superintendent was not amused. "Come," he said to Mr. Markady, rising from his desk. "I'll show you our facilities. The boys may accompany us if they wish."

They trooped out after him into the hallway, but as he began pointing out the schoolroom, the game room, and so forth, with Mr. Markady mumbling words of appreciation at appropriate intervals, Eli felt a tug at his sleeve and heard a small voice in his ear.

"Eli—can't we go off, alone?"

"Sure," he whispered back; then, to Mr. Markady: "We'll meet you back in the office. Johnny is going to show me the grounds."

They went outside, across a yard full of dust, baked hard now with the spring rains and sun, and through a screen of trees that looked rather the worse for wear. Out of sight of the main building, they went down a bank to a pile of boulders beside a scrap of a lake. Here Johnny turned and faced the older boy, took hold of his coat urgently, and looked into his face with eyes alive with desperation.

"Eli," he said, "ye've got to get me out of here—Eli, *please!* I know I disobeyed ye, an' I know I done wrong. But, honest, I'll be a good boy. I'll do anything you say. Jesus, Eli— oh, I'm sorry—swearin' is somethin' ye pick up when you're here—Eli, ye don't know what this place is like—"

"Easy, Johnny! Ease off there!" He tightened his grip on the youngster's arm. "That's what we are here for. I can't promise for sure yet, but we are trying to get you out. We want to take you home, to live with Mr. and Mrs. Markady and me. You'd like that, wouldn't you? Your grandmother has signed papers turning you over to Mr. and Mrs. Markady as your legal guardians."

The boy said nothing, just sat down on a boulder, his eyes widening as he thought over this possibility, and it seemed for a moment to Eli as if he might be going to cry. But Johnny was a tough youngster, toughened in a hard school.

"Tell me about it," Eli said gently. "I hear you ran away to St. John's soon after they brought you here."

"Yes," he said. "I busted out. Me an' two others. 'Twas grand, bein' free, while it lasted. An' some real kind people took us in an' fed us—some young whores who was real pretty, an' a old whore who owned the place, an' was the others' mother or somethin' an' made a real pet out o' me till the cops come. But when we got caught an' brought back we was whipped—" His eyes clouded with pain, remembering.

"Tell me," Eli encouraged him.

"About the whippin'?"

"Yes."

"Well, there's a man here they calls the Whipper. Ye see 'im goin' into the school, or down the hall, he's on reg'lar duty, like the other officers. Ye see 'im goin' into the gym building, ye know some guy is gettin' whipped. That's where they do it, in the gym. . . .

"Eli, ye know I usta get licked in school—well, that ain't nothin'—just a fly bite. Unless ye been whipped the way they do it here, ye ain't never been hurt. The Whipper takes down yer pants, an' ties ye down over a thing they calls the horse, an' lays into ye with a split leather strap till the blood runs down yer legs, an' ye can't scream no more—"

"Jesus, Johnny!" Eli said, horrified.

"I got twenty licks that first time," he recalled. "Ye couldn't believe there'd be pain like it. Ye go mad while they're doin' it—seems to go on forever, it do, an' the screeches like they're comin' from someone else—"

Eli reached out and put an arm about the boy's shoulders, but he was rigid with the memory of torture. "How I hate 'em!" he said with deep, bitter conviction. "An' then, the loneliness—Jesus, Eli, 'tis lonely here!"

"You tried to burn down the school, didn't you?"

"Sure did!" His freckled face lit up with the memory. "Do it again too, did I get the chance! Me an another guy, name of Hill—big fella—but 'twas me own idea. We was sent to the furnace room that day, rakin' ashes, an' we snuck down a lot of old rags soaked in oil from the gen'rator

buildin'! . . . Jesus, Eli! What a blaze! I wish ye coulda seen
it. Boy, did she ever go—like a bonfire night at home. Ye
could see the flames reflectin' in the lake, an' everythin'—
an' the basement windows popped like gunshots—trapped
gas, they said. But they kept the fire in the basement," he
said sadly. "They found it too soon, an' pumped in soda an'
chloride an' stuff—only fer that we'da leveled 'er to the
ground!"

"How did they catch you?"

"Well, they never did, really. But we was on furnace detail, an' all the other guys was accounted for one way or
another, so though we wasn't caught, they just *knew*. They
locked us in the punishment cell. 'Tis pitch-black, ye know
—no windows. We was put in one at a time, an' we was told
we'd be left there till we confessed. . . . But we never confessed." He spoke with a flicker of pride, as one who had
overcome by great endurance.

"Then," he said, "though they never had no real proof that
we done it we was took to the gym an' whipped, with the
superintendent lookin' on to make sure the Whipper didn't
let us off easy—not that there'd be much chance o' that. The
whippin' went on longer'n before, an' I fainted, an' come to
in the doctor's office. I ain't healed proper even yet, after
that last whippin'. Ye want I should show ye?"

"No," Eli said hoarsely. "There'll be time enough later.
Johnny, I promise you we'll not go home without you—not if
we have to go back and camp on the doorstep of the director
till the time of the caplin scull. We never guessed, Johnny
—my God!— We never guessed anything like this, or we
would have been here before."

"The guys don't say much about it, gener'ly," the boy
said. "Some of 'em, they has mothers an' fathers as visits 'em
sometimes, Sunday afternoons—but they don't say."

"Come," Eli said, rising. "We've got to go back and have
it out with the superintendent—but you're coming home
with us—I'll tell you that." He reached out and took the boy's
hand in his, and they walked up through the trees, and

Johnny let Eli hold his hand but pulled away as they emerged into the yard.

"Guys'd say I was queer or somethin'," he apologized, "like the ones spends their nights with the doctor an' gets cigarettes for it."

"Johnny, it isn't going to matter what the guys say once you are out of here. What's all this about the doctor, anyway?"

"Doctor's a queer," he announced. "Ye know what a queer is, don't ye, Eli? That's what they sent the teacher to jail for—cause they said he was a queer. I never knew, before I come here, but ye learn a lot from the guys in a place like this."

When they re-entered the school building Mr. Markady and the superintendent were back in the office, and the superintendent was beaming in his very best Rotarian manner. "It's all arranged," he said. "Penchley, you will go pack your things. You are being discharged into Mr. Markady's custody. I hope you have learned some useful lessons here, and that you will be able to stay out of trouble in the future. Now hurry along."

"They sent the papers down with us this mornin'," Mr. Markady explained to Eli, "signed by the commissioner an' all. I've jest got to put me signature to 'em an' the whole transaction is complete."

So Johnny was sprung, and began his long, painful journey back to the human race. They took him with them to the hotel for the night and got passage by train the next morning.

As the journey proceeded Eli kept trying to talk with the boy, and Johnny kept slipping out of his reach. Following the outburst of confidence at the lake, it seemed the youngster's reserve had returned. He made it clear that he was grateful, but that he wasn't ready to be close and confidential and pally with anybody. Perhaps, Eli reflected, that would come later. He noticed that Johnny had occasional flashes of gaiety, as when he stood out on the brakes, getting soot all over his freckled face and imitating the hooting of the train. But the deep hurt kept returning, and he would withdraw, as under a cloak, for protection from the fingers of the world, even if those fingers meant to be kind.

"He be like a stranger most o' the time," Mr. Markady observed.

"'Tis no wonder," Eli replied. "Did you know that they flogged him half to death?"

"No," Mr. Markady said slowly, "I didn't—didn't know they still did that sort o' thing—though I half suspected something o' the kind. He talked to ye about it?"

"Yes, and it was so bad that I couldn't bear to repeat it."

"So now," Mr. Markady mused, "so indeed? We'll have to be uncommonly gentle an' patient with the lad, I expect, if we are to bring 'im back to himself."

But Johnny's gratitude in part offset his aloofness. "I promised ye I'd be a good boy, an' I will, Eli," he said. "I'll be goin' back to school, I s'pose, as soon as the Easter holidays is over?"

"Of course," Eli said.

"Well, I'll be good in school, then."

"That'll be a relief—and quite a change." Eli laughed.

"Well, I'll be quiet, you'll see. An' I'll do me lessons, even if that mean old Miss Parslip *is* the teacher—an' ye'll help me sometimes with me homework, won't ye?"

"Yes indeed," Eli promised, smiling, "as often as you wish."

He wrote to Christopher from the train, telling of their success, and he mailed the letter from the junction where they changed trains to travel on the branch line to the head of the bay. He hardly more than hinted at Johnny's experiences in the reform school, but Christopher read between the lines and referred to it in his next letter.

"You are to make it up to him, Eli," he wrote. "I don't expect you to love the child as I do. Not everyone has the same talent for those things, any more than everyone has your gift for mathematics. But so long as you are part of the human race, you have a responsibility toward all of its children."

Their return with Johnny, who had suffered only six months of his allotted twenty-four, was a shock to the elders, and to Solomon Marks in particular. They grumbled and made thin lines of their already thin mouths. Sister Leah laid down the law to her Sunday-school class that they were not on any account to play with the young outcast. Johnny's grandmother was sharply reproved in prayer meeting for having abandoned her God-given charge to the agents of the devil, but the old woman replied, with the only spirit that she had ever been known to show, that the whole congregation had abandoned Johnny to the devil the autumn before. At this she was admonished, and prayed over, and brought back to the Lord. But they found out that there was nothing they could do. Johnny's escape from the church and the law was a *fait accompli*.

CHAPTER TWENTY-SEVEN

No better time could have been chosen for starting anew, for it was in the first flush of spring—the great season of healing. And for once the unpredictable Newfoundland weather had decided to produce a classical springtime rather than six weeks of fog and drizzle.

Spring coming, things rustling and growing: the grass pushing up again this year, just as it had for millions of years; the cherries and the chuckly pears breaking out into white, beside the tender young green of the birches; robins murmuring in the white night, and the smell of balsam and poplar giving the air a heavy, resinous tang, bitter and sweet and wild all at once—spring coming and the rivers flowing, and the young things of the wilderness poking their soft noses into the most secret places of the world.

Eli was disappointed in Johnny as the weeks slipped by. Miss Parslip, it is true, was delighted with the reformation that he showed in school. He worked like a beaver, she reported, and actually caught up with his class, for he was quick and intelligent and found the routine of learning no trouble when he applied his mind to it. The teacher tried—perhaps in compensation for former hostility—to treat him as a sort of class favorite, but he fended her off, firmly and politely.

With Eli the youngster was reserved in a different sort of

way. Though never overtly affectionate or confidential, he treated the older boy much as though he were his father.

It was: "Eli, may I go out with Abel Gilmore in his father's boat, to see can we jig a fish?"; "I've done my lessons, Eli. Will you ask me my spellings?"; "How soon am I going to be allowed to go swimming? You know I wouldn't sneak off till you say I can"; "Can I visit Gran tonight?"; "Eli, the weather is warm. May I go barefoot?" (Under Miss Parslip's influence he was beginning to say "may" part of the time, and starting to drop the "be" and "ye" that were so much an integral part of the speech of the Bight.)

The child tugged constantly at Eli's heartstrings, for he sensed in him the continuance of a deep loneliness that he could not touch or heal. When he saw him running bare-footed for the first time that year, crossing the young green grass of the abandoned fields, going all alone to the thickets of alder and swamp maple to think the spring thoughts of childhood without a companion, he wanted to give chase, to force himself into Johnny's confidence and be told his in-nermost dreams. But it was useless. The boy could not be approached that way. He seemed, Eli thought, like a changeling out of an Irish folk tale—a child who wrung your heart without being quite human.

Nevertheless Johnny came back an hour or so later, limp-ing slightly. "I've a splinter," he said and put his foot on Eli's knee and sat stoically while it was dug out. It was deep, and must have hurt, but he didn't wince—just sucked in his breath sharply when Eli dropped iodine into the cut.

Then, impulsively, Eli kissed the small toes lying trust-ingly in his hand. "Be more careful," he said. "If you get your feet cut up I'll have to make you wear shoes."

"I'll be careful," Johnny promised him and turned to go, then turned back again. "You are good to me, Eli," he said. "I want you to know I'm grateful."

But that was all. In a moment he had turned again and run lightly off on some other lonely errand of childhood along the hazy margin of the wood.

With Virginia the boy seemed to be more responsive. Perhaps he saw in her the mother he could not remember. Perhaps the first faint intimations of manhood in his troubled heart were beginning to respond to her powerful appeal. However it was, Eli sometimes found them together, completely absorbed in each other—even, on one occasion, spinning a foolish romance between them, each contributing alternate sections to a story full of knights and dragons and beleaguered princesses.

Johnny had not spoken of Christopher to Eli even once after the day in the grounds of the reform school.

Then he decided to take Johnny fishing. It would be just the thing for a twelve-year-old boy who was too moody and too much by himself, he decided. Eli had no need, of course, to fish for a living, but it was spring, and he felt the sea calling him. Every time he heard the surf he found himself wishing he were slipping down the slope of a big green wave into the valley of its trough.

It was still too early for cod traps, but fish were being taken on jiggers and on baited lines, so Eli and Johnny worked together to put Mr. Markady's long-disused stage back into condition and to refit one of his small boats for hand lining.

They fished only in the late afternoons, when schoolwork was done, on Saturdays, and (supreme blasphemy) on Sundays. But the fish had come early that spring, and were running to large sizes, so that the pile of.split salt-bulk cod in the shed soon began to look impressive.

Hand lining is more like sport than it is like commercial fishing, and for Johnny it was quite an adventure. It was the first time he had worked in a boat with a real fisherman, and the first time he had done anything to earn money of his own. To Eli it was all pretty old stuff, but he still found it exciting, especially before repetition had taken the edge off the pleasure.

You catch the big cod one at a time, on a baited line, or

with a jigger, which is really much the same thing as the heavy plug used by surf casters. Then you haul them in to drop them, flopping, into the bottom of your boat. Since the individual fish sometimes weighed as much as thirty or forty pounds the contest was often enough to put Johnny on his mettle. Boys of his size had been known to lose the struggle and go headfirst over the side, sea boots and all, with nothing but their jigger lines connecting them to the boat.

The jiggers they used were made of lead, which they had poured themselves into a wooden mold the shape of a small fish, except that the small fish had two big hooks sticking out of its snout. This they dropped on the end of a heavy line until they felt it hit bottom. Then they hauled in about a fathom of it and worked it up and down through the water to attract the codfish. When it started to drag, they knew they had a fish and it was time to haul in. Occasionally, when the fish were plentiful, you might get two on a single jigger, one on each hook.

As the fish were hauled over the gunwale the boys would remove them with a flick of the wrist, tossing the jigger back into the water with the same movement. On days when the cod were running well the two of them would soon be knee deep in a mass of live fish, all gasping for water and squirming between their legs.

After some hours of this they would be wet and slimy, and their backs would be aching from the strain of handling the jiggers or baited lines. Then they would reel up their gear and head back for harbor.

Cleaning the fish was no great chore. They worked together at the splitting table, Johnny heading, Eli using the splitting knife. The heads were snapped off across the end of the table, the body passed along to the splitter, who laid open his fish with one clean sweep of the curved, square-tipped knife, so that the guts came away in a single mass and the whole fish lay flat, like an unfolded newspaper. The livers were pushed into a tub to be rotted for oil. The rest of the offal dropped through a hole in the decking of the store into the sea below, where thousands of conners gathered to feast upon it. It took only seconds before the split fish was ready for salt.

Sometimes they worked in the store after dark under the light of swinging oil lanterns hanging from the flimsy rafters. Mr. Markady told Eli that in his own young days he had worked by the light of cod-oil lamps, as all the people of Newfoundland had done for centuries. Those primitive lamps smoked and gave forth a reddish light, and had been replaced, some years before Eli was born, with imported kerosene lanterns.

Virginia would sometimes go down to the store after supper to help them put their fish into salt, as the women of Caplin Bight had always done for their menfolk, time out of mind. She regarded the job as a lark, and was proud to be working for Eli as though she were his wife. His mother had been better than Virginia, an expert in the fish store—as good as any man, and better than most, at judging the amount of salt needed for a good shore cure. But Virginia was very willing, and a lot more fun than anyone's mother to have working with you, and it gave him great pleasure to teach her.

Since the regular fishermen were still working salmon, and none of the trap crews was out, Timmy sometimes went to the store also, mainly to cut out the tongues from the discarded heads. The fish were such monsters that all the tongues were big enough for the pan. He would string them on a wire and sell them to people in the village, ten for a cent. Since it was cash work—small as the returns might be— Elias never thought of forbidding his younger son to do it. A boy in Caplin Bight had the same right to cut fish tongues, wherever fish were being landed, as he had to breathe, and no one would have dreamed of stopping him.

The sea offers little to equal a meal of cod tongues. Mr. Markady, who had sampled sea food from just about everywhere, told Eli that oysters from the Caribbean—little bean-sized things served in Creole sauce—had their place, as did scallops from the Bay of Fundy fried in meal and deep fat until crisp—or baked squid, stuffed and cooked by a Frenchman who knew the secret of using herbs, or shrimp as cooked by a Chinaman in a sweet sauce for a café in Hong Kong, or spider crabs, taken from the deeps of the ocean and served with white wine in Seville, but none of them had the sheer magic of a big platter of cod tongues rolled in salt and flour, fried in pork fat so that they were just crisp on the outside, with the inside partly filled with tender white meat and partly with a wonderful jelly, giving forth the most delicate and appetizing aroma.

When the fish were put away Timmy would sometimes sneak into the Markady kitchen, where they would fry five or six dozen tongues, and Virginia and Eli and Joshua and Anne and Timmy and Johnny would all gorge themselves on them. They were evenings long to be treasured with the thought of home: the lamps bathing the kitchen in liquid gold, the dishes glittering from the shelves above the dresser, the table shining with bright-flowered oilcloth, and platters of smoking cod tongues coming off the stove, filling the house with the glorious odor of their perfection.

The boys fished, it must be admitted, only when they had a mind to. There were many other attractions that spring —not the least of them Joshua Markady's bird boat and his endless stocks of homemade shells. Eli and he were both excellent shots and they began to teach Johnny, going out evenings just at dusk, or mornings at dawn for ducks migrating northward, and murres, and other salt-water birds, such as bawks.

The ducks were rated very high-class meat, but there were some who liked murres even more. The murres—or turrs, as they are more commonly known in Newfoundland —are not counted as game birds in southern countries, but have an enormous reputation in the north. Bawks, on the other hand, which are sometimes called eggdowns, or hagdons, or shearwaters, are not highly rated for food, and are mostly eaten when other birds are not available. They are common in summer and fall, while the other birds are more plentiful in winter and spring.

During their hunting trips they were often wet and cold. But the excitement of the hunt banished all thought of discomfort. If salt spray blew down their necks it didn't matter, for there, dead ahead, showing on the crest of a far wave, between Lattice Harbor Island and the point of the Reach, was a line of black dots on the water—two lines!

"*Now*, boy!" Mr. Markady would whisper tensely when they had approached so closely that his keen old eyes could see the heads turn toward them.

Then Johnny would cut the engine and let the boat coast gently toward the birds as the two men stood, guns at the ready, trying to judge to a fraction of an inch how much the boat would roll with the next wave. People who shoot pheasants or clay pigeons ashore, with both feet planted on solid earth, have no idea of the problems of the turr shooter. His target is moving, and he is moving, and the motions of both are constantly changing. One moment the turrs are obscured by a wave; the next they are outlined against the sky with an underscoring of spray. Up come the guns—and just at that instant the boat seems to drop into a bottomless pit beneath the shooters' boots.

Their homecomings, of course, were a triumph. Wet mitts and bay wool socks and blue Guernseys would be hung behind the stove to dry, and Mr. Markady would tell long yarns about guns and shooting and the bays full of ducks that he had seen on Labrador, while the boys toasted their toes at the oven and Mrs. Markady got a few of the birds ready for a scoff.

A scoff of turrs would sometimes be just a bake, or sometimes a pie, with thick pastry over it, or sometimes a rich chowder. Eli liked them best in a pie, with onions and potatoes and a few rashers of fat pork. When the pie was ready for the oven Eli and Johnny would be shooed away from the stove, and would curl up on the settle. Then Mr. Markady would get out his black pipe and fill the room with its blue haze and talk about his years at sea, while the heavenly aroma of roasting wild fowl mingled with the steam from the wet wool clothing and the strong incense of the pipe and the perfume of crackling spruce logs in the firebox.

Then Virginia would come to share their late supper; presently Johnny would pack away his schoolbooks and trot off to bed, and they would sit far into the night, under the benison of the lamplight, sharing such moments of peace as few men garner out of their lives of struggle and strife.

CHAPTER TWENTY-EIGHT

❧ ❧

But while Eli and Virginia and Johnny drank down great drafts of springtime there were others in the village drinking the poisoned cup of mixed dogmas. In the little Church of the Firstborn the burgeoning of the year brought neither joy nor peace. For Brother John's ecclesia it had been a turbulent winter, and as the sun rose higher above the sea, drawing Caplin Bight gently but powerfully into the ambit of summer, the signs of trouble did not decrease but rather continued to multiply. With the unfurling of the first green leaves the pastor's sermons grew more and more infused with flights of his fanciful oratory, drawn from the prophecies and the Apocalypse, while in private he became more and more gloomy and distracted.

Eli saw him from time to time, flitting about the village like a black ghost, grown thinner than formerly, and with a few strands of gray starting to show in the dark mane of his hair. He got frequent reports on events inside the church from his young brother, who came regularly to the fish store in the evenings.

"Ye should've heard him last night," Timmy reported to Eli and Johnny as they worked at the splitting table one Monday afternoon. "A fair treat it was. He had this text out o' the Book of Leviticus, where the Jewish high priest curses a goat—ye know it, Eli."

"Yes," Eli said, "the scapegoat. It was sent out into the

desert to be eaten by a demon, taking all the sins of the people with it.'"

"That's it," said Timmy. "The scapegoat. Well, Brother John stood up in the pulpit, like this"—and the youngster drew himself up, trying to look black and tragic—"an' says as how it is fittin' that one should suffer fer the sins o' many, an' 'tis the Lord's righteous will an' so on. An' then he says as how the shepherd should suffer for his sheep, an' take upon hisself their iniquities. An' after that he launches into a prayer, callin' down the wrath o' God on his own head."

"He's beginning to sound like Jehu Gilmore," Eli commented.

"Yes," said Timmy. "Jehu was hollerin' out too most o' the time, but Brother John couldn't fetch the others. Father says as how 'tis an unsound doctrine, an' him an' Elder Thomas Gilmore of Matthew talked it over up to our house after church, an' they've called a meetin' of the elders for tomorrow night."

Eli subsequently heard the results of that meeting too. Brother John admitted to them that his attempts to recompute the chronology had ended in failure and that no amount of wrestling with God had vouchsafed to him any newer vision. And Thomas Gilmore of Matthew told him plainly that he feared this might be because he was straying from the "truth once delivered unto the saints."

Brother John denied that he was straying, but the elders pointed out to him that novelties, undeniably, were creeping into his teaching. The "truth once delivered unto the saints," it turned out, was the body of religious doctrine that they, the elders, had been taught in Sunday school. Brother John, perforce, humbled himself before this rebuke and promised to examine his heart and his texts for purity of doctrine. But from that day forward the trumpet of his voice gave forth an uncertain sound.

Meanwhile Sister Leah became ever more rigid and withdrawn and uncompromising and scornful of the weakness of the flesh.

"She looks like a hawk, ready to pounce," Timmy told Eli, "an' every time she gets the chance she pounces on Brother John. She took it up with him in prayer meetin' last week, sayin' the Lord needed a strong rod fer the execution o' His wrath, not one as would bend with every wind that blew. An' Sunday evenin' she sat through his sermon, while he talked about the love o' God an' the remission o' sins, lookin' at 'im like he was one o' the boys in her Sunday-school class who she was goin' to report home for a lickin' because he didn't know his texts."

But if Sister Leah regarded Brother John as a moral delinquent she never mentioned it. It seemed to be his failure as a religious leader that she could not forgive, and by her attitude toward his progressive degeneration delivered a rebuke more telling than any words could express.

His decline as a spiritual leader proceeded slowly. Throughout the winter he had sunk gradually from his pinnacle of the year before toward a nadir that the congregation could not overlook. He seemed to have lost his touch, so that when his sermons were not wild they were insipid. Once he was confined by the elders within the narrow limits of the "faith once delivered unto the saints," he seemed to lose his inspiration altogether, and, just about the time the first salmon were being taken in the nets beside the sunkers and along the shore to the north, it reached the point where they decided to call a meeting of the congregation to discuss the pastorate. Nothing of the sort had happened since the dismissal of Pastor Tishrite three years before. Only on rare and solemn occasions were such meetings called.

"I think they must be gettin' ready to chuck 'im out," Timmy prophesied. "'E just about made it last night, that's all."

"Well, then, what happened?" Eli asked eagerly.

"Oh, there was a hell of a lot o' prayin' an' carryin' on," Timmy said, "an' we sung hymns, ye know, an' the elders prayed in turn fer God to give Brother John guidance an' light. An' then the elders made 'im answer a whole slew o' questions about how he stood in the faith."

"My God!" said Eli. "He must have felt like a worm."

"No," said Timmy. "He stood up to 'em and beat 'em down, text fer text. When they quoted one Scripture at 'im, he had another right ready to quote back. He got the Bible almost by heart, ye know, better'n any o' the elders. An' in the end he took the meetin' out o' the hands o' Thomas Gilmore of Matthew an' Solomon Marks, who was conductin' it, an' prayed fer the souls o' the flock, an' God's fergiveness on the sinners among 'em."

"What's Solomon Marks doing in all this?" Eli wanted to know.

"Not much," Timmy reported. "He's still chairman of the council of elders, ye know, an' he's supposed to have charge o' the prayer meetin's, but 'tis Thomas Gilmore of Matthew as really runs 'em, an' 'tis him as looks like he's out to get Brother John."

"Good luck to him too," Eli said.

It was Thomas Gilmore of Matthew himself who sought Eli out the next afternoon as he and Johnny docked their skiff with a part load of fish at Mr. Markady's stage.

"Eli," the mill owner called down as they looked up from the boat, "I've a matter to talk over with ye. Can ye leave the fish be fer a few minutes an' come up to me store?"

"Don't see why not," Eli said. "Johnny, you fork up the fish by yourself, will you? And then see that the boat is moored properly."

"Sure, Eli," the youngster said. "You go ahead."

They walked up the short path to the mill store in silence and sat in the dusty interior, where the afternoon sunlight fell through the small squared panes and lit the dust motes like a misty morning in a forest. The mill owner took out his pipe and lit it, spending some time about the job, as though making up his mind how to tackle the subject. "'Tis like this, Eli," he said. "We been havin' a mite o' trouble with the pastor, an' I think ye might be able to help clear it up."

"Me?" Eli said. "What on earth have I got to do with it?"

"Well—nothin', directly. But I do think Brother John got things on 'e's mind as ye might know about."

"Ah, I see," said Eli.

"Ay," Thomas Gilmore agreed, "ye do. Now I heered last summer when ye come back from that trial in St. John's as there was somewhat went on as wasn't fully told. Jest a rumor, 'tis true. But didn't ye stand up in court an' accuse John McKim of tryin' to bugger ye or somethin'? I never did hear the rights of it."

"Yes," Eli said. "I told the court that Brother John was guilty of the crime of which Christopher was accused."

"So now—" Thomas Gilmore mused. "An' didn't it occur to ye that ye should o' come to prayer meetin' an' said the same thing, plain an' open, in the sight o' God an' men?"

"No," said Eli bluntly. "It didn't. Even when I said it in court nobody seemed to believe me, except Sister Leah, and she kept her mouth shut. Do you think they'd have believed me in prayer meeting? My own father didn't believe me."

"No," Thomas Gilmore agreed. "Ye may be right. Ye mightn't've been believed—not then—but things've changed these last few months. I'd say ye'd be believed today."

"Are you asking me to go to prayer meeting," Eli demanded, "and accuse Brother John of leading me into what you people describe as 'unnatural sin'?"

"Well, 'tis true, ain't it?"

"Yes, 'tis true enough," Eli said.

"Then what's stoppin' ye?"

"I don't know—I'll have to think about it," Eli said. "No. On second thought, I won't. I don't belong to your church any longer and I swore to my father that I'd never darken its door again. I'll not go."

"The Lord will not hold ye to an oath taken in haste an' in anger," Thomas Gilmore said.

"No," said Eli. "Perhaps not. But he'll hold me to not being a hypocrite."

"I'm sorry, lad, I don't follow ye," Thomas Gilmore said.

"Look, Mr. Gilmore, don't you understand that I don't believe in your religion any more? Any of it. The God I believe in now is as different from yours as the God of the Jews was from the iron idol Moloch."

"So?" said Thomas Gilmore. "Can it be, lad? Ay—I can see ye mean it. Why, if John McKim have been the cause of drivin' ye so far from the truth he'll have much to answer fer at the throne o' jedgment."

"He's already judged himself and damned himself," Eli said. "Anything else that happens will be only trimmings."

"Then ye'll not do as I ask?" Thomas Gilmore of Matthew said.

"No," said Eli. "If you asked me to go to court as a witness against Brother John I might do it—I don't know—but I'll not be his accuser in a prayer meeting."

"Not even if it was the means o' helpin' Mr. Simms?" the mill owner asked slyly.

This jolted Eli, and he wavered for a moment. But then, he thought quickly, if he hadn't been able to help Christopher in court how could he do him any real good in prayer meeting? "No," he replied firmly, "not even to help Mr. Simms. Christopher wouldn't want to be helped by any such gambit."

"Ay," said Thomas Gilmore. "Well, boy, if ye won't, ye won't, but since ye assure me that Brother John be a fallen man, guilty o' carnal sin, I'll have to follow it up meself, in meetin'. How far did 'e go with ye?"

"Far enough," Eli said bitterly. "We slept like man and wife dozens of times."

"So now?" the mill owner mused, his eyes on the golden beams falling almost levelly through the window. "So indeed? An' ye say his wife knew o' this?"

"After the trial, yes," Eli said.

"Ah!" the other replied. "I see—"

"But you must understand," Eli insisted, "that it isn't that I hold against Brother John. What he did with me did me no harm—none at all. His real sin—the one for which he'll never be forgiven—was his hatred and jealousy of Christopher."

What might have passed subsequently between Thomas Gilmore of Matthew and the pastor, or between him and Sister Leah, Eli never learned, but events moved with dramatic suddenness, and he believed that the woman must somehow have known what was coming, for she was absent without explanation from the following week's prayer meeting—the first time she had missed any church assembly from the day she first landed in Caplin Bight.

There were already wisps and hints of rumors flying about, and the prayer meeting was convened in an atmosphere of foreboding.

"You could feel it in the air, like a thunderstorm comin'," Timmy told Eli the next day. "First one, an' then another, prayed. An' there was speakin' in tongues too. First time in months that they spoke in tongues. What makes 'em speak in tongues, Eli?"

"Oh, for heaven's sake!" Eli exclaimed. "They do it because they're hysterical fools. Why can't you stick to the story?"

"I am," Timmy said, aggrieved. "Well—like I say, they prayed, an' they testified, an' they wrestled with God, ye know—hollerin' out fer guidance, an' fer the Holy Ghost to make 'em do right. An' some o' the women was cryin'. Then Elder Thomas Gilmore of Matthew stood up an' made a long prayer, askin' that if the shepherd be smitten the sheep might not be scattered, an' things like that, an' after he sot down they was all quiet, looking to Brother John, waitin' fer him to get up an' testify.

"An' he stood up at last, only he looked—well, ye remember old Peter Fitzroy, the way he used to look when 'e was drunk on home brew, before he was converted?"

"Yes," Eli said, "yes, go on."

"Well, Brother John looked like that. An' he prayed first, quiet-like, askin' the Holy Ghost to touch his lips and tongue. An' then he said he were a sinful man, an' a leaky vessel, an' a unprofitable servant, an' things like that."

"What did the others say?" Eli asked.

"They was quiet," Timmy said. "Every time Brother John stopped they sat lookin' at 'im, waitin' for 'im to go on. Well, he never did get aroun' to sayin' what he done that was so sinful, but he said that he had been led astray be Satan, blinded be excess o' zeal, be false pride, an' be the deceitfulness o' the flesh. What is the deceitfulness o' the flesh, Eli?"

"Oh, stop asking questions," Eli said. "What happened next?"

"Why, he bust out cryin' like a woman," Timmy said, "an' he wailed some more about the cross o' the flesh. An' then he got quiet again an' said the Lord had told 'im 'e were to lay down the heavy burden of his pastorate an' go forth into outer darkness, bearin' the reproach o' many."

"So he resigned," Eli said.

"Yes. Ye could hear a pin drop, Eli. An' then Brother Thomas Gilmore of Matthew got up an' prayed, thankin' God fer havin' touched Brother John's heart. An' while Brother John sat with his head in his hands Thomas Gilmore said that he moved they accept the pastor's resignation, an' they had a show o' hands, an' they all voted for it—every one."

Eli sighed and reached out to cuff his little brother gently. "Thank you, Timmy," he said. "You mustn't mind that I was impatient sometimes. How did Father take it?"

"Black as the hind end of a smokehouse," Timmy said. "An' no better today either. I been keepin' out of his way, Eli, expectin' a lickin' if I don't."

The pastor, Eli learned, had said nothing specific about either him or Christopher, but his semi-coherent confession was accepted, by those with the will to believe, as at least a partial exoneration of the teacher and himself. Among those with the will were Pleman Pike and Christina Marks, both of whom confirmed, during the day, the story brought to him by Timmy, adding that they had always believed in Christopher's innocence.

But the final explanation came from Brother John himself.

That evening, as Eli walked home from school with Johnny, who trotted gravely beside him like a puppy, making occasional forays into neighboring yards and under stilt-like flakes, where winter's retreat had opened up all kinds of interesting possibilities in the way of oil vats and bark pots and blossoming piles of gear, he was still pondering the likely implications of the pastor's action, when they met him in the Bottom, just as they approached the hill to the Markady gate. As ever, he was black-coated and black-hatted, but gaunter now than Eli ever remembered him, and despairing—almost hagridden in appearance.

"Eli," he said, stopping them in the road, "I wonder could I prevail upon ye to walk with me a little way? Don't say me nay, boy. I have great need to speak with ye. It—it'll be just this once," he added rather hastily.

Eli considered for a moment, his anger and resentment at the pastor contending with curiosity and with the hope that he might be about to hear from Brother John's own lips the confession that he had made in the church the night before.

"Very well," he said at last. "Johnny, we'll forget about fishing for today. You run on home and tell Mrs. Markady that I'll be along later. And go over to the store and ask Virginia to come to supper after she's finished work."

"Sure, Eli," the youngster said, taking the older boy's books. "See you later." And he skipped off lightly up the hill.

Then Eli and Brother John walked up the country road in an uneasy silence—they who had once been so easy and familiar—until the first bend of the crooked path took them out of sight of the settlement, and there they found a rail fence on which they could sit and talk.

"Eli," Brother John began, "ye will've heard be now what took place in the church last night?"

"Yes," Eli said. "Several different accounts, in fact. First Timmy told me about it this morning. Then I heard it again this afternoon from Pleman Pike and Christina Marks."

"'Twarn't aisy, boy," the pastor confessed, "but then, nothin's bin aisy fer me these last few months." He paused, sighed heavily, then went on with greater heat. "If ye should ever wish a foretaste o' life in hell, boy—not that I can imagine why ye would—ye'd have only to live fer a spell with me wife, Leah, once she've found out ye are a sinner. There were a time when I stood up to 'er as a man ought—the woman bein' commanded be the Lord to keep silence before her husband—but she've wore me down, boy—steady, down an' down, till there be nought more I can do—an' the worst of it is that she be in the right all the time, ye see, though 'tis hard put I be to admit it."

He paused again, reflecting, and when he resumed, his voice had become tired, utterly defeated. "I done ye wrong, Eli," he said. "I were a long time comin' to it, but I be forced to face it, boy. I ain't offerin' ye excuses. No—as God be me witness, I been through all this time an' time again. I'll try to explain to ye jest the same. 'Tis a hard thing, Eli, always to choose the right road to follow, amid the devious ways o' Satan and the manifold deceits an' temptations o' the world, with the voice o' the flesh speakin' so guileful, an' the devil goin' about like a angel o' light, deceivin', it may be, the very elect."

His voice modulated, dropped a tone, but still vibrated musically like the low notes of an organ. "I be sorry, boy— sorry for what I done. Leah declares that I have committed the sin unto death—a thousand times she've said it, an' she be right no doubt. . . . No doubt? Why do I say, 'No doubt'? Ain't she quotin' the very word o' God when she say that I be cursed an' cut off from the Lord's elect an' me name be blotted out o' the Book o' Life. Ah, Eli, 'tis true—I have no doubt of it meself. Cursed an' anathema I be in the sight o' the angels o' God an' the four beasts that guard 'E's throne with their eyes before an' behind, cryin', 'Holy, Holy, Holy!' I be condemned past all salvation be the Lord an' 'E's holy apostles fer havin' tasted o' the heavenly gift an' the powers o' the world to come, an' then fallin' back into sin out o' which there be no redemption."

He was silent a moment, turning his night-filled gaze upon Eli. Then his voice came again, more softly, with the same note of supplication that the boy had heard him use years before in his pulpit prayers. "Jest say that ye fergive me, Eli, an' I'll make no further demand upon ye." He paused, then spoke very humbly. "There be nought that I can offer ye in return."

Eli said nothing but gazed in fascination at this enormously proud man whose pride had at last been broken—albeit too late to secure his salvation. And he began, for the first time, to feel an acute sense of pity for the humbled wreck of John McKim.

"I'll not ask Mr. Simms's fergiveness," the preacher resumed, "but I know now that I'd not need to ask. What's between me an' Mr. Simms, or what's between me an' God —that be another matter—I ain't askin' yer fergiveness fer that. But fer the wrong I done to ye, Eli—say ye fergive me fer that.

"There be no fergiveness, I know, fer the sin agin' the Lord. The Lord is a hard taskmaster, Eli. I were a pillar in 'E's holy house, an' a shepherd set apart to feed 'E's flock, an' I were unfaithful to 'E's charge, though me heart bleeds to say it. But I be prepared to endure 'E's wrath an' 'E's everlastin' punishment. When 'E comes in the clouds o' glory, and the saints be cot up, an' the heavens depart I be ready to go down into the pit, bearin' 'E's reproach . . . cursèd from birth an' damned forever an' forever—but I pray ye, boy, that ye may not curse me too."

Eli could not resist the power of this appeal, the seemingly desperate need for a final human contact by this man who was now so utterly outcast, so close to the last desert of despair and unbelief.

"I—I forgive you, Mr. McKim," he said with some difficulty. "I'll not pretend that it's easy. For a long while I have hated you with bitter hatred and contempt—but that's all finished now. I'll hold against you nothing that ever passed between the two of us."

The words were like absolution before death.

"Thank ye, boy," the fallen pastor said humbly, scarcely trusting his voice. "Ye've a kind heart—I always knew ye had. I were tormented to think I might o' been the instrument that had put out the flame o' charity in yer soul." And then, very humbly: "I—I still love ye, Eli. Try to think o' me kindly sometimes."

The pastor's big eyes shone with a dark light in the fading afternoon, and were moist with unshed tears, and he put his hand on the boy's arm, timidly, diffidently, and Eli took the bony hand briefly in his own, and pressed it once, and said, "I'll not hold anything against you, Brother John. I swear it—not now, or ever."

The pastor dropped his hand and gazed off across the shimmering ocean. "Good-by, boy."

"Good-by—sir."

So Eli walked off and left Brother John sitting on the rail fence. He never saw the pastor again. The next morning Sister Leah was seen going from house to house, inquiring of her neighbors whether anyone had tidings of her husband's whereabouts. No one, she found, had seen him depart. But that he was gone there could be no doubt, for his boat was missing from its collar in the harbor, and must have put out to sea some time before dawn, before the earliest of the salmon fishermen went out to their nets beyond the restless tossing of the sunkers.

They inquired of the boats that traveled up and down the shore, but none of them had seen John McKim, or the boat in which he traveled. Then, four days later, word came back to Caplin Bight that his boat was tied up to a stage in Broadport. But nobody remembered seeing him there. Had he gone by train to St. John's, they wondered, or in the other direction, to Corner Brook, or Sydney, or the vast, amorphous lands to the south and west?

It was years before these questions were answered. Meanwhile they sent word to the magistrate that he was missing, and the ranger came in his boat and talked with Sister Leah. Then, a little later, she too left Caplin Bight, traveling on the coastal boat back toward the northern regions from which she had emerged three years before.

A week later another meeting was called to discuss the pastorate, and after much praying and searching of hearts they agreed not to send out to St. John's a request for another pastor. Instead Brother Thomas Gilmore of Matthew was elected by an almost unanimous vote to fill the place left vacant by Brother John.

CHAPTER TWENTY-NINE

❧ ☙

One evening late in June, Eli discovered that he was to become a father. No lovelier evening for such a discovery could have been imagined. Over the hill from the Cove came the late voices of the cast netters and the dull screaming of iron sled runners on sand as men, boys, and beasts made the most of the waning light to wind up a fruitful day among the free riches of the caplin scull. Frogs were speaking musically from the marshes, and spirit-voiced snipes from the sky, as Eli laid aside his books to walk with Virginia through a world that, once again, had put on immortality.

They walked up beside the millstream through the wildest part of the afterglow, when the fires of heaven had faded to tattered black and white and the glory of the night came down upon them. Then, as he took her in his arms and kissed her, she whispered in his ear, "I love you, Eli. That baby we talked about—it has started to grow, inside me."

Eli's heart was almost stopped by the whispered words. First he felt a great weakness, then a returning surge of strength, and lastly a climactic wave of joy and gladness and pride. He touched her face with his fingers and his lips, and pressed her close to him in a symbolic gesture of protection.

"I'm glad, Eli," she murmured. "Oh, I'm so happy. I knew it, darling—I knew you'd feel this way about it."

And in their love-making that night, they recaptured all the first fine flowering of their passion.

The next morning Eli went into the examination room in an almost manic state of mind and emotion, and wrote the best paper of his life with unusual speed and fluency from a mind that was crystal-clear and singing.

Of course it didn't last. The first glow of pride at the prospect of being a father (like a hen that has laid the only egg in the world, he reflected cynically) faded, and the worries of approaching parenthood took its place. After all he was not yet seventeen, still very unsure about life, by no means the full master of his fate or captain of his soul. Just what, he began to wonder, was involved in being a father?

He communicated these worries to Virginia that same afternoon. "What are you going to tell your parents?" he asked, as millions had asked before, in the very same words.

"I'm not going to tell them anything," she said. "They'll begin to guess soon enough, and it's better that they find out slowly, so they can get used to the idea. It happened in May, on one of those marvelous nights we had together. . . . Oh, Eli, I wish I could know which—for they were all so different, you remember—each one so separate and distinct—like faces. If I could only tell which night it was, and remember it forever—and link it, you know, with the little one."

"A baby has nothing to do with how you feel at the moment of its conception," Eli said, a little impatient with this flighty romanticism. "It is never anything but an accident—a pure chance meeting of cells."

"I don't believe you!" she exclaimed indignantly. "Cells indeed! You make it sound like that damned chemistry you were studying last night."

"Well, it *is* chemistry, if you come down to it. What's wrong with chemistry, anyway?"

"Oh, Eli! Let's not get into a silly argument!"

"No," he agreed, "of course not. We ought to be deciding what we are going to do about the baby."

"What do you mean, 'do about' it? There's nothing to do except wait for next winter for it to be born."

"Well, you don't just sit around helplessly, without making any plans." He was, he realized, sounding damnably awkward, but he was new to this sort of thing, and groping in the dark. "We could—well, we could think about getting married."

Virginia looked at him coolly for a moment. "I've already thought about it," she said, "and don't ask me to marry you, Eli, because I'd only have to say 'no,' and I love you, and it might be hard to say. Do you think I haven't thought this matter out to its bitter end during the last eight months?"

"Why do you have to say 'no?'" he asked, rather nettled.

"Mainly because you have to go to college," she said, "and that will take four or five years, and then—if you are going to go in for science, as it seems you are—maybe you will be doing years of postgraduate work afterward, and lastly setting yourself up as a professor or a research worker —and you can't do all that and raise a family at the same time."

"It looks like I'm raising one anyway," he pointed out reasonably.

She laughed. "Not the way I mean, Eli. Look—apart from what you may pick up in scholarships, Mr. Markady is going to pay your way through college. It will cost him thousands of dollars, and it will cost you whatever you can earn for yourself at the same time. There'll be no way at all for you to support a wife and children while you're doing it— and even if it might be barely possible, I wouldn't let you try. I'm not going to be a millstone around your neck, Eli. No—I earn more than my keep in Father's store. I'll be able to do it for years to come, if need be. For that matter, he can very well afford to support both me and the baby. And don't worry that he'll kick me out into the cruel world to scrub for a living. I know the fat old brute far too well for that."

"No matter what you say," he objected, "you are in for hard times with both your parents."

"Let *me* worry about my father and mother, Eli," she said. "They'll bluster and they'll bluff and they'll try to bully. They'll try to send me to St. John's to have the baby put into an institution. But when they see I won't budge they'll back down."

"There's one other possibility," Eli said. "I don't know if you've thought about it, and I'm almost ashamed to mention it. But suppose we got married, and while I went to college you went back to live with your parents? I suppose it wouldn't be the first time that something like that has been done."

"I'll think about it, Eli," she said, "but that is as far as I'll go at the moment."

"I can't see how even your parents would try to stop it, can you, once we admit that we're having a baby?"

She gave her little tinkling laugh. "You know, it rather tickles me to think of making Father support your children. In fact I can even believe that he might grow to like the idea of having you for a son-in-law, after he took a while getting used to it—not that he has any liking for you, of course, but before long he'd begin thinking about your value as a business partner, and trying to put pressure on you. . . . Anyway, I absolutely refuse to do anything that might bring you harm, Eli. And I'm not going to be rushed into anything, especially since there's no need to decide in a hurry—far better to make up our minds slowly and be sure of what we're doing."

When Eli broke the news to Mr. Markady the old captain gazed at him under his great bushy brows with something between a frown and a twinkle. "It comes as no very great surprise to me, I must admit," he said. "How far along the way would it be now?"

"Barely started," Eli said.

Mr. Markady grunted. "Heaven only knows why it didn't

happen before. Warn't too young, was ye?" He chuckled at his crude little joke. "Well anyway, lad, ye'll be properly turned seventeen before ye becomes a father—a good respectable age." He paused, looking off into space reflectively. "I never was in favor o' fathers younger'n seventeen." He burst out laughing and slapped Eli on the back with his big paw. "Congratulations, me b'y! If ye keep on till the age I was when I planted David, ye'll father about thirty. . . . Ah, but I wish I was startin' again meself!"

"You don't seem to be much upset about it," Eli observed.

"Upset! Huh! Ain't *me* that's havin' it. Ye plannin' to marry the girl soon? When's the weddin'?"

"I don't know," Eli said. "I offered to marry her, of course, but she doesn't seem very enthusiastic about the idea."

"Don't see why ye can't marry if ye've a mind to," Mr. Markady said. "Rather think ye ought, in fact. I must admit that I'm a shade in favor o' youngsters bein' born in holy wedlock."

"Virginia seems to be reconciled to having them single," Eli said.

"First woman I ever knowed as preferred to birth a bastard," Mr. Markady grunted. "But then she'll likely change 'er mind. Women do, ye know. Good thing she told ye early. Leaves time to make plans. The baby'd be legitimate in the eyes o' the law no matter how late ye put off the weddin'— even if ye had to send fer the minister an' the midwife the same day!"

"I hope it won't come to that," Eli said, smiling.

"Well, ye've the summer to think about it, lad, but married or single I want ye up in St. John's next fall, preparin' fer college."

Eli wrote his last examination, and June passed into July. Suddenly released from the labor of study, he found himself restless in unaccustomed leisure and decided to expand his fishing activities into a full-scale summer voyage.

Eli's old partner, Pleman Pike, had signed on with a trap crew as a full shareman that year, so he kept Johnny on half shares. When she wasn't working in the store, Virginia often went out to the fishing grounds with them, and this provoked a new buzz of amazement. A woman in a fishing boat! Scandalous! An old proverb about a whistling woman and a crowing hen was repeated frequently in the harbor gossip, each time with a wise shake of the head. Heaven, everyone agreed, would be bound to visit vengeance on anything so unnatural as this. Either the boat would be lost or the fish would spoil or—most likely—the woman's blood would turn. But they waited in vain for judgment to fall upon Virginia. She flourished like the green bay tree.

"I hope ye know that ye are fishin' fer fun, an' not fer a livin'," Joshua Markady said, eying the hundred-odd barrels of slop cod that they had now put down into salt bulk. He turned to Johnny. "Havin' a good time at it?" he asked.

"Oh yes, sir," the youngster assured him. "'Tis hard work, but 'tis great fun—besides, I'll have maybe fifty quintals of fish of me very own to be sold in the fall!"

"Well—I s'pose 'tis good fer ye then," the old captain conceded, "but who's goin' to wash out all that stuff, an' waterhorse it, an' spread it an' yaffle it an' pile it an' pack it, come September?"

"If I don't have time to see to it myself then I'll hire three or four girls and pay them ten cents an hour, as Solomon Marks does," Eli said. "There'll be a good price for fish this fall, and 'twill help pay my college expenses."

Mr. Markady snorted. "Price be damned," he said. "'Tis time ye learned, lad, that the men as makes money outa fish isn't the ones as catches it. Why, I made more from a single foreign voyage when we was runnin' the German blockade durin' the war than the best fisherman in the Bight could hope to make in ten years. I can show ye how to make money, if that's what ye want—but I had a notion, somehow, that ye were after somethin' more'n just money."

"Oh well, we'll fish for fun, then," Eli said lightly. "At least we should be able to count on a bit of decent eating prised, for Thomas Gilmore of Matthew was now the social leader of the settlement, ranking even ahead of the merchant in the hierarchy of church elders. But what happened next was even more astonishing. One by one, some of them awkwardly and shyly, the other men on the wharf laid down what they were doing, came up to Christopher, and, following Thomas Gilmore's lead, offered a handshake and a word of greeting.

Elias Pallisher was not among those who did so, nor was Solomon Marks, but a large enough cross-section of the people had tendered some symbol of their good will to make it clear that, contrary to expectations, Christopher was not going to be treated as an outcast. Moreover, the whole demonstration had obviously taken place without the slightest premeditation, out of the good will that came so natural to those people, and as a symbol of their regret at having been in the wrong. Not one of them would ever be able to say to Christopher, as Brother John had said to Eli, "I'm sorry. I did you wrong. I pray you to forgive me." They were not articulate in the manner of John McKim, nor able to rise to a verbal confession of their mistakes, but they could admit them openly and spontaneously, with faces and hands that were far more eloquent than their tongues. These were men who in any case performed most of their speech with their hands: lived by them, spoke with them, communicated with them, prayed with them, fashioned the patterns of their lives by them. Their hands were fluent, and even poetic, while their tongues were often clumsy and uncouth.

Someone handed Christopher's bags into the pony trap, and they set out for the little farm up in the valley in a quite unanticipated atmosphere of approval.

"He hasn't changed a bit, Eli," Mr. Simms said when Christopher was out of earshot. "He's just as he was before, only quieter."

Eli didn't believe this. No man, he was sure, could emerge from a year in prison unchanged. Indeed he suspected

fish for next winter. Besides, Virginia, as well as Johnny, seems to enjoy it."

"And watch what ye are doin' with that girl!" Mr. Markady cautioned. "Girl wants to do somethin' crazy like workin' in a fishin' boat, 'tis her own lookout, I s'pose—but don't ye ferget this one's due to birth next winter. If ye get caught out in a blow she'll likely lose the baby, which I understand the two o' ye are lookin' for'ard to the same as if ye'd been legally bedded for a year."

"First wind squall that shows on the line of the sky I'll head for harbor," Eli promised solemnly.

"Mind ye do—an' keep an eye on this youngster while ye are at it. Ye be a trifle young yerself to be responsible fer so many green hands."

"How old were you when you went skipper to the banks?" Eli asked.

The old captain grinned under his spreading mustache. "Don't be saucy, ye whelp! I'd been sailin' foreign fer years, as ye well know—started when I was no bigger'n Johnny here. When I was growin' up I didn't spend me time with me nose buried in books."

The early days of July on the water were calm and peaceful. Neither Virginia nor Johnny was ever in the slightest danger, and Eli was not chased into harbor by a wind squall even once.

In the mornings there would be just Eli and the small boy in the boat, both half naked and baking in the direct and reflected sunlight that shone from the still surface of the sea as from a mirror or a pool of oil. Eli's olive skin turned almost Negroid, while Johnny's Nordic complexion was overlaid by a tan the color of walnut shells, with little white squint lines—the mark of the sailor—around his eyes.

They worked together at a comfortable pace in easy harmony and unspoken companionship, saying little or nothing by the hour, Eli suiting his own speed to the boy's. After the catch was landed they would take towels and soap and go up to the pool in the mill brook and swim a little and wash off the smell of fish. Sometimes Timmy, released from his father's trap boat, secretly joined in the expeditions to the brook and vied with Johnny in the simple rivalry of age mates.

It was all very pleasant, these well-balanced bouts of work and play, Eli felt. Then the evenings would come, and there would be Virginia, glorying in doing man's work, dressed in bib overalls like the brazen hussy that she was, and—final scandal—whistling through her teeth.

CHAPTER THIRTY

Then, one day, Christopher was back in Caplin Bight. It happened so suddenly as to take his small circle of friends almost as much by surprise as it did the people in general. Mr. Simms, alerted by telegram (delivered by boat from Lattice Harbor) two days before his coming, alerted Eli and Virginia, and they in turn told the Markadys, but nothing else was said about it.

Christopher's appearance on the gangway of the coastal boat, the last week of July, was an obvious shock to the assembled population. Few had imagined that, even after his expected release a year later, he would dare to put in an appearance. But here he was in the flesh, after what seemed only a few months from the day on which he had been banished forever.

Eli and Virginia and old Mr. Simms were all on the wharf to meet him. As he walked down the steel steps, and Virginia ran to him, and he gathered her into his arms, the dockside hum and bustle were frozen momentarily into total silence and immobility. Then, after he had embraced Virginia and Eli and his father, a very strange thing happened. Thomas Gilmore of Matthew, who had been awaiting a small freight consignment for his mill, walked over from the skids beside the deck winches and held out his hand.

"Welcome home, Mr. Simms," he said. "Glad to see ye back."

Christopher shook hands with the man, obviously sur-

that Christopher, far more than most, would be radically changed by imprisonment—that having shared with the outcasts of the earth the dregs of the cup of suffering might make him, in some respects, a stranger to all his friends henceforth. But Eli would mention nothing of this to the old man, so obviously delighted at his son's return, so earnestly believing that the man who had come back to him was the boy who had gone away, first to college, and then to prison. Mr. Simms beamed with pleasure and seemed to have shed—well, perhaps not a decade, but certainly some years from his stooped shoulders.

"Yes, it's very good to have him home," Eli said noncommittally.

The day passed quietly at the farm, and then, in the evening, they went down to the big house on the Point, where Mrs. Markady had surpassed herself in preparing a feast of the most generous proportions, the featured item being roast goose stuffed with green onions and summer savory and flanked with meat pastries. She had brought out from her cellar the black currant jelly, dark red and sharp and aromatic, that she had put up the autumn before, with a flagon of pale green dandelion wine that had been sitting for three years in the dark recesses of a cupboard, nurturing within itself the scent and the sunshine of the summer fields.

So they sat together—three old people, three young people, and a child—and ate and drank in token of their rejoicing, and sat back afterward with glasses of wine, and Mr. Markady with a toddy of black rum, and Mr. Simms with an immense meerschaum pipe that he had cherished for a lifetime until it had taken on the dark glow of mahogany with the translucency of fire.

Joshua Markady was in his best mood of reminiscence that night, and he created for them a vivid picture of a voyage of which Eli had never heard him speak before—an unlucky voyage when, sailing down the parallels with fish for Pernambuco, he had been caught back of the wind—

and of the great islands of floating weeds in the still, tropical sea, and of the serpents that rose up at night out of the glowing depths, scattering drops of green fire.

Then he told of making an alternate port in the West Indies, where the mulatto girls came down to the ship, wearing bells on wrists and ankles—and of visiting the cane fields where "free" Negroes labored like cattle under the whips of overseers, and of the great cane presses and the fermenting vats, and the distilleries where spirits flowed through pipes, and you could buy rum for a cent a glass. And he told also of the endemic sorrow that afflicts those blessed islands that were ruled so long by pirates and peopled by generations of slaves.

So the night grew late in this pleasant companionship, and they were happy and carefree and joyful—and only Johnny, youngest of the group, was sometimes sober and a little thoughtful, and even a little sad.

Eli did not sleep much that night but dropped into restless slumber in the dark hours before dawn, and had enjoyed the doubtful benefit of a few confused dreams when Johnny came bounding into his room, demanding to know did he plan to sleep until noon.

"Christopher is here already," the youngster announced, "an' he says he'll go fishin' with us if we've a mind."

Eli sat up and looked out the window. Dawn was far advanced, and the sky was a tubercular pink. He listlessly pulled on his trousers, ambled down to the kitchen, and began dousing himself with cold water. He felt somewhat hung over from the excitement of the day before, the lack of sleep, and a growing feeling of unease about his position with Christopher and Virginia. Though nothing had been said about it that first day, there was a gnawing feeling that he and Christopher would soon have to face the issue of being rivals for the favors of the same woman.

Eli banished the thought as he shook himself out of sleep and ate his slabs of toast and tea.

"I'm planning to spend a month doing not much except

get the kinks and cramps straightened out," Christopher
was saying. "I tried using an ax for a few minutes this morning. You couldn't believe anyone could get so soft spending
a year at what they call 'hard labor.'"

So they went with him while he rowed and sculled a punt
once again, and jigged fish on a forty-fathom line, and
forked them with the two-tined prong neatly through the
heads, where the puncture would not injure the flesh, and
tossed them in neat arcs over the stage head into the bin
beside the splitting table.

"Suppose I'll be too stiff to move for a week after this,"
he grinned.

They put their morning's fish into salt, and went home to
lunch, and decided to spend the afternoon re-exploring
the woods and hills.

Eli noticed the same reserve between Johnny and Christopher that had existed these past few months between
Johnny and himself—the boy was still unnaturally quiet
and withdrawn and subdued. Christopher, of course, had
seen this at once, and as they sat on the barren hill over-
looking the settlement in late afternoon, with Johnny exploring the nearby scrub for birds' nests, he asked if Eli
knew what was wrong.

"He's been this way all along," Eli said, "nothing you can
pin down, though—obedient and co-operative—almost *too*
co-operative for a boy, especially one who used to be as
willful as Johnny—and he did unbelievably well in school,
you know, after we brought him back here—but he's been
nursing some hurt inside him that I can't reach. For the last
two or three days, since he knew you were coming home,
he has been even more subdued than before—almost as
though he were scared of you or something."

"That's ridiculous," Christopher said. "What do you suppose—" He looked off across the harbor and the infinite
series of blue cliffs marching away into the complex of sea
and sky. "You don't think he could be punishing himself

for what he did last fall? I wonder, now." He called, "Johnny!" and the boy came trotting through the ferns. "Johnny," said Christopher, "you're just about as gloomy as a December afternoon. What's the matter with you?"

"Nothin'," the boy lied, refusing to meet Christopher's eyes but looking off across the hill and scuffing his bare toes in the moss.

"Johnny," Christopher said, "come here."

The boy moved a step nearer, and Christopher, still sitting in the moss, reached up and put his hands on his shoulders. "You're troubled about something," he said, "and I want to know what, because—well, because I love you, that's why—because you are my child just as much as if you were my own son, and whatever it is I won't let it come between us. You've got to tell me, Johnny, because I can't stand having you unhappy—and if things between us are going to be the way they were before, you've got to trust me and tell me your troubles."

Johnny spoke at last—very low, almost in a whisper: "You mean you want me back—just like before?"

"Of course," Christopher said. "What made you think I wouldn't?"

"But I broke my promise to you an' done even worse, I guess, when I busted into the store an' got sent to reform school—not like when they sent you to jail for what you didn't do. They had a *right* to send me to reform school—I broke the law—an' then, ye know, there was all the other things I done afterward. . . ." There were tears in his voice, and his head was low, and he hadn't once met Christopher's gaze.

"Oh, Johnny!" said Christopher. He pulled the child down to him and put his arms about him. "Is that all that's wrong? Why, you young idiot! There's nothing to forgive. Here—look up at me—" He tilted the freckled face toward his own and looked into the blue eyes, which were still troubled and full of pain. "Johnny," he said, choosing his words carefully, "it's your enemies you have to forgive, not the people you love. Others might have something to forgive you, or you them. But there can never be any talk of forgiveness between you and me."

The youngster put his head down on Christopher's shirt front, and the man rumpled his hair gently.

"You've had a pretty rough time," he said. "You've been kicked about most of your life, and you've kicked back a little. That's nothing to be ashamed of. You smashed some cases and windows and things belonging to Solomon Marks —well, God knows the old brute deserved far more than that. You ran away from reform school. Surely you didn't believe that I'd hold that against you, did you?—or that I'd think you deserved to be punished because you tried to burn it down? You mustn't think that I'm on the side of the angels, Johnny—I was with you, all the way. The institutions of the law are full of evil and cruelty, and I could never take their side—against you or anyone else who suffers because of them."

The boy's head was on Christopher's shoulder, and he was crying softly—not hopelessly or in self-pity but with relief and joy. After his journey through the black fires of the underworld and the lonely night of the spirit Johnny too had come home.

"Nothing to forgive," Christopher assured him. "Some of what you did was foolish, but not dishonorable. And through it all, you showed one of the greatest of all human qualities —courage. Even when you suffered a great deal you didn't let them break your spirit." He stroked the boy's hair gently. "I've suffered too, you know, and the experience is something that you and I will have in common all the rest of our lives—something that not everyone is able to share."

Eli left them and walked off across the hill, feeling about as useful as an extra thumb. The miracle that he had tried to accomplish over a period of three months had been performed before his eyes in approximately three minutes.

It's no use, he told himself. I just don't have that kind of way with people. He seems to be able to reach out and touch people instantly in the very center of their hearts. I'll never be able to do it.

When he returned a few minutes later Christopher and Johnny were rolling and wrestling in the moss like a pair of fools, insanely pleased with each other and with themselves. They sat up panting, Johnny's eyes dancing as they had not danced in more than a year.

"Eli," he said, "I'm sorry I was so much trouble to you. You were trying to tell me before, weren't you? But I didn't understand."

"Yes, Johnny," he said, "I tried—but I'm not very good at those things, it seems. You weren't really any bother, you know. You'd be worth a thousand times more trouble than you ever were to me."

"You really did a wonderful job with him, Eli," Christopher said. "You've nothing to blame yourself for—nothing at all. . . . Look here," he added suddenly, "why don't we go in for a swim?"

"In the brook, you mean?" Eli asked.

"I was thinking about the Cove."

"Yes, let's!" Johnny exclaimed.

"No one's been swimming in the Cove yet this year," Eli said. "It'd just about freeze you solid, I expect."

"Let's go anyway," Christopher insisted. "I feel like doing something foolish."

So they went, Johnny walking in Christopher's shadow, holding his hand like a small child with its father. They came to the golden beach of the Cove just in time to see Jehu Gilmore land his tubby black punt, heave its graplin ashore, and take a broken lobster pot up the beach to his house. He offered no greeting as they skirted the sheep-nibbled patch of grass beside his door and made their way to the far end of the beach where the black rocks marched down from the hills above to meet the sands. Then they spent the last hour of the afternoon experiencing alternately the physical shock of the icy water and the soothing heat of the sand.

It was the first time Christopher had seen Johnny undressed that summer, and the white scars of the beatings from the winter before were visible to his astonished eyes. "My God!" he whispered to Eli. "They did *that* to him?"

"Yes," Eli said. "I thought you knew."

"Well, yes, in a way—but it never really came home to me—the extent of the brutality, I mean. Eli—it's unbelievable, that the law would let them do that to a child!"

"Part of the treatment, it seems," Eli said. "Quite the regular thing, so Johnny tells me."

"Indeed," said Christopher, "and I suppose when he doesn't land back in the dock it will be marked down in their records as one more success for their methods."

But Johnny had forgotten all about the marks of suffering in his flesh and was as full of life and high spirits as a baby goat in May. He came dashing out of the water, somersaulted in the sand, tried to do a cartwheel, and landed flat on his back with a thud.

"Here"—Eli laughed—"I'll show you how." And he went wheeling across the sand—a gesture out of childhood that, quite suddenly, made him feel rather foolish.

He was no longer a child, he remembered. And he looked at Christopher, and knew that Christopher knew. It was as though an unspoken message had passed between them— something deep and primordial and biological. For a moment he envied Johnny. Then he went and picked up his clothes, dusting the sand off himself, and began to dress. "You two stay if you want," he said, "but I think I'll go home to supper."

"We're coming," Christopher said, and he too turned with a sigh to the business of dressing.

They crossed the ridge into the Bight with an unspoken tension between them—Johnny all the while frisking happily about, quite unaware of the fact that the two men beside him had, all in a moment, become strangers.

CHAPTER THIRTY-ONE

Eli was now facing the unpleasant necessity of leaving his native village, at least for long stretches of time, and parting from the people who had shaped his life and breathed into him the soul that he would carry with him for all time to come.

The change was not without its bitterness. Until Christopher's return to Caplin Bight, Eli saw himself as the sun around which his little solar system revolved. Now he was suddenly reduced to a planet—or perhaps, he reflected, not even a planet but a dark body on its way out into the night of interstellar space.

When he saw Virginia and Christopher row out across the harbor on Sunday morning and board the little sailboat as it danced before its collar when the lines slipped, and the boat slid past the sunkers, and he watched its white wings retreat through the rattle into Lattice Harbor Run for an all-day cruise, he knew deeply and fully the taste of wormwood in his soul.

From the moment that he had risen once again above her horizon Virginia had turned toward Christopher like a flower toward the warming rays of the sun. The sense of strangeness that had grown up between himself and Christopher was painful enough, but it was a mild affliction compared with the laceration of shame and jealousy that he felt when Virginia began to turn from him toward the renewal of her first love. There was something almost casual in the way Christopher had reached out to take her back—almost as though Eli had never existed.

Christopher sprang the full truth upon him in the kindest way he knew how—suddenly and completely—on the Monday morning after his cruise with Virginia. "Eli," he said as they worked together in the fish store, "I have news for you. Virginia and I are going to get married."

Eli laid down his shovel of salt very carefully and straightened his back slowly. "Married!" he exclaimed, and sat down on the edge of the salt bin.

"There is no need to look so shocked," Christopher said. "We were to have been married a year ago, remember?"

"A year?" Eli repeated. "Is that all it was? It seems like a lifetime."

"I know you love Virginia," Christopher said, "and I warned you that I was going to take her away from you. There is no one on earth, Eli, that I feel sorrier at having to hurt than you, but I've got to do it."

"I must say, you don't sound very sorry to me," Eli said bitterly.

"But, Eli," Christopher pleaded, "it isn't mere selfishness, I swear. If this were just something for myself, I might be able to give it up for you—but it's not—it's for Virginia too, you see."

"For Virginia?" Eli cried. "Chris, do you realize how much there is between me and Virginia? Not just that I love her, I mean. Do you know that she's having my child?"

"Yes," Christopher said gently. "I know. And it makes no difference at all, except that it may hurry matters up a little."

"You mean," said Eli slowly, spelling into words what he had known for many days really, but had not dared to say, even to himself, "that you are taking from me the woman I love—and also the child—the child that is the fruit of our love for each other."

"Nobody owns a child, Eli," Christopher said, "neither the man who begets it nor the woman who brings it forth. If there is ever any human claim upon it, it comes later, by those who nurture it and love it and help it to become human. . . . You look pretty sick, Eli," he added. "I'm sorry I had to do this to you."

"I—I'm not sure how I feel about it," Eli confessed, "except that I love Virginia more than anything in heaven or in earth and I won't let her go if I can help it. And as for you" —he felt a sudden surge of anger, and his voice rose—"all this talk about doing it for her sake, and so on—it sounds like pure hypocrisy to me!" He swallowed hard, realized desperately that he was on the point of breaking into tears.

Christopher came and sat on the edge of the salt bin beside him. "Eli," he said sadly, "go back to Virginia if you wish. I'd do nothing to try to stop your winning her from me fair and square. You're a man now, and you have the right, and you're my friend as well as my rival, and it's up to you to resolve this as best you can. But you mustn't hate me or call me a hypocrite. You know it isn't true. And you know that no matter what happens between me and anyone else, or between you and anyone else, that we can never really hate each other. No matter how bitter our rivalry might be, I couldn't help loving you through it all."

"Yes, I know," Eli whispered brokenly. "It makes it that much harder— If only you were someone I could hate."

They sat for a few moments in silence; then: "Eli," Christopher said, "we are at a kind of an end between us—and perhaps a new beginning too. Your relationship with me was that of a child with a man. It can't go on that way—do you see?—not without stretching childhood long past its limits. The turmoil that you are facing now is partly the fact that, for a little while, you are both child and man." He put his arm about Eli's shoulders. "I'd like to make it easier for you if I could, but there's no way that I can, except perhaps just a little, by talking to you like this. I loved you as a child, Eli, almost beyond expression, and I hope as time goes on that we'll be able to develop a new relationship altogether, completely adult on both sides. But the child

Eli is dead. That's the tragic thing about loving children—they always die before their love is mature."

"Yes," Eli said, "it's true. I've felt the change myself since you came home."

"I'd do anything on earth for you, Eli, but I can't do the things that a man has to do for himself."

"Yes, I know," said Eli. "I've thought about it. I have to go into the wilderness, as Brother John would have put it, and I have to go alone. One of the hardest things of all is growing up—harder than dying, I think. You have to accept such sudden and bitter changes. Your whole life—everything you've loved—goes down the drain at childhood's end."

"I'm glad you found that out for yourself, Eli," Christopher said. "Every man who is going to transcend his childhood has to watch it killed." He sighed, walked to the door of the shed, and looked out over the sea. "But the pain is worth it, for it is also a sort of birth—of the man that you will become—more worthwhile, perhaps, because of the pain of his becoming."

Throughout that day—though his heart was not in it—he and Johnny and Christopher worked at their fish, and Mr. Markady came and watched them and called them, good-naturedly, three confounded fools.

Then, in the evening, he went to seek out Virginia. He caught her at closing time in the store and inveigled her down to the waterfront, where they sat on upended fish drums near the head of the wharf and watched a school of mackerel—the first of the season—cutting like vertical knife blades across the calm surface of the harbor.

"Virginia," he said, "Christopher told me this morning that you have promised to marry him."

"It's true, Eli. Next month, I expect."

"But why?" he demanded passionately.

"Because I love him, Eli," she said quietly, "and want to spend my life with him."

"Oh, Virginia! How can you say it? You've said a hundred times that you love me, and you know that I'd do anything in the world for you—anything."

"Yes," she said. "I've never doubted you, Eli. Oh—if you only knew how I've dreaded this moment!" She sighed wearily. "But then, I knew it had to come. It is true that I loved you, Eli, but you know that I could never make up my mind that I wanted to marry you, even when I found out I was going to have your child. Loving someone and marrying him—that isn't the same thing at all, don't you know that?"

"You mean that you'd love me and still marry Christopher?"

"No," she said, "no, that isn't what I mean at all— Oh, how can I explain it? In a way I suppose I'll always love you, Eli. All the darkness that is in the dark side of me will belong to you forever and ever—but that isn't enough—not enough to make a marriage, I mean."

"Then love me in the darkness," he pleaded, "or in the light, or any way you choose."

"We've got to make an end of it, Eli," she said sadly but decisively, "though I suppose I must go on loving you in the night. But don't you see, I've always been Christopher's. From the day I first saw him, from the day he stepped ashore here and began pacing like a great jungle cat up and down the pier, I've been his. As a dog its master, as a baby its mother, I love him. Loving you was a great adventure, and you helped to heal my wounds when I needed it most, and I'll be a better woman, I think, for loving you. But I *belong* to Christopher, body and soul."

"But you loved me," he insisted, "really and truly. It couldn't have been just an 'adventure,' as you call it. My God, Virginia, we weren't just playing games—at least, I wasn't!"

"Nor I either, darling," she said very gently and sadly. "I loved you. I still love you. The love of you is tearing at me this very minute, like a wild beast with claws. But don't you see?" Her voice dropped almost to a whisper. "Don't you see, Eli? I love Christopher even more."

"It's wrong!" he declared, almost savagely. "I won't believe you. I don't care what you say. It's—it's—*unnatural.*"

"For a woman to love two men, you mean? Yes," she said resignedly, "perhaps it is—perhaps I'm an unnatural woman. It's true, nevertheless. I love both of you—not exactly in the same sort of way, it's true, but I *do* love you both. But it's Christopher that I choose to marry.

"Oh, Eli—it's hard, I know. But you can't have everything out of life, not even, sometimes, the things you want most. Life has to be lived by the rules, it seems, though God knows I have tried hard enough to live it the other way. I can't have you both—though perhaps that's what I really want—your darkness, along with Christopher's light."

"All the while I've been a sort of strange flesh to you," he said, comprehending, "a sort of wicked, dark, delightful adventure, like the Israelites lusting after strange gods."

"If you want to put it that way," she said with a sigh. "I love you the way a woman loves her lover. I could be your mistress forever, for I love you terribly, Eli—but I love Christopher with the love of a wife for her husband."

They were silent for a moment, looking out over the harbor where the little boats rocked in the evening swell. They had reached a sort of impasse.

But Eli still would not let her go. "Virginia," he urged, "come walk with me as you used to do, in the cool of the evening upon the mountain."

He took her arm, and her eyes were dark and compassionate, and infinitely tender, with a wisdom older than thought—a wisdom that reached back through feather and fin and tendril and leaf beyond all human understanding to the ultimate roots of life.

"Ay," she said. "I'll go with you, Eli—this once more."

So they walked up through the settlement in the waning light, and through the fields to the edge of the trees. And they went into the evening forest amid the musk of small animals, and the healing breath of the leaves, and they lay together in love and tenderness, and their love was salted with sorrow and regret.

In a sense, Eli thought, this was their ultimate fulfillment —though how could it be truly said, he wondered, when each time he lay with her he seemed to be fulfilled anew? Yet ever afterward he remembered that night as the climax of his first great passion—a fulfillment that was full of sadness, but full of beauty too.

And when their passion had ebbed, and the tears were no longer wet on their faces, they rose from the forest floor, brushing leaves and dead needles out of their hair and clothes, and walked up, hand in hand, through the aisles of the forest, among the dark and aromatic spruces.

And as they went Eli began to feel a sense of unreality in this land of his childhood, a sense of a deeper reality, inside him, growing and replacing it—the separate themes of his life coming together, uniting, being made one, like numerous strands being woven into a single cable. And it had meaning for him as the notes of a song, meaningless in themselves, take on the colors of thought and feeling when they come together.

It was not a gay or lighthearted tune, he decided, but it was music, nonetheless. The important thing was not that life should be gay, or that its yearnings should be fulfilled, but that it should have a pattern—that it should not be meaningless and ugly, and squandered in trivial discords, as so many lives seemed to be.

He drew a deep breath and clutched her hand tightly. There was a deep resolution forming within him.

So they arrived at the clearing near the crest of the hill, the same where Virginia had danced, and first roused his passion, the year before. She may have thought of this, as he did, but they were walking in silence, each wrapped separately in his own thoughts. Here the last light of the sky broke out upon them, flooding down over the mountain, wild and turbulent, its color washed out to the stark white and black of the last afterglow, filling their hearts with the sadness and the mystery of the world.

The black shapes of the spruces stood up, immovable, against the white fierceness of the sky, and their scent came drifting down, like the memory of childhood, like the incense of everlasting years.

Then Eli looked up toward Virginia, who stood a little above him, black and transfigured against the sky, her hair blowing out in the small breeze, like one of its dark-fronted clouds edged with light, and after what seemed a long time, he spoke. "I can do it now," he said. "I can leave you, if that's what you want."

He said it, though his voice broke saying it; and Virginia, who was weeping gently, did not reply in words, but took his hand and pressed it against her cheek, and he kissed her tenderly, passionlessly—a delicate symbol of love, as he might kiss a child.

So they walked down the hill in silence, into the deserted streets of the village, and she parted from him—in a sense for the last time—and he went down along the shore beside the sea.

CHAPTER THIRTY-TWO

It was the low tide of August in the dark of the moon—
spring low, when the sea sank far down from its accustomed
bourn into the caves and hollows of the shore, and a terrible
pre-dawn stillness hung over Caplin Bight as Eli made his
way along the rocks of the Point to the tiny inlet known as
Mooring Cove, a mere cleft in the cliff, a gunshot from the
sunkers, lashed by the surf of the ocean sea.

But now there was no surf, only the soundless breath of
the Atlantic, swelling from afar, rhythmically, a slow pulse
beat, so silent that he could hear the gushing of the mill
brook a quarter of a mile away, and the creaking of the
great wheel that turned day and night throughout the summer—a sound that would haunt his sleep forevermore—
mingled with the sputtering of small boat engines muffled
in fog and the dry groaning of manila rigging as the mighty
ghosts of his childhood ships sailed and rustled behind the
world.

Tonight, for yet a small space, he belonged to his village.
With the coming of day he would board the coastal boat
and sail out through the sunkers to a world he had so far
glimpsed only in passing.

The small sounds of the night came out around him—the
faint scratching of crabs on the sea-smoothed stones, numberless crabs pursuing their small designs all around him
in the darkness, hunting and killing and eating in the dense
forest of the rockweed that hung, damp and lifeless, above

the black water, then moving on to hunt and eat anew—the all-but-silent breaching of the surface-feeding fish, making small swirls in the inklike sea, gulping down thousands of the new-hatched larvae that floated outward from the rocks on the slack water at the tail of the ebb tide.

Eli found a comfortable perch on the slick basalt and sat there for a long time, meditating upon the eternity that stretched backward through his years in Caplin Bight toward the infinitely far-off miracle of his birth, and the vague promise of the road that stretched before him, through other times and places, toward some other eternity, equally remote.

He could feel, rather than hear, the ceaseless rustle of the small shore life around him—countless snails creeping over the damp stone, grazing on the green scum of algae, like tiny sheep on a pasture—rock spiders that scurried about, trapping the minute sand fleas in the crevices—rough-shelled whelks advancing remorselessly, armed with diabolical weapons that could pierce the hardest shell, seeking what they might devour.

And the sea, rising and falling in a rhythm long established before the first living creature crawled out upon its shore, ordering and directing it all, mother and teacher of life upon the planet—the sea: he could feel it now, subtly, in his blood—the stir, the change, the renewal: without sight of its waters, without sound of its surge, he knew that the tide had turned.

And then, so gradually that its beginnings could not be seen, out of the northeast came the pre-dawn twilight. Diffused at first, without direction, it picked out the contours of the rocks, revealed the shape of the tiny island that lay in the middle of the inlet, and disclosed the rocking motion of silent waters, far down below the tidal pools, where the laminaria kelps—the oldest living things on earth—lay limp along the sea.

The broad band of the rock-clinging barnacles and limpets now stood out whitely around the shore—a fathom-wide chalk mark, stretching away forever between the line of the tides, uniting Caplin Bight to the lands of the north and the south, curving around headland and cove along the thousands of miles of shore line of this mighty ocean-bound island. The lower pools in the hollows of the great flat rocks were full of sponges in a vast variety of fanciful shapes, but all without color in this pre-dawn light, as though color had been drained out of the earth by the long ordeal of the night. In those pools, too, the false corals grew, like tiny rock gardens with fanciful plants among the pale blossoms of the sea anemones.

So gently at first that it could not be noticed, the tide began to flow. The bed of huge brown mussels, which was exposed on the seaward side of the island, now had trickles of water surging through its lower channels, filling for a moment, then emptying again into the sea. And as the surge rose up, advancing and retreating, the mussels opened one by one, spreading their wide valves to the life-giving water, awaiting the larvae and the small sea insects and the granules of photo-plankton that would be brought to them by the rising of the tide.

The northeast sky now had a glowing arc, shading through green and pearl to crimson, with its outer edges lost in the darkness between the stars. And Eli sat, watching the world renew itself from the vast resources of the universe, the rhythm of the tides tying the moon in its orbit to the lowliest limpet upon the rock, the anchored forests of kelp and the tiny floating algae drinking once again their brimming cup of light from the unimaginable depths of space.

The tide was flowing now with urgency, pressing up into the rock pools, entering the caves where the crabs had retreated before the burgeoning dawn, sounding there, with a hollow rhythm, its sad, nostalgic moaning, like the voice of a shell held, empty, to the ear of a listening child.

Far off, behind him, there was a faint cough or two, strangled and tentative—then the subdued chug-chug-chugging of a one-cylinder engine, as the first trap boat circled among the mooring collars of the harbor and slipped between the sunkers into the open bay. The boat put the first gulls, sleeping upon the water or upon the offshore rocks, to flight, and spoke apologetically to the otherwise silent world, never asserting its dominance, but seeking permission, hesitantly, to intrude upon the privacy of nature. Three generations of fishermen had made its voice as much a part of the sea as the mewing of the gulls above it.

One of the big birds came now, banking around the headland on swishing wings—a greater black-backed gull, called by the fishermen a saddle-back—as large as a goose, planing confidently into this small, deserted cove, which was its own special preserve, where it came each dawn with the first light of day to kill and eat the crabs that were tardy in seeking shelter from the apocalypse of the morning.

Catching sight of Eli sitting motionless upon the rocks, the big bird braked in mid-air, hovered for a second, flapping, hoping that it might not have seen aright, then wheeled above him, screaming imprecations, and, catching the light updraft of air from the face of the cliff, rose effortlessly and swept down in a long, graceful arc above the open sea.

The coming of the gull roused Eli out of his meditation. The world and the sea were now washed in blue-green light, and the tide was in full flood, surging up the ranked bastions of the rocks. Within spitting distance, it almost seemed, the trap boats were passing, the fishermen huddled over their tillers, seemingly oblivious to his presence. Soon, he knew, the light would turn to red, and then to gold, and the day would be upon him.

He rose and stretched his muscles, cramped from long sitting in the cool night. He slipped lithely out of his clothes, then stepped down between the rocks into the sea, that rose, chilling, past his groin, and received him, as he slid underneath its limpid surface, with a sort of final cold caress —a baptism of ice. He sank in a long, gliding curve, which imitated the flight of the gull, searching the bottom where monstrous shapes of blue and green and soft brown rose toward him—a vague world where exact form had vanished, and masses and colors were grouped like the patterns of an abstract painting.

His long glide brought him to the rocks on the far side of the inlet, and he clambered out, dripping, the sharp roughness of the tiny barnacles giving perfect purchase for his hands and feet, and he sat, shivering a little, with the sweet taste of the sea in his mouth and the keen smell of the kelp beds rising all around him.

Then he dived from the rock, making a long, straight arrow of his body, and cleft the water cleanly, and swam to the edge of the little island, where he lay face down in the shallows, letting the faint breathing of the water pulse up and down along his sides and trickle across the hollow of his back. He could feel the bands and bulbs of the laminaria slithering under his naked body, and he rolled in them gently, sampling their taste and finding them good—and while the light brightened he lay with the laminaria, man and alga, the alpha and omega of creation.

Then he swam back to the shore and rose from the sea, primordial and renewed. The sky was now blazing with light, and the full flood of the tide had swept up over the land until it had buried most of the zone of life that nestles between the marks of the spring tides along the shore. So rapidly was the water rising that it had reached almost to the place where Eli had dropped his clothes on the coarse black stone.

He picked them up, making a bundle, and climbed over the smooth rocks, through the opalescent light of dawn. And as he climbed, the sun climbed with him, until it stood upon the horizon, blazing like an open hearth, its level rays striking him. So he stretched tall upon the cliff top, washed clean, empty of all feeling except this feeling of cleanness, dipped in the night of the ocean and washed in the blood of the sun.

He faced the sea for a moment and looked down at his cold body, like marble stained red by the raw day. Then, whole and content, he began to cross the dew-wet stones toward the white pillars of the sleeping house that rose above him like an eagle perched upon a crag against the sky.